THE MAGPIE ODYSSEY

THE MAGPIE ODYSSEY

An Irish Journey

Lorretta Lynde

iUniverse, Inc.

New York Lincoln Shanghai

The Magpie Odyssey
An Irish Journey

iUniverse books may be ordered through booksellers or by contacting:

iUniverse
2021 Pine Lake Road, Suite 100
Lincoln, NE 68512
www.iuniverse.com
1-800-Authors (1-800-288-4677)

ISBN-13: 978-0-595-34933-3 (pbk)
ISBN-13: 978-0-595-79647-2 (ebk)
ISBN-10: 0-595-34933-1 (pbk)
ISBN-10: 0-595-79647-8 (ebk)

Printed in the United States of America

MAGPIES

One for Sorrow
Two for Mirth
Three for a Wedding
Four for a Birth
Five for Rich
Six for Poor
Seven for a Secret
…I can tell you
No More.

—Old Irish Folk Saying

For Robert,
who brought light and life into my world,
and accompanied me on this odyssey.

PROLOGUE

▼

A dozen pairs of eyes zeroed in on Colleen Lorrrah when she dodged out of the wall of rain into the small, smoky pub. Her intention had been to take an exploratory walk through the tiny village of Bureen, but the warm lights of the tavern had been an irresistible invitation to seek shelter. That this rough age-darkened doorway would be the gateway to adventure was the last thing on her mind.

Pulling back the hood of her rain-jacket, Colleen shook loose her unruly hair, savoring the feel of it falling down her back. The only place to sit was at a tiny table next to the glowing peat fire. Unconsciously, she fingered back an errant strand from her fair skin, as her deep blue gaze traveled around the establishment, penetrating the hazy blue air. Those who examined her appearance were rewarded with a compelling American and Irish combination. Her face was ageless above a slender, physically toned body. The natural grace in her posture spoke of years in the outdoors, and a reserved curiosity reached out from her eyes. It was mid-afternoon, and a number of people had sought refuge and companionship in this tavern. Most were older, but that made the conversation no less lively.

Some voices wrapped themselves around Irish or lilting English with the accent known the world over. With her arrival duly noted, they returned to their discussions.

Colleen had no defined expectations about what she would find here. It was enough finally to be in Ireland after anticipating the journey for a lifetime. Now the first step was behind her, and she was here, determined to drink in every nuance and experience.

Recovery from jet-lag had taken no time at all, and the anticipation of what might be discovered quivered in her mind, ready to pounce. Anyone seeing her might have taken her for an ordinary tourist, but her mission was different. First of all, no one would have guessed that she was fifty years old. The Lorrah family gift of youthful good health and endurance was hers, defying the occasional times when she felt the years.

A contented smile lit her face, and her mind roamed the path that had led her here.

It had begun miles away, and years ago. As the peat coals embraced one side of her with welcome heat, her memory meandered back across time and distance. Warm embers of thought turned to the untamed rolling hills, rivers and soaring mountains of her ranch-based childhood in southeastern Montana.

One after another, images of her father began to dominate the recollections. Mike Lorrah was rancher who raised sheep in the mountain foothills of eastern Montana. This bigger-than-life man had always dreamed of seeing Ireland. Warm nostalgia and detailed memories of his Irish mother, his Irish grandmother and his many Irish friends added reality and depth to what he told his children. Irish stories, legends and myths expanded the legacy he passed to Colleen and her brother and sister. The truth was, his persona was intertwined with what she felt about Ireland. More than that, he had *created* those feelings in her, building them with one element upon another, castles in her mind.

In spite of the array of circumstances that had somehow prevented him from ever traveling to Ireland, he had a powerful and mysterious connection with the country and its culture. Insisting that his children know about Irish history and mythology, he recounted the old stories, always respectful of tradition and super-stition.

Mike's darker side harbored the curse of less attractive traits historically ascribed to the Irish. Gambling and wild humor were among his passions, alcohol had commandeered a sizable portion of his life. Colleen remembered many times when whiskey held the dynamic character of Mike Lorrah hostage and obscured his core vitality and charisma. These episodes had imposed frustration and grief upon the family, especially her mother.

It took years, but Mike finally triumphed in his running war with his raging demons. It took courage and determination, elements he had in abundance, and he did prevail, but not without casualties. Among these were the loss of several family fortunes and his own health.

There was magic in the man, and she would not have chosen to be anyone else's daughter.

The vast grazing ranges of Eastern Montana had served as the center of his life's work with huge bands of sheep. It had been his own childhood home, and his parents and grandparents had grappled to wrest their living from this region, as well. When he chose sheep-ranching, the decision had not been an easy one to rationalize or defend. The range was in the middle of the Crow Indian reservation, where nearly every ranch ran cattle. Sheepmen were often the subject of derision or open opposition.

None of that diminished Mike's passion for his vocation. He loved raising sheep, and dismissed his own sporadic attempts to switch to cattle ranching as unfulfilling and unrewarding. Besides, the profession repaid his dedication with a good income and some measure of inner peace. The Big Horn Mountains provided a perfect summer range for sheep, and Mike knew it.

His children—Colleen, her older brother Sean, and sister Kathleen—grew up in this life. They lived and worked on the ranch, and went to the same reservation schools as their father. Lodge Grass was a little town that was the base for their ranching operations. It had a declining population of white families, and by the time Colleen went to school, the student population was about three-quarters tribal children and a quarter white children. Nearly all of her playmates were Crow Indian children of her own age and her father encouraged her interactions with them. He wanted her to have the kind of life-long friendships his own childhood had given him.

The older Lorrah children, Colleen's brother and sister, were thirteen and eight years older than her respectively. They had grown up during the early years of Mike's career. In those days, his work for other ranches kept him away from home for long periods. By the time Colleen was aware of her environment, he owned his own ranch, and was in the later years of his life.

When she was fourteen, Mike had a series of heart attacks that left him in tenuous health. From then on, Colleen, the child family and friends described as most like him, served as his companion, driver and right hand. She also became his confidant. The two of them spent hours in the misty mornings and bright days on the mountain and in the hills. He talked to her of places held holy by the Crow Indians. He revealed secret locations that his Indian friends had shown him in trust, and taught her to respect these sites and the beliefs that made them sacred.

Now here she was in Ireland. After all the years of listening to Mike speak of his dreams of this place, and of mystifying and unexplained things, Colleen had the sensation that she was visiting this country in his place. In her fireside seat, she paused. The time had come to assume her place in whatever mysteries the family pattern held, and learn what steps remained ahead of her.

CHAPTER 1

▼

There was *something* about the fire season that year. Ominous portents prowled through the atmosphere .

Colleen stood still on the edge of the rimrock cliffs above Billings and gazed out over the horizon toward Yellowstone Park. It was July 1988, and Montana's summer had been sweltering hot and bone dry. The same heat prickled inside of Colleen.

The atmosphere made her restless and uneasy. Her edginess almost certainly was because of the fire danger, she decided. The rest of her life was in order. With Art, her husband of 20 years, she had just bought a dream home. It was the kind of house they had once believed would be beyond their reach until much later in their lives. High on a cliff, its windows gave a breathtaking sweep of the mountain panorama that formed the northern border of Yellowstone Park. That vista comforted her when she was alone while Art traveled as a charter pilot. From the second floor deck, Colleen spent many solitary evenings watching the weather promenade through the Yellowstone River Valley below.

This night was different, though. Summer thunderheads, so common in the prairie, gathered, and sheet lightning played across the dark track of clouds. Such dry electrical storms frequently brought forest and grassland wildfires, some worse than others. The tension in the air was palpable and thick. The ever-present pinion jays sailed from pine to pine past her deck, mewling their mournful calls to each other. The magpies, on the other hand, were curiously silent. Three of them assembled in the dry grasses in front of her house, and with black-crystal eyes sparkling, seemed to be waiting for something. Her self-imposed watch lasted for several hours; a singular vigil. Finally, she decided to give up her post and get some sleep to be ready for her own work the following day. Rising, she made her way inside.

The next day broke bright and clear, the storm gone without a trace. Colleen's apprehension was not. If anything, this oppressive internal reminder of the tempest had intensified, and was almost smothering her. Despite the cloudless blue skies and calm dry air, something seemed to be lurking just outside her line of sight. It was a feeling she could not remember experiencing before, stirring in the back of her psyche, gnawing at her peace of mind. She tried to ignore it, and anyone who knew her would not have recognized that anything was disturbing her. But that was Colleen's way. Very few people could read her emotions. The tempest was mounting in some very remote, secret recess within her.

Almost against her will, she began to examine her life. What she had accepted without question now revealed its flaws. She was 41 years old, and this year had awakened some sleeping realization inside her.

Circumstances had led her into one job after another, never fully utilizing her intelligence, education or skills. . It was she who had never reached, never risked, to grow professionally. Something seemed to be holding her back.

Now this was coming back to haunt her. Restlessness plagued her days, her life clamored for change, for reasons that eluded her. So she did the one thing she had always done to calm her and help get her thoughts in order. She packed her car and set out on a road trip into her beloved Yellowstone Park.

She was desperate to clear her head. The path to such self-therapy was one her childhood had taught well. Her father always had taken her to Yellowstone Park when her thoughts needed order. Others might consider this strange, but Yellowstone always comforted and reaffirmed her. This place of nature and mystery had been an integral spiritual part of her entire life. Journeys there several times each year since childhood were ritual for her. When she was younger, her father had shown her many remote parts of the Park, explaining how the Indians believed it a holy place. He pointed out that here, unlike nearly any other place in the world, the elements of fire, air, earth and water were married in an eternal dance of power and display.

This lesson in perfect balance created the place for her to gain the same equilibrium in her soul. Now, sometimes she came here with Art, but only when he finally succumbed to her pleas with him to make the trip. More often, she came alone for renewal and contemplation.

This time, her Honda carried her along the tinder dry foothills and up the mountain edge from Gardiner to Mammoth Hot Springs. As she drove, she gazed across the valley to a high crest where she sometimes caught a glimpse of wildlife, and where the landscape always gave her peace. This was traditionally her gateway for meditation as she drove. Not this time. Her breath stopped.

A small tendril of smoke curled up from what was probably a lightning-caused fire on the ridge-top. It was not uncommon to see little fires in Yellowstone in summer, and the park personnel usually did not take action on them, since the park was managed under a "let-burn" policy intended to mimic nature.

This fire was significantly different.

Others might have viewed this small blaze as trivial, but Colleen's spirit recognized it as kindred. In the heat of that day, the air was charged. She felt, but did not see, a spark jump from that infant fire into her heart with the speed of an arrow. Outside of her awareness, that ember found fuel and began to smolder, even before her return trip to Billings began. A drive around the Grand Loop road in the Park did little to soothe her agitation. For the first time in her life, serenity eluded her in Yellowstone. The uneasiness persisted throughout her drive and after she arrived at home, and there was no way to pinpoint the reason.

Contained deep inside her restlessness was a rising, ongoing discontent with her life. Something inside her was beginning to struggle with the status quo. The possibility of a romantic relationship with another man violated her code of honor, and she refused to allow herself to feel deprived or sad about her own situation. The most disheartening result was that she was left unable to pinpoint her real purpose to her life—no children, no career achievements, no mark on the world. Nothing had caused her to feel otherwise, until now.

Now the fires began to burn.

Not just in Yellowstone's forests, but inside of Colleen's spirit.

The fire in Yellowstone spread, greedily devouring acre after acre, driven by desert-dry winds. It burst out of firelines, leaped over rivers and roads, and raged through trees nature had taken decades to grow. It was a holocaust, devastating huge expanses of the Park's woodlands, and it was mirrored in Colleen's soul. As smoke darkened the Montana skies for miles, trepidation made her vision of her world murky. From a secluded place inside herself, the ashes of destruction sifted down, and layered their debris in her heart.

She was bewildered. What was this? How could she experience such discontent at this stage in life? Wasn't she supposed to be settled by the time she attained her forties? The turmoil in her soul dazed her.

With no answers forthcoming to her spiritual questions, all her intensity from these quandaries focused on work. From within the emptiness of her personal life, recognition came that Art and she did not have a marriage. In the eyes of this man to whom she entrusted her loyalty, her future and her heart, she was dismissed as inconsequential. As a result, she now looked for her rewards from her work with a local printing company. What started as a customer service job grew into one of expanding responsibility.

Increasingly, she put in long hours at her office, going early in the mornings and staying late, and taking work home when she left the in the evenings. Colleagues respected and applauded her efforts. All projects she took on showed impressive results, and her office became her refuge. She moved up to supervisory levels, and thrived on the excitement that accompanied the work. Things went on this way until a new president came to the branch where she worked. With his first introduction to Colleen, he recognized her potential. He had a reputation as a demanding and astute man, adept in business and skilled in motivating his best employees.

When introduced to Colleen, he bombarded her with questions and demands for intensive effort. He always behaved as if he believed she could achieve anything, and it suited her. Colleen became his star pupil, gaining more responsibility and more authority. The department grew under her guidance, and ultimately, her synergy with the company led to an opportunity for her first major promotion.

The approach of such a possibility came as a complete surprise, and she failed to envision herself as a candidate. But her mentor urged her to make her mark. The idea was foreign, since she saw herself as less than worthy, and she sensed it would mean even more estrangement from Art. On the other hand, she knew with certainty that she had to go forward or die.

Some force was driving her, and responding to it was her only choice. It hovered in the corner of her memory, but she could not bring it into focus.

Professional success could not quell the burning inside her. Other sources must be found to help cool the heat. The search led her to a career counselor. This woman, respected for skill in advising people in transition, insisted that it was typical for men & women in their middle years to crave new lives. The search was not for excuses, but for validation. This was not the answer. When she could not find confirmation on her own, she looked for it where she always had.

Her father would help her find answers. A drive across town to talk with Mike was the only course of action. Even in her adulthood, he continued to serve as her refuge and guide. This time, the trip to his side felt like a pilgrimage.

Their relationship had remained close during his later years, and she knew he would not make judgments about her thoughts and questions. The two of them had often been described by her mother as "the same person in two different bodies and from two different generations." Of all the people in her life, Mike was the one who understood her. In many ways, he had molded her in his own image. He shared his philosophies with her, told her things which did not make sense to her at the time, but which she accepted on faith, simply because he said them. It was often much later that she learned what the real meaning was.

Parking in the driveway of her parents' tidy, simple house, she climbed up the steps to their front door and let herself in. She entered the living room where he was sitting with her mother. He still wore the long-sleeved western-style shirt and blue jeans he had always worn on the ranch. His frail physical condition belied the strong, swift, dynamic man he had been before his heart began to give out.

In recent years, his body had begun refusing what he demanded of it. His life-style had been one of inactivity and waiting since he and her mother had come to live in the city. But his mind was a volcano of activity as he read mountains of books and talked with his many visitors.

When his history of heart problems had caused the family to decide to move Mike and their mother, Della, into Billings, all three siblings knew this meant the end of something enormously important to their father. Yet, he had been an active willing party in the decision. He told them it would be the best thing for her mother to be closer to her children after he was gone. Besides, Billings was the nearest thing Montana had to a real city, and it offered the people of Eastern Montana and Northern Wyoming services that their small populations would not support in the outlying small towns. There abundant shopping, two college, and two good hospitals that drew people from all over the eastern half of the state as well as Wyoming and North and South Dakota.

Their sadness came in the recognition that there was little life in him after the move. He seldom went out of the house, and his spark seemed to fade. His thinning and graying hair belied the wild black thatch that had always topped his face in younger days, and he had lost the perpetual tan that the outdoors had bestowed on him.

The memory of the day the three adult children moved their parents off the ranch rushed back at her with full intensity. While all the belongings were loaded into a rented truck, Mike watched from his vantage point on a lawn chair on the porch. He was too weak to help, and everything about his demeanor suggested defeat. His eyes devoured the panorama of the ranch as it spread out before him. It was as if he were trying to memorize every detail of the place. The hunger in his gaze, sweeping the elements of the terrain, was heartbreaking for all of them.

Now, as she looked at him sitting in the living room, she was alarmed again by what her instincts showed her.

"My God," she thought, "Have we killed him by taking him off the ranch?" He looked so frail and diminished.

The thought had little time to linger. Her arrival usually caused a rally in him.

"Hi, Colleen!" His eyes lit up at the sight of her, and he sat up a little straighter. "How's my little Magpie?"

She smiled nostalgically at his use of her childhood nickname. A thousand memories of him in earlier days crowded into her thoughts.

Aloud she said, "Dad, I need to talk with you."

A fond and tolerant smile crossed her mother's face, and she said, "I'm glad you stopped by. I was just about to go out and run some errands, but your father didn't want to go. Now you can keep him company."

Colleen cast a grateful look Della. Her mother was still youthful, with a figure that no one would have guessed had survived years of hard ranch-wife work and motherhood. She was neatly coifed, and her clothing fit perfectly. Her open and still-pretty face was the older version of Colleen's sister's, with gray-blue eyes that took in her younger daughter's glance of gratitude and acknowledged it.

Colleen loved her mother, but knew she had always confounded her. And there was no question that her mother loved her, despite the fact that they seemed to constantly seek level ground between them. Her mother found this daughter a mystery, and occasionally let such thoughts slip into her observations.

Once she told Colleen, "When you were born, I had never seen another child like you. It was as if you were a tiny little adult, just waiting for your body to catch up to the old mind inside your head. I felt like you were just watching us and the life around you, just passing time until you could get on with things. It was disconcerting, to say the least."

While Della and she had never been particularly close, her mother never interfered with the special and unusual relationship between her and Mike. If anything, she had encouraged it. It had been at her insistence that Colleen had become his constant companion after his illness, to make certain he would not be alone if something happened to him far out in the range. Colleen became his sounding board, his confidante, and his apprentice. Had she been a son, she might have assumed the responsibilities of running the ranch instead of encouraging her parents to sell it. All that was water under the bridge, and the time had come to have her own turning point. She plunged into the conversation.

"Dad, I just don't feel right with the world."

He was instantly alert, sea-blue eyes electric. He became more animated

"I knew you'd be coming to talk about this one day," he said. "I've been waiting."

If she didn't know him so intimately, such a statement might have seemed odd. But he had always had an eerie connection with all three of his children. In her case, it was almost telepathic. This time, she was cautious.

Mike had never been satisfied with her marriage to Art. He seemed sense that his youngest daughter was not receiving the emotional sustenance she needed, but he had meticulously avoided this subject. She had a sense of his perception, but she, too, had been careful not to speak of it with him.

"I've come to a crossroads," she said.

"I know." His response was simple, but the implications were a complex mix of acknowledgement and prediction. "It's time."

"What do you mean?"

"What I'm going to say will sound strange, Colleen. It even sounds odd to me, but it has to be said. I don't know if I can make you understand this, because I can't define it, but listen to me anyway. There is a place for you in a very significant pattern," he declared. "I don't know myself how you fit. Your instincts are those of a wild thing, and I know you'll go with your gut in the choices that lie ahead."

"What do you mean by a 'pattern'?"

He shrugged.

"The answer will come later. All I can say for sure is that the initial steps will be for yourself. You must strengthen yourself enough, both physically and emotionally, for what is coming. Part of your conditioning will come through achievements and vision. After you accomplish these things, you'll be ready."

"You're talking in riddles, Dad. You've never been this vague with me before."

"It's as much as I can tell you," he said with a sigh. "Once I'm gone, you'll embark on a path that only you can walk. It will be your own vision quest, like the ones our Crow friends make. You'll need help from many different quarters, and it will be there. It won't be easy, but you're the one who must do it."

"Okay, okay," she sighed, knowing that nothing would push him to further define the subject, but also knowing she was unwilling to stop trying.

"Where shall I start?"

"Do what feels absolutely right. Don't worry about what anyone else thinks, even those who are very close to you. Reach, and don't stop reaching until you know your destiny." His statement was adamant.

"Deep inside, I guess I knew what your answer would be," Colleen smiled at him. "You've always trusted my instincts, and you've never discouraged me from trying anything, Dad. This isn't the first time we've talked about this kind of thing, but it's always harder when there are no specifics."

"Here's your 'specific,'" he replied, his eyes searching deep inside her. "You will know. I promise—you will have absolutely no doubts when the time comes."

As if he had physically reached into her soul, Colleen felt his words bank the coals inside her. Subject closed, they moved on, conversation ranging across every area of interest, and talked until her mother returned.

The next day, Colleen accepted the job offer that included advancement into a management position. This step came easily to her, and she was amazed by how right it felt.

More conversations with her father followed. Because it was her inclination to seek more information, she continued to prod at Mike for particulars about "the pattern," but none were forthcoming. He always insisted she would know what was necessary when the time was right, and he would not, or could not expand upon the subject.

For the first time in many years, time moved along swiftly. With her career changes, Art grew more remote and withdrawn from her. Meanwhile, her own strength was growing steadily, as if somehow she had been set free. Her spirit began to take small tentative flights toward new frontiers. By habit and need, she visited her father more frequently, sharing the excitement of these initial steps with him, to the accompaniment of his steadfast encouragement.

Then the edge of the cliff suddenly appeared and she was driven to the precipice, where she stood teetering at the brink.

CHAPTER 2

▼

The first big turning point happened in the spring. The day began normally enough. She and Art stopped by her parents' house to help them prepare their garden. Despite the beauty of the Montana April day, her father insisted he did not feel well enough to come outside. He urged them to go ahead and till the ground so it could be planted. Colleen's senses went on alert. This behavior was odd. Even when Mike's energy was at its lowest, the outdoors would revive him. He would draw up a chair to the edge of the garden, watch the soil preparation, and participate with his presence.

But not on this day.

This day, he stayed inside the house, separate from the work they were doing. He sent Della outside with them, and asked Colleen to come in periodically to tell him about the progress.

All morning, Colleen moved back and forth from the garden to the living room, keeping Mike informed, and asking how he was feeling.

On her third trip into the house, he said, "Stay a few minutes. I have something I must say to you."

She heard a note in his voice that told her what he was about to say would be momentous.

"What's on your mind, Dad?"

"I'm going to leave you today," he said with certainty, sighing deeply.

His remark shocked her.

"Dad, you've said things like this before, but never so explicitly. Don't you think you'll be fine? I'm sure you're just having a down day."

"No." The word was absolute. He paused a beat before continuing.

"You and I have always known you would be here when I died."

It was true. Colleen had lived in other parts of Montana during her life, and yet some part of her had always known with deep assurance that she would be with her father when he died. They talked about this with ease, often to the discomfort of others around them. It had given her peace when she was away from him, because of her honest belief that he could not die if she was not there. There had been a number of close calls with his health, but he had always recovered.

Could it be that the time had come? A chill ran through her.

"Now listen to me." Her father's words became urgent, demanding. "There is very little time to tell you this. You must go on. You're on the right track. Continue to build and strengthen from the inside out. When the time comes, your memory will open and help you know what to do. There are so many things that you have forgotten, but it was necessary for you to put them aside. It is time for you to do your own work first, so you will be ready for a journey. I wish I was the one going, but you must do this."

"Dad," Colleen said, "I don't get it. If this is some big message about what I should do to carry out your wishes after you are gone, it doesn't make any sense."

"This isn't about *my* wishes, Colleen," her father declared "It's much bigger than that."

His words turned to thoughts about his life, painting pictures of some of the days spent with his grandparents and his Indian friends. She listened patiently, waiting for him to return to the original subject. When he spoke of death, his bright blue eyes fixed on hers. His gaze was consuming.

"Remember all those talks out in the hills?"

"Yes," she replied, seeking some kind of solid ground, "they meant a lot to me, Dad."

He smiled with a wistful sigh.

"More than anyone, you know how much I wanted to go to Ireland. Something always got in the way. Now I know that was because you were the one meant to go. This is important. You have to go there. Don't let your life pass without setting your feet on the soil of that country. You'll know when the time is right."

Colleen puzzled over what he was saying. If this was truly the end, and if books and the movies were any indication, it should be the time for profound last minute advice, reconciliations or instructions. But he was telling her that it was vital for her to go to Ireland. It didn't make any sense.

Walking to the window, she looked out across the valley toward the mountains where the Yellowstone fire had ravaged the grand old park. Smoke and flames were whirling in her soul, and there were no answers. Mike could not be permitted to drop the subject.

She turned to ask for clarification. But when she looked at him, the words stopped on their way to her lips. Mike was motionless, eyes closed, head back. He was at total peace where he sat, the conversation ended along with his life.

An initial lurching of her soul made her sit down suddenly, as if all the air had been removed from the room, her own breath gone with it. Then a vast calm settled over her like a gentle warm shower, and she clearly heard her father's voice inside her ears.

"I will be at your side when you need me most, but much of what you do has to be on your own. There will be no need for fear," it whispered.

Then there was silence, as the dust motes drifted in the beam of spring sunlight shining through the living room window. The air shimmered with the presence of the man as he took his leave of the corporeal life.

After some moments alone with her father's body, Colleen rose and went out to bring her mother in from the yard. Della sank into the chair next to Mike's and took his hand in hers. She did not cry, but stroked his fingers, shaking her head and murmuring, "Oh, Mike, oh, Mike. I would have liked to say goodbye to you." Her voice was steady, but without tone. An aura of immense sadness settled over her, making the atmosphere in the room heavy with the weight of it.

Unable to bear the sight of her parents like this, Colleen took action. First, she called Sean and Kathleen to tell them what had happened. A call to the doctor and the hospital's emergency services was next. There was no question in her mind that it was useless, but doing something seemed better than doing nothing. The ambulance and the paramedics' vehicle arrived, and technicians raced to try to revive her father. Lifting him from his chair, they stretched him out on the floor and placed an oxygen mask on him. No response. When they saw that this was unsuccessful, they placed him on a gurney and loaded him into the ambulance. Della insisted she ride along with them in the transport to the hospital. Colleen grabbed the telephone and called Sean and Kathleen again, directing them to come to the hospital.

This done, she asked Art to stay by the telephone and she walked out of her parents' house. Glancing skyward, she saw a lone magpie circling over her. Something about the sight tugged at her memory, but her focus was on getting to the hospital. A turn of the key in the ignition set her on the trail of the ambulance.

At the emergency room, Colleen's first move was to find the doctor and instruct him not to take extraordinary measures. She did this, even though she was absolutely certain that her father would win this battle. Her sister Kathleen and brother Sean arrived with their spouses.

The emergency room staff whisked Mike off to surgery in an effort to revive him, but none of their efforts prevailed. His essence had left his lifeless body behind. The doctor came to the waiting area to tell the family what they already knew. Despite all efforts, Mike had triumphed. He finally was free of the weakened body that had imprisoned his spirit.

There was a peculiar sense of sadness mixed with relief. Colleen couldn't help being glad for him. The family clustered together for a few moments, and then agreed to go back to her parents' house to give her mother company and comfort.

Kathleen and her husband James took Della home, and Colleen stood face to face with Sean. He was obviously in shock. She reached out, put a hand on his arm, and said, "Sean, he's okay now. First time in a long time." Sean nodded solemnly. Her brother, a man of great heart and feeling, had already begun to grieve in his own way.

Colleen walked alone to her car. As she crossed the lawn in front of the visitor's doors, she saw something inexplicable. A solitary magpie now held a motionless position on one of the statues in the hospital grounds. It seemed to be looking directly at her with its glass bead eyes, and when she stopped, it tilted its head to one side, as if in greeting. Colleen stopped breathing for a moment, hearing her father's voice again in her thoughts, saying, "Don't forget, Magpie!"

She shook her head in frustration. How could she forget what refused to come to the surface of her memory?

At her approach, the elegant bird lifted silently off the ground in slow, iridescent flight, wings beating in that pattern so unique to its species, stroke, stroke, glide. It spiraled upward into the sky and seemed to vanish. Colleen paused and thought about what she had seen, ultimately dismissing it as a figment of her grief. Still, an old rhyme her grandmother had often recited surfaced in her mind. It was about magpies—*"One for sorrow, two for mirth…"*

"One for sorrow…"

Back in her car, still at last, she allowed the tears to rise to the surface and spill over. No sobbing accompanied her crying, only a steady stream of silent tears, punctuated by deep draughts of breath. They were tears for herself, sorrow for all the future times that she would not be able to seek Mike out for his understanding and counsel. After a few deep, long sighs, she composed herself. What was it that hovered at the edge of her thoughts?

Unbidden, the image of the "magpie tree" which grew just outside the window of her childhood bedroom rose before her. It had provided home and shelter to numerous families of nesting magpies over the years. In her youth she had always felt a sense of ownership for the old box elder tree, and had even ascribed a personality to it. It had provided much of the companionship she craved as the only child at home on the ranch, miles from town. Embraced by its gnarled branches, she often sat in it and talked to it, describing her day or telling it her troubles.

This relationship with the tree changed with one shining, cornerstone event.

As a child, she always woke with the sun, since her room faced toward the east. Each morning from the time she could get out of bed and walk on her own included a trip to her window to see what the weather for the day might be. This simple act helped set the entire day, even in her earliest years. On this particular day, when she was about ten years old, she pushed back the blankets, padded across the floor to the window, and drew the curtain aside as usual for a glimpse of her tree. Sitting face to face with her, enthroned on the branch closest to her window, was the biggest magpie she had ever seen.

He sat elegantly, only inches from her, and regarded her impassively through the glass. Young Colleen was mesmerized. The brilliant eyes of the bird were filled with intelligence, and the rays of the rising sun reflected glancing rainbows off his prismatic black and white feathers. He sat very still, and she felt him looking straight into her eyes.

"Hi, there," she said. "Aren't you scared of me?"

The bird didn't move. Colleen was excited. She ran from her room to the kitchen, where her parents sat drinking coffee. At her urging, they followed her to her room and looked out the window, but the branches of the tree were empty. They stood with her for a moment, then went back to the kitchen, assuring her that they must have just missed seeing the bird.

As they resumed their seats at the kitchen table, Della looked skeptically at Mike. "Do you think we should continue to allow her to pull us into her imaginary games like that?"

Mike's gaze drilled into Della's. "We must never disparage what she believes. My grandmother taught me that children are born with spiritual abilities on a much higher plane than adults. They exist in a world that we have lost contact with. As adults, we must not destroy the abilities that children are born with by telling them something is not possible. If she believes she saw this, then it's part of her reality. If it's an imaginary game, and I'd be surprised if it is, then that creativity should not be discouraged either."

Chagrined, Della fell into silent thought. This was an issue that had come up between them before, and she knew better than to pursue it.

Disconcerted, Colleen watched them go, then turned back to the window. To her surprise, she saw that the magpie was back. This creature had caused her enough embarrassment for one day, so she did not call her parents back to look. Instead, she went close to the window, and eye-to-eye with the bird, she looked at it for a long time.

Finally, as the sun cleared the horizon and full daylight spread over the fields of the ranch, the bird lifted off. Flying with a silence that was unusual for members of its species, it disappeared from her sight. Colleen dressed and joined her parents for breakfast before setting out to walk the length of the ranch's lane to board the school bus.

At the table, her parents asked her a few questions about the magpie.

"What was it doing?" Mike asked.

"Just sitting there."

"Do you think it might have been looking at its reflection in the glass of your window?"

"I don't know."

Mike leaned back in his chair, his intense sky-blue eyes resting on this child he loved so much. "You'll tell us if it comes back again?"

"Sure," Colleen replied absently, so serious for a child of ten.

Colleen made sure she answered with general statements, but chose not to tell them about its reappearance. Once finished with breakfast, she gathered her books and started her walk out to the main road. Mike walked over to stand by the living room window, as was his usual practice, watching her progress. As he observed her small figure walking briskly up the road, he saw the magpie descend from the sky and trace her path from above and behind.

He was filled with wonder at the sight, and it caused him to recall a conversation with his life-long friend, a Crow Indian named Black Bird Shows. They had been talking, as they often did, about supernatural and spiritual things. In the discussion, Black Bird Shows had introduced the subject of spirit animals. Mike listened to his friend describe a vision quest during which he had seen and recognized his own spirit animal, a raven.

He told Mike he had been guarded by a raven since he was very small, and this fact had led to the giving of his name. His vision had brought him into face-to-face conversation with a majestic bird, which identified itself to him. Mike wondered about this discussion now as he watched the magpie accompany Colleen.

When Colleen returned from school, she was unusually quiet and thoughtful. The next morning, she woke early, and hurried to her window, eagerly opening the curtains to look at the branches of her box-elder tree. There, exactly where it had been the day before, was the magpie. But today it was not alone. Now there were two more of the big birds, both silent, also looking at Colleen. She was amazed and thrilled.

From her stock-still position, gazing with fascination at the bird and its companions, she didn't hear her father come to the door of her room. He stood quietly in the doorway, away from the window, and watched her. Now the triune of birds stayed in place, and with them, Colleen created a tableau that would remain forever engraved in Mike's mind. There seemed to be some kind of silent communication and acceptance between his little daughter and these feathered sentries. A chill of undefined recognition ran up his spine.

Once the sun revealed itself, the birds repeated the pageant of the day before, taking silent flight, wings beating a stroke-stroke-glide rhythm as they spiraled up and up until they disappeared from sight. Now Mike spoke.

"You look like one of those magpies," he said, "cocking your head, and looking out with such bright eyes. With your white skin and dark hair, you might be one of them. I believe they are your friends!"

Colleen turned to respond to his comment. "I think so too, Dad," she said. "I just know they stand guard over my tree when I sleep and during the day they keep me company."

Mike didn't disagree with her. He couldn't. He never discouraged any of Colleen's ideas or dreams. As he had told Della, he'd been taught that children could achieve anything if you didn't stifle their spirits. This conversation would remain between them, with the only reminder of it being his new nickname for her—"Magpie."

Those who heard him call her by this designation would wonder about it, because it did not seem to fit this quiet, serious little girl. She did not seem to bear any resemblance to the raucous, brash birds most people believed magpies were. But others had not seen what Colleen and Mike had. Outsiders had not seen these regal, silent birds which had become her companions. These were not common magpies, and Mike pondered the question of whether they were even real birds. Could they be spectral birds from some unknown realm, come to assume a role in his child's existence?

That morning Mike and Della watched Colleen go through the same ritual as all other school days. She finished her breakfast and went out the door with her books. When she was a few yards up the lane, the open sky above her was suddenly inhabited by all three of the beautiful magpies, their flashing Japanese-lantern wings spread to catch the glory of the sun. They flew above and behind, escorting her as far as the point where she waited for the bus, then soared high into the sky and vanished.

During the week, the child went to school as usual, playing with her Indian friends in both quiet and rough-and-tumble childhood games. On weekends and after school, when Colleen rode her horse and hiked in the ranch's hills and streams, the birds were there. Mike often observed them, and shook his head in wonder.

On one later occasion, Black Bird Shows was visiting Mike, and the two men were sitting on the porch of the ranch house. Colleen came out of the front door, stopped and greeted the men. They asked her where she was going. Her explanation was that she was off to visit "her" grove of cottonwood trees near the creek. It was a place revered by her, and she went there every chance she had. The huge trees formed a lofty cathedral of massive wooden columns topped by a mosaic of leaves high above. Reflected in the peaceful waters where the creek pooled at their base, they repeated the pattern below. The color and drama of the place was glorious. Hours of her time flew by while she sat in the carpet of green grass that grew among the roots of these huge monarchs, staring into the creek at the patterns made by the water and the trout that lazed below, and surrounded by the sounds of nature around her.

Black Bird Shows and Mike watched her make her way across the field toward the creek. As soon as she was a few dozen yards from the house, the magpies appeared. They formed a triangle above and behind her and glided through the air majestically.

Mike turned to Black Bird.

"What do you think of that?"

Black Bird's expression was unreadable. He observed Colleen's progress silently for a few more moments, then turned to face Mike directly.

"It is as you said, my friend," he stated. "And you are right. These are some kind of spirit animals. They will be with her always, and they will see her through everything she must do in life. She will not always see them, but they will be there."

He continued, "There are some in the tribe who consider magpies to be thieves, tricksters and mischief makers, but a few of us know they indicate that all is well for those they befriend. The buffalo use them as sentinels of danger. They serve as guardians to let their friends know what is on the horizon."

Colleen never heard that conversation, and continued to think of the birds merely as her friends and companions.

Now, sitting outside the hospital, the memory of how much she loved the old box elder tree and the birds was strong. Whenever she felt lonely, frightened or confused, the tree was her refuge and the three magpies her companions. The voices of those brilliant black and white birds called encouragement to her. And the long-ago echo of her father's voice told her that she looked ready to take wing herself. Had the time come now for her to do so? Soon, perhaps, but right now there were still some obligations to fulfill for Mike.

The instructions he had given her and the rest of the family during the last months of his life waited to be carried out. Once moved from the ranch, he seemed certain that the end of his life was near. He was emphatic in detailing exactly how he wanted his last rites to be conducted. Most of the instructions were given to all of them at various family gatherings, but a few were reserved for Colleen alone.

Colleen, her mother, brother, sister, and their families sat together at the funeral home and went through the steps of arranging the services. Mike's wishes that he be cremated were relayed to the funeral director.

This was the first cremation in the family, and with some of the more traditional Irish Catholics relatives, it was not well received. Colleen's aunt, Mary Cecilia, her father's sister who had spent her life as a nun, was angry. She had come back to Montana from her convent in order to be present for her brother's funeral.

"This isn't proper!" she exclaimed, dismay on her unyielding face. "What will Father Ryan think?" The parish priest was conservative, to say the least.

"Sister Mary," Colleen responded patiently. "I think he will be less upset about that than he will be about the other thing Dad wanted."

Sister Mary paused, ducking her head as if something was going to be thrown in her general direction.

"What else?" Anxiety chilled the question.

Colleen took a deep breath. "He asked that an Indian holy man do the service," she replied.

Sister Mary was stunned into silence. "What about the blessings he will need to make his way to God?" she finally whispered.

"I don't know about all that. He was very emphatic about the holy man," Colleen responded. "He was so specific that he made us write this down in front of Mother on the day he told us." She showed Sister Mary the paper, with Mike's signature.

Sister Mary turned her head, then not looking at any of them, spine rigid and jaw tight, she rose abruptly and left the room.

The next day, Colleen went to the reservation. She had decided to see Jim Big Elk, an old man who had known her father since childhood. He had been a friend of the family for a long time, and would be able to tell her where to find a tribal holy man. When she stopped her car in front of the little house where the old man lived with his sons, she saw Jim sitting on the little front porch that hung on the house like a forgotten package. His slim, erect body belied his great age and the role he had played as lifetime friend to Mike Lorrah. In some ways, she was surprised to see him so well. His appearance had been that of an old man for as long as she had known him. His face lit up when he saw her.

"Hello, Jim!"

"Ho," Jim responded. His wrinkled face folded into even more wrinkles as his smile widened. "How's your dad?"

"That's why I'm here," Colleen said, surprised how close she was to tears in the presence of this old man's attachment to her father. "Dad died day before yesterday."

Jim stopped smiling, his face realigning itself into sad repose.

"I'll miss him. Thank you for coming to tell me."

"That's not the only reason I'm here," Colleen said. "Dad asked for a holy man to do the funeral service. I'm here to ask you how to get that done, and who should do it."

Jim thought for a moment. "The one who knows him best. Go and see Black Bird Shows. He knows your dad well. He'll help you."

Colleen nodded. Of course. Mike and Black Bird Shows had known each other for years. Their understanding was deep and long, in ways that surpassed mere friendship. Black Bird had been her father's guide and tribal brother, and that they had spent many hours together. But he seemed like such a spectral being that she had mentally relegated him to a category of legend and myth. Now she reproached herself for not realizing that Black Bird Shows would be the one her father would want. She should have known.

'Thank you, Jim," Colleen said, getting into her car. "I should have thought of him. I will see you soon."

Jim was silent, raising his hand to wave her on her way.

As she drove, Colleen thought about Black Bird Shows. Mike Lorrah and he had been children together. Many years ago, when he reached adulthood, he had become apprenticed to his clan uncle, an ancient, respected medicine man many tribal members believed was the incarnation of the oldest beliefs. When the uncle died, he assumed his place as a holyman, performing ceremonies and rituals for the tribe. From then on, he kept to himself, living in a small log cabin deep in the woods along the banks of Lodge Grass Creek, leaving there to conduct ceremonies, and for frequent visits with Mike. The family had not seen him after her parents moved to Billings.

Colleen wondered if Black Bird was still in good health, and if his house was still standing. It was very old and fragile in appearance even when she was a child, and she had trouble imagining that it could still be upright. The approach to the turn in the creek where the house was located brought several memories to the surface of her mind. There had been times when her father had taken her with him to Black Bird's simple dwelling, but on some of these occasions, after the initial social visiting was done he would say to her, "Colleen, you have a book with you in the pickup. Why don't you go out and read for a while. Black Bird and I have many other things to discuss and they are between the two of us." The tone of his voice had given her no room to argue or question, and she had gone willingly to her place in the truck.

On another, particularly vivid, occasion, she had been out riding her horse, and had come to Black Bird's place. Her father was there. She rode up close, intending to say hello, and slid off her horse to walk toward the house. Mike and Black Bird were sitting on the front step, smoking and talking. They were deeply involved in their conversation and did not notice her. Pausing, with a feeling like an intruder, she listened. They weren't speaking English. They often spoke in sign and in Crow to one another, but this was different, a language that Colleen didn't recognize. Suddenly they sensed her presence and both turned toward her at once. Would they think she had been spying on them? Her father didn't look happy to see her.

"What are you doing here?" he asked.

"I was riding, and noticed your truck up the road. I really didn't have a reason, I just thought I'd stop and say hello," Colleen defended her action.

"We're talking business here," Mike said. "I'll see you at home."

His statement was definite, absolute. She left, smarting from the intensity in her father's voice, aware that she had violated their privacy.

Now these memories confirmed for her that Black Bird Shows was the holy man to fulfill her father's instructions, and she knew what she had to do.

Allowing her car to roll to a stop at the head of the little road that led into the thicket of brush and trees that grew along the creek, she got out. Somehow she knew it would only be appropriate to approach Black Bird Shows on foot. Closing the door carefully to avoid the intrusion of a metallic slam on this primeval place, she started down the path. The grove of huge cottonwoods and busy chokecherries reached out and embraced her. The trees were just beginning to get their leaves and the birds laced the air with their songs. From bright sunshine, her path led her through a dappled other-worldly light, as if she had stepped into some other time and place.

Time seemed to expand as she walked, then she emerged into a small sunlit clearing. There, at the edge of the creek, looking the same as it always had, was the ancient little log cabin of Black Bird Shows. It was so old that its soft outlines appeared to grow from the earth, like a large brown mushroom. Next to it was the small humped lodge made of willows and blankets where her father had often taken a sweat with his old friend. The sweat was an important ritual they liked to share, heating their bodies to a red-hot temperature, allowing the poisons of daily living to escape from their pores. It was a poignant reminder of an old friendship, now severed by death.

Silently, as if materializing from the air, Black Bird Shows was directly in front of her.

Colleen started, but only from surprise, not fear of Black Bird. In fact, she felt very peaceful in his presence.

Bowing her head toward him respectfully, she greeted him. "Hello, Black Bird."

He was quiet for a moment, examining her face. "I have been expecting you, Mike's daughter. I felt my old friend's spirit pass me as he went on his way."

This didn't surprise Colleen. Mike had often spoken of Black Bird's ability to perceive what was beyond the comprehension of ordinary people.

"Then you know why I have come?"

"Yes. Mike and I talked many times of what should be done when it was time for him to pass from this life. He told me it is the belief of the tribe he is from that he would need an escort from another tribal person."

"Tribe?" Colleen was confused.

"Yes. He told me many things of his *Irish* tribe. Their beliefs are not so different from ours, the Crow. All tribal peoples share many things," Black Bird Shows explained. "I know what is needed. I will do a ceremony at the church that the other whites will understand. But I will do a private ceremony, too, and you must be there. It will be necessary for what Mike called 'the inheritance'."

Colleen hesitated. "What about my brother and sister?"

Black Bird Shows smiled gently.

"They are not excluded from all things," he said. "It is just that this part of the passing is for you."

Colleen shook her head. "I don't know if they will understand. I'm sure my mother won't."

"I will talk with them. I know the right words," Black Bird Shows said.

There was some consternation among the family's friends and relatives when the details of the service became apparent to those attending. It wasn't about the location. They were accustomed to services being held in Lodge Grass and people being buried in Billings. It was Mike's cremation and pre-services burial that were unexpected to most of the people in their little hometown. There seemed to be something missing when there was no casket, no body. Part of the usual small town funeral ritual involved viewing the deceased, but Mike had been emphatic about the necessity for cremation.

"I won't be needing this body in the next life," he had declared to his children. "I must be free of it. Be sure this happens. I'll be depending on you."

Observing the perplexed expression on Colleen's face, he said, "It's part of the old ways. It has to be done."

It seemed acceptable at the time, but not because of how it might relate to old Irish beliefs. She thought the old ways he was talking about were those of his childhood, perhaps something he remembered of his grandparents.

Black Bird Shows appeared in the church at the appointed time, said several prayers, and sang songs that Mike would have been pleased to hear. Some of the whites in the congregation were discomfited. But most were aware of Mike's affinity for the tribal ways on the reservation, and they knew he had many Indian friends. Colleen had told those closest to the family what to expect, and was a little surprised that her mother, brother and sister had no objection to any of this. The combination of the fact that these were Mike's wishes and whatever Black Bird had said to them must have made them comfortable. She had not been privy to the conversation.

When the church services were over, and all the people had gone to the potluck dinner in the church basement, Colleen was left alone. Earlier in the day, when the family had accompanied her father's ashes to the cemetery, they had stood in the shadows of beloved Pryor and Big Horn Mountain ranges. He could have requested his ashes be scattered over that country, but two of his children who had died in infancy were here, and he had asked to be placed close to them.

The three siblings had eulogized their father at the gravesite while their mother stood quietly but without tears. Colleen had kept her composure until it was her turn to speak. It had been agreed that she would recite the 23rd Psalm. Its references to the shepherd and the green pastures broke her. It was too sharp a reminder of Mike's years following the sheep. Her composure abandoned her, leaving her to sob in total release. Then a strange sensation settled over her. As the tears flowed out, purest peace flowed in. When the graveside rites were over, she was euphoric. More than ever, she felt her father's presence at her side.

The time came for her to drive back to Lodge Grass to meet Black Bird Shows. The location he had indicated was a small distance from his sweat lodge, not far from the peaceful grove of huge cottonwood trees that she had often sought out as a child and young woman.

The trip from Billings gave her time to think about all that Mike had meant to her, and to re-live the hours they had spent together. Once in Black Bird's lane, she parked her car at the same place as before and approached on foot. The regal man was already there, waiting for her. She fleetingly wondered how he had gotten there so quickly from Billings. Had he come in a car? He had refused her offer to bring him to Billings, but she did not recall that he owned a vehicle. Her full attention was directed to what he was saying.

"This is not my ceremony," he said. "Your father taught me this, and said his mother taught him."

This statement immediately riveted Colleen's attention. Her father had never said anything to suggest that his mother, her grandmother, Velia, was anything but the strong Catholic that the family had always known her to be. Something nagged at her, but it was too deeply buried in her subconscious to resurrect. With a gesture the old Indian man indicated the center of the grove, with its soft carpet of grass. The ripple of the creek as it danced along the ancient stones sounded like distant notes from a flute or pipe. Was she imagining things? She had often thought she heard music in the wind and in the creek, but this was more than that. It was most definitely flute music, in a song older than anything she had ever experienced.

Slowly, she walked to the spot Black Bird Shows ordained. Up in the canopy of the trees, the sun played among the new leaves, changing the patterns of light and shadow on the tender spring grasses at her feet. Arms spread wide as Black Bird instructed, she stood with eyes closed as the holy man began to chant in tune with the wind and the creek. He produced a braid of sweet grass, and it ignited from an unseen source. The smoke from the braid wafted about her, purifying her and this place. The old holyman continued to chant. Colleen knew a little of the Crow Indian tongue from her friends in the reservation school she had attended. But the language Black Bird Shows was using in this ceremony was not recognizable.

Failing to remember that she had once heard him and her father speaking it, she decided it must be some ancient Crow dialect that she had never heard. Whatever it was, it began to weave its spell.

The world began to spin around her. The lines between the current world and what her father had occasionally called the "otherworld" blurred, then vanished, and Colleen felt herself cross over. Light and music poured over her, then into her, as she became one with the plants and rocks and water. Strength and a sense of ancient knowledge flowed into her heart.

The embers that had slept in her soul after the trip into Yellowstone were fanned into an inferno, consuming her doubts and her fears. All sense of time and place were lost as implausible colors swirled around her. She felt herself take wing. In that flight, she was not alone. A single magpie soared and circled with her, over the hills of the ranch, and two more of the birds joined them over the sacred Bighorn and Pryor mountains. Finally, the flight took her over the ocean and then above hills and mountains that looked somehow strange and familiar at the same time. This climaxed when all these sights disappeared into a vortex of color and sound and mist.

When she became aware of the "real" world again, she was lying on her back in the grass and wildflowers, arms still spread wide. Black Bird Shows was nowhere to be seen. She was alone, and filled with the internal fire that had been given her.

Colleen stayed in that position for a long time, recalling her feelings during this ritual. A strong impression lingered that she had been flying through the air, and had connected with all of nature. Engraved in her mind were the many sights revealed to her, including lush green hills and another grove of trees. It had been strange to her, and much older than the one she found herself in now. A sense of purpose had come to her, but what it was remained a mystery. Where was Black Bird Shows? Her intuition told her that he had not left completely, and as if called, he now appeared at the edge of the grassy clearing in the grove. His face was transformed.

"The medicine your dad gave me for you was very powerful," he said quietly. "When he taught me this ceremony, it didn't seem like much. He did not tell me what would happen when I did it for you. He taught me these words. I do not know them. But when I said them, there was big fire. It burned without burning anything, but it was big. Then I did not see you any more. When the fire was gone, you were here again. Did you dream?"

Colleen was slow to respond, unsure of what she had seen. "I don't know. It did not feel so much like a dream. I felt like I was in another place." Then she described the experience as best she could. When she finished, she waited expectantly for the old man to interpret everything for her.

But he only shook his head. "It's big magic," he said. "Your medicine and this vision are as powerful as anything I ever saw. Your dad said you would have to learn what it was all about, so I believe you will. I will keep you in my prayers."

Bowing her head reverently toward the old holy man, Colleen said, "Thank you, Black Bird. I know you have done everything my dad wanted, and you are right. I will make it my task to find the answers."

The old man passed a glistening black and white feather around the spot where she stood, said a few words in Crow, and stepped back, still facing her. His expression was quizzical, as if he saw something in her face he was not expecting. Taking backward steps into the shadow of the trees, he moved until she could not see him any more.

Hugging herself, she futilely tried to hold the impressions close, knowing it would be impossible to tell her husband or anyone else about this experience. Uncertainty about even returning to her work nudged at her thoughts.

Deep in thought, she walked back to her car. Sliding into the driver's seat, her reflection in the visor mirror caught her eye. The face that presented itself was unnerving. A glow emanated from inside her pale skin and an intense light gleamed in her eyes. She drove home.

Several days of contemplation passed, and the experience in the grove took its place in her heart. She felt like there was something she was supposed to do, but whatever was lurking in her memory refused to surface. She went back to work. Easing back into the "real world," the events of the previous week came to reside in a secret corner of her mind. Days passed, and with the passage came the realization that the time was not right to act. Her heart recognized it was just another step in the journey her father had hinted about.

After that, life began to accelerate, but not directly toward whatever it was was that her father wanted her to do. Instead, her professional life shifted again, with another career advancement. This one required her to move to assume an executive position in Chicago. With Art's vague assurances at hand, she packed her belongings and moved to start her new job, certain that he was not planning to move with her.

Time proved her right. Art never joined her. The intensity of her work caused her to set aside the final conversation with her father and the events with Black Bird Shows. Eventually, she nearly forgot about them. Her twenty-plus-year marriage was dying a slow death, and she was building her career. There were few differences between her and most of the other people of her generation, with profession and the acquisition of material things a main focus. Her ascent in the company began, and work consumed her totally.

Art continued to withdraw from her, and while it seemed inevitable that a marriage without passion would end the same way, it still constituted a loss of more than 20 years of each of their lives. Finally she approached him with the proposal that they divorce. Almost as if they were making a corporate agreement, which, in fact, they were, the two of them constructed a business-deal divorce. This done, she embarked upon life alone.

CHAPTER 3

▼

Indecision had never been a part of Colleen's style. Her actions as a single person were sure, whether in work or in personal life. There had always been a feeling of direction and destiny underlying all other influences in her life. Once committed to a career the undercurrent was even stronger. Whether it was travel or her work, a self-assured woman took these steps. What had come in the wake of her divorce?

Like a cliff-diver, she plunged into her work, producing real achievement. At the same time, strength and confidence grew inside her by leaps and bounds. The company advised her to develop a professional image, with career clothing and makeup. Her long hair was tamed into a neat, tailored coiffure that left no doubt of her business persona, although she refused to have it cut. Gym workouts developed her physically and management training developed her intellectually. To be sure of her safety in her new, big-city environs, a series of self-defense courses were in order, rewarding her with great pleasure at her body's natural response to the discipline. It was an almost magical transformation. The pragmatism of it all overshadowed many of her more idealistic and spiritual thoughts and beliefs for the more practical world of big business.

As the new work and new location became more comfortable, she began to explore Chicago. Her forays took her to many parts of the lively city, where her greatest pleasure was derived from its Irish history and Irish people. With the imprint of her father's love of the culture, from stories about his grandparents and his great-grandparents, she permitted herself to soak up all the city had to offer. Even when Mike acknowledged the tribulations of his ancestors while they tried to achieve the American dream, he told of how they retained their ways .

His regard for these people had a level of awe that seemed a little excessive for who and what they had been.

As a child, when Colleen had pleaded for more stories about them, he often left the impression that he would go just so far in the telling, and no further. As her teen years and early adulthood passed, she continued to press for more stories, but usually found herself listening the same ones over again. Finally she had resigned herself to this, and while pushing here and there for more information, knew the limits. Now the Windy City provided the opportunity to become acquainted with its Irish community, sitting with new immigrants in pubs, and developing friendships of her own with Irish people.

Participating in talk of the "troubles," and the peace process, she was quick to express a desire for peace between the peoples of Ireland. Long experience and study had made her well-informed on the issues. Her father had shared news articles about the events in this turbulent place with her all her life, and many of the stories she read moved her to tears of frustration and sorrow. It seemed these conditions would never release the Irish people, and the circumstances seemed so futile.

Thinking about the Irish-American community in Chicago made her smile. It had not been possible to get to know many Irish people on the Crow Indian reservation. There, white people had been the minority in the schools and general population. Her brother, sister and she were fourth generation on this reservation, and while well accepted—her brother, father and grandfather were all adopted members of the tribe—they were still white. Her father enjoyed a brotherhood with the elders, and was included in or welcome at many private ceremonies. Tribal members understood his respect for the importance of these rituals, and they trusted him not to reveal the secrets. Her earliest memories included awareness that her skin was a different color from most of her childhood friends, even though the Indian children included her in their games as one of them. Her family had felt at home there, but all of them were constantly aware that they were guests in the world of the Crow, even the world of the children.

Her parents encouraged her to respect and acknowledge the tribal way of life, and reminded her that she would never be truly Indian. That did not stop certain elements of the culture from calling out to her. The singing, drumming, and tribal structure all seemed to tug at ancient memories inside her. She couldn't put her finger on it, and it was not a comfortable subject to discuss with her mother. Her father listened while she talked about it, but didn't embellish her thoughts with any comments of his own. This frustrated her. On a few occasions she had broached this subject in talks with her grandmother, but Velia's reserve kept the conversation at a distance. As Colleen recalled it now, her grandmother was willing to share some things with her, but seemed reluctant to discuss these mysterious feelings in detail. Such discussions crossed into a forbidden area, and her grandmother always changed the subject to something less intimate, less pivotal.

Once in the Midwest, a long way from eastern Montana, and removed from the Crow Indian reservation, the world was very different. The rhythm of the city was all around her, the work was demanding, and the Irish-American community was fascinating. For the first time, here was a pipeline to her heritage, a true channel to the genes that created her. Every restaurant and pub called out to her to eat the food, sip the Guinness, listen to the songs and the speech patterns. The music was in her blood, and the sound of the voices was in her ears.

Gradually, something outside her understanding began to happen. Memories she had long suppressed began to surface, buoyed by the music and the talk. One summer Saturday, walking along the Navy Pier, she heard a trio of outdoor musicians playing old Irish melodies. As if the music had fingers, it reached out to her, entered her soul, and began to tug on her recall.

The aire they played transported her to her grandmother's yard in the mid-summer of her tenth year. She crouched next to her grandmother in the garden, where they were alone together that day. Her grandmother was singing to herself as she worked. The song charmed the child Colleen.

"What are you singing, grandma?" Colleen asked.

Her grandmother paused. "A song *my* gran' taught me," she replied. "Why do you ask?" Her sky-blue eyes rested intently on the child.

"It sounds like magic," Colleen had replied, not knowing why she felt that way.

Recognition flashed in her grandmother's eyes. "What seems magical about it?"

The child rocked back on her heels in the soft dirt and looked off into the distance. "I don't know. I guess the way it makes me feel. It's like it's inside me, whirling around."

Her grandmother smiled a secret smile. "Perhaps it is," she said. "It's an Irish song, and only the Irish hear it that way."

"Like Daddy?" Colleen was excited.

"Like your daddy, but not like everybody in the family."

"But Daddy says we are all Irish," Colleen declared.

"We may all be Irish in blood, but we are not all Irish in our souls."

At that moment, several of her cousins arrived at her grandmother's gate, and the discussion was set aside. Now, that conversation shone as a link in the chain of events that had taken her to the ceremony with Black Bird Shows. But the two occurrences did not connect to each other in any logical way. As if it were smoke, the memory dissolved into a mist that tantalized her but prevented her seeing clearly to the horizon. A nagging feeling insisted that something more was expected of her, but whatever it was, it defied definition.

Returning to the present, she realized the group was finishing the aire. The small crowd of listeners had disbanded, and she found herself standing alone. The musicians were eyeing her curiously. Fishing into her bag, she pulled out a five-dollar bill. It fluttered into the fiddle case the musicians had set out and she walked away quickly. The breeze off Lake Michigan pursued her with the sounds of boats and water, on her stroll back into the anonymity of the city's streets.

This incident magnified her sense that there was a curtain across her life, and family secrets lurked behind it. There was no dread about these mysteries, nor was there a compulsion to uncover them. But she was curious. A telephone conversation with her mother caused her to venture into the subject of her Irish heritage.

"Mom," she began, "What did Dad ever tell you about his Irish background? Did he know anything about his grandparents and great-grandparents?"

There was a moment of silence on the other end of the line. "He never said much. When we were first going out together, he did talk about being Irish quite a bit. He called himself 'Irish Mike,' and seemed to think about it a lot, but I could never get him to explain anything about it."

As their conversation continued, Colleen's mother announced a new outlet to deal with her grief over Mike's death. "I took a lot of notes on my conversations with your Dad in his last years, while he was so sick, "she said. "I'm going to do something with them now."

"What do you have in mind, Mom?"

"I'm going to write them up. I think the life your dad and I lived would be an interesting story to some." Her mother went on to talk about taking a creative writing class, and joining a local author's club so she could get some critiquing and some ideas of how to approach such a project.

Colleen was intrigued. "I didn't know you had kept notes on that stuff, Mom," she observed. "What gave you the idea to do that?"

"I knew your dad was very sick, and I knew he might not live very long. I always liked writing, and thought I should get down some of the things he knew and thought before the opportunity passed. You probably don't know I always kept a diary. Between the things I was able to learn from your Dad, and my own daily journals, I believe I have a pretty complete story."

Colleen was nonplused. This was one of the last things she had expected of her mother.

"Mom," she said, "I'd be really interested to read some of your rough draft materials when you get going. Do you think I could do that?"

"Of course, dear," her mother replied, promising to send pieces along as she completed them.

Colleen was captivated by this conversation, and immediately talked with her sister about it. Kathleen wasn't particularly surprised. She had been closer to their mother than Colleen all their lives, and had an inkling that their mother might do this at some time. Colleen's surprise caused her to smile.

"It's good for her. Mom knows what she wants to do, and I'm really glad she's decided to do this. Think what we gain from it. She and Dad talked about a lot of things in his last years. Now this will let us be in on the conversation. It's part of her grieving process, a way for her to work through how much she misses him."

This conversation satisfied Colleen, and didn't raise a lot of questions at first. Soon, pages began to arrive from her mother. Most of the material revolved around stories and history that Colleen had heard growing up. But the more she read, the stronger the small tickle of dissonance became in the back of her mind. It was an engaging story, filled with many memories and family history information. But something was missing. It was like smooth water in the deep part of the river, with many currents just under the surface, out of sight. This feeling led to a question-and-answer conversation with her mother.

"Is there anything you are leaving out of your book, Mom?"

Della hesitated for a long moment. "Why would you ask that, Colleen?"

"I don't know. I guess I like what you are doing so much that I just want more and more."

The older woman contemplated her daughter's answer. Another pause. Then:

"I've found someone to help with the editing," Della shifted the subject. "One of the instructors at the local community college said she would be willing to read it for me."

"That sounds great, Mom."

Colleen was relieved to change the focus of the conversation. Pushing her mother further about feelings she couldn't define herself would be nonproductive. It was typical of their lifetime relationship. They had never communicated as well as she and her father had. Some family news rounded out the rest of the call, and they left it at that.

Less than a day after this discussion, Kathleen called. When Colleen answered the telephone, her sister said, "I just had a very strange conversation with Mom."

"Really?" Colleen's mind raced. "What was it about?"

Kathleen paused for a moment, then, her voice very quiet, she said, "She came over to see me, all upset because Sean was going to do some research in Lewistown."

The intensity in her sister's tone was acutely apparent. Their brother, Sean, was a skilled historical writer who focused primarily on Montana and the west. He did deep research to assure the authenticity of his work, and often spent several weeks in any location that he planned to use as a setting in his books.

"Why would she be concerned about that?"

Kathleen's voice was almost inaudible now. "Remember how we were told that Mom and Dad got married in Lewistown?" she reminded Colleen.

"Oh, yes. That's right. They got married secretly, and never told her parents because she was so young," Colleen recited the story her parents had related so many times during her childhood.

"Well, that's what upset her. She is terrified of Sean looking up the marriage records," Kathleen stated flatly.

"Why? So they eloped, what's the big deal?" Colleen was genuinely puzzled.

"It turns out they never did get officially married. Sean won't find a marriage certificate there or anywhere else."

That little flame flickered inside her again to illuminate what had been bothering her as she read the pages of her mother's manuscript. How strange. She had no knowledge of this family secret, yet the sense of it had been with her. Her father had never shared this particular piece of information with her.

She reassured Kathleen. "I'll fly home for Mother's Day," she said. "I'll talk with her then."

Kathleen's voice relaxed.

"Good. You always know how to ask questions like that. I'm never comfortable about confronting her, but she's used to you doing that."

Colleen laughed aloud, recognizing the latitude her status as youngest child gave her.

"That's true," she agreed. "Besides, we all need more information about this little surprise. Meanwhile, see if you can get Sean to change his story with her so she doesn't have to be so scared."

When Colleen hung up, introspection took over. What a burden this must have been for her parents. Somehow they had managed to keep all three children from knowing that they had never officially married, but how many people in the family or, for that matter, in their hometown, had known? It was curious, and at this point in their adulthood, it was of no real concern to any one of the three siblings. If only their mother had known how little impact such news would have had on them.

On the other hand, such a secret would have been far more unsavory for people of her parents' generation. If such a thing happened now, in an age when people often lived together without formalities, such news would hardly have created a ripple. But having her parents at the center of such a subterfuge still came as a surprise.

The opportunity to talk with her mother came over the Mothers' Day weekend when they were out for an afternoon of lunch and shopping. Della Lorrah sat, calm in neat pastel blouse and slacks, across from her youngest daughter. Her face held a look of interest, as if she was waiting for a conversation to begin. Colleen knew this discussion could make her mother uncomfortable, but she broached the subject in the only way she knew how. Facing her mother squarely in the little restaurant, she plunged right in.

"Mom," she began. "Kathleen told me what you said to her about your marriage to Dad. Want to fill me in?"

Della looked around the restaurant furtively; as if afraid that everyone she had ever known was there and might hear. When she saw that they were the only people in the establishment, she leaned forward toward Colleen, elbows on the table, as if to create a small private space within which they could converse.

"It's really difficult for me to talk about. It's not something I'm very proud of."

Colleen gentled her own approach, trying to put her mother at ease.

"Tell me about it."

Drawing a deep breath, Della began to speak.

"Most of the story we always told you kids was true. I met your dad at a country dance, and it was pretty much love at first sight. He was so handsome. Probably the most handsome man I had ever seen. He was tall, his hair was pitch black, and his eyes...they were so blue. I felt like I was hypnotized. When he came across the room and asked me to dance, it seemed like a spell was cast over me."

Colleen knew the story, but she had never heard her mother speak so frankly about the event. But nothing prepared her for what her mother said next.

"It was really like magic. I felt a fire start inside me, as if his eyes were the sun focused through a magnifying glass," her mother recalled. Colleen's spirit warmed in response.

"What happened after that?"

"He took me in his arms and we had that dance. I was lost to the world. We only danced the one dance that night, but after that, we saw each other every time we could. I was under his sway from then on. I don't know exactly when it happened, but within several months we became intimate, and before I knew it, I was expecting your brother."

"When I told your father, he told me that he would stay with me forever, but we would not be married in a church. That horrified me." There was a distant look in her eyes.

Colleen was perplexed "I'm confused. What was his reason for that?"

Her mother looked up, startled from her reverie. She continued without answering Colleen's question.

"He saw how hurt and shocked I was, so he took me to visit someone. It was Black Bird Shows."

"Black Bird Shows? The same Black Bird Shows who did his funeral?"

"The very same. He was a younger man then, but of course, we all were."

"Why did he take you to him?" Colleen asked.

"To witness our vows." It was a matter-of-fact statement.

"I'm sorry, maybe I don't understand," Colleen said. "I thought you didn't have a formal wedding."

"We didn't, in the Christian sense," her mother responded. "Black Bird Shows served as a witness, while your dad spoke his vows to me in a language I didn't understand. He told me it was old Irish, and that this ceremony had been traditional for hundreds, maybe thousands of years in Ireland. He said it was part of something called 'Brehon Law,' and that if we were in Old Ireland, someone like Black Bird Shows, only less a holy man and more a magistrate, would officiate After that, he took me to see his grandmother, and left me with her for a day. She explained more about these beliefs, and made it seem acceptable. I felt at the time that it was the right thing to do, although I don't remember now what she said. I just stopped worrying about it."

"After that, my only real concern was my own parents. You know what strict church people your grandparents were. I knew they would be disappointed because I was not finishing high school. I couldn't bear to tell them we weren't officially married. So your father and I told them we had eloped to Lewistown and been married by a justice of the peace. We even had an announcement run in the local paper to make it more real."

This reinforced the Lewistown elopement story that the siblings had heard all their lives. Colleen could recall asking her mother about their wedding when she was a child, and she remembered being told this tale. Since it meant that her parents had not had a big formal wedding with white dress and veil, her childish interest had quickly waned and she asked no further questions.

Now here was the truth, and she wanted to help her mother understand that she and her brother and sister really weren't troubled by it.

"You know that this doesn't make any difference to Sean, Kathleen and me, don't you?" she asked, quick to comfort Della.

Her mother smiled shakily.

"I do know that. Common law would have been legal, anyway. But much later in our relationship, your dad and I did finally get a legitimate marriage license and have a justice of the peace ceremony, not too long before you were born. Your aunt, Sister Mary Cecilia, told us that we were jeopardizing our children's entry into heaven, and such family pressure was finally too much for your dad. So one weekend, we went off and made it all legal. We did it in another county, clear across Montana, just to be sure that it was done."

"Mom, I'm sorry you have carried this burden for so long. We all had a great family life, and I hope you can relax with this whole thing now."

"Well, after the close call with Sean's research, I just felt you children should know now," her mother said. "In the event you or Sean should take up interest in family history again, I didn't want you wondering why you couldn't find any information."

Colleen made a mental note to research more about "Brehon Law," and again reassured Della. Her mother looked at her steadily.

"Now that you know," she declared, "we won't need to discuss this again."

Colleen agreed, but her heart told her there was more to learn in the future, and any further information would come from a different source than her mother.

CHAPTER 4

▼

The talk with Della renewed her interest in the family history. At the time, one of her cousins on her mother's side was researching the backgrounds of her maternal ancestors. That work had been straightforward and helped greatly by the many public records available. Colleen wondered about her father's family. In what little spare time she had, she set out to trace back through the generations. There were only stories from childhood to start with. It was not long before she discovered that there was almost nothing in the way of documentation. Her biggest frustration was that the opportunity to ask her grandmother these questions had been missed. Now with her father and her grandmother both dead, it was hard to tell how much information would be forthcoming from any surviving relatives.

The likelihood of spending some time with her father's sister, the nun, Mary Cecilia, seemed tenuous at best. The events surrounding Mike's funeral had left Sister Mary angry, and she had summarily cut off most contact. Colleen sensed that her aunt and her mother had exchanged words about the service, and whatever had passed between them had resulted in a real alienation.

But now some time had elapsed, and Sister Mary Cecilia had retired from active service to a convent where meditation and prayer were the daily activities. That cloistered place was in Illinois; only about two hours drive from where Colleen was living. Maybe Sister Mary would be willing to see her if she asked.

A telephone call secured permission for a visit. Although she did not talk with Sister Mary, the office relayed her message and the old nun's agreement. What would she find?

Her approach to the convent revealed a gothic exterior and surroundings. It seemed a little daunting and austere, but once inside, the polished dark woodwork glowed with a quiet warmth. A novice came forward to ask what her business was. She explained to the girl, whose face looked like that of a Christmas tree angel. The novice disappeared down a corridor, walking with ghost-like silence and grace along gleaming terrazzo floors. Shortly, she returned to say Colleen should wait in the anteroom for Sister Mary Cecilia.

A short time passed, and the wraithlike figure of her aunt appeared in the doorway. Her habit-attired appearance startled Colleen. How small this woman looked. The years had aged and diminished her and she was dwarfed by the architecture here. There were more lines in her face than Colleen remembered, but she still had the same electric blue eyes as Mike's. Colleen looked hopefully into those eyes and was rewarded with a quiet smile from her aunt.

"I am so glad you have come," her aunt greeted her softly. "Thank you."

"Do you have some time to talk with me?" Colleen asked.

"I'm retired," Mary Cecilia said. "I have all the time you might need. But let's go out near the grotto and enjoy this glorious day."

Once they were in the peaceful garden at the side of the convent, Sister Mary gestured toward a bench near the spring that flowed from the rocks there. They sat down and listened for a few moments to the sound of the water and the birdsong that emanated from the nearby shrubs. Several of the more courageous small birds ventured to the water near them for a drink.

"What can I do for you?" Sister Mary asked.

Colleen was surprised by the shift from the anger displayed at Mike's funeral to this warm, friendly reception, but she chose to accept the change as a gift.

"I'm doing some family tree research," Colleen began, and then corrected herself. "Actually, it's more family history research, and I believe you may be the only one who can give me specific information. No one seems to know where Aunt Willow is, and you are the only one left from Dad's generation."

Sister Mary's expression became wary. "I don't remember very much," she stated.

Colleen was not daunted by this proclamation. "I know that you took care of your grandmother in her last days, and it would help me to know where she was born, and where her husband, Daniel, was born. I know they were Irish, but I don't know what part of Ireland they came from, and that makes it hard to trace the family."

Sister Mary said, "I really don't know those things. If I was told, I've forgotten. They were good people, even though they did have some unusual beliefs…" She stopped suddenly, with a veiled expression on her face, as if she feared she had said too much.

Colleen's mind went on alert. "Unusual beliefs?" she asked.

Sister Mary recovered quickly. "I mean, they were old, and tended to talk in mysteries sometimes. Being Irish, they had a lot of odd superstitions, but I never paid much attention. I refused to be influenced by such ideas. I knew the Church's way was the right way."

Colleen changed tactics.

"Well, if you don't remember about them, maybe you'd be willing to tell me how you came to choose the religious order for your life work, instead of marrying and raising a family. What led to that choice?" she asked.

Sister Mary was thoughtful and she took a moment to compose herself. "I just always knew it was the thing I should do." she replied.

Colleen pressed. "I've seen dozens of photos of you as a young woman. You were lovely, and the photos showed you with lots of young male admirers. You were obviously very pretty and very popular. Was there a particular turning point?"

"I was always a good girl, and even then I was devoted to the Church. I worked hard to please my mother and grandmother," Sister Mary recalled. "When grandmother was dying, I went to live with her to give her the help she needed. She liked to talk about many of her old-country beliefs and when I heard what she had to say, I knew she was senile. After listening to all that immigrant nonsense, I decided it would be my place to put an end to all that superstition in the family. The true way was through the Church, and I was the right one to take that path." Her voice took on a revivalist's ardor.

"Was there a specific event that caused that decision?" Colleen prodded.

"I don't remember," Sister Mary declared.

Colleen was frustrated. Certainly there was much more that her aunt was not saying. "Is there anything else you can think of that might help me?" she pleaded.

Sister Mary looked into the spring for a long moment. "No!" Her answer was absolute and somewhat abrupt. "I'm afraid I can't be much help to you. Maybe your cousin Roisín can help. I know she did some research on the family at one time, because she got the old family bible and many of your grandmother's photos after she died. You might try asking her about this."

Roisín, the daughter of her father's other sister, Willow, would be next on her list. Willow had been the "wild one" of her father's family. In her departure from the state after three failed marriages she had disappeared with a man no one in the family knew. Colleen wished she could talk with her. Her childhood memory of this vibrant woman with the glossy auburn hair and dancing blue eyes brought to mind a strong-willed personality who was never afraid to say what was on her mind. At this point, however, no one in the family knew where she was, or if she was even still alive. Her two daughters and one son were very young when they had been left with their father, and they were very bitter about what they considered to be her abandonment of them.

There was no doubt that Mary Cecilia was deflecting her questions, so Colleen shifted the conversation. She asked after her aunt's health and if she needed anything brought to her from the outside world. Her aunt shook her head, then thanked her for coming and said she was grateful to Colleen for reopening family communications. Sister Mary said nothing about Della, and Colleen didn't venture into that arena. The disagreement that had divided these two women did not involve her, and it was unlikely that she could repair whatever damage had been done.

Asking permission to visit her aunt at the convent again in the future brought as warm a response from Sister Mary as she had used in her greeting. There was no doubt that she would be pleased to see her niece again. Colleen sensed an underlying trepidation in these assurances, but chose to overlook it, determined to maintain contact.

Returning to Chicago, Colleen began to make time in her heavy schedule to research the family history. It was troubling that so little was known about the ancestors who had produced the family. She believed it would be a gift to her nieces and nephews to have such information. In addition, if she really were going to Ireland someday, it would be important to know where these people had come from. There should be records on almost anyone who had ever lived in the United States, but where did one begin? She was driven by a compelling desire to learn all she could

Once settled in Chicago at her apartment and at her new job, Colleen decided the best place to start doing family research would be the nearest Family History Center, an arm of the Mormon Church. It felt a little strange and presumptuous to enter the door of the library there as a non-member of the LDS Church with no intention of joining. But a telephone call had reassured her that all were welcome to use the facility, so it was worth investing a Saturday to give it a try.

Just inside the door, a cheerful, older woman greeted her from behind the front desk. She looked like someone's drawing of Mrs. Santa Claus. Smiling up at her, this little guardian spoke first.

"Can we help you find something?"

Colleen looked down at her pensively.

"I'm not sure where to begin. I have some ancestors I'd like to try to find, but I don't know how to do this. Do I need to be a member to use this facility?" It was probably best to ask again.

"Oh, no, dear," the woman's bright smile embraced her. "I'm not a member myself. My name is Jeanette Smithers, and I've gotten so much help here that I decided to volunteer some time."

She gazed at her new customer with sparkling eyes, her apple-pie features warm and open.

"Tell me whatever you already know, and what you hope to find out."

Colleen recounted the small smattering of anecdotal information she had about her great grandparents.

"What I really want to do is find out where their ancestral home was in Ireland," she finished.

Jeanette showed her the microfiche files, the computer disks and all the library materials. The availability of microfilm from the central Family History Library in Salt Lake City was explained, and she pointed out how much information was available on the Internet. It was enough to send the senses spinning with possibilities.

"I knew this would be simple, once I knew how to do this," Colleen declared.

Jeanette's response was a cautionary smile.

"I hope it *is* simple for you, dear. Many of us find out that people moved too often or census records were inaccurate, or files were destroyed in one way or another. And you can't believe how many people had the same name or changed their names. Even though we are one of the larger family history centers, you will still find gaps, some of them very big and deep. But it's fun. It's a lot like playing detective, and I think you'll enjoy it."

Colleen spent the entire day scanning the available materials. She reviewed the notes she had hastily scrawled from memories of conversations with her father, her mother, and her aunt. Jeanette helped her order several census microfilms, thinking there would be a good chance of locating these people in the places where family oral information suggested they were at certain times in their history.

Her mind was exhausted when she left the library, but logic told her she was on the verge of discovering all about these Irish ancestors. How difficult could it be? The cousin who assembled the family history about her mother's ancestors had found family bibles, hundreds of photographs, and many, many written records. There was no reason that the same kind of information would not be available on her father's people.

The weeks went by, and the microfilms began to arrive. Among the some of the census materials were indications that her great grandparents had lived for a time in Garryowen, an all-Irish settlement in Iowa farm country. A glance at the map told her it was not far from Chicago. A weekend trip took her there in search of any information the parish records might contain. A couple of wrong turns made her curse the flat Iowa farmlands for lacking the kinds of landmarks of her Montana terrain. Finally, what remained of Garryowen came into sight, almost by happenstance. A community hall of sorts was first, then a large and beautiful old Catholic church commanded the landscape. The most interesting part was a small churchyard with numerous headstones. Walking among them, it became apparent that nearly every marker was inscribed with the name of the deceased, and the county of his or her birth in Ireland. It was with a feeling of deep excitement that she talked with the priest. It was pure luck that she found him on the premises, she discovered. The parish had a visiting priest arrangement, and he was only there on certain days of the month.

The cleric listened to her explanation, then offered the bad news.

"You'll have to contact the Church Archives in Davenport, Iowa, for any records. They are no longer stored at St. Patrick's."

Colleen accepted this setback, and found herself little surprised by it. This kind of obstacle seemed to be becoming routine in her family history research. Looking once more over her shoulder at the church, and wishing the building could tell its history, she drove back to Chicago.

Her mail waited on the floor of her entryway where it had landed after being dropped through the mail slot in the apartment door. One welcome piece was waiting among the bills and advertisements. The Big Horn County clerk and recorder had responded to her letter requesting a copy of her great-grandmother's death certificate. Its contents confirmed what she had been told as a child.

Her great-grandmother had died in Lodge Grass, where her father Mike had grown up. Then a note at the top of the document caught her attention. The most important fragment of information on the certificate almost jumped at her. It was the location of her great-grandmother's birthplace. There, in plain, clear letters, her place of birth was listed as "Ottumwa, Iowa." This confused her. She thought this woman had been born in Ireland.

It would be easy enough to check this information. Her company had clients in Ottumwa. When she called on them, she reasoned, a side-trip to the courthouse would be easy enough. That should yield a copy of her great-grandmother's birth certificate, and put her well on her way to gaining all the information she wanted about her Irish ancestors.

Nothing could have been further from the truth.

Her visit to the courthouse revealed that the county had no records as far back as the birth date of her great-grandmother. Refusing to be discouraged, Colleen went to the Ottumwa St. Mary's Catholic Church. The church secretary told her that a few parish records were kept, but the archivist would not be in until Monday. Would she like to leave a written request for the information? Further inquiry resulted in the most frustrating information. The census records that would help her most had burned, and there were no school records available.

Stymied at every turn, she began to see that these elusive ancestors would not be so easy to trace. Her disappointment increased with the realization that she would have to backtrack. How could this be so difficult? After all, there were family members who had kept track of relatives and ancestors, some who had passed family stories down, who had even known some of these people she was searching for. But at every turn, with every question, there were huge roadblocks. Of course, recordkeeping was haphazard in the early years of settling America, and people who moved as frequently as her ancestors often were missed in census counts, especially if they were Irish immigrants.

All these events caused her to focus on her cousin Roisín, whom Sister Mary said had done some family tree research on her father's side of the family. Colleen wrote to her. Her letter pleaded for any and all information Roisín might have uncovered. The response was quick, with a large manilla envelope arriving at Colleen's door. It contained some research information, most of which Colleen had already discovered. There also was a letter from Roisín. In her typical chatty fashion, she related what her children had been doing, inquired after Colleen's health, and reported on the weather in her area. Tucked inside a small paragraph in the note was a mention that Willow had re-established contact with her children after all these years. The paragraph riveted Colleen's attention. She snatched up her telephone and dialed her cousin's number.

Pouring out her thanks for the information received, Colleen acknowledged the years of non-communication.

"I know we haven't had much contact in the last few years, so I feel a little strange asking for your help at this point. There have been a lot of dead ends in my research, and I really appreciate all you have sent me."

Roisín assured her that she was delighted to hear from her, and said, "I would have sent you more, but I'm afraid most of it is gone. A few years ago, our home burned, and I lost most of my research and photos."

Colleen felt like someone had slapped her. More information unavailable.

Aloud, she said, "Oh, Rosie, I'm so sorry. I didn't know about the fire. I hope you and your family are all okay."

Roisín smiled at her cousin's use of the childhood nickname, and replied, "Oh yes, we are, thank God. We weren't even home when it happened, so we were safe. We did okay with our insurance, and have a new house now, so we're fine. Trouble is, it's impossible to replace some of that stuff, like all the old family information and pictures."

"I understand. But your letter intrigued me for another reason. You mentioned that you had heard from your mother. I thought no one knew where she was."

"It turned out that her fifth or sixth husband or live-in or whatever he was, died, and she is alone. Guess she had some time to think about all she's done, and she's probably looking for us to take care of her in her old age. She hasn't taken particularly good care of herself, with her lifestyle, and I don't think she wants to be a lonely old woman. We still haven't seen her or anything. We just got a note from her saying where she was."

The tone of Roisín's voice made it apparent that she was still very angry with her mother.

On the other hand, it was amazing that Willow had made any contact at all. She was anything but family oriented. She had simply vanished, and had not communicated with anyone for any reason, with the rare exceptions of a few postcards she had sent to Mike. These came from exotic locales like Alaska and Mexico, and never had a return address.

"Rosie, may I have her address and telephone number?" Colleen asked. "I do want to talk to her. This family tree research is driving me crazy, and she might remember some things."

"Sure." Roisín laughed, a small bitter laugh. "Don't let her talk you into taking care of her or giving her money or anything. She's in New Orleans, which is just far enough away for me."

Once the good-byes were said, Colleen immediately dialed Willow's number and sat breathless, listening to the distant telephone ring.

Suddenly the voice she remembered vividly from childhood answered the telephone. "Yes?" The reception on the line was as clear as if her aunt was next to her, speaking into her ear.

"You won't believe this, Aunt Willow, but this is Colleen, Mike's daughter."

"Colleen!" her aunt's voice bubbled. "Why are you calling?"

"Well, I'm working on some family tree research, and thought you might have some memories you'd be willing to share. I never asked Dad or Grandma enough questions, and Sister Mary says she doesn't remember anything. So I'm calling to ask if you'd be willing to talk with me," Colleen explained.

The answer was immediate.

"Hell, yes, I'd be glad to talk to you. Never had any hesitation to say what I thought in the past, no reason to start now," Willow laughed. "It's what always got me in trouble!"

Colleen laughed with her, partly with relief that Willow would be willing to talk, and partly because her aunt's mischievous high spirits were as contagious now as they had always been, even over the telephone.

"Talking with you on the phone is grand," Colleen told Willow, "but the fact is, I'll be in New Orleans for a convention in a couple of weeks, and if you'd be willing to spend part of a day with me, I'd like to see you face to face."

"Sure, honey. I haven't got anything going on, just sitting here passing the time. I'm not so sure you'll want all the information I can give you, but I'll pass it on to you anyhow, and you can sort it out," Willow's voice sang over the line.

Colleen was ecstatic. Her secretary arranged for her to arrive in New Orleans a day before the start of the convention, and she began to think about what she wanted to ask her aunt. In addition to any memories Willow had of her own grandparents and great-grandparents, Colleen was curious about why Willow had separated herself so totally from the family. What had happened? Would she talk about it? Colleen suspected that Willow might be the vital link between present and past, and in anticipation of this conversation, looked forward to the trip eagerly.

When the plane touched down in New Orleans, Colleen stepped off it into the heaviest, stickiest air she had ever experienced. Her previous trips to this city had been in cooler seasons. The atmosphere was sultry and palpable. After picking up her rental car, she went to her hotel, dressed in the coolest thing she could find in her suitcase, a light cotton shift and sandals, and sat down on the hotel bed to call Willow.

"Hello, Colleen!" her aunt said as she picked up the telephone. "You got here right on time. When will you be coming over?"

Colleen should have been startled that her aunt knew who was calling before she identified herself, but years of having her father do that on her calls had prepared her for it. Maybe Willow didn't get many calls. She noted it in her mind, but said, "Any time you say, Aunt Willow!"

Willow gave her a few quick directions and Colleen went downstairs to get the car. Her walk—just a few steps from the hotel to the parking lot—left her feeling like she was pushing the heavy wet air ahead of her. Settling into the vehicle with its life-saving air conditioning was a huge relief.

In a few moments, she was making her way through the streets of this grand old city to a series of old apartments. They were fashionably seedy, but seemed like the kind of place that would fit her aunt's rebellious tendencies.

Parking her car in one of the few shady spots on the street, Colleen gathered up her notebook and climbed the stairs to the balcony on the second story. There was no doubt which apartment was Willow's. She found herself in front of a bright red door. She rang the bell and stood, while the slightest breeze stirred the fabric of her shift.

The door to the apartment opened, and Colleen turned. At that moment, she found herself looking into eyes identical to her father's, the face of a woman who appeared far younger than her 78 years.

"Welcome!" Willow cried, throwing her arms open wide and encircling Colleen in a hug. "I would have known you anywhere, Colleen! You look exactly like your father! God, I miss my big brother!"

Colleen was delighted to see how little Willow had changed. Her auburn hair had some streaks of white in it, but they did little to diminish her vitality and youthful appearance. Her skin was creamy and almost without lines. She was dressed in a funky, floating, roaring twenties-style wood sprite confection of sheer gauze and seemed ethereal in the dark doorway.

"Aunt Willow! What did you do to stay so young all these years?" Colleen asked with a grin.

"Made a deal with the Devil, I guess!" Willow laughed heartily, the sound light on the air as a wind chime. "Come into my humble abode!"

Colleen stepped inside the door, and it was like crossing into another world. The air inside the small dwelling was cool and kind. A silent ceiling fan turned slowly, and the shuttered windows filtered the hot sunlight into a soft glow in the late afternoon. The apartment was an eclectic blend of old and new, but mostly old. Soft chairs and couches offered welcome and comfort and some kind of incense touched the air so lightly that it could not be defined. Colleen felt her spirit settle, and she gazed directly into her aunt's eyes.

"I made some cool tea," Willow said. "Would you like some?"

"It sounds wonderful, Aunt Willow," Colleen replied. "I like your place here. How long have you lived in New Orleans?"

"I don't know," her aunt responded from the nook that served as her kitchen. She came back into the room with two tall glasses filled with a greenish tea and a lemon slice. "I guess I've been here for about 12 years. The town seemed to suit me."

Colleen had to agree. New Orleans was a distinctive place, a little wild, a little mysterious, completely unique. If her Aunt Willow had been a place instead of a person, she would have *been* New Orleans.

'What brought you here? Last I heard, you were in Alaska or the Northwest Territories," Colleen said.

An impish smile accompanied Willow's answer. "Guess it was my sixth or seventh 'companion,' Alton."

Colleen knew better than to pursue this subject. Her aunt had been in the company of many men, a lifestyle since the earliest days of her young womanhood. The idea of any one relationship holding her for long was so unlikely that it did not merit further discussion.

"You decided to stay here rather than going to any other place?"

"I did," Willow replied. "There are many reasons, not the least of which is that we have roots here, you and I."

Colleen was intrigued. "We do? I had never heard that!"

With this implicit invitation to continue, Willow commanded, "Sit down, horsey, and we'll talk, you and me!"

Colleen was ready to listen, but not ready for what she was about to hear. Willow settled herself on a velvet chaise, and placed her tea on a table at the side.

"My great-grandparents—your great-great-grandparents, Margaret and Richard Hughes, came to the Port of New Orleans when they fled Ireland," she began.

Suddenly, here were the subjects of Colleen's search, the parents of her great-grandmother, Anna. She had encountered this particular path of Irish migration previously, but had not suspected that her own great-great-grandparents had come this way. Her full attention focused on her aunt, eager to hear what she knew.

'They were fleeing the famine, right?"

Willow regarded Colleen solemnly.

'That was the story that served them at the time, and it's the story that was passed down through the family," she declared.

'You sound like that's not the whole story," Colleen countered.

'It's not."

Willow pulled out an exotic looking cigarette and placed it in an elegant gold holder that would have been ludicrous in anyone else's hand. She lit it, took a long drag, and blowing blue smoke into the atmosphere, continued her account.

"They fled Ireland because they were being hunted by both the Catholics and the Protestants," she said. "They were of the 'old religion' of Ireland. I don't know if you know what that is, but it is sufficient to say neither church approved of it."

Colleen felt a little thrill. The conversation with her mother about the early days of her 'marriage' to Mike crystallized in her mind. She wanted to ask her aunt a million questions, but Willow had audible momentum in her story, and this wasn't the time to interrupt her.

"It was a little like the witch hunts in New England in the 1600's. But with so many people fleeing Ireland to escape the famine, it was easy for them to lose themselves in the masses of immigrants. They came here in the hold of a cargo ship that had delivered cotton to England. Such ships took their cargoes to England, and used human beings—Irish human beings—as ballast in the lowest holds on the return trip."

"They landed here, lost themselves in the crowds of immigrants, and found a number of odd jobs. Yellow fever was rampant here in New Orleans at the time. Your great-great-grandmother helped as many people as she could with old Irish remedies and cures. After a while, both of them got tired of witnessing the miserable circumstances and the wretched deaths of so many people, and they decided to go on upriver toward Missouri. When they reached St. Louis, your great-great-grandmother was able to make a little money treating people for various kinds of illnesses and injuries. Problem was, they didn't blend in there as well as they had here amidst the voodoo and other practices that were common in New Orleans. After a while, the neighbors started looking at them strangely, ostracizing and finally threatening them. By this time, your great-great-grandmother Margaret was pregnant, and she insisted that Richard take her away from there. She missed the cool climate of Ireland, and wanted to go north, so they did."

"Aunt Willow," Colleen broke in, "this is fascinating. How did you learn all this?"

"Your grandmother, my mother, Velia, and her mother, Anna, told me this when I was a young woman," Willow replied. "It sounded pretty unbelievable then, but enough things have happened since that it seems perfectly logical to me now."

"Did that have anything to do with your leaving home?"

"In a way. Both grandmother and mother wanted me to carry on some of the beliefs. It seemed to be part of a big dream they had for me. All their talk was about a pattern that had to be carried out, and how it maintained its strength through the daughters of the family. Mary Cecilia was been the logical one, as the oldest daughter, but she was pretty put off by the whole idea," Willow recalled.

"For me, it seemed like too much responsibility, and I am too self-centered. I had all kinds of exciting plans, and the discipline of learning all the old things they thought were so important was not among the experiences I wanted."

Colleen thought again about her conversation with Sister Mary. Was this a clue about why she had taken up the religious life?

Willow continued, "I don't know what finally happened, but I had the feeling that when Mother and Grandmother couldn't persuade one of us girls to continue these beliefs, they chose Mike." Another drag on the cigarette fueled her for the rest of her observation.

"He never really told me that, but the timing was about right. I always wondered if it wasn't a part of his drinking. He had to know this made him different from anyone else, and there were so many things that couldn't be explained. What I do know is that he spent a lot of afternoons visiting with our mother, and he spent even more time with our grandmother in the year just before she died. Sister Mary was too frightened by all this, and just didn't want any part of it."

Colleen finally glanced up from the notes she had been scribbling to look at the grandfather clock ticking away the hours in the corner of the apartment. The time had flown by, and it was time for her to take her leave.

"Aunt Willow," she said, "I have just one more question. Do you have any idea where great-grandmother's family came from in Ireland? I plan to visit there someday, and I must be able to find the town they came from."

Willow took a long pull on her cigarette and blew out the smoke, sending a blue mist out to encircle her small form.

"I don't know for sure, but I think there is a place named for the Lorrah family. I also seem to remember that the Hughes family came from someplace near there. You might try looking it up that way. Your great-grandmother once said something about her parents coming from County Cork, but I don't know if that was where they were from, or where they got on the ship."

Colleen stood. "It's going to take me some time to digest all this, Aunt Willow. I think I'd like to go back to the hotel now," she said. Smiling warmly at her aunt, she hugged her and thanked her for all the information.

"Wish I could tell you more, honey," Willow said earnestly. "Guess you are still going to have to do a lot of research yourself. Thank you for spending the day with me, and for letting me see you. If there is anything to all this, I wonder if you aren't the one in this generation to learn what our history has to teach us. Best of luck to you, honey. My thoughts will be with you wherever it all leads."

She paused, then spoke solemnly, a rare occasion for this free spirit. "On second thought, I don't need to wish you luck. You are destined for great deeds, I believe."

Colleen wondered what she meant, but Willow made it apparent that the conversation was finished. She opened her arms to her niece, and declared, "Go with the goddess! *Slán abhaile*! (Safe home!)" Colleen had heard this Irish farewell many times from her grandmother and her father in earlier times of her life, but now it suddenly implied far more than it ever had before.

Shaking her head, Colleen hugged her aunt and said good-bye, all the while wondering if this would be the last time she would ever see Willow. She returned to the hotel and prepared for her convention meetings the following day. Once back in the mainstream of her work, she set aside her notebook with all she had written down, and told herself she would get back to her research very soon.

Her aunt, and all she had learned from her in that discussion had been another benchmark along the road to Ireland, where the more things changed, the more they remained the same. Thousands of years of traditions and oral history only served to preserve the past. The next step in the journey came because things were changing fast in her career.

The company was about to move her again.

CHAPTER 5

▼

Intuition told her she was about to experience something extraordinary when this transfer took her to the Rapid City office of her company. The Hills mirrored her homelands, haunting in mystery and legend. The Sioux Indians, whose lands these were, practiced a kind of mysticism different from but parallel to that of the Crow Indians, but the feeling was the same. Once settled there, she was reminded daily of her life and friendships in the small reservation schools she had attended, and events that had seemed unimportant when they had occurred in childhood took on new significance as she remembered them.

Although she swiftly became acquainted with most of the community leaders, it took Colleen a bit of time after her arrival to meet one of the most remarkable people in the community of the Black Hills. Samuel Aaronsberg came across the room to introduce himself to her at a community event several months after she had come to her new assignment. The local grapevine had made her aware of him for some time, but circumstances had not placed them in the same location until now.

As he approached her, her curiosity was piqued. Although he had a large presence in the region, he was not large in stature. In fact, he was small, but the deference he received from those in the room was obvious as he made his way to where she stood. His gray hair, a neatly trimmed beard, and decidedly exotic appearance registered with the information she already had. Locals talked about the fact that he was Jewish, and that he had fought to maintain his identity in a place where there were very few Jews. It was common knowledge that he had built upon his father's business to create a powerful corporation. What she was not prepared for was the electricity that emanated from the man.

His intense amber eyes burned into hers when they were introduced, and he bowed very slightly when he shook her hand. "My apologies for taking so long to meet you," he said. "I would like to have a conversation with you at your convenience."

Colleen was taken aback. She had not expected that he would have concerns about the fact that it had taken time for them to meet. Whenever she started work in a place, she viewed it as her responsibility to get out and make the acquaintance of community decision-makers.

"Any time you'd like." Her response was instantaneous.

"After this reception?"

Although startled by the immediacy of his request, she didn't hesitate.

"Certainly."

They both moved about the gathering, meeting and greeting people and fulfilling their public roles. She thought briefly about their encounter, certain that when the reception ended, he would forget his request.

But when the event wound down, he was waiting at the door for her. He had somehow picked up her coat from the coat check, and helped her into it.

"There's a coffee shop not far from here," he said. "They have wonderful chocolate chip cookies and great coffee. We can talk there."

Once they were seated and their coffee ordered, Samuel looked intently at her.

"This will sound peculiar," he said. "but I had a sense of your coming. Seriously. I honestly knew you were coming. I wanted to meet you sooner than this, but I've been traveling a great deal."

"What do you mean, a sense of my coming?" she asked.

"I could feel it. It was in the earth, the wind, maybe even in the prairie grass, I don't know how to describe it."

He shrugged.

"Well, I've heard a lot about you ever since I got to town," she noted. "You hold a pretty auspicious position in this community."

"Three generations of my family have been in the Black Hills, and I raised the fourth here, too. My sons have all moved away now, but they grew up here."

In her direct way, she could not resist asking a question from the heart of her curiosity.

"It's unusual that people of Jewish background stay in these small western communities," she observed. "Why do you think you did?"

His response was unexpected.

"Most would say that it was because I inherited a business that couldn't be moved. But it could have been sold any time. The truth is that I love this land, this place. And more than that, I feel a particular affinity to the tribal people here. Jews are tribal, of course, and being here among the Sioux gives me more comfort than I get when I spend time with Jewish communities in large cities. The Sioux still know what it is to be a tribe. I do what I can to help them, and I stay because their aboriginal tribalism feels so right."

Colleen was amazed. "That is what I always felt on the reservation where I grew up," she said. "But I'm not Jewish. I'm Irish. Yet, there has always been a great comfort with the Crow Indian people. My family was three generations in Crow Indian country, and even though those of us in the fourth generation have moved away, it's as if you never really leave."

Samuel nodded.

"My theory is that tribal pull leads you to seek your homeland, or substitute the nearest thing. Tribal people tend to be drawn to others of like ethnic history, sometimes even when they have no specific connection. I see it all the time with gentile friends who go to visit Israel. They are drawn there even when they have never been there, and then they are startled by the familiarity of the place. It's like a magnet for them, calling them to set foot where they have never lived."

Thoughtfully, Colleen agreed. What he was saying had a ring of truth for her, and it led to exchanges of more stories about their friendships with the Indian tribes in their respective home territories. The conversation carried them on deep into the evening. When Colleen looked up, she was dumbfounded to see that the coffee shop clock said it was nearly eleven o'clock.

Her expression was apologetic when she spoke to Samuel.

"I really have to go," she said. "I have an early day tomorrow. I would like to continue this conversation sometime. It's rare that I find a kindred spirit in these matters. In addition, you have a lot of knowledge about the history of this community that would be very helpful to me. I hope you'd be willing to share some of it."

His response was swift, and seemed almost impulsive.

"Of course. Let's have dinner tomorrow!"

With anyone else, she would have been uneasy in the face of such urgency and intensity. With Samuel, it was part of his persona, and probably how he got most of his business done so successfully. She pulled out her calendar.

"It will have to be after seven, if that will work for you."

"Done!" he exclaimed, and helped her with her coat. He saw her to her car, and said as he bid her goodnight, "This place has been waiting for someone like you. Welcome to the Black Hills!"

During her drive home, she reflected on the dialogue that evening. Something deep inside her had clicked into place when he talked about tribal people, but she could not quite pinpoint it. Once inside her house, sleep eluded her, so she wandered to where her books were shelved and ran her fingers across them until she stopped at some of her father's reference books on Ireland. Pulling down a history of the country from prehistoric times to the present, she took it to bed with her. As the words flowed from the pages into her mind, understanding came that the Irish population had always been tribal. In megalithic and neolithic days, the people were tribal in the same sense that the American Indians were and continued to be, and later, in the same way, had labeled their tribes as "clans." Black Bird's reference to her father's "tribe" came streaming back, and she began to string together some of the subjects her father had talked about.

Samuel and Colleen established a routine of talking frequently. They had dinner or lunch together on numerous occasions, and despite an age difference, found common ground on many subjects. Samuel shared all she asked for regarding the nuances of the historic, business and social fabric of the Black Hills, and they discussed philosophies. While she learned volumes from him, Colleen was unaware that Samuel was learning much from her as well. He was curious about her interest in Ireland and things Irish. He listened intently when she talked of her family's beliefs and about the "old religion." And he began to accept unexplainable things he had always dismissed before.

All this came to a head one evening, when Colleen was preparing to spend her customary evening of solitude on the prairie on a night of the full moon. This was a practice that she had begun by instinct when she was very young, first slipping out of the house alone. The night called to her, and she could not resist the summons. Once her parents discovered this practice, her father encouraged it without question, even on school nights. She could recall him cajoling her mother, "It's only one night a month," he would say. "Let her do it. It's good for her."

The personal ritual continued to soothe her core throughout the years of her marriage to Art. He usually became so involved with watching television on the nights he was home that he scarcely noticed. All she usually had to do was to say she was going for a little walk in the night. He'd murmur acknowledgement, nod, and return his attention to the program or sports event he was watching without further comment. Her return to the house usually found him fast asleep.

It was her practice to travel until discovering a private place in the grasses of the prairie. Then seating herself on the ground, surrounded by the solitude and peace of nature, she held a vigil during the full moon's entire journey as it rose from the horizon and moved through the sky. This always settled her spirit, and banked the fires in her soul, so she fiercely avoided missing it.

This changed during her time in Chicago, because there was no appropriate place for this personal observance. In addition, the city lights generally diminished the moon, so she had temporarily abandoned the practice. But there were consequences. Throughout the entire time that she was deprived of this personal ritual, she felt restless and uneasy. Now, back in the West with access to the prairie, she was determined to never miss the opportunity.

On this night, she accepted a dinner invitation from Samuel at a local restaurant, but cautioned him that she would have to leave early to go to the prairie. His curiosity was piqued when she told him this.

"What is this about, now?"

"I don't think I can explain it, but I spend the night of the full moon on the prairie. I'm sure that sounds strange to you."

"What do you do there?"

There was no tone of judgment in his question.

"I don't know how to define it. I *connect* with the earth, somehow." She groped for the right words.

He agreed to dine early. Upon her entrance at the restaurant, he rose from the table to greet her, then stopped halfway out of his chair.

He was staring at her.

"You look…I don't know, you look *luminous*! I've never seen you look like this."

Colleen had never given any thought to her appearance on these nights.

Since her previous existence with Art and later when single had been so isolated there had never been anyone in a position to observe her closely. Samuel, on the other hand, had powers of insight that missed little around him, and his perception of people was very acute.

"I'd like to go out there with you."

"No, Samuel. This is something I have to do by myself. It is for me alone."

Because he was her friend, he accepted this. But on a number of later occasions, he attempted to discuss it. Each time, she shifted the subject, mostly because her inability to account for what happened to her at these times. She didn't remember. All she knew was that there was an irresistible compulsion for her to go back to the prairie for every full moon. Afterwards she somehow returned to her house to sleep dreamlessly.

What she didn't know was that Samuel once attempted to follow her, only to be frustrated by the fact that the tiny road enabled her to disappear. He sped up, trying to catch sight of her car, but it, and she, vanished abruptly; leaving him no clue about where she had gone. He stopped his car, rolled down the window to see if he could hear the sound of her engine, but could not. All he heard were the whispers of the prairie grasses, the rhythmic sound of what he thought might be drums, and far away, the cry of a magpie.

For Colleen, her ongoing contact with members of the Sioux tribe and the religious observances they held were enduring reminders of her own life among the Crow. News from home continued to find her, and one day a letter from one of her female friends in the tribe brought stirring news. Two of her friends and classmates were now becoming tribal holy men as their middle age brought them into readiness.

Conversations and experiences with these men when they were in their teens surfaced in her thoughts. Like all teenagers, they had talked of things important to them. Richard Pretty Eagle and the friendship the two of them had shared came to mind first.

She remembered a day of watching him work with a young wild horse. When others "broke" horses with much pain for both horse and rider, Richard spoke quietly, and touched the horse in ways no one could understand. Similar methods would later come to be called "horse whispering" by white horsemen who practiced them. For Richard, it was not a method, it was his innate nature. The horse accepted bridle, saddle, and rider as if it had always been so. Even at thirteen years of age, Richard's skills placed him in demand for training the horses of both Indian and white people.

Remembering Richard was always peaceful. He was quiet and calm, and seemed to be shy to most people. His friendship with Colleen was companionable, but very strong, as if he understood her as well as the horses he worked with.

It was different with her other friend, Thomas Sky Horse. While their friendship started in high school at Lodge Grass, it deepened in college. Like many tribal people, Thomas left the reservation to go to college, and attended the same one as Colleen. Thomas only stayed for one year.

The pull of tribal alliances and family was too strong, and as a young man, he could not continue to live at a distance from the tribe. While at college, he was lonely for anyone from home, and sought out Colleen for conversations about how homesick he was. Around the same time, in the mid-sixties, Colleen had begun to seek the "meaning of life" herself. They had many philosophical conversations. Even then, Thomas shared his dreams of becoming a holy man or medicine man with the tribe. He had two uncles who held this station, and he was the heir apparent. Fascination and fear about the prospect held him in thrall. Such a move would not happen until he was much older, and he worried aloud to her that he would not live up to his family's expectations.

It had been Thomas who first revealed the vision quest experience to her. Because he was so far from home, and because no one from the tribe was available, he placed his trust in her. Staying in college had become a growing struggle for him, and he pleaded with her to accompany him on his quest. They drove in her car to the canyon of a small stream called Magpie Creek, two hours from the campus. He had already been fasting for several days. Directing her to turn off the main road and drive up a small trail, he continued to guide her until they found a small road leading to a trailhead where she could park. There, while she stood by, her friend constructed a sweat lodge near the cold course of Magpie Creek. He cut limber willow branches, arched them and lashed them together, placing his lodge near a turn in the stream where the water formed a deep pond. She helped him cover the bowed construction with blankets and light the fire to heat the stones. They worked all afternoon.

When all was ready, Thomas told her to wait at a distance, while he stripped off his clothing and stepped inside the lodge. Colleen settled at the base of a huge spruce tree, and began her vigil. She was patient, remembering her father's conversations with her about his own participation with some of his Crow friends in the sweat. The sound of Thomas's voice, but not the words, carried to her as he said his prayers. Late afternoon passed into night, and still the prayers flowed from him.

Colleen was relaxed, but watchful. Then a deep exhaustion came over her, and she dozed. After an undetermined amount of time, the sound of a splash brought her fully awake.

Where had that come from? Her eyes darted about, seeking the source of the sound.

In the light of the night's full moon, the ripples spread on the water of Magpie Creek. Prayers finished, Thomas had sealed them with a plunge in the ice-cold waters of this mountain stream. After he had been under the water for what seemed a very long time, she became momentarily alarmed. Finally, his head silently broke the surface of the water, droplets streaming along the shoulder-length strands of his blue-black hair. He swam to the shallows and stood. In the moonlight, he looked like some nature spirit, entwined with the forest and the stream. His tall, straight form, which had served him so well on the basketball courts during their high school years, was regal and elegant.

Emerging from the water with gliding steps, he wrapped one of the blankets from the lodge around himself. Noticing her watching him, he motioned for her to come to where he stood. Silently, he gestured toward a trail she had not detected. She gathered her backpack and one of the blankets and followed him as he led the way. They climbed for nearly an hour; finally reaching the top of the ridge that overlooked the canyon on three sides. Thomas selected a spot and motioned for Colleen to go to the shelter of the trees nearby. Seating herself on a blanket she spread on the ground, she prepared for her watch. From the shadows of the trees, she observed as the blanket he had covered himself with dropped to the ground. Completely nude, he sank gracefully to a sitting position with his legs crossed, assuming the bearing of a young prince. She was not conscious of his nudity, but rather of a glow that seemed to emanate from him.

Mesmerized by the beauty of his image, she stared. Suddenly, a cloud drifted over the moon, and the forest descended into darkness. When the cloud drifted away, the scene had changed. Now it appeared that Thomas was on the other side of a sheet of water. The moon was gone, and something curious was happening to the sky. From nowhere, the Northern lights had appeared. Flaming across the sky, they moved and shifted, dancing overhead as Thomas sat completely motionless.

The word her father always used to describe the aurora borealis came to mind. "Nightfire," was his name for this phenomenon. On many occasions he had quietly awaked the child Colleen from her sleep, wrapped her in a warm blanket and carried her out of the house. In the yard, they would gaze up and watch the lights display themselves in the sky over the ranch house. She remembered perhaps twenty such times with him. Basking in those memories as her friend sought guidance from his gods, she pulled the blanket close around her. Despite her efforts to stay awake, sleep swept her to another plane.

Dawn broke, and the warmth of the sun touched Colleen's face. It disoriented her at first, but she quickly became conscious. For a moment a small twinge of guilt prodded her for having slept as her friend tested himself. Then Thomas's cautionary words echoed in her ears.

"Don't try to do what I am doing. Just be there for me. This is my quest. Yours will come at another time," he had said.

As she wakened fully, her eyes moved quickly to Thomas's spot. He was still there. She recognized that he was not aware of her presence. In fact, he seemed to be in another place, on another level of consciousness. Arising, and wincing at the stiffness the mountain cold and damp had caused in her young body, she stretched. Her steps were quiet, but her senses were alert, always keeping Thomas in her sight. Looking back down the ridge, she made sure the car was still where they had parked it. It was far enough off the main road that it would be invisible to the casual passer-by. Returning to where she had spent the night, she ferreted in her backpack for a bottle of juice. A deep drink revived her, and her paces back and forth warmed her. She nibbled at an apple and stretched her cramped muscles.

A sound demanded her attention. It was the low cry of a magpie. Colleen looked up and saw something she had not seen since leaving home for college. Three magpies circled overhead, not over Thomas, but over where she stood. As if satisfied to find her safe, the birds wheeled about twice more, then one by one, flew out of sight. A deep peace descended over her, bringing the knowledge that she was where she belonged. Resuming her seated position, she pulled out a book and began to read.

Time glided by quickly for her, and as the sun traveled its circuit across the sky, Colleen marveled at the strength her friend demonstrated. Erect and proud, he sat, meditating and communing with unseen forces of nature. He took no water, and he was on at least his third day without food. At midday, she rose and walked back down the trail to her car. The sight of sweat lodge greeted her, and she stepped past it to the creek bank. The water where Thomas had taken his plunge the night before glistened below. The pool looked impossibly deep for such a small watercourse. Although the stream was crystal clear, the bottom could not be seen. Drawn to the very edge, and peering into the depths, she was unsure of what to expect. There appeared to be a flash of prismatic color, undefined, out of the ordinary. There was a mystery here, but it was not her mystery.

Returning to her station, she continued to watch. When evening came, the skies began to cloud over. Would Thomas be too exposed on the rock ridge he had chosen? His warning not to disturb him once he began his vision quest was absolute. Clouds continued to gather, and it was obvious that they were storm clouds. A distant rumble of thunder sounded as they accumulated, and then it drew closer. The sky roiled about, and she glanced up nervously at the height of the trees above her. This was not the safest place to be. Moving to the preferable shelter of a group of rocks that formed an outcrop, she found it was still possible to see Thomas from there. Now lightning began to play across the sky. The appearance of this powerful display reminded of her father once again.

This was sheet lightning, racing its illumination across masses of clouds but not connecting with the ground. Each flash lit the area like daylight, and still Thomas sat, impassive as a bronze sculpture, wind stirring his waist-length black hair across his shoulders and chest.

Suddenly Colleen witnessed something outside her experience. Even between the flashes, he was completely visible in the darkness; his body was luminous from the inside out. Now a strong wind came up, and thrashing the clouds, swept them to the east.

The sky cleared and the full moon dominated the night sky once again. Now her eyes took in another sight that snatched her breath away. Thomas was no longer sitting on the ground. He had levitated above the rock-strewn ridge, and hovered perhaps four feet above the surface. His face was rapturous. Colleen was stunned. This phenomenon lasted for what seemed an eternity, but actually (as Colleen analyzed it later) probably for about five minutes. It was too much for her to take in. She fainted.

When full consciousness returned to her, it was morning again, and Thomas was standing over her, wrapped in the blanket he had brought with him up the mountain. She scrambled to her feet to face him. Looking into her friend's eyes, she tried to determine if she should break the silence. Above them, the three magpies were circling again.

Thomas's demeanor had changed. His calm face showed he was at peace, and it was apparent before he spoke that he had made a decision about his future. Noting the concern in her eyes, he broke the silence.

"I'm okay," he said simply.

"Did you receive your vision?" Colleen asked, knowing the answer.

"Yes. I'm going back to the 'Rez.'"

"Are you sure?"

"Yes." He was emphatic. "I have much to learn, and not much time to learn it. When you come home next time, find me. It will be time for you to discover your way."

They loaded everything back into her car, and drove to the campus in silence. Colleen hated to see Thomas abandon his formal education, but it would be of no use to try to dissuade him. She took him to his apartment. He got out, took his belongings, and shook her hand.

"Thank you," he said. "I will go with you when your vision time comes."

They said their good-byes, and Colleen drove back to school and to her dormitory. She would miss Thomas. The two of them were like brother and sister in many ways. He had crossed all cultural barriers, and helped expand what her father had taught her about Crow beliefs.

Looking back, she recognized that all the signs had been there at the time, predicting what was to come.

Thomas's route would be very different from that of Richard Pretty Eagle. Richard always had a quiet assurance, as if he knew it was his destiny to hold such a sacred position from the day he could walk, and his preparations began early.

Thomas was not so sure. As it turned out, these doubts would nearly destroy him before he was ready to assume this honored position.

CHAPTER 6

▼

The next time Colleen saw Thomas, she was working in Billings. When she looked up to find him standing silently at the door to her office, it was apparent that he had changed. He told her he was married now, and had been hired to work at the same business she worked for. He remarked that it had necessitated a move off the reservation and away from the tribe. Jobs on the reservation were nonexistent. His care-worn bearing spoke volumes about his state of mind. The dignity was still there, but his self-confidence was diminished. His face looked drawn and tired. She motioned for him to step into her office, and asked him to sit and talk for a while. He seemed uncomfortable.

"Thomas, are you still working with your uncles to learn the holy ways?" she asked.

His response was evasive. "No. That's set aside for now."

"Why?"

"My uncles say I'm not ready," came the solemn answer.

What could possibly have caused that judgment? It was apparent that the time was not right to ask.

Colleen had already risen to mid-management level in the company and Thomas quickly earned his way to become a lead man on the night crew. Then word began to come from Thomas's boss that he was performing very well most of the time, but that there had been occasional grave lapses when he either did not show up for work or performed poorly at the simplest duties. Finally it came to a head. Thomas missed three days of work and ended up in the drunk tank of the local jail. Because of their friendship and because of her past experience with other employees' alcohol problems, Colleen was asked to work with Thomas once he was released from jail.

When he appeared at her office, all the damage the three days of drinking and one night in the tank were stamped on him. His hands trembled uncontrollably, and his almost black eyes were bloodshot and scared. He looked beaten and hurt. Colleen hated seeing her proud friend in this position. But her training had prepared her to help those who were ready. And Thomas was ready. Colleen had never seen anyone more ready. His red-rimmed eyes averted, he said dejectedly, "Guess my job is gone, right?"

"That depends, Thomas. You have some choices to make. You can lose your job because of this, or you can choose to go to treatment. If you go to treatment, it's not going to be easy. You're going to have to be even further away from home, from the tribe, and from your wife and little girl."

Thomas was immediately on guard. "What do you mean 'away from home'?"

Even though he did not live on the reservation at this time, he was only an hour away from it. Home and family were all-important tribal connections that provided the support he had always relied upon.

"Can't I go to treatment right here in Billings?" he pleaded.

Colleen was calm. "Thomas, I checked on the treatment methods here. The local center does not understand the tribal aspects of your life. They work with white people, and they don't know how important your beliefs are to you. You will just have to trust me when I tell you I found a place in the northern part of Montana that will serve you better. You willing?"

Thomas shifted in his chair and sighed. "I guess. You wouldn't send me the wrong way. No reason to make this harder than it has to be. What do I have to do?"

Colleen got up from her desk and came around to sit down in the chair next to him. Eye to eye, she said, "Go to this address and talk to this doctor. He's made the arrangements for you, if you go through with this. It has to be your decision, Thomas. No one else can decide it for you. I can tell you that if you do, and the treatment is successful, your job will be here for you."

Thomas squared his shoulders. His body language told her what he had decided.

"I know I can't go on like this," he said. "I don't have the money for it, and my wife is tired of it. I'm going to do it."

Colleen leaned back in her chair. She held out her hand to shake Thomas's. "I'm glad, Thomas. It takes a lot of courage for you to make this decision, but I don't think you'll be disappointed."

Thomas went through with it. He had even gotten on a small commuter plane to fly to the treatment center, although he had never flown before. In many ways, it was all in a day's work for her. She did not foresee the consequences of her actions that day.

Thomas's treatment returned him to work a changed man. He was delighted with his new life, and stopped by to tell her. Colleen insisted she had not had a very big role in his success, that he had taken the action that had rearranged his life for the better.

Thomas moved back home and commuted to work from the reservation, a daily drive of some 60 miles round trip. Colleen was curious, but Thomas did not share much with her. She heard from others on the reservation that he was dedicating himself to the practice of "medicine" with his uncles, and he was also working with other tribal members as an alcohol counselor.

Eventually he left the company, and Colleen lost track of him as her career took her to other locations around the country. The incident was not forgotten, but she simply assumed that Thomas was doing well, and that he would be satisfied trying to help others from the tribe.

Then one day she got word that he had come back to work for the Billings site. It sounded like good news for both the company and him, but she was curious. Making a mental note, she decided to stop by and see him on her next trip to Montana. Thomas worked nights, so even though she tried a couple of times, she always missed him.

Next, he became a prime candidate for a promotion to another branch of the business, and the management from that property called her for a reference. The human resources manager from that property approached the subject in the usual professional check-the-references fashion, and after they had discussed Thomas's qualifications, the HR woman paused.

"Colleen," she said cautiously, "I don't quite know how to ask this, but during his interview, Thomas said something odd. I just have to ask you a question. Thomas told me you saved his life. Is that true?"

Colleen, startled, replied, "I know the incident he is thinking of, but I never thought of it that way. He's giving me too much credit." She told enough of the story to the woman, then encouraged her to hire her old friend.

Thomas was hired for the job, and Colleen called him there. She was amazed that he had been willing to leave tribal lands to take this new job, and she told him so.

Even over the telephone, the smile could be heard in Thomas's response.

"Have to go away so I can go home," he declared. "I just want you to know that I really thank you for saving my life."

"Thomas…you saved your own life. You had to make the decision and do the hard work."

Thomas shrugged verbally. "That's not how I see it."

They talked about his work for a while, then he told Colleen his biggest news. "I'm learning how to be a holy man," he said.

"Thomas, that's wonderful! Are you doing that there in Missoula?"

"No," he responded. "I drive back to the reservation for ceremonies."

Colleen gasped.

"Thomas! That's 400 miles! Isn't that a lot to take on with this job, too?"

"The people here have been real helpful to me, and I use vacation and personal days to take part in ceremonies. My uncles have taught me how to use my spirit to keep from getting tired."

Colleen was skeptical.

"That's a lot of driving…eight hours each way. Are you doing okay?"

"Yes," he said eagerly. "Last time, I went on a vision quest with my brother. He was fasting up at the Medicine Wheel, and I was there to be with him. I decided to fast with him for part of the time, and I had an important experience. I got in the middle of the medicine wheel, and I actually flew above the ground again. It was amazing."

Colleen started. As she had dialed the telephone to call Thomas, she had been thinking of the medicine wheel on the top of the Big Horn Mountains. He father had taken her there several times, and had talked about the mysterious wheel. "It's old," he had told her. "No one knows who built it or when it was built. It is oriented to the solstices, and it has always been here. The Indians consider it a very holy place, and so do I."

Colleen remembered how she had felt as she had stood on the narrow ridge next to this ancient site. Stone formations thrust themselves up from the cliff edges, ancient ramparts standing guard over this sacred ground. The narrow ridge that led to the flat area where the wheel was located was dramatic, a fitting platform for those who sought the magic of the place. She had never ventured past the edge of the wheel itself in previous visits, since it was fenced off, and to do so would have felt like an intrusion. It had left a strong impression, and she had tried to imagine its builders. It had been impossible to conjure up a picture of them, but she believed she could feel an intense power here. Her father agreed. They had stood side by side in the cold edge of the mountain winds at the

10,000-foot elevation. "It gives you a chill, doesn't it?" he had asked. "I always feel awed when I come here. It's kind of haunted, I think."

That feeling came back now as she listened to Thomas's story. Then the direction of his conversation changed. Intensifying his voice, he made an unexpected statement.

"Your time has come, my friend. That's what my last vision told me. You must have your vision quest now," he asserted.

"Now?" Colleen was shocked to hear this suggestion. They had talked about this on other occasions, but she had thought that was all it was, just talk.

"Now." His answer left no doubt. "When can you go?"

Colleen recognized the gravity of this discussion. "I can take some vacation. I could be ready in a day or so," she said.

But Thomas had a specific time in mind. "We have to do this when the moon is full. That is five days from now," he said. "It must be this way."

"I understand," Colleen said. "When do I start my fast?"

"Three days before we go. You'll do your sweat at my family's sweat lodge," Thomas declared.

"It's in your hands, Thomas," Colleen was already preparing herself.

And so they had gone. Colleen told her own family that she was coming to Montana for a camping trip with some friends, a partial truth. She drove over from Rapid City, straight through to the land that Thomas and his family owned. They had a permanent sweat lodge there at the edge of Pryor Creek. All had been prepared, the lodge frame draped with blankets, the rocks pulled from the fire and placed in the center of the structure. Thomas's wife, Janine, and her sister, Doris, helped Colleen ready herself for the sweat, and when she asked about the prayers, Thomas told her that Black Bird Shows would be there to help her. She was surprised. "I haven't seen him since my Dad died," she told him. "What is your connection with him?"

"He's one of my uncles," Thomas replied.

Although Colleen had lived her entire life on the reservation, she still did not completely understand how these relationships worked. She knew they were very different from those of the white culture, but until now, she had not realized that Thomas had this connection to her father's old friend.

As she primed herself to enter the sweat lodge, Black Bird Shows appeared, again as if out of the air. He greeted her warmly, and scanned the skies after his hello. Sure enough, there were the three magpies, spiraling above the sweat lodge and the small gathering in front of it.

Black Bird had brought a new wool blanket, and he held it out to Colleen. She had never seen one quite like it. It was a deep emerald green, and the patterns on it were trees and flames.

"This is for your quest," he said. "Your dad had it made from the wool of sheep he raised, and left it with me. Now the time has come for you to have it. You will wrap yourself in it."

Colleen thanked him, taking the blanket out of his hands. Caressing the almost silky softness of the gift, and she felt the presence of her father with her. She laid it carefully on the grass beside the door of the sweat lodge. Black Bird stood side-by-side with Thomas, and they slowly turned their backs so she could strip off the clothing she was wearing. She wrapped herself in the blanket to enter, and was immediately hit by a wall of scalding air and steam from the sizzling rocks. She spread the blanket on the ground, and sat, completely unclad.

Black Bird and Thomas did not enter the lodge, but seated themselves on either side of the door. Black Bird began to chant a prayer, in the same language he had used when he performed the ceremony with her after her father's death. Again, she heard the strange words that were not in the Crow language, and again, she felt transported by them. She did not understand the language, but she knew now that it was a very old form of Irish, and that her father had taught it to Black Bird. Time passed quickly, and after about an hour of reverie and meditation in this intense heat, Janine entered the lodge and poured water over the still searing hot stones. A wave of superheated steam filled every crack and crevice and Colleen felt as if all the air had been removed from the interior of this little structure. Every toxin left her body through her pores, and she nearly stopped breathing. The heat sterilized her body and her mind, and she knew the time had come for the cold-water plunge in Pryor Creek.

She lunged for the door, strode across the grass, oblivious to her state of nudity, and stopped at the edge of the water. It was crystal clear in the afternoon sun, and she looked for the bottom of the stream. A sense of dejá vu came over her as she realized that the water depth was unfathomable.

With eyes wide open, she stepped off the edge of the bank. When her feet, then her legs, then her entire body entered the water, the sensation was one of passing through a doorway. The water was deep, and as she sank, it closed over her head. Looking up, only patterns of light and dark were visible above her. The cold water cleansed her skin, and accelerated her heart. She stayed down for a long time, relishing the feeling, and when her face finally broke the surface, she still did not feel desperate for air. Swimming to the shallower part of the creek bed, she set her feet firmly on the bottom. Janine and Doris brought her blanket to her, and wrapped it around her as she waded to the bank. Her mind was alive and clear.

As she stepped out of the water, Janine put a hand on each of her shoulders, and spoke to her quietly: "Some of what you learn on this quest, you will not remember until you need to. Do not be surprised by this." Colleen returned her gaze and nodded.

The two women led her to the car, where Thomas and Black Bird awaited her. They were in the front seat, so she stepped into the back, still wrapped only in the blanket. She noticed that her clothing and other possessions were on the seat beside her. The men were watching the sky. Three magpies were circling, waiting, and once she was in the car, the birds turned one more time, and flew off toward the south.

Thomas started the car, and followed their lead. Before turning onto the main highway, he drove to the grounds of the Chief Plenty Coups home.

Plenty Coups was a famous Crow chief and visionary who was revered by the tribe. It had been his wisdom and vision as a leader that had brought the tribe prosperity and good lands in the early twentieth century. Near the house, which was preserved as a museum, Thomas stopped the car, and helped Colleen get out. She placed her bare feet on the spring grasses and pulled the blanket a little tighter around her. He walked with her across the grounds, and down a small hill to a freshwater spring that Plenty Coups had considered sacred.

It bubbled out of the roots of a massive, aged, cottonwood tree. Thomas spoke.

"Black Bird says you are to drink from this spring before you start your vision quest," he said.

Colleen knelt and cupped her hand to the water. The spring looked very much like her grandmother's spring on the ranch, and she felt comfort in that comparison. The memory of the spring where her grandmother gathered watercress came to her, so clear and sharp that her own visits there could have been in the past week, and not in her childhood 40 years ago.

She recalled all the times her grandmother Velia had taken her there, but the first visit was unsurpassed for its wonder and magic. Her parents had brought her to her grandmother's for the day, since they business to do in Billings. This was a special treat, since she usually spent time with her grandparents on occasions when her cousins were there. But today even her grandfather was gone, and she would have her grandmother all to herself. At 10, she felt very grown-up. Her grandmother sat her at the kitchen table, gave her a glass of milk and some shortbread, then she joined the child.

"Colleen," she said, "How would you like to see my spring?"

"What spring, Grandma?" The child was instantly interested.

"Well," her grandmother answered, "It's a spring where I gather watercress. But if I show it to you, you must promise me that you won't tell anyone. It has to be our secret."

A thrill ran through Colleen. Her grandmother had always awed her. The child knew how devoted her father was to his mother, and she had often witnessed the unspoken communication between them. Now this grandmother was offering to share a secret with her! She knew this was an important moment.

"I'd like that a lot, Grandma!" Colleen exclaimed.

Her grandmother took a bowl from the cupboard and set it on the table. Removing her apron, she folded it carefully and set it on the counter. Then she turned her full attention back to Colleen.

"Your dad told me about how grown up you are. He told me you spend a lot of time in the grove, and he said he thinks you are ready to see the spring. I believe he is right. But I want to be sure you understand that only certain people can know about it."

"I won't tell anyone, Grandma," Colleen promised solemnly.

They left the house, Velia with the bowl in one hand and Colleen's small hand in the other. Colleen was filled with anticipation as they walked away from her grandparents' neat white house. She had explored much of the ranch between her family's home and that of her grandparents, but the path her grandmother chose was brand new to her. It began in a small opening in a chokecherry thicket and when they stepped out on the other side, they were on a soft, grassy—no, mossy—path that led along one of the many sloughs on the ranch. Lodge Grass Creek, which meandered through the ranch for four or five miles had changed courses many times in its long history and had often left these sloughs where its previous channels had been. Cattails sang a green song in the breeze and red-winged blackbirds joined in the concert in their search for nesting materials among the cattail heads. The day was crystal clear and perfect.

Velia paused and gazed up into the blue of the sky. Soaring above them were the three magpies. Velia smiled and began to walk again.

They descended a path down a small slope, where the track turned to rocks arranged in stepping-stone order. Finally they came to an elegant tree of a type that Colleen did not recognize. It grew in a curving pattern near some other shrubs. The path circled the shaded base of the tree and Colleen looked closely at the shrubs. They were like the holly that she had seen in pictures and at Christmas time. But she had never seen it growing anywhere else on the ranch, or in Montana, for that matter.

Nestled at base of the tree on its far side, an even bigger surprise awaited. It was a diamond-clear pool of water, and a strong flow ran from it in a sparkling little brook. It appeared to originate between the roots of the tree, as if it were being constantly reborn. Colleen was fascinated.

Velia settled into the lush grass on the bank of the spring, and patted the ground next to her. Colleen hurried over and knelt by her side. When she placed her hands on the grass and leaned over to look into the spring, she gasped with surprise. Clear as it was, she could not see the bottom.

"Grandma! That is really deep!" She was amazed.

"It may have no bottom," her grandmother said. "It is a sacred spring, and at certain times of the year, it is possible to communicate with another place through it."

"What other place?" The child tried to understand.

"That will be for you to know at a later time. For now, it is enough that you learn to gather the cress with me." Her grandmother left no room for other questions about the bottomless spring. Colleen watched how she picked the finest pieces of watercress, and how she made sure enough was left to provide for new growth. When the bowl was filled, there was one more thing to do. Velia reached into the water with her hand, scooped up some of it and drank. She had Colleen do the same thing. Then Velia stood, brushed off her skirt, and took the child's hand again. They walked in silence back to the opening in the chokecherry thicket. They stepped through, and continued to walk toward the house. A few steps beyond, Colleen turned and looked back. No opening was visible in the shrubbery. She remembered that she was never able to find it again without her Grandmother accompanying her.

Now, at the medicine spring of Plenty Coups, she did the same thing. She scooped a drink of the cold water to her lips and drank. It was delicious and she felt the cold of it spread through her like a conscious thought. It connected her to the earth it flowed from and she recognized its source as a doorway to another dimension in herself.

Colleen did not speak as they returned to the car. There was no need for words, but instead she sat quietly as they drove along. They traveled south for some time, then turned and started up a long mountain road. When she saw the road, she recognized it and realized where they were going. This was the road that led to the Medicine Wheel.

They parked the car a mile or so from their destination and began to walk. Pulling the blanket tight around her, Colleen looked with trepidation at the stony road. Her bare feet would be defenseless against the sharp rocks. She cast an inquiring glance at Black Bird and Thomas. Both men looked back at her steadily, deep brown eyes compelling and peaceful.

Softly, a feeling of trust and calm settled over her, removing all her questions. Her first tentative step brought the astonishing realization that the surface felt smooth beneath her feet. The path took them across a narrow ridge of rock, carved away by glacial forces in ages past. They entered a plateau leading to a sloping flat ridge. There, in its ancient splendor, lay the Medicine Wheel.

The enigmatic ring of stones sprawled flat across the slight slope of the high flat ridge. The "spokes" of the ground-level configuration reached, spider-web of white, to spread the slightly irregular circumference. The outer edge was punctuated by rock cairns at intervals and there were signs of the visits of hundreds of native people. A fence surrounded the composition, no doubt erected in later years to protect this sacred place.

Even the enclosure had become part of the rituals practiced here. Medicine bundles, ribbons, bits of feathers and plants and other items decorated it.

None of the Crow tribal elders knew for sure what the origin of this ceremonial pattern was, or who had constructed it. There were a number of legends about it, but they were beside the point. What was important was that this mystery had been in place for as long as there had been tribal memory. All recognized it as one of the holiest places in the Big Horn Mountains. It was a magnetic site, drawing the most devout of vision-seekers to search for their spirit-world messages here.

Instead of placing her near the circle itself, Thomas took her to a rock outcropping nearby. From this vantage point, Colleen could see a sweeping panorama of the plains and rolling lands of Wyoming, as well as the surrounding mountain terrain. Scanning the area, Colleen saw that the three magpies had taken up perches on the pinnacles of rock that jutted out, castle-like, from the ridge. They formed a triangle, marking off an area. Keeping the blanket around her, she chose a flat spot inside the triangle, and seated herself. Black Bird held out his hands to her. In them was a bundle, wrapped in deerskin that had been tanned to a warm golden color. At her questioning look, he explained, "This is yours now. It was your father's medicine bundle. I have kept it for him, just waiting for this day."

Stunned, Colleen took it gently from his hands. Why did her father have a medicine bundle? More importantly, why did she not know about it? Until now, she had believed that such items were the sphere of tribal members. Loosening the soft deerskin strips that bound it, she unrolled it and contemplated the items that rested inside. There was a bunch of white sage, a sweetgrass braid, three black and white feathers which were immediately recognizable as magpie feathers, one tiny beaded Crow moccasin, a small, angular piece of black-brown stone, some sea shells, and an intricate triangular amulet of bronze-colored metal which was woven with obscure and complex serpentine designs.

Waves of heat and power radiated from the objects as she arranged them on the deerskin wrapping in an order that satisfied her. Holding her hand a little above the objects for a few moments, she felt the emanations connect her with a new plane. Now, she turned to look out over the cliff.

Even though her self-imposed fast had gone on for three days, she felt comfortable. Her vigil began, and the two men withdrew to a spot some distance away from her, where her form was in their line of sight. The first day passed uneventfully. The magpies sat still, black-and-white sculptures on the pinnacles, and the wind blew steadily, but the skies were clear, and the day was quiet. When night fell, Black Bird lit a small fire for Thomas and himself, and they smoked silently, watching the small sparks rise toward the night sky. Colleen pulled the blanket closer against the night chill, but felt no muscular discomfort from sitting for so long. As the darkness became complete, the moon rose on the horizon. It was huge, and lit the landscape with shimmering silver light. Colleen looked up, and saw that the magpies were still there, motionless and watchful, her guardians.

A few owls and bats ventured out into the night, but they circumvented the spot where Colleen sat, as if they understood something extraordinary was happening there. The night passed quickly, and Colleen's mind was filled with thoughts of her father, his connection with the land, and his friendship with the Crow people. She had originally agreed to this quest to satisfy Thomas's need to see her through it. But now, the desire to accomplish it was compelling. Why did she feel this way? There was no answer, but deep in her spirit the knowledge was absolute that it was essential.

The real surprise was how well she felt, having had no food for the past three days, and only a sip from the sacred spring to sustain her. As the sun rose, a reverence that could never be recaptured outside of her home country settled over her. Reflected sunlight blazed in the drops of dew, the colors around her intensified, and the stones took on a razor-edged clarity. All this created an awareness of her vision quest beginning to take effect. She sat patiently.

The second day moved along, and the layers of Colleen's life began to peel away, exposing her core. She leaned forward to welcome whatever might come.

The magpies watched her, and so did Thomas and Black Bird Shows. Suddenly, in the midst of the rocks before her, on the ledge at cliff-edge, a tiny flame sprouted directly out of the rock. Colleen looked at it, then into it, as it began to grow. The flame swelled to a height of at least six feet, as it danced before her. A tiny fragment split off from the large fire, and hovered in the air directly in front of Colleen. Then it leapt at her chest, and re-ignited the old fire inside her soul. The heat spread inside her, and when she looked down at her body, that glance revealed that she was becoming transparent. Her skin was no longer opaque, but had transformed to translucence.

The internal flame illuminated her body with a golden light that glowed and shimmered. Then, where the large flame had been, a tree suddenly appeared. It was a mighty cottonwood, balanced there on the edge of the cliff, with massive branches thrust into the air. Colleen recognized it. It was the oldest, largest tree from her own grove on the ranch.

The magpies slowly took flight, one after the other, and formed a regal procession, climbing high into the sky. Then they circled, down, down, each landing on a separate branch of the tree. At its roots, in the solid rock, a change began. The rock appeared to liquefy, then form a pool at the base of the tree. Colleen knew what the pool was. Her grandmother's sacred spring glittered there. It looked bottomless.

Rising gracefully, she allowed the blanket to slip off her body, and stepped toward the cliff's edge unfettered by clothing or cover. Unable to see the tree, the flame or the spring, Thomas and Black Bird Shows froze where they sat. Was she about to plunge over the cliffs? Colleen walked to the edge of this ethereal pool, and saw rock steps leading down into it. As the two men watched in bewilderment, they saw her descend into what appeared to them to be solid rock. As Colleen's steps carried her down the stairs, she took a long look at the mountains and the prairie spread out below, then dropped into the watery depths. When the water closed over her head, she found herself in a very different world. She was not aware that Thomas and Black Bird Shows had bounded to their feet and run to her position. When they reached it, she was nowhere to be seen. Her body had vanished cleanly into the rock, before their very eyes.

Colleen paused at the bottom of the watery stairs and scanned her surroundings. This world was very green. Stone walls divided the fields of green into neat patterns, and a brilliant blue sea lapped at the base of the hill that below her in the distance. A familiar figure waited for her by the shore. Her feet glided down a soft, green path, and she was completely oblivious to her lack of clothing.

A soft breeze kissed the grasses and her face, while the three magpies hung suspended in the air, ever watchful. As the distance closed, the figure on the beach turned to face her. It was her father. Suddenly several other people appeared next to him. His mother, Colleen's grandmother, stood there, holding out her hands, and his grandmother, whom Colleen recognized from old family photographs, smiled a welcome.

Then, out of the air, dozens more people appeared. Colleen instantly knew some were ancestors, reaching back many generations. Others were transparent and fluid, spirits of this watery world she had entered. With joined hands, they formed a circle around Colleen, and her father stepped forward. He entered her mind as a thought, speaking no words. His presence touched her psyche, and his love soothed her soul.

As his spirit moved about inside her, he planted a message that she could not comprehend at that moment. It was there, but when she reached out to her father in question, he shook his head. The knowledge came to her that the message would become clear when it was needed. One thing was very evident, however. This place was Ireland, and she was expected there.

Now the wind picked up, and the seas ran high. Waves crashed against the rocks, sending up plumes of spray in stunning proportion. Clouds rolled in, altered the light, and a sent down a soft rain, washing her skin and hair. Now the watery stairs of her entrance were directly behind where she stood. Turning, and without deliberation, her foot sought the bottom step, and she started her climb.

When her form emerged at the rock's surface, Thomas and Black Bird were shocked to see not only that their charge was reappearing, but that she was dripping wet. Water streamed from her long, red-black hair and glistened, jewel-like, on her white skin. She was radiant. With elegance and grace, she turned, sat on the green wool blanket, and faced out over the cliff again. She closed her eyes and was very still. Beyond her, the magpies reappeared and flew in steady, repeated slow circles over the medicine wheel, tracing its circumference again and again. It was an awesome sight that transfixed her human guardians.

The rest of the day and the night passed without further incident, and as the morning of the third day dawned, Colleen opened her eyes, rewrapped the medicine bundle with deliberate care, and arose from her place. Cradling the medicine bundle, and pulling the blanket tight around her, she walked to where the men were seated. Every fiber of her body was invigorated and she had never felt more intensely alive.

We can go back now," she said to her two sentinels.

Thomas spoke. "Did you learn what you needed to know?"

He struggled to understand what he had seen. Something very mystical had happened, and he was a little afraid of his own feelings.

She gazed silently at both of her beloved friends for a long time.

"I know where I'm going," she said. "The rest will come later."

CHAPTER 7

▼

Colleen learned that Janine had been right. When she first returned to herself from her quest, the vision was clear in her mind. As she put her clothes on next to the car, the revelations started to recede into the back of her mind. Frantically, she struggled to force the memory to remain on the surface, but it retreated slowly and silently. Donning the trappings of her everyday life seemed to put more and more layers between her and her vision.

Thomas and Black Bird drove her back to Thomas's home, and in the light of day, everything looked very different. Janine and Doris had removed the blankets from the sweat lodge, so only the graceful willow-branch arches remained, and the water of Pryor Creek looked ordinary to her.

Placing her belongings in the car, she allowed her hands to rest longingly on the blanket and the medicine bundle she had received from Black Bird. A subtle, warm vibration emanated from them, comforting her. When she looked in the rear-view mirror of her car to adjust her hair, something strange caught her attention. In the rich red-black of her mass of hair, a small white streak shone. It surprised her, but not enough to cause her to question where it had come from. The memory was with her in a subtle form, just outside her reach. Starting her car, she drove back toward Billings, and by the time she arrived at her sister's home, the feelings left by her vision formed a vague sensation tucked into a deep recess in her mind.

The next day, she took leave from her sister, brother and mother, ignoring to the puzzled looks in their eyes. Their eyes mirrored their confusion over the change in her, more than the change in her hair, but when they asked about it, she shrugged it off.

When Kathleen asked about the streak in her hair, her reaction was ambivalent.

"It's probably been there for a while, and if I seem different myself, I'm probably just tired after the camping trip," she rationalized.

Her sister knew otherwise, from pure intuition. Kathleen had always had an extraordinary sense about her family members, particularly this younger sister who had so often been her charge.

"You don't look tired," she insisted. "You look…this is probably a strange word…but you look somehow *transformed.*"

Her sister had developed an increasing ability to read her that no one else in the family had, now that their father was gone. Somewhere inside Kathleen, the same genes resided, and the same genetic memories were there. Kathleen had been aware of her father's extra-sensory abilities when it came to his children, and she had known about some of his premonitions.

She did not disbelieve, she just accepted it and never dwelled on it. Once her own children were born, the same extrasensory family abilities became apparent, and she marveled only at the fact that they seemed so natural to her.

Kathleen had lived a sane and level life, and had been the solid base around which the rest of the family revolved. Her marriage to a wonderful man gave her three beautiful children. After they were grown, she had lovingly cared for her parents in their later years. She was still their mother's best friend, and her intense love for both her brother and sister knew no bounds. This dedication had resulted in her worrying about Colleen during her younger sister's divorce. Now that Colleen was alone, Kathleen watched over her as she had when her younger sister was small.

"I don't know why you think there's been a transformation," Colleen responded, "I still feel pretty much the same."

Kathleen, Sean and her mother walked her to her car. As they got the last bits of information and advice exchanged, they agreed to spend Christmas together. Colleen settled in for her drive back to Rapid City. As the miles rolled by, she leaned back in the seat and let thoughts of her work take over her mind. This was common for her after every vacation break. Each time she attempted to recall anything about her vision quest, all that remained was the memory of arriving at Thomas and Janine's home, taking the sweat, and walking away from her quest site at the Medicine Wheel. Her thoughts rested briefly upon the blanket and the medicine bundle Black Bird had given her, riding peacefully now in her back seat. They could only be regarded as wonderful gifts. Deep inside, she knew there must be more to the experience, and while the memory was beyond reach, a deep, tranquil feeling remained.

Once back in Rapid City, a visit to a hairdresser took care of the white streak in her hair. There was still no memory of where the streak had come from, and she was uneasy with the thought of trying to explain it to anyone. At her office, she pitched herself into her work with an intensity that startled even those who had worked closely with her. Her arrivals at work were far earlier than they had been, and she didn't go home until long after everyone else had left the building. Her energy seemed boundless. The end of the day would find her at home, sitting in front of her computer, feverishly researching Irish immigration and genealogy. The need to find her ancestors had become a compulsion.

Some fragments began to come to light. She found census records that referred to her great-grandfather's mother, Dr. Flora Daly. This enigmatic woman had been a mysterious medical doctor who practiced in the Black Hills of South Dakota, not far from her office. Very little about this great-great grandparent had been mentioned by anyone in the family. With the opportunity provided by proximity, a little weekend research was in order.

A Saturday drive took her to Deadwood, where she talked with the curator at the Historical Museum. Some photographs and documents acquainted her further with "Dr. Flora," and revealed that somehow this woman had managed to establish and build a homestead deep in the hills at the same time that she maintained a medical practice in Deadwood, and one in Sundance, Wyoming. The logistics of two such endeavors, miles apart from each other, were beyond belief. Old news articles described the large numbers of patients the beloved doctor had treated in both communities, and there were notes about the steady stream of people who sought her out at the remote homestead as well. The newspapers also indicated that no patient ever was turned away, whether white community leaders or outlaws, Chinese or Sioux Indians.

A footnote in an obituary stated that her great-grandfather Frank Daly had inherited the homestead, and noted that her great-grandmother Anna Hughes Daly had continued the healing practice at the homestead, then later in Sundance. Using the news articles, she tried to locate Dr. Flora's grave in Mt. Moriah Cemetery, the famous Deadwood resting place of Wild Bill Hickock and Calamity Jane (who had been one of Dr. Flora's patients). Despite detailed records kept by the cemetery stating she was buried there, there was no sign of the grave.

The papers in the historical collection also gave a property description of the homestead, and Colleen knew she had to visit the place. After obtaining a detailed map of the area, she ventured along the dirt roads in the hills to locate that property.

The area was confusing to Colleen. The land had to be close, but there were no clues to help pinpoint the exact location. Finally, she allowed the car to roll to a stop, and got out for a panoramic look beyond the limits of her Honda's windshield. Standing quietly for a moment, a motion caught her attention. A burst of black and white flashed at the edge of her vision, and a quick turn presented a sight that caused her to gasp. Three magpies had landed on the branches of a large dead tree near her. They were looking directly at her with black-jewel eyes glittering, quiet, heads cocked. When it appeared they were sure that she could see them, they lifted off deliberately, one at a time, circled her car, and began to fly toward the west.

All she could do was trust her instincts and past experience. Colleen got into the car quickly and turned west. The birds stayed a few yards ahead of her, and before long, the property that matched the legal description she had brought with her appeared before her. Parking, she left the car and began to walk toward the cluster of trees in the small canyon at the back of the property. Inside the wooded area, she found a beautiful spring. It was pure and clear, and when she reached toward it, she was amazed to see the small bubbles rising from the depths of it. It was a sparkling pool, and the effervescence gave it life. Scooping up a handful of the water, she tasted it. As she swallowed, the details from her vision quest suddenly surfaced for a moment, sharp and defined, then submerged again. This jolted her.

This spring was probably part of the reason so many people were willing to travel long distances to seek medical help from Dr. Flora and later from Anna, whose travels had brought her west with Frank. Apparently, these two friends had brought something mysterious and ancient to the pioneers and Sioux Indian people they had treated. As Colleen contemplated this discovery, it tied definitively to her conversation with her aunt Willow. No wonder these ancestors had kept a low profile. The west would have been a good place for them to come to escape the scrutiny of more "civilized" communities. This place had sheltered them, giving them the chance for a peaceful life. Colleen mused that these little gold mining camps and western outposts accepted all comers, strange beliefs or not. It was a good sanctuary, allowing the freedom to practice even the most unusual beliefs without fear. And it had ultimately resulted in Margaret's daughter marrying Flora's son. What a perfect blend of families. Next, Colleen wondered if there was any possibility of uncovering what kind of relationship these women had with the tribal people in those days. Her work had opened the door for a fresh avenue of research.

Returning home, she telephoned one of the local Sioux tribal members she had met since coming to Rapid City. Her request for a list of the oldest, wisest people in the tribe yielded the name of Nellie Black Robe. Nellie was known to be at least 95 years old, and this elder was known to still have a very sharp mind. Colleen called Nellie's granddaughter, with whom she lived, and asked if she could visit to ask Nellie some questions about the history of the area. The granddaughter told her that the old lady spoke little English, but that she would be happy to interpret for them. Colleen thanked her. Searching through her cedar chest, she looked for a gift to take to Nellie. After some careful thought, she selected a beautiful shawl that had once belonged to her grandmother Velia, and folded it carefully.

When she pulled up in front of the tiny house on the south edge of Rapid City, she felt a moment of recognition. It looked like so many of the homes that her Crow tribal friends occupied. Although it was small, it was very neat, and in the back yard, clean laundry waved at her. She walked respectfully up to the front door. Her knock sounded on the solid wood and she stood quietly waiting.

A middle-aged woman came to the door. The woman was trim and elegant with salt and pepper hair, and her warm brown eyes examined this visitor with reserved, but keen curiosity. Colleen introduced herself, and restated her interest in talking with Nellie. The woman said her name was Alice Black Robe and that she had been the person who talked with Colleen on the telephone. Her fluid gesture was an invitation to enter the house and come into the tidy living room area. There, a very small Indian woman sat in a comfortable rocker. She was ancient, and her hair was snow white. Her eyes were set deep in mahogany colored skin, which folded into a mass of wrinkles when she smiled at Colleen. Despite her obvious age, she appeared to be in good health and Colleen observed that she had all her own teeth.

Alice said, "I told her you were coming, and she said a funny thing. She said she had a dream about you last night."

Colleen's expression showed surprise, but she smiled and responded, "I hope it was a good dream."

Alice repeated this comment to her grandmother in Sioux, and the old woman chuckled, nodding.

Colleen turned to Alice, and said "Please tell her I'd like to know about some white medicine women who lived in the hills in the 1890's and the early 1900's.

They were Dr. Flora Daly and Anna Daly, and they worked with patients in Deadwood and Sundance."

Alice relayed the information and Nellie's expression became very animated as she responded in rapid Sioux dialect.

Colleen listened without comprehension, looking from Nellie to Alice as this exchange went on, then she focused on Alice while she told her in English what Nellie had said. "She remembers hearing her parents talk of them. Once, when she was a girl, she went with her parents when they took her little brother, a very sick little baby, to see the second one, Anna. Everyone had tried to treat him, medicine men, local medical doctors, everybody. But he just kept getting sicker and sicker. They put him and Nellie in their wagon and made the long trip to the homestead. Anna was there, and she invited them into her house, something very few white people did. She put her hands on the baby and he stopped crying for the first time in several days. But he was so sick and weak. Anna picked him up in her arms, and asking the parents to come along, took him out of the house to a spring that was not far from her house. They went, and Anna put her hand in the water, and put some drops on the baby's lips. The baby was very still, and the parents were scared he was dead."

Colleen was mesmerized. "What happened then?" she asked.

Alice continued. "She took them back into the house, and they waited. Night came and still Anna held the baby in her arms. He lay so still. She sat in her chair and continued to hold him. Finally morning came, and the sun came in through her window. It formed one single ray that touched the baby as he lay in Anna's arms. The baby woke up, looked around and held out his arms to his mother. Anna gave him back, and told the mother to feed him. She put him to her breast and he nursed long and deep, for the first time in many days. After he finished, he smiled and went to sleep. Anna told them that the baby would begin to get stronger day by day, and that he would recover."

"Did he?" Colleen already knew the answer in her heart.

"Yes," Alice replied. "That baby was my great-uncle. He got well, and lived a long, good life. He became a very respected person in our tribe."

Colleen turned toward Nellie and smiled. "Thank you for talking with me," she said. "I needed to know if my ancestors were who and what I thought they were."

Alice translated, and Nellie spoke at length again. Alice turned and said to Colleen, "She says that these women were known to have great magic by members of the tribe. They were revered and respected, and the Sioux trusted them totally. More than that, they were held in awe for the magic they could work.

They could cure most ailments and they could make any kind of plant grow. They had many excellent treatments and they never turned anyone away. We all mourned the old one when she died, and we missed the young one when she moved away."

Colleen reached into her bag and pulled out the tissue-wrapped shawl that had belonged to her grandmother Velia, Anna Hughes's daughter. Respectfully, she offered it to Nellie. Nellie held out her ancient hands and took the shawl reverently. She laid it in her lap and stroked it tenderly.

Colleen said, "Please thank her for me. This information is very important."

Alice passed this statement on to her grandmother, who smiled and nodded at Colleen. She said a few more words to Alice, who said, "She says you look exactly like she remembers your great-grandmother, and she knows there is magic in you, too."

Colleen smiled. "That would be nice, but somehow I don't think so. I'm just an ordinary person."

With that, she stood, said good-bye to Nellie and to Alice and went to the door. As she turned the knob, she looked back, and saw that Nellie was still looking at her intently, as if trying to memorize her image. Colleen waved and stepped out the door. She mulled over what she had heard. It all fit in with what Willow had said, but it seemed beyond belief. Yet, there must be something to it, since so many small pieces of the puzzle were starting to match up.

CHAPTER 8

▼

As Christmas approached, Colleen found herself feeling more and more troubled by the impending trip to Billings for the holidays. The idea of the visit was a burden, and the feeling was inexplicable. Ordinarily, seeing her mother, her brother and her sister and her nieces and nephews was something to be anticipated with joy and eagerness. This time, she felt a dark dread in her heart. It would have been impossible to back out of the plan on such short notice, so she confirmed her plans to stay with her brother and sister-in-law.

It had been one of the most intense winters in recent Montana history. Old timers sat about in local coffee shops and talked about how they could not remember a harsher or colder time. There was a substantial amount of snow and temperatures were frequently sub-zero. Even though Colleen had worked hard all year, she planned for a very short holiday. Her work had become her life, and she hated taking any time off. This visit was scheduled for just five days. As the holiday grew closer, the more oppressive the weight on her heart became. It was a huge encumbrance that rested upon her shoulders, and she was disconcerted. Perhaps it was a mid-winter blues period, but there was no reason for it. Work was going smoothly, and recognition for her efforts was abundant in her company and her industry. In addition, her health was exceptionally good, giving no reason for concern.

Clothes and Christmas gifts were packed into her car. Perhaps her anxiety was just the result of dreading the drive in winter conditions, but she had prepared properly. Extra food, blankets and winter supplies were included in the car, and the road reports indicated that the roads were clear and dry. It was too cold to form ice or snowpack on the road. When she could delay her departure no longer, she started the journey. Throughout the six-hour drive, she kept expecting that car trouble or an accident would justify the apprehension, but the ride was totally uneventful.

Upon her arrival in Billings, she stopped at Kathleen's house first. The family would gather for the holiday dinner and gift opening there. Besides, it was her practice to touch base with her older sister whenever she needed some reassurance. Her brief visit with Kathleen did little to alleviate her angst, so after a while, she prepared to leave, gamely putting on a cheerful face. It was Christmas, after all, and she was intent upon avoiding causing Kathleen reason to be concerned about her.

Then she drove out into the country. Sean and Lydia had bought the house on the cliff from her and Art after her transfer from Billings. It was good to see the house again. Its location had always been a delight and she had found peace for her soul here. Even with the divorce, there were few very unhappy moments here. She parked the car away from the house a bit to give Sean and his wife, Lydia, access to their garage. From there, it was simple to tug her suitcase out of the car and go to their door. They saw her coming and threw open the door to greet her.

"Happy holidays!" her brother emphasized the greeting with a warm bear hug.

Lydia embraced her, too, and urged her to hurry out of the frigid air and into the house.

"Get inside!" she exclaimed. "The television weather just said the temperature is twenty-six below zero!"

The three of them scurried in amidst clouds of frozen breath.

In the warmth of the foyer, Colleen looked around. The house welcomed her, but trepidation continued to afflict the mood of the day. What could the reason for her edginess possibly be? Sean and Lydia looked good, and the home had flourished under their care. A lush Christmas tree dominated the great room, and the fireplace crackled merrily. It was the perfect holiday scene.

Internally, Colleen scolded herself.

"Snap out of it. There is no reason to feel like this. This is going to be a wonderful Christmas."

Thus lectured, she put on her best smile, and settled in for an evening of visiting.

The talk went on until nearly midnight, when they finally, reluctantly, parted company and went to bed. Colleen washed her face and crawled into bed. She would stay in the guest room, on the opposite end of the house from Sean and Lydia's master bedroom. A deep sleep engulfed her immediately.

At two in the morning, Colleen came wide-awake with every sense working overtime. It was very light outside. The luminous dial of her watch couldn't be right. Had it stopped? But the alarm clock on the nightstand confirmed that it was two o'clock. She sat up bolt upright and stared at the window. A red glow like that of sunrise shown through the curtains. Hurling herself to her feet, she dashed to the window, reaching out to open the drape. Nothing could have prepared her for what was outside. On the outer wall and above her head, the entire back side of the house, including a covered second-story porch, was violently ablaze. The fire was entirely on the exterior of the house, and it was gigantic. The flames had already devoured the floor and roof of the porch and there was no doubt that speed was of the essence. She felt no panic. A deep calm settled over her, and she turned from the window and raced purposefully up the stairs toward the master bedroom. Jerking open the door, she shouted at Sean and Lydia.

"Wake up! Fire!"

Jolted from their sleep, they plunged out of bed. In the hallway of the great room they looked toward the end of the house where the flames were in full attack.

"Call 911!" Colleen ordered Lydia, who moved quickly to the telephone."

Leaving Lydia to her call, Colleen returned to her room, and moving in deliberate, preternatural calm, put on warm clothing, including boots and coat. Some inner voice assured her that she had time for this. Gathering her belongings into her suitcase, she carried it quickly back up the stairs.

Sean and Lydia stood on the landing in front of the entry door, waiting for her.

They were wearing their coats, and Lydia clutched her most cherished possession, her grandfather's violin.

"Are you ready?" Sean asked.

She nodded, and he opened the door.

With that action, the fire imploded, shattering all the window glass inward, and the fire ripped into the house. Deafening noise accompanied the smoke that ballooned at them ominously. There was a hurried exchange of questions. Could they get to the water hoses? No. They were put away for the winter. Could any of the neighbors help? No. This fire was too big for anyone else to risk their lives. Far off in the valley below, they could hear the fire sirens and see the flashing lights of the engines as firefighters started toward the distant road that would bring them up the steep rimrocks.

They turned away from the structure reluctantly. All three wanted to go back and try to do something, anything, but that last look made it obvious that the fire was far too colossal. The sight of the towering flames sealed the decision. Safety had to be their first concern. As they retreated, a blanket of calm settled over Colleen. Her dread departed, and now an inner voice was clear and recognizable. It was her father.

"Well done, Magpie! You were here so your brother and Lydia would be safe. In achieving this, you have been strengthened by this fire."

Colleen would have wondered if she was having an audio-hallucination, except for the fact that she had heard that voice numerous times since Mike's death. She accepted it now.

The raw violence of the sub-zero air attacked them, creating a dissonance between what they could see of the flames and smoke and what they could feel on their skin. It chilled all three of them to the core.

It was imperative to put space between them and fire, and at that moment, a deputy sheriff arrived. He urged them to get into his car where there was shelter from the cold. They obeyed him like children, and once in the car, turned to look again at the fire. It was gathering strength, burning, burning, plundering all the possessions Sean and Lydia owned. Lydia burst into tears, keening with her grief. Sean comforted her, and watched in stunned silence as the drama continued to play out.

The house was many miles from the nearest fire station, and the icy condition of the streets made the fire department pumper trucks take a long time to arrive. The flames ravaged the structure, taking the exterior of the house first, then feasting on the interior. The sounds were horrendous, breaking glass, crashing timbers, small explosions as it found the usual most volatile household materials and, finally, the deep roar of the fire as it satisfied its ravenous appetite for destruction.

Lydia couldn't watch, and Colleen couldn't stop watching.

Now the fire fighters arrived and committed themselves to the hopeless struggle to battle the fire in the arctic cold. Sean, Lydia and Colleen recognized that there was nothing further they could do. After watching a while longer, Sean and Lydia went to stay the night with their mother, and Colleen went to Kathleen's home. Once there, sleep evaded her. She felt relieved of the trepidation and anxiety that had haunted her for the past weeks, but adrenalin still coursed through her. When morning arrived, she arose, showered, and began to dress. The sight of herself in the mirror shocked her, because her face emanated the same strange glow. This must have been what her sister had pointed out after her vision quest. More than that, she leaned toward the mirror and lifted up her hair. Hidden beneath the outer layer of it was another white streak. Colleen sighed. Recalling the sound of her father's voice at the site of the fire, she contemplated it for a few moments with no conclusions.

Further self examination confirmed that she had indeed been strengthened. Like superior cutlery, the fire had tempered her spirit and created a nucleus of refined steel inside her. A hardened resolve demanded that she move forward. What should her mission be? What better undertaking than the mysterious assignment her father had set out for her?

Behind closed eyes, she relived the previous night's drama. In her mind's eye, she could see herself, emerging from the fire. At the last moment, with her father's voice in her ears, she felt a fragment of that blaze, a powerful shard of flame, leap from the depths of the inferno into the banked coals inside her. Now her own fire was ablaze, fueling her future. Her hidden memories moved closer to the surface. Something inside her soul told her the time for the journey had come.

CHAPTER 9

▼

Colleen paused and looked around, remembering when preparations had begun for her journey. Following the fire, she had kept close tabs on her brother and his wife. They were saddened by the material items they had lost, but they recovered their equilibrium quickly, and began to make plans for their future. The house on the ranch was available, and they decided that was where they wanted to be. The big place had always been a family refuge, and with Sean's career as a writer, it would be the ideal place for them to heal. When their parents left the ranch, the family had decided to keep the house vacant, with the ranch foreman taking care of it. It symbolized the hope against hope that their parents might somehow be able to return there. With Mike's death, Della had told her three children that she did not intend to go back. Kathleen and James planned to stay in Billings, and Colleen knew the time was not right for her to live there. All agreed that Sean and Lydia's residence there would make it feel like home again, and the matter was settled. It had a feeling of destiny, and the siblings knew better than to try to change it.

Colleen was frustrated by research attempts that still had not revealed the exact location in Ireland where her ancestors had originated. The family name had pinponted a likely place to start. A town named Lorrha in the West of Ireland had been mentioned in one old letter to her grandmother. Something about that place name struck a chord. But more importantly, some obscure Irish historians suggested that the original family stronghold for the Hughes name was located further north, near a little spot-in-the-road village—Bureen.

Several attempts to call her aunt Willow in New Orleans resulted only in a recorded message that told her the telephone had been disconnected. How frustrating. Now that she couldn't reach her, there were a million questions to ask. A check with her cousin Roisín, produced only a disparaging comment.

"That's typical. I don't know where she is, either, and frankly, I don't care."

Willow's whereabouts were completely unknown and Colleen was out of ideas about how or where to find her. That avenue closed, the next best thing was to make another try at getting her aunt Mary Cecilia to divulge what she must know.

This second visit to the convent home resulted in a discussion that was even more frustrating. The winter weather forced them to talk in one of the gloomy old reception rooms. The dark surroundings, smelling of wax and old wood, added to the dismal mood of their conversation. After the usual formalities and inquiries after her aunt's well being, she ventured onto what she knew was forbidden ground. Sister Mary met her declaration about her intention to travel to Ireland with disparagement.

"There's probably nothing for you to see in that country," she said, face impassive. "No one knows anything about those relatives, and it seems like a lot of trouble for you to go there and not find anything out. I don't think you should go."

Colleen was patient. "Sister Mary," she replied. "I don't feel like I have any choice. It has become an obsession for me. Dad wanted me to go, and everything he ever told me about it made me want to."

Colleen tried another approach.

"Did I tell you I had a nice visit with Aunt Willow a couple of months ago?"

Sister Mary Cecilia looked shocked and disconcerted. "You did? Where?"

"In New Orleans. I learned she had been in touch with Roisín, so I thought she could be helpful in my family history research. I had to be there for a convention anyway, so I arranged to go visit her. We spent a wonderful afternoon together, and she told me a some very interesting things," Colleen explained.

Sister Mary was concerned. "What did she tell you?"

"She told me the Hughes great-great grandparents had immigrated to New Orleans, then worked their way up the Mississippi to St. Louis, and on to Iowa. She said they had some unusual beliefs that made them feel they had to keep moving. It was a fascinating story," Colleen recalled.

Glancing around to make sure they were alone in the room, Sister Mary leaned forward to speak in a low and intense voice. "I hope you didn't believe everything my sister told you. Her imagination is very active and wild and she makes things up. If she told you anything at all about me, it wasn't true."

Colleen realized that this discussion was not going to make any inroads, so she rose, keeping a calm demeanor with her aunt, and said, "Actually, she didn't tell me anything about you. I just wanted to let you know about this journey, in case you had any thoughts about places I should try to visit, or things I should look for in trying to trace the ancestors over there. I didn't know if you might recall anything that great-grandmother Anna told you. Even the smallest piece of information could have given me a clue, so I thought I would check with you one more time. No matter what, I am grateful that you were willing to see me again."

As a farewell gesture, she took both her aunt's hands in hers. "Sister Mary," she said warmly, "It's important that you know I'm not trying to pry into your thoughts or feelings about all this. I just have a sincere and deep need to know. You are very dear to me, and the last thing I want to do is make you uncomfortable."

Sister Mary did not reply, but merely nodded, squeezing Colleen's hands. Her face was serious, apprehensive, almost grim. They stepped apart, and as she watched Colleen go, Sister Mary saw the three magpies circling overhead. A shudder wracked her, and she wrapped her arms around herself. Then, averting her eyes, she crossed herself, and hurried back inside, crossing the reception area to the hall. Overwhelming her was a chilling sense of long-hidden things about to be revealed. Deep inside, the knowledge had always rested that this time might come, but she had prayed long and hard that it would not. Now it had arrived, and a helpless feeling flowed through her, seeping through her shield of lifelong religious faith.

Upon her return, Colleen made airline reservations, and requested a nine-month sabbatical from work, starting early in January. Her boss was surprised. Bill Sloan was a hard-driven no-nonsense man, an unabashed admirer of Colleen's work. He had been a superb mentor from the time she came to work for him, and his hard-driven style had set a pattern that she imitated and sometime exceeded. In every annual performance evaluation, he tried to encourage her to relax, but to little avail.

"Colleen, are you all right?" he asked, looking at her intently. "You usually won't even take a full week of vacation, and now you are requesting nine months on the very shortest notice. Is everything okay with your health, your family?"

"Sure, Bill," she said, "I just have something I have to do. It has nothing to do with work, and everything to do with me."

Her boss leaned back in his big executive chair, and smiled. "You know the company encourages periodic extended sabbaticals. We believe that it keeps our executives more creative. But I've pushed you to do this several times, and you've always refused, even though your work is consistently in such good order that you could have gone any time. You can't blame me for being curious. What finally got you to do this?"

"It's not something I can define for you right now," she said. "I'm sure it will be more clear when I come back. I'll leave telephone numbers and other information so people can reach me if they need to."

Colleen had always been private at work about her personal life. Bill knew any further attempts to question her would be futile, so he nodded at her and settled for what he had heard. Whatever the reason, he was certain the break would be good for his star employee. He watched quizzically as she thanked him and left his office.

The next weeks were filled with tying up loose ends at work, and with settling things at home for her prolonged absence. She started working out and pushing for a higher level of fitness, to make sure that she would be as strong and as well as she could for the trip. Renewed attendance at self-defense classes pushed her body to its limits. She arranged for a house-sitter, giving a delighted new sales manager from her firm the opportunity to live in very comfortable surroundings for nine months.

This arrangement necessitated the storage of her possessions out of the way of her new tenant. She packed away her home office files, her personal items, and then she started on her clothes. The contents of that closet had a peculiar effect on her as she worked. As she re-hung the fashionable executive items in the cedar storage closet, she suddenly paused. Setting aside this wardrobe was sweeping away the professional persona she had assumed in the evolution of her career. With every tailored suit, every silk blouse, a layer of her professional self was stripped away. The essence of her inherent spirit began to emerge from the cocoon she had languished in for so long.

A sense of lightness enveloped her, leaving her feeling almost weightless. The realization of how she had subjugated herself to the trappings of her career was so profound, that she dropped to her knees on the floor of the storage space. The warm aroma of cedar surrounded her, and her spirit set itself free. The feeling was intoxicating, and she rose to her feet, reaching back for the pins that held her hair bound up in the neat, sophisticated style she favored for work. The mass of it tumbled down around her shoulders and over her back, forming a dark frame for her face.

Racing up the stairs, she began to pack the things that would sustain her for a long period out of the country. Once clothes and sundries were organized, she looked around her bedroom for anything that might have been forgotten. Her father's medicine bundle caught her eye from its prominent position in the glass cabinet she had had built for it. Something about it seemed to be calling out to her. On impulse, she unlocked the cabinet and reverently cradled the precious thing in her hands. Taking a silk scarf from her dresser, she wrapped the bundle carefully and placed it in her carry-on bag.

A stop in Chicago allowed her to quiz her Irish friends about what to expect when she entered the country. Each of them reaffirmed that, for her purposes, Ireland was best visited outside of the tourist season. After these reassurances, she boarded the Aer Lingus flight for Ireland at O'Hare. This would be her first overseas flight, and cautions about jet-lag made her worry that she might not sleep on the flight.

It turned out that sleeplessness would not be a problem. Settled in her seat, she watched the teal-clad flight attendants move smoothly through safety demonstrations and pre-flight activities. Her eyelids grew heavy as soon as the flight began to taxi to its place for takeoff, and she drifted into sleep, lulled by the thrum of the plane's engines.

The ability to fall asleep easily in nearly any environment had come from her years of business travel, along with some methods learned in meditation classes. The result was that she always arrived at her journey's end rested and ready for all work demands. The last conscious thought she had before dozing was that an overseas destination did not seem to diminish this gift.

Her slumber patterns were unusual for their depth, so much so that whenever the subject of dreams came up, she always insisted that she did not dream.

This time was different. First came her usual deep sleep, but then there was a shift into a dream state, a very defined move. It was a condition that seemed like wakefulness. In the dream, she found herself looking into a pool of water identical to her grandmother's spring on the ranch. Watercress glistened green and lush at the sides of the water, and the depth of the spring was unfathomable. Her unconscious-self stepped through the surface of the water and suddenly, she found herself in a green world, greener than any place she had ever been.

Looking around the verdant field where she stood, her sight rested on a path that led across it to the edge of a wooded area. All but the field and the trees directly in her path were obscured by a bright, shining vapor, so like the mist remembered from the early morning sojourns into the Big Horn Mountains with her father. All was silent.

Following the path, new to her, she was most assuredly lost. The only solution seemed to be to continue to travel forward through the mist, as if guided by an invisible line.

The mist became brighter yet, and there was no visibility through it until tree shapes began to emerge. Now the trees defined the path, and she continued to walk, with more purpose. The trek was long, but finally an opening in a grove of ancient trees stretched out before her. Stopping and standing very still, she gazed across the opening to the other side, to a particularly regal tree with white bark. The vapor began to dissolve from around this tree and it stood shimmering in sunlight. Gradually, its form began to shift, and the shape of a man emerged. He was an older man of small size, with smooth skin and white hair. As the sun touched his face, she realized that he was looking at her intently with brilliant blue eyes.

His gaze was tactile, rather than visible. His charisma focused on her. Frozen in place, she was unable to move or speak. Speech would be unnecessary with this man. Pulling at her mind was a connection to him like the one she felt with her father's spirit. There was no fear, and she considered it a natural phenomenon, as natural as weather, as natural as fire.

As the dream continued, she understood that this man was waiting for her, expecting her to do something. This was so confusing. What could this tree-being want from her? What was she supposed to do? As she watched, the man's simple clothing was transformed into a tunic that appeared to be from a very ancient time. Before her startled eyes, a wall of flames rose around him and he disappeared. Her attempt to call out produced no sound. She was rooted to the spot where she stood, and when she looked down at her feet she was stunned to see that she, too, had become a tree. Her roots plunged deep into the soil of the place. As this realization came to her, another being emerged from the flames. Her first impression was that he was a wild animal. His eyes were deep and green and fingers of the fire burned in their depths.

Everything about him appeared to reach out for her and she longed to run to him. His form began to shimmer again and he also reverted to tree form, thrusting roots into the ground.

The flames died down, and where the first, white-haired man had stood, now there was a pool of clear, pure green water. All the trees in the grove were living spirits, and she had joined them. The silence continued for a very long time, and then the mists parted, and the sun was there, playing through the green leaves and grass.

Abruptly, the silence was broken by a voice, and it seemed very loud. Colleen felt herself ascending to the surface of the water corridor that had brought her into this otherworld, and as she broke that surface into a million glistening slivers, she was conscious that the sun touched her face. Her eyes blinked their way through some confusion to full wakefulness. That loud voice had been the flight crew, announcing the landing time at Shannon airport. She shook her head as vivid memories defined every detail of the dream. Overseas flight must have a real effect on her, she mused, if it could cause such an odd images.

Her window provided a sweeping view of the Shannon estuary and the patchwork fields below. The forms of birds flying and sitting in the water could be seen, and the muted light played on the surface of the water. Excitement blossomed inside her and all her senses were alive with anticipation. It was so green! Someone had once told her that she would see at least thirty-seven shades of green, but that seemed a conservative estimate. As the plane descended, the details of the neat stone walled fields became clear, and the landscape seemed to throw open its arms in welcome. The biggest surprise was the clarity of the day, despite the rain . She had anticipated gray rainy weather, but instead, there was a light mist falling on the countryside—a soft day.

Deplaning in the shining vapor, Colleen collected her rental car, which had to be one of the smallest vehicles she had ever seen. She examined the steering wheel and instruments on the right side with some trepidation. Sitting in the parking lot, she went through the motions of shifting with her left hand, located all the controls and dials, then started the vehicle and pulled out slowly. Signs on the road leading out of Shannon reminded the novice driver again and again to stay on the left side of the road, and to look in the other direction for oncoming traffic. After a little nervous practice at navigating the opposite side of the road, she found that she was very comfortable with it, and relaxed into the rhythm of the drive.

The map from the rental car company guided her north toward the thatched cottage she had leased in Bureen for the nine months of her planned holiday. If anyone had asked, it would have been difficult to explain why she had chosen that particular accommodation, but when she had reviewed all the Irish Tourist Board literature, the picture of the cottage had reached out and grabbed her. It epitomized what she had always imagined Irish homes to be like.

In addition, it was located in the area near what might have been among the original holdings of the Hughes and Garrett families. The road took her through the tiny community of Lorrha, which had seemed to suggest the origin of her father's last name. She stopped there long enough to look at the ruins of the old church whose bell was still rung daily. So far, little information had surfaced on this name or how it had become the last name of the family. With no clear information, and with travel exhaustion to overcome, it seemed logical to return here on her way out of the country.

CHAPTER 10

▼

Bureen was a delightful village, and the sight of the cottage validated her choice of lodging. Although her plans included some tourist attractions, it was important to have a base from which to explore. This one would make her feel more like a part of a single community. It suited her wishes on all counts. The thought occurred to her that this little dwelling was probably similar to the home where her ancestors might have lived, although this one had a few modern conveniences. The key from the rental agency turned easily in the quaint green half-door and it swung inward on well-oiled hinges, inviting her to enter. She was relieved to find running water, indoor plumbing, a minuscule refrigerator, a two-burner stove, and some ineffective-looking electric radiators to supplement the peat fireplace in the parlor-dining room. The layers of quilts and blankets piled on the bed would have to be enough to keep her sleeping hours warm.

It had been late morning when she arrived, unpacked, and ate a small lunch. Settling in included stocking her cupboards with some food she bought in a diminutive shop nearby, and then it was time to begin exploring the area. When she ventured out, it was still raining softly, but not enough to deter her interest, or the activities of the residents of the area. Bureen was small, with neat rows of houses along its one winding street. Many were old, but some were newer, and there were several small shops. The big Catholic church building dominated the landscape as it did in so many Irish towns, and there were three cozy pubs clustered together, balancing that influence and providing a social center for the community. The village was located near several wooded areas, and she could glimpse the Atlantic Ocean some distance away. She stayed out walking for a long time, and her return to the cottage revealed that someone had lit the peat fire. The miniature stove did a decent job of heating a bowl of soup, and she seated herself before the small fireplace to eat it.

After her meal, she donned her jacket again to walk across the grassy square to the pub. The rain seemed to be a constant, but she had made sure to bring good rain gear for protection from the elements. A waterproof jacket, good sturdy shoes, and a pair of Wellingtons for walking about in the fields comprised her new wardrobe. Now, in early evening, she entered the combination store, pub and gathering place of the town. It was not so typical of Irish culture for a lone woman to walk into a pub unaccompanied, but she hoped that the locals would chalk it up to brash American behavior, and welcome her anyway.

She looked up as the barmaid (what an odd title for the tiny white-haired woman) came up to face her across the well-worn table.

"What would y' like?" the woman asked.

"Smithwick's, please," Colleen responded.

The woman looked at Colleen piercingly, smiled more to herself than at Colleen, and nodded.

"Anythin' more?" she asked expectantly.

Colleen smiled warmly, shaking her head. "No."

The woman turned away, walked back to the bar, and placed a glass under the tap, pouring a miraculously perfect head on the golden liquid.

When she returned, she set the glass down in front of Colleen, paused, then asked, "Would y' be the visitor in the Keefe cottage?"

"Yes," Colleen replied, inviting further comment.

The woman smiled, now, directly at Colleen.

"Welcome home," she said, and strolled back to the group of men about her age who were arrayed on mismatched stools at the bar. They took up quiet conversation again, and Colleen knew she was the subject by the glances they periodically sent her way. Almost as if they were one person, all of the men rose and went out the door. Before long, the other one or two patrons of the pub meandered out into the street, and Colleen was alone in the establishment with the "barmaid."

She sipped her pint and ventured a comment across the room to the older woman. "That was a nice greeting, 'welcome home,'" she said.

The woman came around from behind the bar and stood next to her at the minuscule table. "Twasn't meant lightly," she said, her brilliant blue eyes penetrating Colleen's. She ran a hand through her snowy hair.

"What do you mean?" Colleen inquired.

"We get dozens of tourists, mostly American, who come here, lookin' for their *roots*, as they say. Every one of them says they're Irish, and most are Irish descendants. But some of 'em have strange ideas about Ireland, and they don't know what they are asking for."

"I'm not sure I am any different than that," Colleen observed ruefully. "I had ancestors who are said to have come from this area, but there are very few records of them in America, and I don't even know where to start here in Ireland. I am mostly going by intuition, I'm afraid."

The older woman smiled, in recognition. "Then that makes you truly Irish!" she declared.

"What made you notice me, other than the fact that I am obviously American?" Colleen was curious.

"Ye have a look about yerself, very much like several women from this area," the woman observed. "Would y' be needin' help in your search?"

Colleen was relieved. "Yes, I do need help. I don't even really know where to begin. My name is Colleen Lorrah, which suggests a connection with the old town south of here. I have no real information on the Lorrah family, but several family history experts in the States told me this area might be a good place to start looking for earlier members of the family. The ones who immigrated had the last name of Hughes."

The older woman gave a sharp intake of breath, and uttered something that Colleen could barely hear, but which sounded something like 'O' Hay-ah'"

Then she spoke aloud, "Are those the only Irish names in your family?"

"No. Those are the people I have the most information about, and the ones I know for certain were immigrants from Ireland," Colleen admitted. "They may have left from this area and came to the United States during the famine, since the first records I was able to find are at about that time, and an aunt of mine said she believed that was when they emigrated. I don't know exactly where they came from, and I don't know who their families were."

The woman sat back and looked at Colleen carefully. Again, she breathed a word almost outside of Colleen's range of hearing, but which sounded like, "O-Hay-ah."

"Does that name mean something to you?" Colleen asked.

Now the older woman was cautious. "It might," she said slowly. "But I'll have to have some time to find out. Why don't y' come here again tomorrow to see what help I can give you?" The woman rose, gathered some glasses off the next table, and started to move away from Colleen.

Colleen felt unsettled. Why had the name caused such a change in this woman's demeanor? It wasn't exactly a negative reaction, but rather one of distancing, of separation. And what was that word she had uttered? She wasn't sure what to say next. Trying to keep the woman talking, she asked, "What is your name?"—so I can ask for you when I come in again."

"You can ask for Anna."

Colleen wondered if she'd found a person who was just a little crazy. This was in a strange country, after all, and she recognized there were many customs she didn't know about. But somehow she also doubted that this odd conversation was one of them. Why not go along with it? She already was settled into her cottage, had little more to do for this day. Besides, it was important to stay awake until later in the evening to continue getting her body into sync with the new time zone.

"Anna was my great-grandmother's name," Colleen said, trying to sustain the thread of conversation.

But the woman drifted to the back bar area and began washing glasses without acknowledging this comment. Such abruptness was perplexing, but it was obvious that no further conversation was going to happen at this time.

Colleen finished her pint and went out into the street to walk and see more of the community. She wanted to think about these sights, to try to imagine her ancestors' lives when they lived in this country. First she returned to the cottage, where she pulled on her new hiking shoes and then she began to explore in earnest. At the edge of town, some of the small side roads through fields and woods beckoned her. Colleen was somewhat surprised to find such a rural environment in this small country. She had expected the towns to be much closer together, and that there would be few back-country areas. Hundreds of sheep watched her progress from stone-fenced fields, and the low voices of cattle sang out from the farmyards. In the cloudy skies, many varieties of birds flew overhead, and all was bucolic.

Her thoughts returned to the brief conversation with Anna in the pub, and the older woman's reaction to the name Hughes. Originally, Colleen had believed it might be a British name that had come to Ireland with the English invasion and married into the local population. Could that give it a negative connotation among the locals? All her attempts to trace it in America had turned up no clues.

Anna's strange behavior was a puzzle, and she tried to guess what their dialogue might be like on the following day. What was the reason the woman had changed her manner so suddenly? She hoped whatever it was wouldn't be an obstacle to a comfortable conversation.

Around a corner, strolling along an old stone fence, she was amazed to find herself face to face with a magpie. It sat quietly watching her, diamond drops of moisture sparkling off its brilliant black and white plumage. Somehow this species was not something she had anticipated seeing in Ireland. It watched her approach, then lifted off effortlessly and floated away without sound on the still air.

As the twilight came on, and the lights began to glow in the pubs and homes around the village, Colleen returned to her cottage. Exhaustion took control of her. The time change, the exchange with Anna, and all the walking had left her bone tired.

Once she stripped off her clothing and crawled into the layers of warm bedding, she fell into a deep sleep and did not awaken until almost noon.

When she woke, she prepared a pot of hot tea and a dish of porridge to ready her to step out into the soft misty day and cross the common area. Anna was waiting for her in the warm interior of the pub.

"Hello," Colleen smiled her warmest smile at the woman.

The bright blue eyes regarded her carefully, and then Anna spoke. "Mornin'," she said.

Colleen felt a little unsure of herself, so she ventured, "You suggested that I come back today to see if you had any ideas regarding my family research."

"Aye," Anna nodded. "Tell me more about what y' do know about your people."

"Hughes is a family name for me," Colleen began. "The ones who appear to have come to America during the famine were Richard and Margaret Hughes."

Anna nodded sagely, as if this was what she had expected to hear. Then she reached into the pocket of her skirt and pulled out a small black wood frame, no bigger than a man's wallet. She held it out. It appeared to be quite old, so Colleen delicately picked it up out of the woman's bird-like hand. Holding it next to a small window to see it more clearly in the limited pub light, Colleen stared at it, jolted by the fact that she could have been looking at a photograph of herself. Gazing from inside the frame was a woman, probably in her twenties, dressed in 19th century clothing, whose features were a mirror-image of her own.

"Who is this?" Colleen's voice held an uncontrolled urgency.

"It's me own grandmother's cousin, Margaret, who sent it from America to show she had arrived there safe and sound," Anna said.

"Why didn't you tell me about this last night?" Colleen was genuinely puzzled.

"I wanted to be sure me memory had not tricked me," Anna said simply. "Me grandmother always believed Margaret would come back, but she never did, and I guess no one could blame her."

"What do you know about why she left?" Colleen wanted to know everything.

"M' grandmother never talked about it, but I think she thought it was because of the Great Hunger," Anna replied. "Those were bad times."

Anna continued. "It seems m' family's been waiting for one of ye to come back, and now here y' are."

"What made you believe I'd come here?" After all the years with her father's "feelings" and "hunches," she was unwilling to dismiss any such intuition.

"I didn't know t'would be yourself," Anna responded. "But I knew someone would return. There's the legacy, y' know."

"What legacy?"

"Ah, so y' haven't been told. There's much to tell before y' understand about the legacy," Anna cautioned her. "It's not material—it's a spiritual inheritance."

Great, Colleen thought. Not only is this woman a little crazy, but she's into some pretty strange beliefs, too. I can see it all now…it's probably some racket the locals run on visitors.

Still, there was no way anyone here could have known about her quest for the Hughes ancestors, and certainly no way to fake a photograph like the one here in her hand. Was all this a coincidence, or was something profound going on here?

"I have plenty of time to listen," she said to Anna.

The little woman rose from her seat at Colleen's table, and a younger man appeared as if on cue from a back room. Anna nodded toward him, and he raised a hand, acknowledging her signal. "Michael'll watch the pub," Anna declared, and, turning back toward Colleen, said, "Come."

In the rain, Anna led her up a small path through wet, glistening grass and vines, and they approached a wooded area. Without hesitation, Anna made her way through the trees as the light changed in subtle ways around them. They walked in silence, Anna in the lead, Colleen following.

At last they came to a clearing. Actually the trees seemed to part and form a pool of grass where a small cottage stood, timeless and patient. It was built of stones, in the old style, grass, wildflowers, mosses and other plants had taken a foothold in the thatched roof, and the mossy walls made it look like it had been produced by nature, rather than by man. Seeing Anna in front of it, her filmy white hair haloed around her face, reminded Colleen of pictures in one of her father's childhood books of stories about fairies and woodland spirits. Anna led Colleen to the small split door, and opened it. She stepped inside, seeming to melt into the interior, and gestured for Colleen to follow her.

They stood in the semi-darkness of the cottage, and Colleen was aware only of the concentrated silence that permeated the place. There were bright areas in the room, touched by the light filtering in through the tiny windows, but the corners were shadowed and mysterious. Colleen's skin prickled. There was an awareness of all the people who had lived here over time, men, women and children. Their presence was as real as if all those souls were now standing in the room with her and Anna. She felt, rather than heard, them breathing, and there was something else, too. There was a perception of people who had been in this spot before there was a house here. The earthiness of their existence was palpable, their communion with nature and in the seasons of the place. There was a sudden realization that the grove of trees surrounding this cottage had been here before the settlement of people who lived in houses.

"Why have you brought me here?" she asked Anna.

The older woman smiled quietly. "Be patient," she replied.

So there they stood. Anna with her endless serenity, and Colleen with all those spirits swirling around her, unseen, unheard, but felt deep inside. She knew Anna must have a purpose, but she couldn't guess at what it might be. She couldn't be silent.

"Anna," she asked, "whose house is this? Is it yours?"

Anna turned to her. "In a way of speakin'," she replied. "I lived here when I was a wee girl. But I don't own the house. No one can own a house like this. It is part of the forest."

"I don't understand."

"Y' will," Anna ordered, "Now just wait and be quiet."

The statement was so commanding that Colleen stopped talking. Standing in the silence, listening and waiting, breathing quietly, she tried to calm herself. This was a strange adventure on her first visit. Had it been a mistake to allow this woman to lead her away from her own rental cottage and possessions? It occurred to her that she wasn't sure how to find her way back, even if she lost patience and walked away from here.

Suddenly, the muted light that had been coming in the window dimmed. It was the same effect as when a cloud obscured the sun, not an unexpected event in Ireland, but the timing made Colleen feel unsettled. She looked apprehensively toward the window to see what the cause of this change had been.

Then, the hair stood up on the back of her neck. Her sense of the previous inhabitants of this place was disturbed, like a ripple in the water of a smooth pond. Something had changed inside the cottage.

She turned to look back at Anna, and instantly saw the figure just beyond the older woman. It seemed to materialize out of the darkness of the corner near the peat hearth. It was the shadow of a man.

He stepped toward them, and the light coming in the window brightened again, illuminating him as if he were created by it. When his face emerged from the shadows, Colleen was jolted by the energy that emanated from him. She prided herself on her ability to analyze character in any new person she met. But she'd never had this experience before.

At first glance he appeared to be an ordinary man. He was small, no more than five feet tall, a matched set with Anna. He had wavy silver-white hair. His ageless, brilliant blue eyes were on her and the corner of his mouth turned up slightly in the hint of a smile. The banked fire in Colleen's chest ignited again.

She felt an instant recognition, despite the fact that she had never seen him before. An ancient fire burned steadily behind his eyes, and she let out a long sigh, realizing that she had not been breathing.

Anna chuckled. "Brendan, this is Colleen," she said.

He didn't speak. He reached out his hand to Colleen, and without even knowing it, she mirrored that gesture. When their hands touched she started. The contact was electric. Colleen felt a curtain, long drawn over her emotions, rend from top to bottom. Feeling exposed and vulnerable, she spoke, directing her words to Anna.

"Who is this, Anna?" she asked, voice trembling.

"He is me brother, and he has a part in the events that brought you here," Anna said, reassuringly. "I'll leave you to talk. He'll see that you get back."

This said, Anna turned and vanished out the door.

Colleen would have panicked and run, but she was frozen in place. She had never had a first contact like this with anyone in her life, and she was afraid. Her heart was a frantic drumbeat, hammering in her chest, and her breathing came is quick gasps. Attempting to gain some of her usual sense of control, Colleen tried the direct approach. Pulling herself to her full height and aware that she towered over him, she asked, "What is your reason for being here? Who are you?"

He spoke, and his soft voice struck a chord deep inside her. "M' name is Brendan," he said.

"So Anna said," she replied, "But that doesn't explain who you are, or why she wanted us to meet."

"Anna doesn't explain," he said forcefully. "She has no need to give reasons. Forces come together for her, and it is her way. Nothing she does is without purpose, and she creates events that make changes."

Colleen heard his words, but she was most aware of the voice that spoke them. It was as if that voice reached out with fingers of soft sound to soothe her restless soul. The impact was indefinable, but profound. Suddenly, forgotten memories of her grandmother and her father came to her with shocking clarity. Looking into the depths of the cobalt blue eyes of this man, she remembered so many things. In his eyes, she could see the sweeping panoramas from the top of the Big Horn Mountains, and the vistas beyond the horizon that her father had shown to her. The recall of her vision quest at the medicine wheel tantalized her, and she could recall the small secret clear spring of water where her grandmother had spent hours sharing the mysteries of the old religion. How could she ever have forgotten these things?

She knew Brendan's presence was somehow responsible for this clarity. "Tell me what I should know," she pleaded.

Brendan smiled now, a real smile that warmed his demeanor and settled Colleen's fears a bit. "Y' are surprised, of course," he said gently. "Sure, you didn't expect this when you came to Ireland from Montana."

"How did you know that?" Colleen gasped, dumbfounded.

"Anna knew," he answered. "She's been waiting for you for a long time."

"So she said, but I don't understand any of it. How did she know I'd be coming to Ireland? How did I end up here instead of any other place on the whole island? How…" Colleen stopped for a breath as Brendan broke her headlong charge with a small warm laugh. It sounded like water splashing on the rocks of a brook.

Colleen stared at him. "I guess it is no more strange than the feeling I have that I know you," she said at last.

"Where do ye believe we met?" he asked.

"This will sound strange," she said. "But I've seen you in dreams." A pause. "This sounds contrived, but it isn't." Rushing to qualify this statement, "I mean, these weren't daydreams, or anything. There was just a real awareness of your existence."

Brendan stopped her with an upheld hand. "Nothing y' can say will sound strange. Come with me."

Colleen followed him obediently from inside the cottage to the circle of trees outside the cottage. The mist had gone from the grassy area, and a muted light played on the leaves of the trees of the grove and danced in the blades of grass.

Brendan motioned her to a low stone, and seated himself across from her, leaning forward toward her, elbows resting lightly on his knees.

His wizened demeanor reminded her of the Crow Indian stories about the sage and magical Little People who lived in the Pryor and Big Horn mountains.

"Anna has left y' with me so I can help y' begin to understand why your journey led to us," he began. "I do believe I know who y' are. Y' are a grandchild of Ireland, descended from the millions who left us in bad times. We have known of ye for generations. Y' are part of our tribe, the O'Aodha (he pronounced this word O'Hay-ah). Y' are the daughter of Mike Hughes Lorrah, the last in a long line of spiritual leaders—some less informed might call them druids—from this family. The time has come for such people to return to Mother Eire. We lost the old ties when those of your da's great grandparents' generation left Ireland to avoid persecution. Anna was born with some of the skills, but not all. The line of spirit people with full powers goes back many generations, but certain conditions are required to produce descendants with powers at full strength. It only can occur in people from families of three children, and is most powerful in the third generation of three children.

"Mike had two sisters, his mother had a brother and a sister, her mother had two brothers, and her grandmother had a brother and a sister, and..." Colleen paused.

"But what does this have to do with me? I had two brothers and two sisters!" she protested.

Brendan looked unwaveringly into her eyes. "How many survived infancy?" he asked.

Colleen was circumspect and solemn. "Just the three of us," she replied. She wondered if he could know that her other sister had died at birth, and her other brother had drowned at two years of age in Lodge Grass Creek.

"So 'tis your place to carry on," Brendan told her. "Your ancestors had to flee to America to make sure future generations would be safe. Anna tells me you grew up among the Crow Indians. The path led to where you could be born and raised among the members of this tribe because their beliefs and way of life were enough like the Old Religion of Ireland and of the Celts to sustain you and start to prepare you."

"You received enough guidance to bring you to us so the power you carry could be used when it was needed. Now you will need to understand the foundation of the Old Religion. It will require that you know more of the goddesses who ruled this land before the Church, and more of nature."

"This is crazy," Colleen insisted. "I would have known if I had some wonderful 'power.' I'd remember something. But I don't know what to do, or why I am here, or if I would even want to do it if I did know."

"That will come in time," Brendan assured her. "Many of the things that happened in your childhood were helping prepare you for this time. Some part of you must know that."

Colleen was silent. She had to admit that there were too many mystical things in her personal history to ignore. Brendan noted her implied agreement, and his voice became gentle.

"It's no wonder that you are confused. Anyone would be. You don't remember what you once knew. Anna will help you. As for you and me, we have talked enough for today. Go now, return to your cottage, and we will talk again." Brendan was firm.

"But there are so many things I want to ask!" Colleen cried.

"Another time," he stopped her with a raised hand. "Until then, Anna will answer most of your questions. That is not my role."

'How do I get back to the cottage?" Colleen asked.

'Go out to the path," he replied. "You'll know the way."

Colleen looked toward the path, and when she turned back to take her leave of Brendan, she was alone. Wonder filled her, along with fear, but she stepped out on the path and started down it into the mist that hung over the grove. When she emerged from the cluster of trees, she paused and looked around her to get her bearings. The day was waning, and twilight was approaching. Something caused her to look skyward, as if she had been told to do so, and immediately she saw three magpies. They were hanging in the air as if awaiting her, and when they recognized that she had them in sight, they wheeled and flew slowly ahead of her.

A shadowy presence watched her depart from the area near the cottage. Feral eyes of luminescent green observed her hungrily, following her every move. The man those eyes belonged to stood still, blending with the forest around him, and silently contemplated what he was feeling. He had been alone for a long time, isolated by his own choice from people except when the voices of the past called him into action. But the old ones had told him of her arrival, and he had come here to catch a glimpse of her from a distance. Once she had walked out of his line of sight, he sighed heavily, turned and vanished into the trees.

Darkness was descending as she entered the village, and as she passed the pub, she saw the lights come on. Had so much time passed? She made her way to her cottage with little trouble, and when she looked skyward again, the magpies were gone. A shiver ran up her arms, and she hugged herself for warmth, even though she was not cold.

Entering the cottage, she took off her jacket, and turned to start her peat fire, only to find it was again already burning brightly. Her conclusion was that Anna must have had someone light the fire again, and with this thought, she settled into the rocker next to the hearth. She leaned back, gazed into the fire, and reflected on the day.

Brendan dominated her thoughts. Even with her eyes closed she could feel his blazing blue eyes on her. No, not on her, *inside* her. Brendan had been able to look deep into her center, to the secret space where so much of her essence lived. Leading the parade of thoughts were the dreams that had inhabited her sleep on her journey and since she had arrived here. The realization came that each dream included some manifestation of Brendan and of other more untamed beings, as well. Was her dream on the plane, with its brilliance and spirit, the first? Suddenly, she knew with certainty that other dreams had preceded that one, night after night, and she could no longer imagine herself as the person who declared she never dreamed. The dreams were ancient, yet integral to her. As if to emphasize this reality, sleep and dreams claimed her again from her place by the fire.

As before, the doorway to the otherworld was through a deep clear water passage. Again she found herself back in the grove, and Brendan was with her. He was not visible; she could only hear his voice. He was not speaking to her, but to someone else. His first declaration was that she was heir to the spiritual lineage of the O'hAodha, and that she was here to continue the "work." There was at least one other presence with them in the grove, but Colleen was not afraid. It was as if she was the audience to this conversation, although the participants were aware of her. As Brendan continued, she began to wonder who he was speaking to. Her attention focused on a giant ash tree, which seemed to be receiving his words. She waited to hear a reply from the other. But when it came it came it was from the air around her, reassuring and stunning.

"Then all is right with the world," said the strong, peaceful voice of her father.

The concept was so astonishing that she woke from her deep sleep.

"That can't be," she told herself. "Dad is dead. I must be so afraid that I dreamed about him to reassure myself."

Then came the answer to her thoughts, from all around her in the darkness of her bedroom. "I promised I'd be there when you needed me," said her father's voice, strong and clear in its presence. "And so I am."

She slept again, deep and without further dreams.

CHAPTER 11

▼

Colleen spent the next several days walking and surveying the area, chatting with local residents she encountered on her wanderings. She was welcomed, and everyone treated her as if she had lived in this community for a long time. She mused that a number of them could possibly be relatives of some kind, although there was no documentation to confirm the notion. The lay of the land became familiar to her, as did the history of this place.

Local legend said the area was one of the strongholds of the legendary ancient Irish race known as the Tuatha de Dannan, and the people of the village held this to be a truth, not a myth. These magical entities were purported to still exist here, but not in physical human form. The local people believed that they took the form of fairies or woodland beings, or—and this piqued Colleen's interest because of her dreams—of trees. In the pub, she listened to old and new folklore. The men and Anna talked about Cuchulainn, the "Hound of Ulster;" of Maeve, the warrior queen; of Finn McCool, and of some more recent legends about fairies and banshees.

One evening, the men started telling stories about a mythical hero they insisted was alive and active at present. They called him *MacCumhail,* and told tales of his daring interventions in the on-going violence of Northern Ireland. The stories told of him arriving just in time to prevent fanatics and terrorists from carrying out activities that might otherwise jeopardize the peace process. It was said that no one had ever seen his face, and that he seemed to appear out of thin air to stop the villains before they could do any damage. Colleen was skeptical, and asked a few questions, but the men declared him real—a descendant of Finn McCool. Her father had told many stories of the ancient legend—*Fionn*

Mac Cumhail. This warrior being was reknowned in Irish myth. There were stories telling of his exploits in battle, hunting, sorcery, and unity with animals and nature. They included saving the High King's Palace at Tara, gaining vast wisdom from a taste of the Salmon of Knowledge, and defeating the wicked King of the World, *Daire Donn.*

The men in the pub insisted their current hero came from a long line of warriors, fighting for peace in the only way such transgressors could understand—stopping violence with violence. They had dozens of accounts of such adventures, and delighted in repeating them after a few pints of Guinness. After growing up around cowboys and sheepmen who loved a good story more than almost anything else, Colleen was sure they were testing her gullibility as a newcomer. This made her even more determined not to give them the satisfaction of thinking they were making her believe such tales. The one thing that prevented her from doubting completely was the absolute consistency of the story from one person to the next. Every person who talked about *McCumhail* reported the same things. No one had ever seen his face; no one knew where he came from or where he went after his interventions were over.

He was a mystery to everyone, but all the people Colleen listened to were grateful for his actions in stopping terrorists in their tracks. And there were fascinating parallels to Indian mythical heros whose verbal histories had been handed down for generations in the Crow tribe. Such heroes had saved individuals and entire family groups from evil-doers by wielding inhuman strength and cunning with the help of animals and unity with mother earth.

Meanwhile, her explorations continued. Much of this touring was done in the rain, and she continued to be grateful that for the purchase of a good rain jacket so she did not have to struggle with an umbrella. She walked the back roads, and the fields, examining old churches, ancient court tombs and dolmens, and the ever-present stone walls and hedges.

The feeling that she had been here before was a constant companion. So many things seemed familiar. The sight of sheep in the fields, and so many people with features and coloring like hers settled her soul and suggested that perhaps she had come home. She wished her father could be here in person, seeing all these sights, and at the same time, there was a sense that some part of him was right there, sharing and participating. Afternoons and occasional evenings were spent in the corner of the pub with Anna, listening as the older woman told her of her ancestors, and the beliefs they had held.

Anna insisted that these people had descended from the Tuatha de Dannan, a statement Colleen viewed with grave doubt, and she told her they had been spiritual leaders. Anna had never used the word "druid," and Brendan had suggested it was not appropriate. Colleen finally asked about this one more time.

"Anna," she said. "Would the name for the station these people held be that of "druid'?"

Anna was thoughtful for a moment, then responded. "Some might say so," she replied. "I suppose it describes some of what they did. It's not that we don't approve of the name, only our family never called it that." Her explanation went on to say that this word had come to be used in an all-inclusive way by people who did not truly understand all facets of the old religion.

During the daylight hours of almost every day, Colleen spent long periods of time with Anna, listening, learning, and to her surprise, remembering. She clearly remembered her father's mysterious ability to locate lost people and things, the lush gardens he had grown with what seemed to be no effort at all, his preternatural ability to reach out with his spirit to his children. She recalled her grandmother, too. There were memories of her grandmother's magic, and a sense of the small fringe of sadness that always seemed a part of Velia's life.

Every evening, she joined locals in the pubs, listening to more talk of history, of current events, and of myth. Over time, she gained enough knowledge to feel comfortable taking a stand on the peace process. Like most of the locals, her heart's desire was to see peace become permanent, and the violence come to an end.

At the end of each evening, she made her way back to the cottage, where, lulled by the sounds and smells of rain on the countryside, Colleen slept soundly, a deep sleep, barely breathing, not moving, only her spirit active with the brilliant dreams that visited her night after night.

Finally a sunny day dawned, the mist and rain were gone, and the light sharpened the edge of everything around her cottage. Colleen felt peaceful and rested, but very anticipatory. Dressing helped organize her thoughts, as she pulled on jeans, a shirt and an Aran sweater. Once she tied the now well-worn walking shoes, she stepped out of the door of her cottage. Her strides took her to the little store, intending to buy food for herself. Anna stood expectantly behind the counter.

"Good morning," Colleen greeted the ageless woman.

"'Mornin' yerself," Anna replied, as she turned toward the back room.

"Michael!" she called. "I'll be leavin' now. You're on your own with the store."

A stocky young man with a thick mop of rusty colored hair came from behind the shelves he was stocking. Silently he nodded to Anna, casting a sharp glance in Colleen's direction. Then he shrugged and went back to his task.

Then she turned toward Colleen. "Come," she said simply.

Colleen regarded Anna thoughtfully. Inside, she was a little amused at how easily this little woman ordered her about. But what she was learning from her was intriguing. Anna struck out in a direction toward the edge of the little village, motioning for her American friend to join her. This time, the route led in what seemed to be the opposite direction from the one they had followed before.

Colleen fell in beside her. "Where are we going?" she asked.

Anna replied. "Back to the cottage. I have something for y' to see along the way." They walked in silence down a narrow road, past neat stone-walled fields of intense green, and Colleen smiled at the small bands of sheep that grazed in them, feeling very much at home.

Finally, they turned into a gate onto a path that led to the door of the small, neat, ancient cottage. Flowers she had not noticed before (or had they leapt from the ground overnight?) grew profusely on each side of the small door, and Colleen experienced all her feelings from the previous time she had been here. But there was more. There was a prickling feeling that she was being watched by hundreds of eyes.

Anna motioned for Colleen to follow her as she set a brisk pace past the house down a path toward the sea. When they reached the waterline, the tide was at its ebb. Anna led her to a grassy bank where they could overlook the rocks of the shore. A good breeze brought all the smells of the sea and the hills to them, and Colleen, having learned by now that asking questions was usually nonproductive, waited to hear what Anna might choose to say. There were stone steps leading down to the shore, and Anna started down them, gesturing for her to follow. Next to a small, grotto-like opening in the rocks of the low cliff, she stopped and pointed for Colleen to look down. There, at the edge of the tide-line was a small crystalline pool of water. Colleen was astonished at the clarity of it, and at the fact that it was obviously not seawater. She turned to Anna.

"What a beautiful little spring!" she exclaimed.

Anna smiled, pleased at Colleen's recognition of what it was.

"'Tis a sacred spring, a sea-well," she declared. "Been in the possession of our clan forever."

"Do you mean a holy spring?" Colleen asked, remembering reading about all the holy springs and wells credited with healing powers and named for the multitude of saints in the Catholic hierarchy.

"Not holy in the sense of those the Church has claimed for itself, stealing from the old religion," Anna replied. "This one is sacred in the old beliefs, and it is tied directly to the powers of our clan, which Brendan has told ye about. Because it is so hidden by the sea, the church never discovered it, so it was never converted to a church site."

Colleen looked at the spring with wonder. It was an enormous step for Anna to reveal this treasure to her, and she looked at the older woman questioningly.

To Colleen's astonishment, Anna wordlessly reached out grasped her wrist. She guided her hand toward the water, and without any warning, plunged Colleen's fingers into the water, holding them there.

When the ripples of this motion settled, pool was quiet for a moment. As they watched, the water began to effervesce around her hand, slowly at first, then with more and more intensity until the entire pool was frothy with iridescent, bright bubbles. Anna pulled Colleen's hand out of the water, and together they stood up straight again. The older woman smiled with satisfaction.

"I had to see that for meself," she said. "T'wasn't meant to surprise you, but this last bit of proof was necessary. You most certainly are the one I have waited for."

"What do you mean?"

"You'll get your answers soon enough, lass. Not today." Subject closed.

She brought a dumfounded Colleen back up the stone steps to the grassy slope, and invited her to sit down. Anna arranged her skirts around her, and put a hand to her wispy white hair, gazing far out to sea. Colleen watched in fascination, as whatever the older woman was remembering transformed her face, softening lines that had been there forever. Finally Anna took a small breath and spoke.

"It's time for you to leave us here in Bureen," she said. "Y've learned all y' need for the next step."

Colleen nodded slowly, not really understanding, but willing to hear what else her strange new friend would say.

"I have written some directions here for y'. Y'll be takin' a road to the north, and there's someone there for ye to meet," Anna continued, reaching into the folds of her clothing and producing a piece of tightly folded paper. Y'll be packin' up your things and gettin' ready tonight. We'll be havin' a wee send-off, up at the pub. Come when you're ready."

Taking the paper that was offered, Colleen shook her head and smiled at the news of the planned party. Why was she always the last to know what was going to happen next? But the entire village knew better than to argue with Anna.

She tried a question. "Who is this person I am to meet?"

"He's the one who can help with your work. He lives in the country outside of Derry, and he knows what you need to know," Anna replied. "His name is there on that paper. Maddie O'Hanlon at the bed and breakfast I've written there will know where to find him."

Colleen opened the folds of the paper, read down through the directions, then looked at the name at the bottom: Andrew Finnegan. Something stirred inside her, like a breath of wind on banked coals. Who was this man? What would he contribute? a calm settled over her, that familiar feeling of pre-assignment resting easily on her spirit. It was the knowledge that she had something to accomplish, even though she did not know yet what it might be.

Again, the Colleen was the object of attention of the enigmatic being from his vantage point in the trees. His green-fire eyes had taken in what occurred at the sea-well, and he remembered the events that had brought him to this place many years before.

That evening, Colleen finished gathering her things from their various places around the cottage, placing all in order. How long would she be gone from here? Although it was strange for her to allow another person to direct her actions, she trusted Anna. She decided to take enough with her to cover several weeks. Once all her traveling items were in place near the door, ready for an early morning departure, it was time to step outside and walk across the grassy space to the pub. Inside the open door, the happy chatter and laughter that settled on the place every evening awaited. There was Billy Flannery, at the bar, talking to Anna in Irish. Joe and Brendan sat at one of the little tables, deep in some political conversation. No longer strangers to her, several people had taken up places near the fire, where she had sat when she came in this place the first time.

When she stepped through the door, Anna looked up immediately and motioned for her to come over. "And how's our guest of honor tonight?" Anna asked.

"I'm fine. I hate to go from here. You've all made me feel so welcome," Colleen said.

"Y' *are* welcome," Billy said sagely, "Y're family."

Colleen perched on a stool next to him. "You certainly have made me feel like family. I wish I had more information about the ancestors I had from here. It still seems like a mystery to me."

Anna regarded her quietly. "It'll all come clear, darlin'. It'll all come clear."

CHAPTER 12

▼

Colleen was wide-awake at sunrise, and she quickly got ready to go. Dressed in a pair of jeans, a sweater, and those well-worn walking shoes, she quietly stepped outside. Carrying her rain jacket to the car, she observed that it was actually sunny. The day promised to be one of those clear-blue, almost painfully beautiful ones that only Ireland can bestow upon those favored visitors who happen to be in the right place at the right time. Colleen got into the car, and eased the door shut quietly to avoid disturbing any of the people who had participated in her send-off until the wee hours. A turn of the key resulted in the quiet hum of the engine, and she pulled away from the cottage and the tiny village, with a pang of sadness at the leaving. This little community had stolen her heart, as if she had known it all her life. Although what lay down the road was unknown, there was a feeling that she would be a very different person when she saw Bureen again.

Her travel began with a turn to the north onto the main road. There were no other drivers out at that time of day. Ireland is not a country of early morning risers, she had learned, a real difference from how life was experienced on the Lorrah ranch. But for those few precious hours the road, perhaps the entire country would be hers. After several hours, the directions on the paper, which lay unfolded now on the passenger seat, directed her to turn off the main road. The car bounced onto a narrow, wooded tributary that meandered up into the mountains. The instructions were clear, and she marveled at the country around her. The road crossed numerous small farmsteads, then began to run alongside an exquisite sparkling stream. There were trees and flowers everywhere, and every so often, the stream would tumble over rocks in a small waterfall. It was an enchanted place.

Then the track began to climb. The mountains were substantial, and the trees looked like the old native forests of Ireland, not the new tree plantations that were slowly replacing the bogs. There were numerous species of these venerable old trees, and they were mixed randomly, giving the forest a primeval countenance that reassured her and soothed her eyes.

It was hard to say how long she had driven when at last the road topped a rise and the overlook revealed a small mountain valley. A diminutive village burrowed into a hillside, crowned by a huge steeple that rose from the ubiquitous Catholic Church. The route wound through the town, and she parked in front of a pub for lunch. It appeared that she was the only non-local in the pub, and the patrons scrutinized her silently. This was a bit strange, since her experience had been that no town in Ireland was unaccustomed to hoards of tourists. This group was cool and distant, eyeing her cautiously, and responding to her only when she initiated conversation. The waitress served her without comment. As she finished her bowl of soup, a glance at her watch indicated how late in the day it was getting. The travel had covered many miles, but she felt as if no time had passed.

Counting out coins for her lunch, she asked the scowling bartender about the road to Derry. His directions matched those she had on the paper, and his curiosity was apparent. Perhaps she could win him over with a little friendly conversation.

She smiled warmly, and said, "I am meeting a new friend there."

The bartender received this information with only a raised eyebrow and a guarded gaze. She returned to her car, shaking off a chill inside her. Driving away, she did not notice that one of the pub's customers had come out onto the street behind her, and stood, his piercing eyes keenly watching her depart.

The roadway gave her another moment or two of the splendid view, then rounded a mountainside and entered the forest again. The trees closed in behind her, and she slowed, picking up the unfolded piece of paper on the seat next to her. There was no question that she had driven according to the directions, and this was the right track. And yet…

Now, inside the woods, it was starting to get dark. The border crossing into Northern Ireland had not come up yet, and she wished to reach it soon. The idea of exploring unknown territory alone after dark was disconcerting, even though she had no reason to feel anything but very safe in this country.

Finally, the border crossing with its attendant guards and check station appeared just ahead of her. Although common knowledge indicated that there was currently little trouble at this spot, the fact that this would be her first encounter with a military checkpoint made her jumpy. She slowed her car, then stopped and rolled down her window as the young soldier approached. He looked like a high school student, although that was impossible. Were they all this young?

"Hello," he said, bending down and examining the inside of her vehicle through the window with keen eyes. "Where are you from?"

"America," she responded with measured courtesy. Then smiling, "Just on vacation."

"Shouldn't be travelin' alone at night, miss," the guard said.

"I know," she replied. "I'm afraid I didn't allow myself enough time. I'm just trying to get to the Ballysheen area, though, so I'm close to my destination."

"Do you have a place to stay there?" he asked.

"Yes. The O'Hanlon bed and breakfast."

How much should you tell anyone, even the guards? But it would not be wise to appear to be hiding anything, either. She was grateful that Anna had arranged for her lodging.

"Be careful," he admonished her. "It's easy enough to get lost in the night on our country roads. And don't stop for anyone. Enjoy your visit." He waved her on.

As Colleen departed, her uneasiness increased. The feeling was not to be ignored, since past history had proven that her instincts were usually accurate. As time passed, it got darker, but still nothing seemed out of place. She scolded herself.

"This is just a different country, a different culture. It's just the strangeness of it all."

Still, the itchy feeling in her subconscious that something was amiss wouldn't be ignored. Switching on the overhead light, she examined the directions again. She was on the right road, small as it was, and it should only be a few miles until...

She slammed on her brakes. In the middle of the confined road, there was a pile of large rocks. The car skidded to a stop just short of them. Breathing hard, she was glad she had been alert enough to see them and not crash into them. With a long shaky breath, her hand reached to shift into reverse.

It was too late.

A dark, older model car was behind her, lights out, blocking the way. She reached to engage the locks, but not fast enough. The car door flew open, and rough hands pulled her from the car. Stumbling to her feet, she found herself staring at two men, their faces shrouded by black, ski-type masks. Their clothing was paramilitary camouflage, and they wore black leather gloves. Both had pistols tucked into their belts. Cold fear squeezed Colleen's heart, and she could not breathe. Finally the taller man, who seemed to be in charge, spoke.

"It's her," he spat out the words to his partner.

The shorter, stockier man spoke directly to her. "You aren't going to do it," he said.

"Do what?" she asked, choking out the words past her fear-constricted throat.

"Help those weak-kneed peace mongers," he declared, "Don't be so stupid. Did ya' think we wouldn't know? Did ya' think we wouldn't know what you've been sayin' in the pubs? Idjit!"

"I don't understand," Colleen whispered. Visions of the worst possibilities hovered in her mind like a dark shroud. Her mind raced, but none of her self-defense training had prepared her for a surprise attack by two well-armed men.

"I'm only trying to visit another part of Ireland. I'm just a tourist and I don't know what you're talking about."

"Sure," said the tall one, "And I'm the Pope!"

"Please let me go," Colleen pleaded. "I'm expected in Ballysheen." Perhaps if they thought someone expected her, they might not detain her.

The short one laughed, an ugly, humorless sound. "Lots of tourists never show up where they're expected. No one will ever come to look for you."

Colleen's frightened gaze darted about, frantically searching the surroundings for identifiable landmarks and weighing her options. There were no lights, no other cars, and no escape. Even the air was absolutely still. Now the tall one stopped talking. He gripped her arms so hard it seemed he must actually be grasping the bone. His face was so close to hers that she could smell the sour whiskey on his breath. In concert, his accomplice reached into one pocket of his camouflage shirt, and pulled out a length of strong rope. He bound her hands tight behind her back. Once she was secured, the other produced a filthy, stale smelling black cloth sack and pulled it down over her head.

"Now we'll be takin' a little ride," his voice told her, ratcheting up her terror.

Deprived of vision, Colleen felt another sense kick in, an extra intuition she knew she had not used since childhood. Another presence was nearby, in the woods. Her captors seemed unaware of it. She sensed it coming toward them at lightning speed. Were these ruffians only part of a larger gang? Were more thugs involved in this attack?

The sounds became clear to her. A breath of wind moved the air. Leaves murmured, high up in the trees, as if something passed through them. The grass stirred, whispering at her feet. All of these night sounds converged to sing an ancient concert. It was a symphony of myth and history, in the voices of thousands of Irish who had come this way before. The sound increased in Colleen's ears, yet her tormentors continued to be oblivious to it. What they had noticed was that their captive had become silent, and it made them apprehensive.

The first one taunted her. "Don't have anythin' to say? I thought you American bitches knew everythin'."

"Aye," the other chimed in, "Don't know so much when you're bound and blinded, do you?"

Didn't they hear? Colleen heard and felt the music rise to a demanding crescendo, now joined by thunderous drumming—authoritative, war-like. It reverberated in the ground she stood upon, it resounded inside her.

"What the..?"

The second man's words were cut short by a grunt of pain. The first man suddenly let go of her and she stood still, unable to see. It was the sounds that told her her tormentors were under an attack of some kind. The noises were swift, brutal and left no doubt that her captors were on the defensive. Whoever or whatever their assailant was, no words came from him. His approach had been absolutely silent.

She jerked her head, trying to dislodge the hood, but it was secure. Instinct told her to step back from the sounds of the assault, but where should she put her feet? Finally all she could do was wait. The sounds of blows landing on human flesh, and the cries of rage, then pain, then panic from her tormentors came to her. It was over quickly. More swift blows, a few groans, and then nothing.

Now there was only silence, and she wondered what her circumstances were. Was she still in the hands of the highwaymen? Was there something even worse in store for her now? What should she do?

In the darkness, a hand touched her arm, causing her to flinch and wrench away. Then a voice spoke quietly, next to her ear, a gentle, sensuous male voice that caressed her soul and quieted her fears.

"I have to keep you blindfolded, but I will untie your hands if you do not fight me."

Something about the voice persuaded her to trust the man behind it. It was unlikely that she could be in any more danger than she had been with the two men, so with a nod, she indicated her mute agreement. Now the hand on her arm was leading her around to sit in the passenger side of a car, probably her car. Obediently, she sat and waited while the man stepped into the driver's side. The engine started, and the car backed up and turned around.

Now she spoke. "What happened to those men?"

"They won't attack anyone again."

The reply was cryptic, and Colleen was certain she didn't want to know any more. She stopped speaking. After some time had passed, the car turned off the pavement of the small secondary road and lurched along a rougher course. Finally the car stopped, the driver got out and walked around to open the passenger side door, reaching in to help her out. That gentle touch was a surprise and caused her to shiver a bit. What made her feel she could trust someone she could not see, and feel so many emotions at the sound of this voice and the touch of this hand? What was happening?

Once out of the car, the man led her along a short distance over what felt like turf, then stopped. From behind her, he removed the stifling hood and she looked around. They stood in the center of what appeared to be one of Ireland's ancient stone circles, in the full moonlight. The stones were tall and elegant, seeming almost translucent. Pure magic touched the scene. Velvety grass fields fanned out below this hilltop location, their green silvered by the moon, and a lake glistened below. There was a gurgle of water trickling down the rocky slope nearby, and the splendor of it all was spellbinding. Her rescuer remained at her back with a hand on each of her shoulders. Then he stepped around her and stood, partially illuminated by the moon.

Colleen was as dazed as if she had been struck by lightning. Although he was obscurely lit, and his face was not visible to her, his form was tantalizingly familiar. He had been a part of her vision at the medicine wheel, one of the people in the strange green water world. She could make out his body in that silver light. His size was probably average, but he was powerful, with broad shoulders and well-muscled arms. The luminescent moonlight glinted off the gloss of his thick hair. While his face was indistinct, his eyes were dazzling. The emerald green gaze held an inner flame, ablaze in the moonlight, as they looked directly into hers. That glow reminded Colleen of the way wolves' eyes cast back a strange fire at night, an extraordinary blaze that humans don't possess. Something in her soul stirred and began to ignite. She was speechless.

The man looked at her, deep inside her, for several moments, and she thought she might have glimpsed his smile, as if in recognition and welcome. He spoke and his voice carried the traces of thousands of years of Irish music and myth.

"Are you hurt?"

"No, thanks to you. How did you happen to be here?" Colleen regained her speech as the shock wore off. "How were you in the right place in the right time to rescue me? How did you know I needed your help?"

His quiet smile revealed itself in his voice as he answered. "You will learn. I am the descendant of warriors, and I have the instincts of a warrior."

Eyes wide as a child's, Colleen nodded remembering her father telling such stories, urging him to go on.

"I came because your *need* called me."

His answer was simple enough on the surface, but it was underlain by a million obscure nuances.

"I thought it was my fear that screamed out into the night," she said ruefully.

"It was surely that, too," he confirmed, a small chuckle of agreement emanating from his throat.

The music that had announced his approach in the woods began to inhabit the night air again. This time it was gentler, an enthralling composition that wove threads of sound around them in the circle built so many centuries before. The resonance was intoxicating, as were the sights and the scents of the night.

Her rescuer seemed to affirm this state, and said, "You have been sent. You are all I knew you would be, and more."

Colleen was puzzled.

"Who told you anything about me? What were you told?"

"I can't say," he remarked, "I have been alone for an eternity, having contact with no one but a few trusted souls. Solitude is not my desire, but I can trust no one, so I remain alone. The past teaches that trust is fragile, not to be wasted on those who do not deserve it."

He continued. "When you drew near, I could feel your approach. The earth told me, the wind told me, and your guardians came on ahead of you."

"Guardians?" Colleen was genuinely puzzled. If she'd had guardians, she thought wryly, she would not have been in the predicament she had found herself in tonight.

The stranger looked deep into her eyes again, as if in wonder that she did not understand. Then he looked off, behind her. He placed a gentle hand back on each of her shoulders and turned her around. First she saw three pairs of eyes, glittering with the power of the moment, regarding the scene with silent, motionless dignity. There, sitting on three of the stones that comprised the circle, the white portions of their feathers glowing luminously in the moonlight, were the magpies.

CHAPTER 13

▼

The man seemed to change then, withdrawing into himself, and altering his demeanor with her. As if the familiarity had embarrassed him, he took his hands from her shoulders, and stepped back a pace or two. Perhaps he had revealed more of himself than he had intended.

"You must get back on the path to your destination," he said, voice low. He turned quickly and walked back toward the car.

"I can get there on my own," she responded sincerely, snapping back to reality. "But I want you to know how much I appreciate what you did back there."

His gaze rested levelly on hers. "There's no more danger to you here. You'll be safe enough. Go on to O'Hanlon's as planned. You'll hear from me again one day." It was a command.

Colleen was tempted to point out that she was not there to take orders from him, but stopped the words as they rose to her lips. After all, he had put himself in jeopardy to protect her. Starting to walk to her car, she turned back to check her directions. The stranger had vanished, gone as suddenly as he had appeared. She was alone in the Irish countryside.

Where had he gone? Why had he not stayed to answer the multitude of questions that now occurred to her? Her frustration gave way to a small flutter of panic. Despite her assurances to him, she really didn't know where she was, and possessed no idea of how to get back on the road. Her rescuer had assured her that the men who attacked her would not be back, but she had no way to know that for sure.

Feeling a little foolish, and totally off-balance, she stood just outside the stone circle. The soft grass underfoot welcomed her. Not knowing what else to do, she trudged back into the center of the circle, and sat, cross-legged as was the custom among her Crow Indian friends. The stones glowed in the moonlight, and the music wove intricate patterns through the trees, a peaceful song. It faded only slightly, and the scent of flowers and grass wrapped around her isolated figure. Fear was replaced by a strange sense of comfort.

Time passed, and her mind drifted to a different plane. There was no way to estimate how long she sat there, but when awareness returned, the moon had moved very little. What should she do now? A sharp cry reached her from the sky. A look skyward showed the three magpies were now circling, circling in the night breeze, black and white wings flashing like strobe-lit dancers in the moonlight. They soared toward her car. Taking their cue, she rose to her feet and followed.

She slid into the drivers' seat and sat there for a moment, suddenly aware that the car still smelled of the essence of the enigmatic being who had saved her. It was a heady blend of woods and earth and something else—a light scent of smoke. a quick survey around the interior of the car, revealed the set of directions Anna had given her, open neatly on the passenger seat. Her belongings were still in the back seat. Looking at the car, no one would ever guess what drama had unfolded here. The magpies awaited her from their stations in the grass before her car. Once she started the engine and they provided a graceful lead as they lifted off toward the main road. From the shadows of the forest, green-fire eyes watched her go. The stranger sighed, shook his head as if to clear his thoughts, and melted into the night.

Entering the highway, the first thing she saw was a road sign directing her to Ballysheen. Once the sign appeared, the magpies vanished. Relieved to have concrete directions, she followed the sign's indications, reaching the edge of the village almost instantly and O'Hanlon's B&B within seconds.

The door opened a crack in response to her knock, then was flung wide as an apple dumpling of a woman greeted her. Her kind face showed concern.

"Ah, lass, I was beginnin' to worry about you," she chirped with the voice of a lark, "I expected you long before this."

"You must be Maddie O'Hanlon," Colleen stated the obvious.

"I am."

"I'm Colleen Lorrah."

"Where've y' been, darlin'? I thought y'd be here much earlier."

Colleen's voice shook. "I was waylaid," she began, and realized that her tears were very close to the surface.

Maddie reached out and took her hand, leading her into the house. Colleen sank into the nearest chair.

"Oh, darlin'!" Maddie exclaimed. "Are y' all right?"

With an act of will, Colleen tried unsuccessfully to compose herself. Drawing in a shuddering breath to calm herself, she tried to speak.

"Yes, I'm fine."

Then in a tremulous voice, she tearfully poured out the story of what had happened to her. Maddie listened attentively, while she moved about, pouring tea for them both. Alarm displayed on her cheerful face when Colleen described the attack by the two men. When the story led to the rescue by the mysterious stranger, Maddie's expression changed from fear to astonishment, then eager curiosity. She leaned toward Colleen.

"Did y' see him plainly?" she inquired in an ardent voice.

"No," Colleen replied. "Why do you ask?"

Maddie took a sip of her tea, then set it back in its saucer, and sat down in the chair next to Colleen.

"No one has ever seen him clear enough to describe him," she said thoughtfully. "But if he was who I think he was, he's a legend in these parts."

"What can you tell me?" Colleen was eager for any scrap of information about this phantom.

"Everyone hereabouts calls him *MacCumhail.* When there's trouble, he shows up. All the militants and rebels, both the lads and prods from all the factions, have felt his wrath. Even though the man has never been seen clearly, the descriptions of the encounters are all the same. He comes from nowhere, stops whoever's doing violence, then disappears."

Colleen remembered the identical tales she had dismissed in the pub at Bureen, and smiled ironically. Perhaps it hadn't been a case of jesting with the newcomer, after all. She nodded at Maddie, encouraging her to continue.

The older woman took another sip of tea, then continued. "All the factions have put a price on his head, with little success. He doesn't seem to be tied to anyone or any cause. No one knows his purpose or his reasons, but we common people believe he's an angel for peace."

Colleen was thoughtful. "The men who attacked me said something that might correspond with that idea. The short one referred to 'weak-kneed peace mongers.'" She paused, then smiled, "Although, I suspect he would change the 'weak-kneed' part of that comment now."

Both women laughed, then Colleen yawned.

Maddie rose from her seat and gathered their cups.

"It's not good to be on the road so late," she observed, glancing toward the windows pensively. "Let's get you to your room, and get you settled."

Colleen liked this kind woman, and now, in the safety of her lodging place, she suddenly realized she was exhausted. Her host led the way to the room reserved for her, and set her bag down on the floor. Maddie stepped back from the door, and looked directly at Colleen.

"Truth is, I'm closed for the season," she declared. "I'm giving y' this room for Anna's sake. She said y'd be all right if I wasn't always around. Y'll have a key, and I'd be grateful if you'd lock up each time you leave the place."

This was surprising news, but Colleen had discovered that surprises were part of nearly anything that Anna was connected with. She nodded at Maddie, fingering the key she had been given.

"I understand," she said. "This room is lovely."

It was a large and comfortable room, decorated with a distinctly feminine touch. Books lined a shelf along one wall, and a bouquet of fresh flowers gave off a beautiful scent.

"Anna told me y' were important to her," the older woman said. "So I wanted you to have a special room. This one's not a guest room. T'was my daughter's." A shadow crossed her face, "I've kept it as it was when she lived here. She died some years back."

"Oh, Maddie, I'm so sorry," Colleen was dismayed to think of this kindly woman suffering such a loss.

"Y'll be the first to sleep in her room since," Maddie stated. "But it's time. Anna said there's no better person for it."

Colleen set her bag down gingerly, feeling as if she were in a shrine. "How long ago did you lose her?"

"T'was many years ago," Maddie replied, a distant look in her eyes. "Although it seems like just yesterday. She got caught in a crossfire during some of the troubles."

Colleen felt helpless, wondering how many families had experienced such horrors during the violence that plagued this beautiful country. She asked no more questions.

Maddie came back to the present from where her memories had taken her. She pointed out the bathroom and other amenities, and told Colleen that she'd serve breakfast whenever she woke up. Then she stepped out of the room, and left her to herself.

Colleen was so fatigued she could hardly get ready for bed. She wearily peeled off her rumpled clothing, dropped it on a chair, then rinsed off her face and collapsed into the softness of the bed. When she switched off the light, the room was flooded with the silver glow of the full moon. It touched her skin and gave all in the room an unearthly sheen. Then she saw no more, and if she dreamed, she did not know it.

The depth of her exhaustion enfolded her in dark satin sleep, almost akin to death. When morning arrived, a single beam of sunshine found its way around the curtains that draped her window and nudged at her closed lids. Blinking her eyes open, disoriented, she looked around the friendly room. As full wakefulness came, she tried to sit up and moaned under her breath at the soreness in her muscles. It seemed she had slept in an awkward position, and in addition, her wrists hurt where the ropes had bound them the day before. Gritted teeth got her into an upright sitting position, covers still pulled around her nude body. Then she flexed her shoulders and back a bit, trying to stretch some of the soreness out of them. Her gaze travelled about the room, trying to orient herself.

Abruptly the experiences of the previous night descended upon her in an avalanche of emotions. Terror and relief mixed with wonder and curiosity as she remembered her rescuer. The tones of his voice echoed in her ears and memory tried to recall any details of his face. The blazing blue-green fire of his eyes came back with crystal clarity, but his features eluded recall. This frustrated her.

"I know that face" she declared to herself, "But it hovers somewhere past the edge of my memory and dodges my efforts to retrieve it."

What effortlessly surfaced in her mind with total recall was his touch on her skin. Every detail of that contact etched on her spirit. The darkness and all the turmoil of the event obscured the rest.

Finally she gave up and tossed the covers aside, easing out of bed. The dawn was just breaking outside the room's curtains. Her bare feet took her to the window to peer between the drapery folds. Gazing steadily back from a tree branch in the shining mist were three pairs of brilliant black-jewel eyes. The sight of the magpies comforted Colleen. When the visage of her rescuer evaded her, she had begun to wonder if the birds might have been fantasy. But here they were, attached by a lifetime of invisible threads. Smiling, nodding, and acknowledging their presence, she ambled across the room to the shower.

The hot spray helped her come totally awake. Finishing dressing with a quick brush through the mass of her unruly hair, she went down the hall to Maddie's little dining room for breakfast. At a small table, a place had been set with a traditional Irish fried breakfast. The smell of the eggs, tomato, hot breads and bacon increased her appetite ten-fold. The food was hot, and she was hungry.

"Maddie!" she called, "Is this plate for me?"

"Mornin', darlin'!" Maddie chirped. "Sure 'tis. How did y' sleep?"

"Deeply." A simple reply told all.

"Good," Maddie said as she scurried about, pouring juice and setting a basket of still-warm brown bread next to her. "Have y' recovered from the misadventure last night?"

"Yes," Colleen smiled at her gratefully. "Your kindness helped me very much. Thank you."

Maddie brushed off her thanks. "It never should have happened," she declared. "Anna will be very unhappy to hear of it."

Changing the subject, Colleen said, "I don't know if Anna told you, but I'm trying to do some family history research. When she sent me here, she gave me this name. She said it was someone she believed could help me."

She fished the folded piece of paper from her picket, smoothed it out, and handed it to Maddie. The older woman looked at the name on it, and nodded.

"Andrew Finnegan. Yes. He'd be the genealogy expert who comes here to Ballysheen town on Wednesdays. He donates time to anyone who needs help at the Heritage Center. A number of visitors here and in other towns as well have been helped. Haven't Anna and I both known him for years?"

The Irish way of making a statement with a question always made Colleen smile. She was relieved to know that some expertise would be available for her search. In the back of her mind, however, the feeling persisted that something more was expected of her. Was she on the wrong track, spending time talking to a genealogist? This brief self-debate brought the decision that Anna would not lead her astray.

"What time does he usually get to the center?" she inquired.

Maddie leafed through a dog-eared calendar on her kitchen counter. Colleen glanced around the room and into the kitchen while she waited. There had been little time or energy for such observation the night before. It was an older home, heated with peat, and she noticed for the first time that the kitchen stove was fueled by peat, as well. It was a welcoming place, but it was a little shabby, too. After noting the ever-present photograph of the pope on the wall, the St. Bridget's cross in the rafters, and the small statue of St. Jude in a wall niche, Colleen wondered what she should do next.

Triumphantly, Maddie tapped her finger on the calendar. "Last week he was here at half-ten," she observed. "I'd guess that'd be his usual time."

Colleen finished her breakfast and rose from the table. She thanked Maddie and said, "I'll gather my notes and go to the center."

Maddie nodded. "Let me tell you how to get there," she said, "It's walkin' distance from here. You can't miss it."

When Colleen stepped out the door a half hour later, she was greeted by brilliant sunshine left by the lifting curtain of fog. The fog that had been over her mind lifted as well, and lightened her steps on the street. As her stiffness lessened, her long legs covering the ground easily. A love of walking was bred into her, each step making the natural connection to the land, a feeling she had experienced when hiking about her family ranch.

It took very little time to cover the distance from Maddie O'Hanlon's to the door of the tiny building that served Ballysheen as library, museum and heritage center. But for a small wooden sign that designated its use, a passing tourist might mistake it for someone's home. Since this small town was off the beaten tourist track, the presentation of these facilities was unpolished. Colleen's hand was just reaching out to open the door when it swung inward, causing her to break her stride.

Awkwardly, she caught herself and regained her balance, coming face to face with a serious, bookish man in his fifties. He peered at her through thick wire-rimmed glasses.

"Sorry," he said gravely. "I was just leaving for some supplies. May I be of some help to you?" His speech was almost totally clear of accent.

"I'm looking for Andrew Finnegan," she answered.

"That would be myself," he stated, looking closely at her face. "Were you sent here by someone?"

"Anna Hughes gave me your name," she replied.

Suddenly he realized they were standing there, door partly open, with him on his way out and her waiting to be allowed inside. He blinked behind his glasses but did not change the rest of his expression.

"Please," he apologized. "Won't you come inside? My errand can wait. Are you Colleen Lorrah?"

"Yes," she said. "I guess Anna did tell you I was coming to talk with you."

"She did. But I thought you'd be older," he said. "She said you were fifty."

"I am," Colleen declared. His less than tactful observation did not bother her. She was accustomed to people misjudging her age. This quiet, studious man probably didn't give such things much thought anyway.

She followed the scholarly Andrew Finnegan past a few neat, modest displays to a much less neat, small desk in the bookstack area, and stood politely while he shuffled some books and papers off a wooden chair. His brisk gesture indicated that she should sit, and when he had taken his place at the desk, she reached into her leather folder.

'Here are a few of the facts I have been able to find about my great-great grandparents. I'd like you to tell me if I have enough to continue searching, or if I should give up," she said as he took the materials from her and began looking through them.

He turned the pages, reading all the information with deliberate care. He was silent in this process, and never looked at her. He wrote notes to himself on a sheet of white, unlined paper. He wrote in small, neat cursive strokes, choosing the information he wanted from her materials with order and precision. Finally he finished and sat back, gazing reflectively at his notes, but not at her.

She waited. He still did not speak.

She stared at him. He was staid and dignified, his head of thick, curly, dark-brown hair sprinkled with threads of silver. He reminded her of many of the academics she had known in her college years. Quiet, deliberate and non-responsive, such people had often been an annoyance for her quicksilver, curious mind. Lively verbal exchange was her preference, and she always learned faster through dialogue.

But this was the person Anna had recommended. And Maddie had confirmed that his ability had helped many people who had found little success in family history searches before working with him.

Finally, unsure if he even remembered she was there, she felt compelled to break the silence.

"Is it hopeless?" she asked.

He looked up quickly, apparently startled by the sound of her voice, and even by her presence. He blinked, then stared.

"Is what hopeless?" His direct, unblinking gaze was disconcerting, even through the thick lenses of his glasses.

"My family history search," she reminded him. What did he think she meant?

"It will take work," he declared. "But nothing is ever hopeless. Your information so far gives no real connection here in Ireland, except for anecdotal information. Your notes suggest that some of the people you talked with about Lorrha and those you met in Bureen might have information, but if they do, you haven't put it down."

"You're right," Colleen nodded, embarrassed by his implication that she had not been very accurate in her materials. "I wasn't sure what you might need. I have more notes from those conversations. What would be most useful to you?"

"I need something that might connect them to a parish church. The priests often kept the most detailed records of the community."

She leaned back in the chair, considering what his reaction might be when he knew their *real* religion. Oh well, she might as well tell him about it. His attitude toward her made her feel there was nothing to lose.

"This may sound peculiar," she began, "but what little I've learned suggests that these people practiced the 'old religion.' I'm told it may be why they went to America, to flee persecution here."

Her eyes never left Andrew's face as she revealed this information. At her mention of the old religion, a slight change flickered in his expression, but it passed quickly. He continued to look at her with his cool, academic presence, leaving her uncertain she had seen a reaction at all.

Deciding that she would outwait him this time, she stopped speaking. He dropped his eyes back to the paper he had been writing his notes on, and scrawled a few more lines. Silence filled every nook and cranny in the room. A fly buzzing on the windowsill attracted her attention. More time passed. She curiously noted that in this level of quiet, she could actually hear her own wristwatch ticking.

Still, he did not speak or look at her. She considered standing up and walking out, wondering if he would notice her departure. Just when she was about to do this, he raised his head, and caught her in a piercing gaze.

"I'm sure I can help you. How badly do you want this information?"

Here it comes, she thought. The pitch for the big fee.

"It depends on the cost," she said, taking on her assertive American female executive persona. "I've spent a lot of money and time to come here, and I've invested substantial personal effort in the states to get what little information I have. Every time I thought I was getting close, I've found a dead end or a false direction. Here in Ireland, this search seems to have a multitude of peculiar leads, with strange pieces of information I don't know how to use. The ancestors are important, but what my father said to me when he asked me to do this seems to have little to do with them."

The tears of frustration standing in her eyes embarrassed her, and she averted her gaze. When she looked up again, Andrew was no longer seated at the desk. He had moved to the window, where he stood, hands in pockets, gazing out to the green foothills.

"You must finish," he said, almost under his breath. If it hadn't been for Colleen's extraordinary hearing, she would not have heard him.

He turned back to her and in a cool, professional voice, stated, "I don't usually do this, but since you are a friend of Anna's, I won't charge you for anything but materials. Will that be satisfactory?"

Colleen was disconcerted. "No. That's not what I meant. Your time is valuable. I want to pay your usual fee. I'll ask that you let me know periodically what the costs are, and let me pay as we go. Also, please allow me do some of the work, since I love research. If you'll tell me where to look, I certainly can do the basics."

"That will be fine," he said, sitting down at the ancient desk again. He tore off a clean sheet of paper and scratched some more notes on it.

"Take this to the priest at Sacred Heart," he ordered. "His name is Father Callan. Tell him what you know and see what records he can find for you. If your people come from Ballysheen, they would have left some traces in the church or the community."

Colleen bristled a bit at the brusque tone he used in giving these directions, orders, actually. Couldn't he be a little friendlier? At this moment, she felt like she was inconveniencing him. A fleeting thought about what he would look like if he smiled danced through her mind, then she dismissed the idea. Men like this take themselves and their work too seriously.

Still, she couldn't help wondering about him. After having been single for some time, her few social and business dates made her realize that she had little right to judge others whose work interfered with their personal lives. It was rare that she missed Art, but there were times when a longing for companionship arose. It wasn't that she had not resigned herself to the idea that she would be alone for the rest of her life. It was rare for a woman of her age to find a new life partner, and she had accepted this with no regrets. This acceptance aside, whenever her path brought her into contact with an intelligent, interesting man near her age, she allowed herself to speculate.

Andrew Finnegan was such a man. His intelligence was apparent and self-contained. His disciplined, careful courtesy was refreshing, after the tough, demanding corporate men in recent years. She mused that he was a relatively attractive man, too. His thick hair framed a strong, open face, and there was real depth behind those glasses. But he was so solemn, so formal. What must his personal life be like? Did he have family, or was he a recluse? What did he do besides assist helpless Americans in their search for roots?

She made a stab at conversation. "What is your profession?" she ventured.

He looked at her steadily, as if sizing her up. In measured tones, he replied, "I teach."

Subject closed.

Had she intruded? "When shall we meet again to talk about this research?" she asked, searching for safer ground.

I'll be back in Ballysheen the day after tomorrow," he said. "We can talk then."

"Time?" she asked.

"Half-one," he said, gathering the papers. Dropping them into his worn leather case, he motioned toward the door. Meeting over. She rose and walked ahead of him into the sunshine. When she turned to say good-bye, he already was marching down the street. This dismissal was annoying, and she shook her head as she walked back to Maddie's.

Entering through the front door of the bed and breakfast she encountered Maddie, who was already bustling about the kitchen, making tea.

"How did you find Mr. Finnegan?" Maddie asked, pulling out a chair for her.

"A little cold and unfriendly," Colleen replied honestly. "I know he comes highly recommended, but he is so formal...distant, really. I guess I expected someone like you or Jeanette." She described the family history center librarian for Maddie.

"Andrew Finnegan makes me feel like I'm intruding on Ireland, Ballysheen, and him."

Maddie nodded thoughtfully. "I've seen that in him, meself," she agreed. "Anna says he had a tough go of it in the past. She knows him better than I do and she has every confidence in him."

"But we'll see that y' meet some of the lads who are a little friendlier," Maddie continued. "I'll be takin' ya' to the pub m'self."

Colleen, nodded with a smile, then moved the discussion to the assignment Andrew had given her. "I'm supposed to talk to the parish priest at Sacred Heart," she said. How do I get in touch with him?"

Maddie smiled. "That'll be easy, love. He'll be in the parish office in the mornin'. You'll have no problem talking with Father Callan. He's truly a friendly one. Everyone loves him."

"That will be a welcome change from Mr. Finnegan," Colleen observed.

Maddie made a light supper for both of them, then went off to her own room while Colleen settled into the snug little parlor in front of the peat fireside. After being caught short by Andrew Finnegan, she wanted to review her research before talking with the priest.

Reading through it all again, the desperation that must have driven these great-great grandparents to leave their beautiful country became even more apparent. Pieces of their history must be learned to accomplish whatever her father had sent her to Ireland for. Regardless of his cold demeanor, Andrew had given her hope that it was possible to fill in some of the gaps in her information. When the fire began to die, and when a glance at her watch showed it was almost midnight, she rose from her seat and ambled the hall to her cozy room. She undressed, folding her clothes neatly into the dresser drawers, and then rinsed her face. The act of pulling back the down comforter on the bed, brought the realization that she was again very tired. The waning moon shone outside the window, casting a soft light when even after the bedside lamp was switched off. It seemed she had barely stretched out beneath the covers before she was fast asleep.

In the middle of the night she woke—or was she dreaming? She usually slept soundly through the night, so what had caused her to wake? She lay still, listening. There were no sounds except those of nature outside. Still, there was a sense of being watched. A chill went through her. Were her attackers back? Had they somehow tracked her to Maddie's? She was very alert.

Slowly she raised her head and peered into the darkness of the room. In the shadowed corner, barely visible, was the outline of a man, standing very still. The green fire of his eyes revealed that he was watching her.

She spoke. "Who are you? What do you want?"

Acknowledging that he had been seen, he stepped from the darkness into the dim moonlight. Now there was no doubt. It was her mysterious rescuer from the night before. Relief flooded through her, and she squinted at him, again trying unsuccessfully to make out the details of his face.

"It's you! I'm glad. I thought…"

The resonance of his words reached across the room to where she sat, holding the covers around her nude body.

"I came to see if you were recovered from last night," he said.

"A few bruises, and some shaky moments," she admitted. "But I'm fine. You didn't give me a chance to thank you, though." She stared into the darkness.

"No gratitude needed," said the voice. "It never should have happened. Not to you."

Her hand stretched out for the light.

"No!" It was an order and a plea. "I can't have you see me. You'll be far safer if you never see my face."

"I don't understand," she said.

Her desire to catch full sight of him was intense. His voice made her feel things she had never felt. There was fire and strength in that voice. The presence of this man made her fearlessly accept the fact that he was in her room. But even that was puzzling.

She had locked her door and windows before getting into bed.

"How did you get in?"

"Through the doorway of your dreams," he answered.

She was stunned. She realized now that she *had* dreamed of him. She remembered worrying about the attackers as she fell asleep, and she remembered wishing she could be sure of her safety. "But how…"

"Your fears called me," he said. "So I came."

"Please," she pleaded. "Talk with me for a while."

"Only if you don't try to see my face," he said.

Reluctantly, she agreed. Her ardent desire was to see the face of this vibrant, heroic stranger was demanding, but she craved his company even more.

"Please sit down," she invited, pointing toward the chair near the bed.

He moved across the room, lithe as a young panther. It was just barely possible to see his lean, muscled body in the pale glow of the night. It appeared in the darkness that he was dressed in a rough knit dark sweater and denims. He moved without sound, and settled gracefully into the chair.

"I'll stay until you fall asleep," he said.

She could see the green incandescence in his eyes more clearly now. It came from deep inside him, and stirred long forgotten emotions and reactions inside her. After the encounter with poor, stiff, formal Andrew earlier in the day, the warmth and intensity of this man were even more overt.

They sat quietly for a few moments, then he spoke.

"You are a beautiful sight."

It was a statement of fact, not insincere flattery.

"I'm ordinary," she said, "and I'm beyond the age where men say I'm beautiful. Although I have to admit it is wonderful to hear such words."

"I've waited for a long time to see the likes of you," the stranger said. "You just don't know how beautiful you are."

Colleen felt herself grow warm.

"What do you want?" she asked him.

"To be at your side along the way you must travel." The answer held promise and mystery.

"What do you mean?"

His voice reached out to her, weaving a web of intrigue.

"You will play an important part in events that were set in motion long ago."

She leaned forward, still grasping the sheet around her. That voice seduced her spirit and gave rise to a spreading warmth inside her. It was the intensity of the rush that comes with sensuality. She had not felt such sexuality since her adolescence. Outside, she could hear the wind rising, beginning to play night music in the trees.

"But I don't know what is expected of me, "she whispered.

"I'll be here to help you learn," he said, "but not yet. Continue with the path you have chosen, and I'll come to you when the time is right."

Colleen recognized that this statement was his opening to take his leave. He had promised to stay until she fell asleep. But when she started to ask him to stay, he cocked his head as if listening to something. Then he reached across, put his fingers to her lips, and shook his head with regret and urgency.

"I must go," he stated. "I'm needed elsewhere."

"Wait!" she protested. "You said you'd stay until I fell asleep!"

He placed a hand on each of her bare shoulders, easing her back into the pillows. Then he bent down, tucking her in like a child. He placed a light kiss on her forehead and murmured, "Back to sleep now."

She tried to keep her eyes open to see him leave, but sleep was a dark pool that claimed her first.

CHAPTER 14

▼

The loud and impertinent morning song of an Irish robin called her from sleep the next day. The little bird sat on a bramble branch outside the house, shouting his greeting to the day. His voice was impossibly large for a bird so small. The mist sparkled in the air and on the grass, predicting another sunny day to come. Colleen recalled every detail of the previous night as she dressed for breakfast, but decided not to share it with Maddie.

The older woman had already been out and she was bursting with news from the next village.

"Do you remember me tellin' you of *MacCumhail*?" she asked Colleen, excitement echoing in her question.

Colleen nodded without comment.

"Well, he appeared again late last night. Some ruffians from the Protestant side were gettin' ready to bomb the church in Kilskerry, and he stopped them. Sounds like they never knew what hit 'em. They were found this mornin', tied to one another in front of the RUC station, with their bomb ripped to pieces and scattered about their feet. They were so bruised and frightened that they confessed everything. Said they'd planned to blow up the church when he came out of nowhere. They insisted he was too strong for the both of 'em, and that he was so swift that he seemed to be in many places at once. They asked to be locked up, so he couldn't get to 'em again!" She clapped her hands and laughed merrily. "Isn't that *brilliant*?"

Colleen looked amazed and thoughtful. So that was where he had gone last night. For a moment, she wondered how the night might have turned out if he had been able to stay.

Breakfast was set out before her, and this time it was more modestly sized. (She had begged Maddie to ut back to porridge only. Her appetite had diminished with her arrival here, and she felt the need to run on leaner fare.) Genetics had blessed her with a spare body, but instinctively her metabolism told her she would need less food in the coming days. Maddie was bewildered and a little hurt, but eager to please this guest who had already begun to fill a lonely spot in her own heart. She gave the younger woman a motherly pat on her arm as Colleen set out for the church.

"Good luck to ya'!" she exclaimed from the door.

Colleen stepped into the filmy mist, zipping her jacket over her wool sweater to repel the damp air. Her strides took her to the edge of the village, all the while thinking of how ancient the cobblestone streets must be. It took a brief time to reach the simple old church, which occupied the grounds where early Christian monks had once established a tiny community. Her guidebook had mentioned that the site was chosen for the pagan religious significance it held in the lives of their prospective converts.

How often this had happened in Ireland and other countries as well. The early Christian mystics found that compromises incorporating aspects of pagan beliefs made conversions easier. So days sacred to the pre-Christian peoples were adapted to become Saints' days and holy days, certain ceremonies were customized, and sites of sacred wells, equinox observations and other acts of pagan worship were appropriated as Christian. In some cases, the monks themselves had blurred the lines between their beliefs and those of their new congregations.

As she approached the steps of the neat little church, her mind scambled to remember some of the Catholic rituals she had learned as a child. It had been a long time. The front door was open, and invited her to step inside. Eyes adjusting to the darker interior, she found herself in a simple chapel area. She genuflected in the aisle, then glanced around for a door or hallway that might lead to the priest's office or study. There was an archway, and as she started toward it, the parish priest came toward her. He was a small man with a merry, round face and startlingly black hair. His attire included the usual black shirt and white collar, but he was dressed against the morning chill in a well-worn black cardigan sweater.

"You're Colleen Lorrah," he greeted her warmly. "Andrew Finnegan stopped by yesterday to tell me you'd be along. I got out the old books and records from what should be roughly the right time period, so we can have a look if you're ready."

He motioned amiably for her to follow him down the hall. "I hope we can make this easier in the future. These old things are heavy, and they're dusty."

He opened the door and ushered her into his study, which was a wonderful contrast to the dim light of the church. Here, large windows permitted vast amounts of light to flood into the neat room. The walls were white, with paintings of Irish landscapes neatly arranged on them, and the priest's desk stood in the corner, facing the entrance door. In the center of the room was a huge library-style table with a neat stack of very old, very large books on one end.

Colleen was delighted. "How kind of you!" she exclaimed. "I would have been happy to help you move them!"

Father Callan grinned at her. "No need. It was good exercise and it was time for me to do a little cleaning in the archives, anyway."

"Show me how to look at these!" Colleen implored him.

"Better than that," Father Callan agreed. "Tell me what you're looking for, and let's see if I can help."

They sat down at the table, and Colleen explained what she'd been able to find in American records. Then, pausing a moment, she looked trustingly into the cleric's eyes, and related to him what her Aunt Willow had told her about the ancestors' practice of the "old religion," including the story of their subsequent persecution for it. Words flowed from her in a cascade as she rushed to tell all. Finally, she took a deep breath and paused, awaiting his reaction. He had begun to lean forward as she spoke, and the only expression she saw on his face was one of rapt attention.

"Fascinating!" he exclaimed. "I have an idea of where to look!"

He continued, "In the mid-1800's, there was a priest here who kept a sort of personal journal in addition to the day-to-day church records. I had seen the book a few times, but when I asked my predecessor about some of the passages, he dismissed it. He insisted that this priest had been something of a 'throwback' to the ancient Christian mystics, or that he had gone a little mad."

He quickly restacked the old volumes on the table, working his way down to a crudely bound, slim sheaf of papers.

"Here it is!" he declared.

Carefully, he untied the thongs that held it together, and began to lay the sheets out side by side on the big table, reading as he went. Colleen stood and leaned over to peer at the document. When she saw it was written in old Irish, she sat back down and waited.

"Here!" Father Callan pointed at a passage on the page, "Listen to this from 1849!"

He read once to himself, formulating the translation for the second reading.

"Comes Maighréad Hughs, a strange girl, who comes not to confession, nor to daily prayers. A number of farmers call on her to cure their sheep and birds sing from whence they perch on her shoulders. She hears voices no one else hears. Some believe her sainted, but I know these doings to be evil, and she must be exorcised of these demons."

He looked up into Colleen's drawn face.

She felt physically ill. If such beliefs had been held in recent times, her own father would have been seen as an enemy of the Church.

He read on.

"Do these fools not see she has caused a plague on the potato crop?' I shall exhort them from the pulpit and we shall pluck this evil girl from our midst."

Uneasy, Colleen asked, "Is there more?"

Father Callan shuffled through a few more pages. "Yes, yes, here." He began to read again.

"In the matter of M. Hughs. I have shown the faithful the truth about this sinful girl, and they have agreed we must drive the evil from this place. But a defender for her has appeared from Achill—one Richard Garrett. He took her up and they have fled from this place with others escaping the famine. We are concerned that their continued freedom, wherever they are, will extend this curse on the land."

"That must be when they started their journey to America," Colleen said thoughtfully. "But something isn't quite right. Margaret and Richard's last name was Hughes after they were married. Shouldn't her name have been Margaret Hughes Garrett?"

"Not quite," the priest said. "He notes here that he has heard of them again when they sought protection among the Protestants. They found no mercy there, either. The Church of Ireland did not want the burden of any of the Catholic famine victims. So they refused any who dared to ask for help. Being in the same community, they had no doubt heard of her peculiar ways as well. That gave them all the excuse they needed to drive her out of town. In those days, it wasn't unusual for people to change their names when they got to America. They must have decided to use her name. No, no…she was definitely Margaret Hughes."

Tears stung Colleen's eyes. "Poor Margaret. Poor Richard." She sat quietly for a few moments.

"Is there any earlier information about the family?" she asked.

"Could be. That's were I'll be putting you to work," Father Callan put the 1800's church record book in front of her. He showed her the way the pages were laid out, with births, deaths and margin references to local events that happened at certain points in the history of the community. Colleen bent to her task.

Referring to her own notes, she made a calculated guess about the approximate date of her great-great grandmother's birth, and turned to that period in the book. The spidery script used by the person recording these records was difficult enough to read. In some places, the ink had faded. In others, the dampness had caused it to blur, but she examined each entry carefully.

Aside from the birth dates for Margaret Hughes and her siblings, the only other notes of importance were the dates of death of both her parents. They had died very young and on the same day. It appeared that Margaret and her sister and brother had been forced to fend for themselves from a very young age. Her brother was older, and Colleen guessed that he had helped to provide for his younger sisters, but once they were orphaned, the children no longer attended the church. There was no reference to confirmation for any of them. She wondered why they had turned away from Catholicism, but decided she would probably never know the answer. She showed this page to Father Callan, and he looked at it, then turned the book sideways, reading a note in the margin.

She watched his face. He frowned in concentration, then gasped. "This notation says the elder Hugheses died for no apparent reason. The children found them dead in their beds, and when they came and told the priest about it, he accused the children of killing their parents. From the dates, it looks like the children were only eleven, nine and seven years old, so hardly likely murderers. But they were accused, and chased into the woods by the townspeople. Somehow they survived, although the only information we see later is about Margaret. She appears to have resurfaced after the new priest came to the church, and while he no longer viewed her as a murderer, he still believed her to be evil. What a sad time for those children." The kindly priest was contemplative.

Colleen wrote detailed notes, stood from where she had been sitting at the table, and helped stack the books before leaving the church. She had reached a limit on data for that day. The information on Margaret and Richard Hughes had been painful, but not unexpected. What was exasperating was that she still had not found information that would help her understand what her father had wanted her to accomplish. Everything in the church records and everything her Aunt Willow had said was a logical progression for Richard and Margaret to have left Ireland and sought their future in America. But what kind of mission did her father have in mind for her? The family history research was interesting, and helped explain some of Mike Lorrah's behavior and some of his enigmatic skills. What it did not explain was many of the other events that had occurred since her arrival in this beautiful country. And it did not explain the presence of her magpie guardians or the appearance of the mysterious stranger. She could not shake thoughts of him from her mind as she walked toward Maddie O'Hanlon's cozy house.

During her stroll, she noticed that it was growing dark outside. Had she been in the priest's study that long? Had the discoveries of her research made the day seem more dismal?

Stepping inside, she heard Maddie bustling about in the kitchen.

'Is that you, lass?" The cheery voice called out.

The woman could make her feel very young again.

'Yes it is, Maddie," Colleen replied as she walked into the warm and cozy kitchen. Wonderful smells emanated from the oven.

"Maddie," Colleen scolded in a kind voice, "I don't need any complicated menus. I just want something light."

"Oh, it will be that," Maddie stated with certainty in her no-nonsense way. "I'm only serving a little smoked salmon and brown bread with tea. But someone gave me apples, and I wanted to bake a pie. With a guest here, it gives me reason to cook. When I'm alone, I don't get that excuse. You'll help me eat it, won't ya'?"

Colleen couldn't help laughing. This woman was irresistible. She felt grateful that she had such a wonderful place to come back to each night, and she mentally thanked Anna for arranging her lodging with Maddie. With a smile, she seated herself at the kitchen table, and watched while Maddie scurried about. And when Maddie asked about the day's research, Colleen dutifully reported the events of the day to her, like a child home from school.

CHAPTER 15

▼

It was almost noon before Colleen awoke. The time on the bedside clock surprised her, and it made her feel disoriented. It was not like her to sleep so late. A ranch upbringing had set a lifelong practice of rising early. She hurried to get out of bed, showered and threw on her clothes. A walk through the house looking for Maddie proved fruitless. It appeared that the older woman had gone out and not returned. Putting her keys into her pocket, Colleen strolled down the road to the heritage center. The door was open, and Andrew was the only person there.

Looking at her intently, the genealogist said, "I thought you'd be here this morning. It appears that there is some news about your ancestor search."

His statement was accusatory, as if she was late for an appointment. It raised her hackles. "I'm sorry," she said irritably. "I didn't even know you would be in Ballysheen in the morning. I thought you said half-one."

"It depends on other commitments," he said. "It happened that some of the old documents at the college gave some clues about your ancestors. Tracking back from the information that you and Father Callan found, I was able to pinpoint the location of the Hughes family stronghold. It is located on a high point above the lake, and we'll have to do some hiking before we get there. Do you have hiking boots?"

Colleen's attention focused hard on what he was saying. "What do you mean, stronghold?"

Andrew gazed at her through his thick glasses. His look made her feel that he thought she was not particularly worthy or very bright.

"The stronghold was generally where the clan chieftain made his home and safeguarded his people. It usually had a central residence and protective walls to prevent raids. There are hundreds of ruins of such structures all over Ireland. Some can be traced and some cannot. This one had a few references to it over the years, and I happened to find one that gave me an idea where it might be. I already went to check it, and there are parts of it still standing. It is not easily accessible, and will require some hiking. If you want to see it, and I assume this would be important to you, since what you say is that you are here to trace your family, then you'll have to cover part of the distance on foot. So—what do you want to do?"

Feeling put in her place, Colleen stifled her annoyance with this arrogant man, and replied, "Of course I want to see it. I'll go back to the house and get my boots." Starting to walk away, she turned to Andrew and said, in an effort at peacemaking, "Thank you for the extra trouble you went to in order to find this."

Andrew nodded curtly.

As soon as she was out of his sight, Colleen blew out a long breath. She hated to be treated in a condescending manner by anyone, and this man's approach particularly rankled her. It would be more enjoyable to work on her family history if the man were more understanding when she didn't comprehend all the cultural nuances found here.

Once she was suitably shod, she returned to the heritage center, this time driving her car. There had been no indication that it would be needed, but she was not willing to walk back a second time if it was, nor did she want to give Andrew a second chance to chastise her. She left a note on the dining table for Maddie, telling her that her guest might not be back for dinner.

It took less than ten minutes to accomplish this, but Andrew stood waiting at the front of the heritage center. He had several bundles with him including a couple of daypacks, and he was wearing sturdy boots as well. Had he been wearing them when she saw him the first time?

Without the tweed jacket, he looked less formal, but Colleen was still very much aware of the distance he kept between them. The car had barely stopped rolling when he flung his bundles inside and slid into the passenger seat.

"Take the Market Road," he ordered.

Colleen shifted into gear and followed his directions. They drove in silence for a time, and then she ventured an attempt at conversation.

"I've never seen you with a car. Do you drive?"

"No." Silence seeped into every corner of the vehicle.

She tried another tack.

"Do you have family nearby?"

"No."

"Where do you teach?"

"The North, mostly."

More silence.

What was necessary to break through the barriers this man cast around himself? It was not that she expected effusive chatter, but after a few meetings, she was accustomed to having people warm to her. When they didn't, it was usually viewed as a personal mission to find the key that opened them to her.

"What do you teach?" she asked, looking away from the road and directly at him. When she moved her gaze toward him, something gave her the brief impression that he had been looking at her. By the time her glance had his face in direct view, his eyes were fixed on the road ahead of them.

"Lessons of history," he replied.

Quiet once again.

"Tell me more," Colleen was growing frustrated now.

"Nothing to tell."

"How long have you been helping with family histories?" she asked.

"About ten years."

Impatiently, she tossed out a flip question. "Do you ever speak more than three words at a time?" The edge in of her voice was audible and unmistakable.

To her surprise, he laughed, a brief hearty laugh, so unexpected it seemed almost like it might have come from a different person. She looked at him quickly, but the laugh had already settled into a small, ironic smile.

"Andrew," she tried again. "What is it that makes you so reserved toward me? Do I say the wrong things? We don't have to be close friends, but I'd really like to be on more congenial terms while we work together on my research."

"It's just not my nature," he said with an almost imperceptible shrug. "If you don't find my services useful, you'll do well to get help elsewhere." This was a matter-of-fact statement, without resentment or defensiveness.

"Andrew, that's not what I meant, and you know it. If you come so highly recommended by Anna, then I know you will probably provide exceptional assistance. But it appears that we will have to spend time together to accomplish what I need to, and I'd like that time to be a little more pleasant."

This was spoken earnestly and she looked directly at him as the last sentence was delivered. He did not return her look, but continued to stare out the windshield. When she paused for a breath, he gave a single, almost imperceptible nod, but did not speak.

Colleen sighed a long sigh, and concentrated on the road. Shortly, Andrew indicated a turn off into what appeared to be a farm lane. The tiny track led into a farmyard, past an old, shabby farmhouse, and into the pasture beyond. Just inside the walls of this field, Andrew told her to stop the car.

"We walk from here," he said.

They pulled on their rain jackets, and he handed one of the backpacks to her.

"What's in this?" she asked.

"Food and supplies."

"How long will we be?"

"Several hours."

He began to walk, never looking back to see if she was following. Colleen hurried to catch up, silently grateful for the genes that had gifted her with long legs and an easy stride. Staring at Andrew's back, gave her cause to wonder if it was part of the Irish male's culture to show so little attention to a hiking companion. Matching him step for step, her eyes darted about, noting their route. If he should leave her too far behind, it would be important to be able to find her way back.

The green path crossed the meadow and led to a small opening where they climbed over the stone wall into the next field. This meadow sloped up the hill to the edge of the woods. Soon they entered the trees and followed a course that grew ever steeper as it climbed up the hill to a high ridge. The deeper their trek into the forest, the larger and older the trees became. Finally they found themselves treading between moss-clad tree trunks under a high canopy in dappled light. The trail no longer showed signs of animal or human use, but traveled green along openings in the forest growth. The primeval atmosphere would have inspired awe in anyone. An occasional fox and a vast variety of birds came into view. The verdant ceiling altered the light of day, obscuring direction and time. Colleen glanced at her watch—one o'clock. Would she have enough daylight time to finish this journey?

Just then, Andrew stopped abruptly. The trail dropped off into a ravine just ahead of him, then crossed a stream below and immediately climbed the steep hill opposite. She came up next to him and looked at the terrain.

"This is spectacular, Andrew!"

For the first time since starting into the woods, he looked at her, peering through the lenses of his spectacles thoughtfully. His eyes rested on her a moment longer, then he started walking down the trail without comment. The descent was quick and easy, and the stream was simple to cross where some huge rocks provided the means to keep their feet out of the water. He stepped aside and permitted Colleen to go first. Halfway across, she paused on the largest of the stones and looked into the green depths of the water where it pooled in a small turn.

Andrew stepped across to the same broad stone, and his gaze followed hers. What she had seen caused both of them to catch their breath. Just at their feet, resting quietly in the back current, was a huge salmon. Its scales reflected the muted light with a golden glow, but the overall appearance was prismatic, rainbow colors shimmering off it in a constantly changing pattern.

"That looks like a picture in an old book my father used to read to me," Colleen said quietly, fearful of disturbing the beautiful fish. "It was a legend about Finn McCool."

"Like the Salmon of Knowledge," Andrew whispered.

"Yes! How did you know?"

"It's an Irish story." His tone was wry.

Colleen ignored the rebuke. "Did your parents read it to you?"

"My ma did."

She recalled that this creature had an important role in Irish mythology and water lore. Legend said this fish could give any who came in contact with it great wisdom.

Colleen spoke again. "I can see how some of the myths and legends originated, if these things really exist in nature."

Andrew was silent, then quietly declared, "Most myths and legends have a basis in fact and reality."

The statement was so emphatic that Colleen pulled her eyes away from the fish and stared at him. He stared back, his eyes drilling into hers, as if trying to drive this thought home. Caught in this unrelenting scrutiny, she felt trapped, as if he was correcting her. She broke eye contact by looking back into the water, but the salmon had gone. No ripple or bubble marked its departure, but an opalescent trail remained in the bottom of the stream.

Andrew passed by her on the rock and gained the opposite bank, starting the long climb up the steep slope. Not wanting to be left behind, she crossed from the last stepping stone to the grassy bank, noting it was a long step. She was feeling annoyed that he did not even glance back to check her progress, and she was surprised at how steep the trail was. It took her reserves of energy to keep up with Andrew. Exhaustion was threatening, but her pride would not let her admit it. The trail became rocky where Ireland's constant rains had washed away soil and plant matter, leaving large shards of broken stone exposed. Andrew continued to set a fast gait, and Colleen pushed hard to keep up. Suddenly, a rock shifted under her foot and threw her to the ground in a clatter of stony debris. Instantly, her guide leapt back down to her side.

"Are y' hurt?" he asked, his accent more pronounced in his concern.

"I think I might have scraped my knee, and maybe an elbow," she said, wincing Thankfully, she hadn't fallen all the way down the steep bank.

"There's a little spring of water up ahead," he said.

He took her hand and helped her to her feet.

"Can you walk?"

"It was just a little tumble." The words were said bravely. "I'm sure no harm was done."

Cursing her own clumsiness, she started moving more slowly. "I always get myself in trouble when I move too fast."

"I should have paid more attention," he said. "I'm so used to hiking alone, I forgot to think about you. I should have known I couldn't expect you to keep up with me."

Colleen wasn't appeased. Even this statement sounded like criticism. How could he not be aware of a companion? The pace he had been setting was more than thoughtless. It was competitive and punishing.

Her attention focused on her knee. Warm wetness coursed down her shin; she was bleeding. Every painful step seemed to aggravate it and increase the blood flow, but there was no way to be sure of this without looking at it. The tough black denim of her jeans had resisted the rock, so whatever damage her knee had suffered could not be seen.

When they reached the place where the slope leveled off, there was a tiny brook coursing through the thick grass, just as Andrew had promised. She sat down and tried to roll up the leg of her jeans. She struggled. Damn tight legs— she couldn't clear the knee.

She turned to Andrew. "I'm going to have to take off the jeans to wash this cut Could you please turn your back?"

He shrugged and walked away from her wordlessly. She was even more annoyed. He certainly didn't seem to care about her injury. He was lucky it had not been more serious. She glared at his retreating back as he entered the woods.

She tugged off her denims and blanched at the sight of the gash just beneath her knee. It was bloody and still oozing, but the jeans had kept stones and most dirt out of the wound. She sat down again at the edge of the little rill, glad for the relative dry space in the grass under the tree canopy. She dipped her hand into the clear, cool water and rinsed the cut. The cold of the water stung, but it cleansed the area effectively. A burrowing into the pack Andrew had given her produced a bandanna, but no first aid kit. Here was the first flaw in the perfect Andrew Finnegan. Good planning demanded that hiking gear included a good stock of first aid supplies. It was her first thought when she packed her own gear.

With the bandanna pressed against the gash, she tried to think. There were footsteps behind her, and she turned her head to look over her shoulder. Andrew was approaching her from the edge of the woods. She grabbed for her jeans, and cried out, "Wait!"

But Andrew continued to stride toward her. Colleen was horrified.

"Andrew! Please! I'm undressed!"

Andrew stepped around her, reached into the little stream, and sprinkling water into what appeared to be some leaves and mud in his other hand, mixed the elements into a pasty concoction. He kneaded it, looking intently at the potion, then picked up a little slippery moss from one of the stones on the bank. He added it to the compound. Finally satisfied, he turned toward Colleen. Never taking his eyes from her knee, he moved her hand and the bandanna. Then he applied the earthy mash to the cut. Colleen was about to protest, but the goo was already in place. She stopped in mid-objection, amazed. The pain left her instantly, and the bleeding stopped. Andrew put her hand on top of the poultice, rose, and started to walk back toward the woods.

"Take that off in about five minutes," he said.

Colleen was speechless.

When the time was up, she cautiously lifted the bandanna, peeled back the partly dried balm, and gasped with surprise. Not only had the bleeding stopped, but the cut looked clean and appeared to have already begun to heal. Curious, she collected some of the material into the bandanna, and stuffed it into her jacket. Looking around to see if Andrew was in sight, she stood, pulled on her jeans, and picked up her pack. Sliding her arms into the straps, she turned in time to see her companion emerging from the trees.

"What was that stuff?" she asked.

"Just a little remedy."

"Where did you learn to do that?"

"From an old woman who took care of me when I was wee," he replied.

"Took care of you?" Colleen's curiosity was aroused.

"After my parents died." His response was terse.

Colleen was not about to be cut off.

"Andrew," she said firmly, "Why are you so curt with me? You make me feel like I am intruding whenever I try to make a little personal conversation."

Colleen stopped, embarrassed at her display of annoyance. Had she overstepped herself?

Andrew stared at her. She waited.

At last his voice came, so quiet that she had to lean toward him to hear.

"No. That's my way of keeping my distance. Anyone I've been close to has died. It is easier for me to be alone."

The agony in his voice was so obvious that Colleen wanted to reach out to him.

"Can you talk to me about this?"

Now a feeling of shame washed over her. How could she have been so annoyed with him?

Andrew spoke again, slowly. "All I can say is that "The Troubles" cost the lives of both my parents and my brother and sister. I was left an orphan. Then Evleen, an old midwife in the South, gave me a home. She raised me and taught me much, but she was very old, and died when I was seventeen. I've been alone since."

Colleen was cautious. "Where do Anna and Brendan fit into your life?"

"They are sister and brother—Evleen's cousins."

"Sister and brother? I thought they were husband and wife!"

"No. Neither ever married. But they filled a void in my life, like an aunt and uncle."

Colleen contemplated what she had heard.

"What about your adult life? Friends? Relationships?"

The old barriers came up instantly. He shook his head, averting his gaze.

"Let's move on," he said abruptly, his reserve solidly back in place.

Reluctantly, Colleen fell into step behind him. There had to be much more to know, but it was obvious that Andrew wouldn't share it easily. She scolded herself for misreading him. It was pain, not arrogance that caused his reserve.

As they hiked, Andrew's thoughts were on the fateful day his parents were killed. From deep in the recesses of his mind, his memory wrenched him back.

It happened in Derry in 1955, when he was seven years old. His entire family had been awakened from sleep to thunderous pounding on the thin wooden door of their Bogside flat. His mother came to his room, pulled him and his older brother from the narrow bed they shared.

"Shush, boys," she hissed.

Taking each of them by a hand, she urged them toward a small, dark closet where their older sister already cowered. Pushing them inside, she said, "Be quiet now. Your da' and I will deal with this."

Packing them all tight into the cramped, shadowy place, she shut the door behind them. They huddled there silently, holding their collective breath and listening to her receding footsteps as she rushed from the room.

Just then, a resounding crash heralded the onset of shouting. Rough male voices exchanged curses and muffled threats. The children heard their father's anger through the flimsy wood of the closet door. "Out with you! Me family's got no part of this!"

Then their mother's voice, clear, strong and bell-like, "Not so, Michael! These are the Protestant bastards who killed me brother!"

Their father's voice next: "Jesus, Bridget! No!"

The two older children broke from their fear-filled paralysis now. The boy whispered, "They need me! I've got to help them! Wait here!" and bolted from the confines of the closet. Disregarding his command, his sister grasped a broom and followed him toward the clamor.

Young Andrew sat, stunned. He hated fighting. He had always cringed silently when his parents exchanged words, walked away when his brother and sister fought with one another, and at eight years of age, he had somehow managed to avoid the street fights that broke out among boys his age in this Catholic slum.

He had heard more taunts and threats than many children, first because he was Catholic, like everyone else who lived in the narrow, dirty, wretched streets of Bogside. He was Catholic in a place where that was the kiss of death for hope. The Derry ghetto was unkind to him and his fellow residents. Because of his peaceful ways, his own playmates often ridiculed him as a coward and a weakling. His father spent much time with little or no work, and his mother was treated like dirt outside the shelter of their own neighborhood when she walked to her meager work at the factory. He tried to understand the talk of his da' and the other men, but their dark words of rebellion and sedition passed over his head.

His parents had been more concerned lately, because several of their male friends and acquaintances had been jailed and beaten in the past several weeks. Tensions had been running very high with the men in his father's circle of friends, and their conversations grew more and more angry. In recent days, there had been talk of retaliation, but he had only heard fragments of it. Then someone had attacked two Northern Ireland RUC police officers, and left them badly beaten just inside the ancient wall of the city. The message of that location was unmistakable, since the wall marked the separation between the destitute Catholic population and the prosperous Protestant neighborhoods. The same attack had left two civilians injured as well.

The civilians were men whose names had been mentioned around the hearth by his father's friends on more than one occasion. The general line of discussion implied that these two were informants and traitors who had crossed the line to sell information to the Protestants. It was believed that they had been responsible for beatings and incarcerations of several men in this very neighborhood.

After the attack on the RUC, there had been no more gatherings in their home. The men stayed separate from one another, and silent on the subject. Their mother and father had ordered the children to come home straightaway after school each night. The dark overtones of these warnings frightened the children, but this was not the first occasion that they had been through a time like this. They knew the danger was real, and did not question what their parents dictated.

Now it had landed squarely upon their doorstep. As young as he was, even Andrew had no doubt about that. He hugged his knees, frozen by the fears his parents had so strongly instilled in him.

The shouting continued.

In his panic, he could not make out the words.

Suddenly the retort of a shot echoed up the stairwell, and penetrated his immobility.

He scrambled from the closet and rushed to the door at the head of the stairs. When he reached it, what he saw etched itself into his soul. His da slumped against the wall, clutching his chest, while a fountain of crimson poured through his fingers.

His mother stood at the top of the stairs. Behind her back, she was clutching a knife, which the boy recognized as the big butcher knife from the kitchen. She brought it around her, screaming, "Get out of my house, you bastards!"

One of the black-masked men in the doorway reacted instinctively to her motion, raising his gun and firing before she could do anything with her pathetic weapon. She crumpled like a silk shawl dropped to the floor. From behind him, the boy heard his sister and brother run up from wherever they had been in another part of the flat. They dashed past him where he had stopped and huddled on the upper landing, through the door and directly into the chaos below. The girl fell to her knees by the deathly still form of their mother. The brother, his face contorted with the howling rage pouring out of his throat, charged the attackers unarmed. The masked men, startled by the ferocity of his youthful fury, fired directly at him, then at the sister when she looked up in horror. The older boy dropped in mid-flight and thudded down the stairs. The girl fell across the broken body of her mother, a sacrificial shroud of blood and nightshift.

"Christ, man, stop!" one of them shouted, "They're only children!"

The second man stopped, and looked at the carnage on the stairs through the slits of his mask. Both men stood still for a moment, then the one who had shot the children finally spoke. His voice was calm and filled with an icy cold the boy would remember for the rest of his life.

"They're just filthy Catholic spawn," he said. "Good riddance."

The men turned and stepped quickly out the door into the night. Somehow they had not seen the boy at the top of the stairs. He fell to his knees, eyes filled with tears, and knelt there a moment before curling up on his side on the floor, hands over his ears. After a few silent moments, the neighbors finally ventured from their tenements, and they found him there.

These people sheltered him and sent word to his father's home village. His aunt came to Derry for him. She was his father's sister, and she had never left the community where his father and she had grown up. Gathering the child's meager possessions, she brought him back to her old stone cottage near the small hamlet.

Although she was much older than his father, his Aunt Evleen had gladly taken over raising him. Recognizing how wounded his spirit was from the violence that had claimed his family, she opened her heart and home. Her husband had died before they could have children of their own, so she bestowed all her love on the boy.

At first, young Andrew was dazed by the events that brought him to her. It took some time, but the peaceful pattern of their life in the woods began to heal his pain. The woman was gentle and kind and she intimately understood the natural world that surrounded them. Gradually, he grew aware of the beauty and magic of the forests and fields. He started begging his aunt to teach him about the mysteries of it all. The slums of Derry had harbored little plant and animal life. Dirty streets and buildings and peat smoke so thick you could hardly breathe obscured the few natural things that clung to existence there.

Life with Evleen in the cool, clean surroundings of the woods, provided a splendid classroom with plants and birds and wild creatures. At first, he sat very still and observed all these things closely. Then he peppered his new "mother" with questions about the flora and fauna. Her knowledge was extensive, passed down by oral tradition through hundreds of generations of her family, and she joyfully taught the boy.

She showed him hundreds of herbs and medicines. He learned to walk so quietly through the ferns that he could come up next to a bird or fox without it hearing him. They spent hours in her green canopied classroom of trees, learning about nature and about the old religion.

At night, he read the books that lined the spartan shelves of her snug little cottage. When those were finished, she brought him books from the library in the village. It never occurred to him to ask why he did not go to school, and he never questioned why the only visitors he ever saw were the woman's cousins, a brother and sister his parents had never mentioned to him. If he suspected all this might be to protect him from further harm by those who had destroyed his family, he did not bring up the subject.

The reality was that he didn't want to ask. For the first time in his life, he was living a completely peaceful existence, and it suited him. Away from the filthy streets, he was no longer tormented by other children. His new "family of one" treasured him and his keen mind was being filled with the knowledge he craved. It was the answer to many of his prayers.

Always with him was the emptiness left by the loss his parents and his siblings, but he had no desire to return to Derry. The hideous events of the their deaths still invaded his dreams, and brought stark wakefulness many nights. When this happened, the child was soothed back to sleep by the woman. Evleen knew when the nightmares invaded, and would come to sit in the chair next to his bed. When he was small, she would tell him stories or have him listen to the birds and breezes of the night. As he grew older, he did this for himself.

Finally, he banished the dreams through an act of will, and the memories only haunted him when he was awake.

With him absorbed in these recollections, they hiked in silence for about a half hour, finally topping the ridge in the midafternoon. There, in a swale on the brow of the hill, were the ruins of a towerhouse. Colleen looked at this 'keep' with awe, as Andrew turned to her and spoke for the first time since they had started walking again.

"This is the Hughes, or O'hAodha, stronghold from the fourteenth century." He gestured to a point beyond the old stone tower. "But come this way. There's something else you should see."

She followed him, past the building, and slightly over the ridge of the hill. There, perched majestically where the view of the countryside swept the entire horizon, was a deep circular ditch and a matching ridge. Colleen gasped. "Is this a…"

"Ringfort," Andrew finished her question with a statement. "Yes. Probably tenth century."

Colleen walked to the edge of the ditch and stood, surrounded by ancient stone and earth. A light haze softened the edges of the scene, and standing there, all her questions were voiced in one.

"What can you tell me about this place?"

Andrew was thoughtful. "Some of what I found came from written mentions, some is oral history, and some is legend. But even in the mythical, there are often grains of fact. As a historian, I never dismiss any related information."

Colleen waited, and he continued, "The O'hAodha were the primary clan in this region. Several of them descended from great leaders, one man and one woman—Rowan and Dana. Some modern scholars might have called these people 'druids' or even gods, but their leadership was more than religious and more than governance. They were like a combination of royalty and priest-class. These lands were theirs, not as a result of conquest, but because they were so powerful and skilled that they were recognized almost as god and goddess. Of course," a small contrary smile appeared briefly on his face, "some of that is definitely myth."

"What happened to them?"

"They and their people appear to have flourished here in a completely peaceful existence until the English began to conquer this country. They did not become involved in the clan and blood feuds between chieftains, and the Vikings and Normans seemed to avoid this area for some reason. The O'hAodha and their successive generations lived here in the ringfort. The purpose of that fortification was primarily to protect their livestock from predators. The stronghold was not built until news of the English attacks began to spread across the land. That is in recorded history. Even then, when the English attacked, the O'hAodha created a great cloud of fire, to shield their people and escaped, rather than fight. The invaders did not find any of them. They melted into the forest and back into the life they had lived before they settled in one place."

"Their enemies took the land, but not the spirit of the land. English journals of the time recorded occasional and supposed sightings of them, but never actual contact. As a result, local Irish natives insist until this day that they were descendants of the legendary 'Tuatha de Danaan,' and that they became one with trees and nature, or that they became *sidhe*, or fairies. More realistic explanations suggest that they became nomadic and possibly nocturnal. They probably lived off the land and moved under cover of darkness to avoid detection. Incidentally, it was because of their name and their association with fire that Ballysheen was named. In Irish, the name of the place is Baile Tine, roughly interpreted as Town, or Home, of Fire."

Colleen was fascinated. "What do you think?"

"My guess would be that they became something like your American Indians, mobile and self-sufficient, relying on their spiritual beliefs and upon nature to sustain them. They probably blended in with the native Irish when they could. I imagine some intermarried. They were peaceful and used their powers to try to create peace." He laughed ironically, and continued, "unlike my ancestors."

"What do you mean?"

"Like many other men of his time, my great grandfather participated in the Rebellion," he said, "and most of my male ancestors carried a weapon and fought to try to take back what was ours. I suppose I'd be a disappointment to them if they could see me. I'm an educator, not a rebel, and all I want is to live long enough to see peace in Ireland."

Colleen disagreed. "You teach," she declared, "and there is no greater weapon than knowledge."

A strange look passed over Andrew's face and he disengaged from the conversation with no response to her statement. Colleen discovered that it was growing easier to recognize when he was finished talking, and that it had begun to frustrate her less.

"I'd like to spend a little time here," she said. "Would we have enough daylight for me to do that?"

Andrew hesitated, then nodded. Something about his manner indicated that he wanted to leave soon.

"I'll only take a few minutes," she said. "Then I'll ask you to write down directions, so I can come back on my own. Is that acceptable?"

Andrew nodded, and leaned on a rocky section of ruined wall.

Colleen meandered back to the brow of the hill. Standing in the misty air, looking out across the vista, she could feel the presence of those who had gone before.

"This was the home of some of my ancestors," she thought. "No wonder it feels so peaceful to me."

At last, she pulled herself away from her musing and turned quickly back to the path. In this moment, she caught Andrew staring at her thoughtfully, the late afternoon light reflecting off his glasses. The effect was disconcerting, and the moment he saw her turn, he stood and walked away from her to take the lead. Now he set a slower tempo, and when they reached the treacherous stone rubble, he took her arm and supported her. She thanked him once the difficult stretch was transversed. He nodded and continued on. Carefully watching where her feet were placed with each step, she also watched Andrew's back as he led the way. His stride was easy and graceful, and he looked like he took good care of himself. He was lean for someone who spent a lot of his time in libraries and record offices. But then, Colleen thought, it's impossible to know what he does in his leisure time. He does not have a car, so he probably walks a lot, as so many Irish do.

Why did Andrew seem so isolated? What little he had said about his own background suggested painful events that contributed to his restraint, but there had to be additional factors. There was reason to suspect that she might never know the answer. Everything in his demeanor signaled that more personal questions would be rebuffed.

Once on more level ground, he increased the speed of his stride. She hurried to maintain the pace. Several times he glanced at the sky, and once he lifted his wrist and looked at the watch.

"I hope we haven't made you late for an appointment," she said.

"Next one is after sunset," he replied.

Before long they reached her car, and after they got in, she handed him a small notepad.

"Please write down some directions to help me get back here. I want to come back alone," Colleen said.

Taking the pad, he quickly pulled a pen from his shirt pocket and started to write as she pulled out of the farmyard onto the road. There was no more conversation.

When they arrived in the village, she stopped in front of the heritage center.

"When will you be back in Ballysheen?" Colleen asked, not wanting to make the same mistake she had made today. "Should I plan to work with you again at any specific time?"

"It will be about a week," Andrew replied. "In the meantime, you can go out to the stronghold anytime you want. I told the farmer you might return."

Colleen pondered his efficiency. This man didn't miss a beat.

He left the notebook on the dashboard, and removed the daypacks from the back seat. She waited until he had put the things inside and emerged from the building. As he started to walk along the street away from her, she permitted herself a look at his notes. They were detailed and precise, as expected.

Upon her return to Maddie's house, she saw her host had a guest.

"Anna!" she cried happily. "I didn't know you were coming to Ballysheen!"

"I came to check on you!" Anna's bright blue eyes twinkled. "Maddie tells me that you've seen the priest and Andrew and she says you've met up with *Mac-Cumhail*."

"Then there's not much more to tell you, is there?" Colleen teased.

Anna chuckled. "You won't get away that easy. Has Andrew been helpful?"

"In his own way," Colleen's voice told more than her words.

Maddie stood, as if on cue. "I'm on my way to the bakery. Why don't the two of you catch up while I do that?"

Colleen was taken aback. This was an intense reminder of her mother's instincts about the times when she had needed private conversation with her father. She wanted to talk to Anna.

Once the door closed behind Maddie, Colleen spoke her mind to the older woman.

"It's about Andrew. He said you and Brendan are like family to him," Colleen began.

Anna, expression focused, nodded, but did not speak.

Colleen continued, "He's done a very professional job so far, but he's so reserved that he is almost unfriendly. I'm used to more warmth from people I'm dealing with. He told me a few facts about his parents' deaths, and I can understand why that would make a person protective, but it was so long ago. Is there more to the story?"

Anna nodded. "Aye. Poor Andrew. While Evleen raised him, he was very much to himself. They were private and separate from the people of the village nearby. And he needed that kind of life. He never forgot seeing his parents killed…"

"He saw his parents killed?" Colleen was horrified. He had said they were murdered, but he had not revealed that he had been a witness to it. Anna nodded solemnly.

"When he was just a wee lad. Evleen raised him well. She helped him continue to believe that peace is the only way for our land, and why revenge brings no solution. We women know this, but our warrior men believe otherwise. And once the goddesses were set aside by the Church, bloodshed became a way of life for our people. The women recognized this, but they were set aside, too, and no longer seen as equal." Anna's thoughts seemed to drift as she made these statements.

Colleen patiently brought her back to the subject at hand, "What about Andrew?"

Anna blinked. "Oh yes. Andrew studied the old ways with Evleen, and they sometimes went to Church, too. He found his own way to reconcile these separate beliefs. After she died and when he was old enough, he came back among people and went to university. His studies were history, anthropology and sociology, and he set out to work with those who needed him. He never lost his balance, but found he could best deal with aggression by helping the victims.

Eventually he began working with school children in Derry, trying to help them know that not all men are brutal."

Anna paused, lost in thought for a moment. Colleen was composed, attentive, but not intrusive. After a time, Anna resumed. "He was happy in this work, and began to be more open and outgoing. He made some friends, and, in time, developed an interest in a girl. He fell deeply in love with one of the teachers at the children's school. But he was too shy to do anything about it. He worked closely with her, and he served as her friend, but the truth was that he worshipped her, if only from afar. The girl never knew but he just stayed close, and worked with her and the children every day.

"What happened?' Colleen asked. "Does he still feel this way about her?"

"It was terrible," Anna said with an effort. "During the days around the Battle of Bogside, now some 25 years ago, he heard fighting had broken out beside the school. It was just as the children were finished and leaving for home. Andrew was racing toward the door when the gunfire started. The girl he loved already was running to try to put herself between the children and the gunmen, and he couldn't reach her. When she came out the door of the school, the crossfire caught her, and several shots struck her before his very eyes. She died right there in the schoolyard, bullets from both Protestants and IRA bleedin' the lifeblood out of her. Her bravery saved the children, and when the gunmen saw what had happened, they fled into the alleyways, never to be caught. Andrew tried desperately to save her, but she died while he was holding her. The loss was so awful, he never recovered. It was never reported in the papers, but that didn't make it less terrible." Anna shook her head slowly, with great sadness.

Colleen heard the heartbreak in the older woman's voice. "What did he do after that?" she asked.

"He came to Brendan and me and stayed for a few months' time at the old cottage. I think he tried to tell us about the tragedy, but never would tell us the girl's name, and we did not ask. All that time he spent deep inside himself, and I thought that he might die from the hurt of it. Then one day, he said he'd decided that the way to honor her was to go back to teaching. Once gone, he now only comes back occasionally to visit. We have not been to his home, but he does let us know what he is doing. I knew he had started to do family history work here, and I knew this would be the right person to help you. Andrew is a good man, Colleen...never a better one."

The sound of the door opening ended this conversation, and Anna turned her attention to Maddie and the cakes her friend had brought back from the bakery. When Anna announced that she had to leave to catch the bus back to Bureen,

Maddie insisted that she take one back to share with Brendan. Colleen was disappointed that Anna was leaving so soon.

"Couldn't you stay overnight?" she pleaded.

"No, darlin'," Anna smiled at her. "Brendan needs his evenin' meal, even though it'll be a little late."

Anna took her leave and Colleen waved at her from the door, then stepped back into the house. Her thoughts churned in a tangle, baffling her attempts to process what she had seen and heard in this day. The thing she knew for certain was that her opinion of Andrew was shifting, but she could not be sure of what it meant.

CHAPTER 16

▼

Retracing their steps, Colleen drove to the place where Andrew had taken her. More than anything, she considered it important to see it alone, without the distraction of having someone with her. The mist and fog complicated his detailed directions, but she arrived without delay, pleased that she had not made any wrong turns. The countryside was blanketed in the glistening wetness, and looked even greener than normal. As she parked her car in the farmyard, the farmer, attired in oilcloth coat and mud-caked Wellingtons, raised his hand in greeting. In typical Irish fashion, he left his tasks and came to where Colleen's car was parked.

"Mornin' miss," he said, smiling broadly.

Colleen was surprised to note how handsome he was. More importantly, he was friendly and engaging, unlike Andrew.

"My name is Colleen Lorrah," she began.

He nodded. "Andrew Finnegan told me y' might be by for another walk in the hills. Y're welcome to it." He paused, then offered, "I'm Kieran O'Leary. Be sure to ask me, if I can do anythin'."

"Thank you, Kieran. I think I'll be fine. I just want to go back to the place Mr. Finnegan took me yesterday." His eyes followed her gesture as she pointed toward the path, and he started to go back to feeding his milk cows. Then he turned.

"Will y' stop for tea when you come back?"

She smiled. "I would like that."

Her own Wellingtons were useful as she started up the passage. Careful of her footing, she noted each landmark along the way. Today's walk was a pleasure, simply because she could move at her own pace and because the silence that resulted from the fog brought tranquility. The ravine proved far more reasonable when traversed cautiously, and she paused to see if the salmon might show up again. But all that presented itself was crystal water in the deep green pool, so she sighed and moved on. All her senses were sharpened, since she was alone and solely responsible for her own welfare. The moisture could be heard dripping off the trees, and the rushing water murmured as it descended the steep slope. Her own steps sounded a rhythm that kept her company, and in the distance, she could hear the mellow chime of a bell on one of the farmer's cattle.

At the top of the rise, she paused a moment near the rill where Andrew had put the organic mixture on her gashed knee, and thought about what had happened there.

The man was still a puzzle to her, but her opinion of him was improving. Thanks to what little he had told her, and to what she had learned from Anna, it was easier to comprehend why he was so abrupt. Admittedly, he had been very helpful in her family history research, so it would only be fair to be more patient with his behavior. Why couldn't he be as friendly as the farmer, Kieran?

Hiking on toward the stronghold, her approach to the massive, ruined stone walls was marked by the cessation of the rain. The fog continued to eddy around her, and it gave the place a sense of timelessness. She stood still, listening.

The first sound she could hear breaking the silence was that of something passing through the air. On the rock wall directly in front of her, one of the magpies landed. Soon the other two glided in on glistening wings, and took up their positions nearby. As they did, she heard faint strains of the same ancient music that had come through the trees the night *MacCumhail* had rescued her. The music spun around her, wrapping her in a wispy web of sound. She was captivated. She experienced a connection with the people who had occupied these lands in the past, and felt they were with her as she stood in this place. It was as if they were just outside her peripheral vision, with their voices a pitch out of range of her extraordinary hearing.

Her strides took her in the direction of the ringfort, and as she approached it, she noticed something she had not seen on her previous visit. Off to her right, next to a huge holly tree, there was a monument of rocks, smaller than most of the dolmens she had seen, but structured similarly. A large capstone perched elegantly about four feet above the ground on top of three delicate pillars of stone. In the shelter of the capstone, centered between the three "legs," was a perfectly circular pool of clear, sparkling water. It fed a tiny stream that flowed toward the ringfort, then vanished on its way, dropping beneath the limestone that broke the surface of the grass. Colleen was fascinated.

She dropped to her knees and looked reverently at the pool. Obviously the people who had come before had venerated this spring. Dozens of egg-shaped stones had been placed around its perimeter, and some of them still sat where they had been placed on the capstone. The holly tree was festooned with dozens of strips of colored cloth, all tied on carefully. Colleen had never seen anything quite like it, although she recalled that Crow tribal members often tied bits of fabric to trees in sacred places..

The magpies flew to join her near the pool, settling to form a brilliant black and white triangle on the holly tree. She remembered reading that the sites of most holy wells and sacred springs include a tree, forming part of the order required for whatever magic the spring delivers. What was the primary attribute of this one? Some were said to heal specific ailments, some to provide wisdom, some to answer individual requests. When she had read about them, she concluded that these beliefs were probably the genesis for modern day wishing well legends. From this vantage point, the fog obscured the fortress, and she could only vaguely see the contours of the ringfort. But she could hear the sound of the water pouring out of the spring and into its course across the limestone. She could hear something else, too.

Assuming as still and unobtrusive a position as she could, she crouched there. In the mist, she was sure she could see movement, but there was no way to be sure. The music continued to surround her, and the magpies remained in their places. Her squinting did not make the forms become any more defined to her. She rubbed her eyes, and the impression of figures disappeared. It was a relief, and it brought the recognition that she had been very anxious about who they might be. Was there any possibility that they could be those of the men who had previously attacked her? Just as she was about to relax her vigilance, there came a sensation of someone standing very close to her, and her muscles tensed, ready for flight or defense.

By some trick of the fog, or her own imagination, a voice seemed to emanate from the stones of the small monument over the spring. It was *MacCumhail*.

"You belong in this place," he said.

"Where are you?" She looked around quickly.

"You won't be seein' me," he responded.

"What do you want with me?"

"I just want to look at you and talk for a while," he said.

"What am I doing here?"

"You've come where you are needed," he said simply.

"For what?"

"You know in your heart."

"No. I don't know in my heart! Or in my head, either!" she exclaimed with frustration. "I have been trying to discover what the purpose of my being here is ever since I came to this country! I don't feel any closer to an answer now than I did when I first arrived!" Tears stood in her eyes.

Now he spoke in silken tones, touching her core. "It only seems that way. Your visions and dreams have led you here, and your bloodline has given you many gifts. You will know for sure e'er long. It'll all come clear."

"I want to know now!" Colleen felt like stamping her foot. "I sense so many things inside myself, and I dream strange dreams, but I am alone in this and no answers are forthcoming. And if there are 'gifts,' I sure don't know what they are."

MacCumhail was silent during this outburst, but when she stopped speaking, he told her to close her eyes.

Colleen did.

From somewhere behind her, she felt his hands stroke her hair, and then move gently along her shoulders. As he caressed her neck and back, he soothed her.

"You are not alone in all this, Colleen Lorrah. But you alone are the key to what must happen. Generations have waited for all the right elements to come together at a time when peace could begin to return to Eire. It required the return of some of Ireland's best exiles and it meant that other tribal peoples would have a role as well. Many descendants of our emigrants have come back, and the goddesses have searched through them all. But we have actually been waiting for one. You are the one."

"But what is expected of me?"

"First, a deep understanding of where you came from, who your ancestors were. Your lost memories must awaken. Then a blessing upon you from kindred tribal people, who recognized you and helped along the way, and finally, timing that all of Eire could understand and accept."

Colleen shook her head, eyes still closed. She was languid with the pleasure of this man's touch, and did not want this moment to pass. Part of her was surprised at how easily she could accept his touch without ever seeing him clearly, but the sensuality of the moment was too gratifying to stop.

"Tell me more," she begged, wanting to prolong the sensation.

"There is little more to tell at this time, except that you will soon understand what is expected." He sighed deeply, as if from the depths of his being. "I must go now, but I am never far from you. I've waited a long time for you to come here, and you are taking a larger piece of me with you each time we part. I want you to understand that."

"Please don't go!" Colleen was distressed. "Please! I don't want you to leave!"

Still behind her, he put his lips close to her ear. "I am always with you. If you truly need me, I'll be there. But Mother Eire demands my first allegiance. When the fates have been fulfilled, perhaps I can rebuild my own life. But for now, I must leave you, though it tears my heart to go."

Abruptly, he was gone. Colleen could feel his absence as if some physical part of her had been wrenched away. She was distraught. An unbearable loneliness settled over her like a heavy shroud. She sat staring into the water for a very long time. Outside her view, MacCumhail ran from where she was.

He moved swiftly through the forest, tears streaming down his face. When he was far enough from where he had left this beautiful woman, he stopped and raised his face to the sky. He planted his feet, dropped his hands to his side and cried out to the goddesses.

"Why?" His voice was a plaintive lament. He felt helpless. Falling in love was not a part of his calling, and it divided his existence unbearably. If any of the insurgents learned of his attachment to her, she would be in mortal peril. He had an arduous role to play in the future of Ireland, and now his concern for Colleen's safety was rapidly becoming a distraction. He knew he had to be at the pinnacle of his abilities to anticipate and apprehend the enemies of peace on both sides. Personal emotions could not be permitted to interfere. On the other hand, he could not counter his passion for her. His heart and mind were captivated. He desperately needed these precious moments with her.

An ethereal form materialized at his side. The timeless deity extended her hand to touch his hair and to calm him. After a time, she spoke.

"Ah, my champion. You cannot succeed alone. This woman brings you the answers to your questions about the future. She holds the key to your crusade and the key to who you really are."

He sobbed, a single, sorrowful sound, then rested his fearful eyes upon his muse. "Why didn't you tell me before? I am so unprepared."

He was desperate.

Again, the dulcet tones of the shimmering presence came to him.

Comfort emanated from the voice.

"The time was not right before this. It is only now that you are both ready."

CHAPTER 17

▼

When Colleen had contemplated this encounter with *MacCumhail* long enough, she descended from the O'hAodha ancestral site on the trail, and went up to the farmhouse door. Her knock was answered by Kieran. His smile told her he was pleased that she had taken him up on his offer. Without his raincoat and his Wellingtons, he looked very different. She guessed that he was about her age, maybe a few years younger, and she looked around the house for signs of a woman's touch. Catching her gaze, he guessed what she was thinking.

"I live alone," he said. "Never married."

"Why not?"

"When I was the right age, my da' became very sick, and I took on all the work on the farm. There was so much to do that I never went courtin'. Then, after Da' died, I still had my Ma' to look after. She wasn't well, either. But she was alive for many years, and did some of the woman's work around the house. By the time she died, it just seemed too late. So I kept to m'self, and here I am now."

Colleen was amazed. She had heard stories of bachelor Irish farmers, but this was the first one she had ever met. He was tall, and startlingly attractive in his flannel shirt and wool pants. His eyes were blue, and he had sandy hair that showed very little gray. It was impossible to guess his age, but his skin showed some of the signs of the many days spent outside. His body was strong and well-muscled, broad across the shoulders and narrow at the waist. She was intrigued.

The conversation between them flowed naturally. Colleen was curious about farming in this climate, and she asked many questions. She also asked Kieran about his schooling, and learned that he had finished the primary and secondary schools, but the rest of his education had been self-taught. Reading was a passion with him, and he followed the national and international news in the papers with avid interest. Yes, he did go to the local social events, ceilis and parties, and he did stop by the pubs in Ballysheen for an occasional porter. She wondered why the local women weren't flocking to his door, and finally asked that question.

"I guess I just like my own company better," he shrugged in a disarming way. "Might come to regret it when I'm an old man, but for now, I'd rather not have any distractions."

They finished their tea, and Colleen thanked him for his hospitality. Getting into her car, she drove back to Ballysheen. When she parked and walked to the door of Maddie's house, her thoughts were spinning rapidly. The door opened in front of her just as she reached for the latch.

"Anna!" she was puzzled. "Back again so soon?"

"Aye, child," the older woman's voice was urgent. "It's time for us to talk."

Did Anna somehow know of her most recent contact with *MacCumhail*? No, that couldn't be. There was no way anyone could know.

She stepped into the house. "Where's Maddie?" she asked.

"She's off for the evenin'. It's just the two of us." Anna was matter-of-fact. She led Colleen to the table in the small dining area.

The two women sat, and Anna pushed a cup toward Colleen. She filled it with tea, and nodded for the younger woman to drink it. They sat in silence for a moment as Colleen settled in, then asked, "What did you want to talk about?"

Anna leaned down to reach into the cloth bag she carried whenever she left home. She produced a small linen-wrapped bundle, laying it reverently on the table between her and Colleen. Carefully untying the strip of fabric around the wrapping, she peeled back the outer cloth, leaving the item inside untouched.

Colleen looked curiously to see what it was that elicited such reverence from this wise old woman. It was the texture of a mass of spider web or silk filaments, and it was a creamy, glistening white. It almost appeared alive. Colleen wanted to touch it, but at the same time, she was afraid to. She sat still, waiting for the next thing Anna might say.

Anna did not speak. Instead, she delicately took the fragile thing between the thumb and forefinger of both hands and lifted it up. The airy stuff draped in splendid folds that drifted in the air. It was a garment, shift-style, gauzy and mysterious, with strange designs woven across the bodice. Prism-like, colors and light played across it, highlighting first one part, then another. It was strangely opaque, despite the initial impression of transparency. Colleen was mesmerized.

"Anna!" She gasped. "How beautiful! What is it for?"

"This is a ceremonial dress," Anna said simply.

"Where did it come from?"

"It was spun and woven of the finest wool from the sheep who live in the mountains. The design has been handed down through the family," Anna was contemplative, almost as if speaking from another time and place. "Me grand-mother taught me mother about it, and me mother taught me. But it was never fashioned in the present days. There wouldna' have been a purpose to it."

"Is this very old, then?" Colleen was amazed by the sheer magic of it.

"No. It is very new. It was just made because the time has come for a dress like this to be worn again." Anna looked off into a distance only she could see.

"What kind of ceremony is it used for?"

"This dress is only created when the elements come together for an uncom-mon ritual. When the elements of battle and peace are about to come together for the common good, it is worn by one who represents of the goddess of nature and of harmony."

"How often is that done?"

"It has never been done in its entirety during me lifetime, or that of me mother or me grandmother."

"Then how do you know about it?"

"It is one of the most sacred events of the old religion. It has come down through our bards and oral histories, and no one seems to know how long ago the last ceremony was held."

"What was its purpose?"

"To unify and to bring peace to Mother Ireland."

Colleen allowed herself a wry smile. "Then it has been a long time, hasn't it?"

Colleen was truly confused, now. She had heard *MacCumhail* refer to peace. He said he was a warrior for peace. She had also been closely following the peace process that was part of the agonizingly slow dance between all the factions in Ire-land. She had all but abandoned hope that this country she loved so much would ever find a way to negotiate its way to peace. There were too many tightly held beliefs, grudges, and too much blood-soaked history for any progress to be made. How could peace ever happen here? She had lamented this to friends in the States, and she had sat in numerous conversations in the little pub at Bureen, lis-tening to the old men talk of process and of rebellion. What could the old reli-gion possibly have to do with peace?

Anna nodded wearily. "The troubles have had hold on us for many thousands of years. The elements weren't in place, and the time was not right."

Colleen was fascinated. "Are you saying that the elements are in place now?" "Is there some indication that the time is near?" She continued to gaze raptly at the airy garment as the slightest stirring of the air in the room caused it to undulate between them.

Anna was thoughtful. "The peace talks in the north are surely opening a wee door in the wall between old enemies," she stated. "If there has ever been a time for the ritual it is now."

Of course. Colleen couldn't believe she hadn't made the connection herself. "So what is involved in the ceremony?" she asked.

Anna leaned forward, letting the dress settle back into its linen wrap. Her bright blue eyes burned into Colleen's.

"The goddess of nature and harmony blends her essence with that of the warrior spirit, to create a fire that purifies the path. The strengths of both combine to produce an irreversible force to bring peace. This will happen at Imbolg, at February first, the festival of the goddess. It has always marked the turning point of the year, a rebirth. Each year, we of the old faith gather to welcome the planting weather. This ceremony requires the presence of 'one of three'—a woman, and another 'one of three,' a man. The two souls must become as one. In the past, people from our village represented the goddess and her consort."

"Anna," Colleen was energized. "Do you think I could witness the ceremony when it takes place?" She felt a compelling need to see this rite.

Anna looked at her quizzically, but did not answer. Colleen had an eerie feeling of displacement.

Colleen tried again. "Who will wear that beautiful dress?"

Anna reached out and touched her hand. "Yourself."

Colleen was jolted. "Me? Why? Shouldn't it be someone of the Old Religion?"

"Ah, darlin', have you not seen the signs? After all you've learned, after all the hours with me and Brendan, the talks with *MacCumhail?* How could you not know?"

Colleen squeezed her eyes shut. This was beyond her imagining. Despite the visions, the history of Margaret and Richard, the encounters with *MacCumhail,* she had not been prepared for this.

"But I won't know what to do!" Colleen shook her head, bewildered.

This couldn't be happening. She peered out the small cottage window into the shadows of the tree in front of the house, trying to gather her thoughts for an answer that would not offend her friend. Her gaze was met by the sparkle of the black-diamond eyes of the largest magpie in the three that kept watch over her. As she watched, it slowly glided from its perch, and as it caught the breeze under its wings, it was joined by the other two. Anna's eyes followed hers. A small smile played on the older woman's face.

"Ah," she sighed, "Three magpies. The old saying goes: *One for sorrow, two for mirth, three for a wedding…*"

Colleen was jolted from her reverie. "My grandmother used to say that verse," she recalled.

"T'is the wedding we are discussin' here," Anna said.

"What wedding?"

"The wedding of the forces that will open the way," Anna replied. "You have been taught. And you will *know* whatever you were not taught. The blood in your veins will tell you."

Colleen suddenly remembered that her vision quest had revealed some elements of this eventuality to her. As Janine Skyhorse had promised her, the memory had remained submerged until she needed it. She also remembered the legends from the stories her father and her grandmother had related to her and her siblings. She recalled the details Anna and Brendan had added when they taught her in Bureen. Still, she hesitated, searching for the confirmation inside her heart. Then the voice came to her inside her inner ear. "You must do this, it is your destiny. I will be with you."

It was her father's voice.

Suddenly she was sure.

So it was that she found herself back in the grove at the O'hAodha ancestral site. In the late hours of the evening of February 1, Anna had dressed her in the gossamer shift and brought her to the grove on her bare feet. Despite the cool damp of the evening, the clear skies had permitted the full moon to illuminate their path. They had come a different way than the route Andrew had shown her. Anna directed her to stand near the dolmen. Then the older woman had taken both her hands, and looking intently into her eyes, had told her that the hope of the Irish people was with her on that night. With that, Anna departed, leaving her alone.

Colleen stood there in the silence of the night. The diaphanous dress rested lightly on her body, almost without touching it. Her body felt free and had she not known she was wearing this attire, she would have been sure she was completely unclad.

There was no wind, and no creature moved in the woods. The light of the full moon filtered down through the canopy of the trees in the grove, but revealed nothing. Colleen felt an immense calm, and closed her eyes, waiting. With her eyes closed, her other senses were heightened, and she began to feel others near her. She was unafraid, certain that Anna would not have placed her in jeopardy.

Now a small breeze caressed her face and moved the gown. The music began. It came from a great distance, faint but persistent, intensifying incrementally. It was the same ancient rhythm she had encountered before, but now there were new aspects to it. The pipes beckoned, and now the drums began. The sounds drew closer and the wind swirled through the grove, calling the branches of the trees and the wisps of the mist to dance. Colleen was swept into the tempo of it, and lost all track of time.

Suddenly, she sensed a presence very close to her. She opened her eyes. In the dim light of the filtered moon, she could see the indistinct form of a man, just inches from her. Although he did not speak, she knew immediately that it was *MacCumhail*. He was so close to her, she could feel the heat and energy radiating from his body. From the corner of her vision, she saw the flicker of a flame. Small flames, like those of candles, dimly illuminated the area, but his face continued to be obscured by the darkness.

CHAPTER 18

▼

She was dumbfounded. He was dressed in a tunic of similar wool to her garment, and his eyes glowed in the minimal light.

This was *MacCumhail.* How could this be?

"I don't understand," she whispered, "Are you...?"

He silenced her by placing a hand on each of her shoulders, that touch so familiar to her. Then he bent his head toward her and kissed her on the mouth. The kiss was light at first, a butterfly touch on her lips, then it grew hot and ravenous, and she responded. The candle flared in concert with their craving, and a desire beyond anything Colleen had ever imagined engulfed them both. The music thundered an ancient cadence, increasing with the throb of their unified heartbeat. As one, they moved to an elevated area in the grove, away from the glow of the candles. He picked her up and laid her on a bower of soft, dry mosses and grass, and stood gazing at her as if seeing her for the first time. Her mass of dark hair spread about her head, pillowing her and framing her face, which was transformed with an inner light.

Colleen had never felt anything like this. Her mind was reeling with the shock of recognizing *MacCumhail.* How could she be here with him? What was expected of her? What should she do now? What was this ceremony?

There was no doubt in her heart about what she wanted to do, but she did not know what she *should* do. With all the men she had ever had, in all her sexual encounters, she had found pleasure, but never such power and heat. She felt desire rise from deep inside her, radiating out to her fingertips and feet, to every part of her. She was being taken over by an ancient memory, perhaps a genetic memory, commanding her, body and soul. She lay still in the softness of nature's embrace, and stared at the shadowed face of this man, this warrior. He had come to her again by night. This time, the purpose was not protection, but something else.

He moved. Kneeling beside her, he reached one hand toward her with a silky, deliberate motion. His long fingers gently touched the tender part of her arm and she was jolted by the contact. One look at this hand astonished her. As the fingers traced along her arm, a tiny trail of sparks left a luminescent track on her skin. A current of electricity coursed through her body and she saw his tracings begin to glow.

Now she was no longer quiescent. Instinct guided her hand to his bare and muscular arm. She outlined the same intricate pattern on his skin, with the same result. There was a design to it, one older than the language, older than the country itself, and both knew it as if it were emblazoned on each of their cells.

They continued to trail the luminescent patterns, moving their hands to every part of each other's body. There was no need for words. The pipes, and drums and the voices (oh, the voices!) would have drowned them out anyway.

Colleen felt her body become lighter. There was no sense of the ground beneath her now, but there was a sensation of floating somewhere above it. *MacCumhail*, too, appeared to levitate from the surface of the earth to a plane next to her. In this state, their bodies were free to move in a way that no ordinary human had known or experienced. Colleen was no longer submissive. She was driven to take control of her part of this mysterious event. The splendid ceremonial garment fell away, drifting to the ground, a wisp in the Irish mist. *MacCumhail*, too, was inexplicably undressed. Their bodies blended in the oldest act of passion. The warrior was engulfed, surrounded completely by the spirit of the peace goddess, as the flames rose as high as the tops of the trees, and the music and voices reached a pounding crescendo.

Her mind was not totally separated from all this. Awe was the only reaction, on both a physical and spiritual plane. She was ablaze with the heat, and yet the deepest part of her mind was cooled by tranquility of it. The fulfillment was exquisite. Her needs and desires were satisfied in a way beyond imagining, and a blanket of serenity and knowledge settled over her. At the same time, the arousal was driving her to a level beyond fantasy. Her sexuality, long lost in that innermost place, was responding, consuming, advancing and retreating toward *MacCumhail* in a dance older than the stones, building toward a pinnacle where Colleen was sure she would break into a thousand glistening pieces and fall back to earth.

Even though *MacCumhail* had been readied for this ceremony with all the care his teachers could give him, he, too, was unprepared for the intensity. Here was the face of this woman he had desired since the first time he had seen her, and he was nearly struck dumb by the beauty of her transformation. He was not a stranger to women, but he had never been so consumed by passion. They flowed together like the water of the stream nearby, a motion so natural and synchronized that it rocked them like leaves in a brook. The joining went on, time was lost, and only heat and light and energy existed between them. At last it reached a zenith so profound that it exploded the night into a million rings of light, spreading outward from them. The banked fire inside Colleen's soul intensified to burst into pyrotechnics. And the voices of the music in the night air continued, chanting the age-old word for fire, "O'hAodha…O'hAodha…O'hAodha."

MacCumhail cried out, the sound thunderous in the night, throwing back his head and giving voice to the freeing of his spirit. Echoing him, from some central place in Colleen, a place so secret and sacred that she did not know it existed, her own cry went out into the night air.

That cry flew on the winds, winged into all the corners of Ireland's green land. It whispered from the rafters of venerable little cottages and row houses, it floated into the shadows of new homes and old, and always, it beckoned the women. Each Irishwoman, old, young, north and south, heard it. The smallest recesses of their ancestral female essence responded.

Peace would be the domain of the women. The ancient goddess societies that had last enjoyed peaceful circumstances summoned, intent on superceding the warrior culture.

The warrior system had wrought changes through the centuries, arising in the wake of the invasions. The men had fought and killed and died themselves. Courage and strength were not lacking. There had been great heroes in Ireland's history, but no progress to peace. Peace became something to be discussed as process but not as a clear event or direction. Like drops of water on stone, the rancor had eroded the serenity of the ancients, and left an abyss that defied the dreams and desires of the mothers, sisters and daughters. But it did not kill those longings.

In the ashes of buried memories, coals ignited again and glowed. The voices and breath of wind from the mountains ignited the flames of peace, and the spirits of the women arose from their beds. Women whose men had died in the persistent troubles, women with husbands and lovers, virginal women, old women and young girls, all placed their feet on their floors and walked out of their dwellings into the pre-dawn darkness.

Colleen came to her senses, alert to everything, in the same way she had been aware immediately following her vision-quest. Specifically, she was aware of the man who was with her in the night. They were dressed again, although she did not know how this had happened. All of this was so far beyond her believing. How had this happened between her and a being she had never seen in the light, barely knew? It was the result of a force beyond her, surely. Even though the darkness hid his features, her steady gaze held *MacCumhail's* eyes, a question hovering in the air between them.

He looked back at her with a force that was almost painful.

"I'm with you now," his voice murmured.

"Did you speak?" she asked from her dreamlike state. "I thought I heard someone calling me."

"You were called," came his voice, now close to her ear. "But not by me."

"There are others?" she asked, rousing from her reverie enough to be curious.

"Yes," he replied, "The time has come to complete the circle."

This statement wakened her senses. Clear-minded now, with anticipation, she wanted to know more.

"What circle?"

"You'll know soon enough," came his stirring voice, his touch guiding her to stand and start walking. A fog had come, and it was thick. She wondered how he could know which direction to go.

The darkness and the mist scrubbed out any detail of him. What she managed to comprehend came from voice and touch and those flashing, feral eyes. Now he was a fraction behind her, conducting her through what seemed to be a labyrinth of trees and huge stones.

It became darker and darker as they navigated this maze.

"Where are you taking me?" she ventured.

"Where they await you," was his reply.

Suddenly the mist parted again, and Colleen gasped. They were standing at the foot of a massive hill. Now *MacCumhail* took the lead, keeping her hand in his, his back obscuring whatever might lie before them. The wind was evident, but not cold. Something about this place and how she felt was curiously reminiscent of her vision quest at the Medicine Wheel.

The narrow path he chose led them around the base of the hill, through the damp grass and along the stony path. When they reached a copse of trees, they stood next to the opening of a cave, partially obscured by ferns and holly. *McCumhail* drew her through the small opening, along a slender access, and into a huge chamber with a lofty ceiling. The stones of the inner part of the cavern were phosphorescent and glowed enough in the dark space to dimly illuminate the "room." The music had preceded them to this place, and now it wove its way among the stones to emit haunting melodies. Colleen was transfixed for a time and when at last she turned to speak to *MacCumhail*, he was no longer with her.

Alone in this space, created by the eternal forces of nature, she still could hear the music. There also was the piping sound of water. It flowed over stones nearby and coursed away into the darkness. The gentle sound triggered memories of her grandmother's spring and of Plenty Coups' spring, and the sea-well Anna had shown her. But there was far more power here.

Suddenly, she could hear *MacCumhail's* voice again.

'Stand quietly," he commanded her. She couldn't be sure she heard him in her ears or in her spirit.

The pale light that had illuminated their arrival here began to fade, leaving this place darker and darker. At the same time, the music diminished so she was not sure she really heard it.

In the deepening shadows, Colleen's extra senses began to kick in. Others were here with her. Some were near, and some were further away, but all were most assuredly in this chamber. The melody was intricate, and older than time. As it expanded, the atmosphere became charged with sound as the light increased again. From all around the room, the shadowy forms of people began to reveal themselves.

Like *MacCumhail's* visage, their faces were not clear at first. Colleen tried to not close her eyes, fearful that she might miss something. Ultimately, she lost the battle and her eyes closed against her will. She fought to open them again, but she felt like someone had dropped a curtain in front of her.

Finally the glow penetrated even the darkest corners, and she struggled to open her eyes. Looking straight across the room, she clearly saw the first figure. It was Anna. The older woman's face was luminous and ageless, and she smiled warmly at Colleen, her blue eyes sparkling.

Brendan was standing next to Anna, and he looked much younger than when Colleen had seen him last. She moved her gaze to the next person, and stopped in total surprise.

'Aunt Willow!" Colleen cried, her voice cascading in soft echoes off the crystalline rocks.

"Don't be too surprised, my dear," her aunt's voice bubbled in tune with the water. "You have come here with good reason, but the time is growing short, and there is much to do. Your doubts and questions have to be suspended. The answers will come."

Colleen could not identify the next two people, but the sixth person was another stunning surprise.

She was speechless for a moment, then the words flew from her mouth. "Black Bird!" she exclaimed as the figure of the holy man came into focus. "I can't believe it! How can you be here?"

The ancient Crow Indian man looked young and strong and vital. His response to her was equally strong, resonating in this chamber. "It is always possible to be where we are needed. My last vision revealed this place to me, and your magpies brought me here along the sky-path."

Then Colleen saw Thomas Sky Horse. "I guess I should not be surprised to see you here, my friend," she smiled ruefully at him. "After all, you have been my guide in earlier times."

Thomas nodded. "Yes, my sister. This is your ultimate journey. My uncle and I have known we would be part of it since your vision quest."

Colleen looked around the room to try to see if *MacCumhail* was there, but he was nowhere in sight. She sensed his presence, but she could not see him.

Now one of the personages she had not recognized spoke. The voice was female, otherworldly, commanding.

"Welcome, Colleen," it said, and she found herself standing straighter, focused on the speaker. The woman who spoke was regal, tall, powerful and elegant. The ancient tones of the voice, echoing up from a long forgotten past, continued. "It is time for you to know why you are here. I am Brigid, the ancient bearer of the goddess spirit. Long before the Firbolg arrived, and long before the Tuatha de Danaan were driven from the surface of our beautiful land, all who lived here were at peace."

"The coming of invaders and warriors robbed us of the ability to live in peace with one another. As they intermingled with us, we were no longer in harmony with the natural things. New religions began to replace our Old Religion, taking over our sacred places and venerated rituals for their own. We would have been willing to live side by side, and practice our beliefs in harmony. But the invaders insisted on conquering through violence and death. Many centuries and lifetimes have passed in this way, but enough people sheltered and nurtured the old beliefs that they did not die out in their purest forms. Now it is time for them to return, in their rightful place to bring peace back to our land."

Colleen found the courage to speak.

"What does all this have to do with me?" she asked.

'You are one of three, and now you are joined with another one of three," replied the other person she did not know. "Your blood carries the ancient fire, the *O'Aodha*. Surely you must feel it burning inside you?"

Colleen nodded slowly, solemnly, her veins confirming it with the same molten flare she had intuitively felt throughout her life. She shivered, remembering how it had burned earlier this night with *MacCumhail.*

Brigid continued speaking. "The passion for peace does not kindle in the same way as the passion for war. The peace fire is more enduring and, in the end, hotter. We have been waiting for the time to be right and for the necessary elements to come together. We needed tribal spiritual leaders like our own to come into concert with our energies. Only someone of your bloodline could do this, and it was necessary to find a time in history when all these could coincide to influence events. For too many years, our old religion has been viewed as dangerous and strange. Your own ancestors were victims of this. The world did not understand that it is a doctrine of harmony—harmony with nature and humanity. We are not anti-Christian, we are not militant."

Here she stopped and smiled an ironic smile. "Although we do have one of our own who operates as a warrior for peace, an odd concept."

Colleen knew Brigid was speaking of *MacCumhail*, and glanced around the room again to try to see him. Still no apparent presence.

"It will take both of you and thousands of others like you to pave the way for the peace to come," Brigid continued, "and you will need to know more. For that reason, we have brought together teachers for you."

"One is Willow, who has been with us all her life, although not with the dedication needed to fill the role given you. Willow is a bit too pagan to devote herself to peace alone," Brigid smiled tolerantly, "and your other teachers are here because we knew you would trust them. The Black Bird and the Sky Horse are both men of tribal integrity, and although they are not of our blood, they are of our beliefs. They have done powerful service in setting your feet on this path. In addition, *MacCumhail* continues to have an important role in helping you complete this circle."

"What..." Colleen started to ask, but Brigid held up her hand.

"All knowledge will come to you as you need it. Let the events flow." Brigid's voice echoed in the great chamber as the light suddenly extinguished itself, and Colleen found herself plunged into darkness.

"Aunt Willow!" she cried out. "Black Bird! Thomas!"

But all was silence, except for the sound of the water making its way.

Colleen stood stock-still, afraid to move in the darkness. Then *MacCumhail's* voice was in her ear, and his hand on her arm. "I am with you. Come."

As he led her out, Colleen spoke to his back. "I still don't understand. I want to see my aunt and Black Bird and Thomas. Was all that back there real, or was it some kind of dream? What is next for me?"

McCumhail's voice was clear, and sounded more like he was next to her than in front of her. "More is to come for you on this journey. You will fulfill an age-old destiny. When you return home, you will feel like you dreamed, but the memory will come back when you are ready. This gathering was to prepare you for what is coming. I will always be nearby, so you can abandon your worry."

He finished this statement as they reached the opening. The darkest part of the night, just before the sun was on the verge of rising, greeted her, and Colleen blinked with surprise. Had so much time passed? How could it be nearly dawn?

Now *MacCumhail's* voice was inside her ear. "I will be near. Rest assured, my splendid one." His hands stroked her shoulders for a moment. "I am always watching over you, even when you do not see me."

Colleen blew out a short breath. "I never actually see you!" she cried out.

Turning quickly, she tried to get one more look at him in the rays of the rising sun. But he was gone, vanished past the protective cover of the hilltop's edge.

CHAPTER 19

▼

Drifting back to the village, the events of the night begin to fade from Colleen's mind. She clutched at the memory, but it slipped away like water held in the hand. The same fading of clarity as that following her Medicine Wheel vision quest occurred. Had this been a vision? Or was it something more real?

By the time the edge of the town presented itself, nearly all had been erased, with just a few reassuring fragments soothing her heart. Once at Maddie's house, she let herself in, and was relieved to find that Maddie was nowhere to be seen. Gratefully, she wandered to her room, closed the door and collapsed onto the bed, exhausted. Deep sleep claimed her, with no interruption from Maddie's usual morning knock.

When she did awake, it was nearly dark. She fumbled to find the small light on the stand next to her bed and switched it on. The small travel alarm said it was nearly 5:30 p.m. Why had she slept through the day? She was bewildered.

Colleen sat up, feeling with her feet for the sheepskin slippers she always kept close to her when she slept. She looked down at her body. Even though she had been asleep on the top of the bed and not under the comforter, she was nude. Her nakedness surprised her, and when she noted that there was no clothing tossed over a chair, she felt displaced and disoriented. Going to the small closet, she pulled out a robe, and put it on. Then she ventured out into the hallway.

The sounds of Maddie emanated from the kitchen, and everything seemed normal in the house. Cautiously, she went toward the warm light and her entrance into the room caused Maddie to turn. The older woman greeted her guest cheerfully. Colleen looked at her intently. Was there something else in her eyes? Did she think it strange for her visitor to sleep the entire day away?

It was unfathomable.

Maddie poured her a cup of tea, and said, "Would you be hungry, lass?"

Colleen thought for a moment. "Maybe just a nice piece of your brown bread and some marmalade?"

Maddie cut the bread in thick slices, and set it in front of her. Then she sat down companionably across the table and looked at Colleen expectantly.

"I feel a little strange," Colleen told her. "I don't know why I slept so long. I had no reason to be so tired."

Maddie leaned back in her chair, and an undefined expression flitted across her face. Was it satisfaction? Had she been waiting for Colleen to appear?

The older woman appeared to weigh her words, then speak. "I thought you must need the sleep. Sometimes our travelers have a delayed reaction to all the changes in time from here to their homes. That must have been it."

Colleen accepted this comment, since she could think of no better explanation. On the other hand, she could not ignore all the sensations running through her. Part of her felt grounded and settled, more than ever in her life. What had been a fire blazing inside her had become a deeply gratifying heat, not a relentless force crying to escape her.

Only fragmented flashes of the previous day's experiences permitted retrieval, but she found herself looking forward to the next regular genealogy session with Andrew. This seemed odd, in light of the edgy relationship the two of them had developed so far. Nothing in her conscious thought accounted for such change in perception of the man and the work she was doing with him.

The Imbolg experience rested too deep in her subconscious for her to understand its impact. Colleen had been oblivious to the events which now dictated most of her actions. She returned to her family tree work with Andrew, meeting with him on a weekly basis as before.

As time went on, their relationship had reached a kind of uneasy truce. They were less businesslike, but there was never an indication of friendship or camaraderie. They were like two partners working on research and nothing else. She supplemented these sessions with a rudimentary social life. Maddie and she would occasionally go to the pubs after dinner. Sometimes Kieran was there, and he was unfailingly attentive to her if he encountered her. Maddie encouraged their friendship, and there were times when Kieran and Colleen stayed on while Maddie went home. Colleen had to admit that she enjoyed the attentions of a man like this. He did not seem to expect anything of her, and he continued to seek her out. He invited her to dinner on a couple of occasions, and she enjoyed their talks. It was a friendly relationship, and Kieran seemed very interested in asking her many questions about her own life. He was fascinated by her child-hood on the Indian reservation, and he was very inquisitive about what she was trying to accomplish in Ballysheen. But he seldom kept her company during the day, stating that his farm took up all his time.

For her, the days flowed by, and her research work consumed her. There was less frustration in the fact that digging through reams of pages had brought no results at all.

Then came a turning point.

On one of their ordinary meeting days, when she entered Andrew's tiny, clut-tered office, she recognized things were different. The marked difference in the way he addressed his remarks to her mystified her. His intensity and the anger seemed to have been replaced with a conciliatory tone. It was a surprise, but she discovered that she also felt a certain warmth toward him that had not been there before. Perhaps it was the result of the growing familiarity between herself and this scholarly, private man. They no longer circled about one another looking for neutral territory.

By contrast, there seemed to be something else, something deeper, that could not be accounted for. Why the altered approach toward her? Everything about Andrew's demeanor now emanated solicitude and a completely unexpected open-ness. When the noon hour came that day, he did not hurry off, but asked her if she'd like a bite of lunch with him. He assured her that he had brought extra food, and suggested it might be a better use of their time to eat in his office. In front of her astonished gaze, he brought out a thermos of tea and two neatly wrapped sandwiches. Picking up a bundle of papers from the desk, he laid out clean white paper in front of each of them, and set out the sandwiches and the tea. Then he fished in anther bag and produced two highly polished apples and some cheese.

His hands as he did this preoccupied her attention. Something about them triggered a distant echo, but it hovered just outside her reach.

He took his seat across from her, and bending his head to his cup, he looked directly across the desk into her eyes, as if he was seeking something specific.

' What are you thinking?" she asked.

' How long it has been since I felt comfortable with a woman."

She hesitated, weighing her words. "I don't want to intrude, but Anna told me about how you lost someone who was very close to you. She said it happened during the Troubles in Derry."

A wrenching impression of vast pain crossed his face, and he dropped his gaze. Colleen reprimanded herself. Had this broken the moment, or betrayed Anna's confidence? Then he looked up again, and she was disconcerted to see that there were tears in his eyes.

"Oh, God, Andrew," she said quickly. "I'm sorry. It is none of my business, and I shouldn't have said that to you."

He slowly shook his head.

"No," he said. "It's time for me to let go of the past. It's time I talked about it. When it happened, I swore I would never trust enough to let anyone get close to me again. It is too dangerous."

Colleen assumed that he was referring to the pain of his loss.

"It's not dangerous to trust," she said. "Everyone needs people to share things with."

Andrew looked away from her, past her. "That's not what I mean," he said. "Although that has been missing from my life all these years, too. No one can understand the rest."

This statement was so definitive that Colleen immediately understood she should not pursue it.

"Is there anything you want to talk about?" she asked gently.

Andrew pushed aside his partially eaten sandwich.

"Let's walk," he commanded. "I can't sit still and talk about this."

Ordinarily, his habit of issuing orders annoyed her, but now it seemed appropriate to rise to her feet and follow him outside. His pacing was like that of a caged animal, and she stretched to keep up with him. They began to walk through the village, matching each other step for step, stride for stride, as if they had walked together all their lives. Colleen was quiet, waiting to hear whatever he might have to say. But words did not come as they put distance between themselves and his office.

Once their silent trek brought them the parameter of the small village and began to take them along country roads, Andrew drew a long, shaky breath.

"What did Anna tell you?" he asked in an even voice.

Colleen was quick to jump to Anna's defense.

"She didn't mean to violate your trust," she assured him. "I had asked her why you were so unapproachable," she smiled ruefully at this confession. "She was trying to help me understand that it was your way, and probably not anything I had done."

Andrew stopped and stared at her with surprise and a measure of dismay. "God, no. It wasn't anything to do with you. It was myself. I've been struggling with the feelings that were stirred up in me from the first time I saw you."

Colleen shook her head in confusion. That certainly did not match her recall of their first encounter at his office. This change in his stated view of her was surprising and even hopeful. The reverse of that was that she would always take a careful approach in relating to him. It was not easy to forget how brusque with her he had been in the past. It probably would be best to err on the side of caution. Under his inquiring eyes, she smiled warmly, without replying.

"There is not a lot more to say," he declared. "This is probably more than I should have said."

Andrew became quiet again, and turned them back toward his office. What had been the purpose of this traveling conversation? Colleen tried to analyze why he had insisted upon walking away from the heritage center, and why he had said so little.

"Is that all you wanted to say?" she asked.

"I don't know," he said earnestly. "I just don't want any personal conversations where I work. I don't know what I feel. I'm not prepared to talk about it, even though I thought perhaps I was. I do want to tell you that I have been hearing in the village that you have been seein' Kieran O'Leary. I don't think that's a good thing."

Colleen was shocked. "I don't think that is any of your business," she declared. "Why would you even say that?"

"I have my reasons." Andrew said flatly. "Just be careful of him."

"He's been nothing but a gentleman," Colleen said coldly. "That subject is closed. Do you understand?"

Andrew was taken aback by the force of her response, and he nodded in acknowledgement. But he didn't give up. "Just be careful," he repeated. They walked back to his office in silence.

Bewildered, Colleen mulled over the conversation. Could Andrew be jealous, somehow? What would possess him and cause him to make such remarks to her? It did not ring true with anything else she knew of him. She decided to keep their future exchanges on a purely business basis.

Their return to the office gave him the opportunity to pass some copies of records to her. He had faithfully conceded to her request that she be allowed to do as much of the research as possible. With the papers in hand, she left to go back to Maddie's where there was more room to work.

She bent to her task that afternoon and evening, plowing through the tiny handwritten script. The document copies Andrew had delivered were very old, and the writing on them was faded and difficult to read. Her eyes screamed for relief by nine o'clock, and she set the work aside, stretching out on her bed. Maddie had gone out, taking her leave immediately after the evening meal. She was joining a Spring Equinox celebration, an old custom, and Colleen had begged off when her older friend invited her. Ordinarily, she would have found such an event exciting, but the day had left her feeling unsettled and tired. As the evening wore on, it was a relief to have the house to herself.

When sleep refused to come to her after a time, she got up to stretch her stiff muscles. Opening the front door of the house she stepped outside into the unusual warmth of the night. Perhaps a short fresh-air stroll would help her fall asleep.

After a time, Colleen looked around her. Her walk had brought her without knowing to the hill where *McCumhail* had left her on the early morning following Imbolg. It was immense, thrusting massive bulk upward to the edge of its black outline in front of the star-strewn sky. Alone in the darkness, she tried to get her bearings. The frigid, damp air of this March night invigorated her and made her feel intensely alive. It was a pleasure to stretch her muscles.

Instinct turned her toward the hill. At her feet, she sensed rather than saw, the beginning of a path that led toward the apex of the hill, and something inside her nudged her feet onto it. Her mind was at peace. The assurance came that she belonged here. She began to climb.

The longer she climbed, the higher the hill seemed. But the task did not tire her. The environs of the night energized her far beyond any previous experience. Again, the latent electricity of *McCumhail's* touch was manifested on her skin. It charged every motion, every step. Her footing was sure, even in the darkness, as she made her way through grasses, low-growing shrubs and over pebbles in the path.

At last the pinnacle of the hill loomed ahead, and she could see more imposing shapes in the waning moonlight. Now she recognized this place from her many exploratory trips. It was an early megalithic cemetery, where a number of passage tombs dominated the top of the rise. She was thoughtful.

The people who had taken their final rest in this place had been of a far earlier time, a time prior to history, a time prior to clans and warrior cultures. They were people who lived when the inhabitants of Ireland were at peace with the world around them. Theirs were lives of nature, of harmony with each other and the environment, of a culture dominated by the female aspects of their society. These passage tombs, like breasts of the earth, seemed now to welcome her arrival and invite her to take sustenance for what was about to come.

The only signs of life in this silent place were her trusted companions, the magpies. They had been awaiting her, perched on the top of the largest tomb, and their presence was marked by the luminescence of their white feathers. They sat still, and made no sound. She took her place near them. She could see nothing, but she had a keen sense of anticipation.

The dawn began to emerge slowly. And with it, sounds began, murmuring at first, the rustling of grasses and leaves in the night air. Now that haunting music started, distant and tantalizing, just beyond hearing. It was mesmerizing, and Colleen stood stock-still, straining to listen.

The light grew slightly. The mist glistened at its edges, and the dew on the grasses flashed with it. And there were more sounds. No voices, but sounds nevertheless. A gentle breeze caressed the hill. It stirred the mist, splitting it into shreds and streamers, swirling it along. With the wind, the mist began to rise. The vapor dissipated, slowly, like a curtain being raised on a stage before a drama too profound for description.

As the last tendrils faded away, the rising sun shot fingers of light across the glimmering hill. The magpies wheeled up from their place and circled high in the sky. Colleen knew this was her destined place, but had no idea what to do. Stepping carefully and reverently to the top of the passage tomb behind her, she seated herself to wait.

Suddenly, she was again attired in the beautiful ceremonial garment, and she was surprised at how warm she was. Circling her drawn-up knees with her arms she rested her head, waiting. For what? She did not know. She only knew it was coming.

Now the sounds could be heard more clearly. The initial impression was that of the breeze blowing through grass. Then the murmuring told her it was something more. Footsteps. On the rock path. She rose to her feet atop the passage tomb in an effort to see where the sound was coming from.

The haze that persisted in the valley below obscured the source of the sound.

Then forms began to issue from the mist and appear at the base of the hill. Colleen could see them. The women. First one or two, then several, then ten, then twenty. Then twenty more, then fifty and then a hundred. They came steadily, climbing the hill, and when the first rays of light broke the horizon and illuminated the top of the hill, there were thousands of them. Colleen could not believe her eyes. Where had all of them come from? Were they really here physically, or was this the manifestation of their spirits? Colleen couldn't be sure, but their presence was no less real to her.

The women.

They came, old women bent with the years; young women, glowing with the lack of them. Catholic, Protestant, mothers, grandmothers, sisters, daughters, converged at the place that had been the resting place their predecessors in the distant shadows of time. They were humming and singing and making their way to surround the place where Colleen stood. A multitude of Irishwomen from everywhere, faces turned toward her, waited expectantly.

Colleen experienced a thrill of terror in her heart. This task is too big for me, she thought. What am I supposed to do now? She felt alarm, but there was no way to make a graceful departure. She closed her eyes, hoping this was dream and if she opened them again, these women would not really be there.

When she opened them, there were even more women. She drew a deep breath, and exhaled slowly, searching her heart for something to say. Then *MacCumhail's* voice inside her ear said, "The words will come when the time is right. Do not be afraid. This is the purpose for your coming here."

She rose to her feet. As she stood, another voice, that of Brigid, stirred in her soul, and then the words came out of her mouth.

"Why have you come?" she called out to the gathering.

"We were called," came the response. "We've come from our sleep."

Then the voice of the ancient came again into Colleen's head.

"What do you want for Ireland?" she called out across the crowd.

With one voice, the women replied, "We want peace."

"Only you can bring peace," Colleen replied for Brigid.

"How can we do that? We are only women," a white-haired grandmother lamented.

"You have the numbers. You have the power. You are more than half the people in Ireland. You must speak with one voice." Brigid's voice issued from Colleen. "If you do, you cannot be denied."

Recognition ran through the gathering like an electric current.

"We vote!" cried one strong female voice.

"We vote! We vote! We vote!" The chant came in wave after wave of excitement and intensity as the women identified their legacy in peace. The blood of the ancient matriarchal societies throbbed in each of them, demanding that they take a hand in changing the fate of their land.

"Our men have been warriors too long!" came a voice from within the crowd.

"Too many centuries," another agreed. "The warring has to stop! We vote!"

Then the voice of one of the older women came gliding through the tumult. "That's not all we can do," she declared. "We can get our men to vote for peace, too!"

The others looked at her with questions in their eyes, then they all nodded in agreement. Several smiled a secret smile, indicating that they understood.

Brigid's smile manifested itself on Colleen's face. The women knew. Nothing more needed to be said. The rising force of the goddess and the land would do the rest. The women stood a little more erect, prouder. They squared their shoulders and turned to leave the hill. Like the centuries of pilgrims to Crough Patrick and other sacred shrines in Ireland, they had completed the pilgrimage, and they walked with purpose. Each had her mission in her heart, and each would do her part when the time came.

As suddenly as they had come, they were gone. Colleen stood alone at the top of the passage tomb, her long hair billowing about her face. She had a sense of the phantasmal. Had the women been here? Or had she imagined the entire night? Was this a dream or another vision? Even the magpies had departed, and it was time for her to descend.

CHAPTER 20

▼

All of Ireland was watching the procedures at Stormont by now. As Colleen traveled the countryside surrounding Ballysheen, it was the number one subject of discussion. In the pubs, talk continued about the peace *process*, but now there was more optimism in conversations. There was an air of expectation that had not been there before. The peace talks had their ups and downs, but there appeared to be some progress. Colleen heard the discussions, and she heard the hope in the Irish voices. When the Good Friday agreement was completed, there was a collective sigh of relief in the Irish winds. The agreement between the British and Irish governments and the political parties in Northern Ireland was created in an attempt to end nearly 30 years of bitter and violent fighting and set a path for peace in Northern Ireland.

It tugged at her heart as she thought about the numbers of people who had died on both sides leading up to this point. She often contemplated what Andrew must have suffered in the loss of his first love, and her knowledge of his tragedy made her even more aware of the hundreds of other people affected by the hostilities.

When she saw Andrew for the first time after the agreement, he was pleased, but cautious about its meaning. "There is yet much to do," he said quietly. "There are many who would have peace fail."

She came to understand what he was saying when the newspapers reported the violent protests over the Drumcree marching ban. She wanted to talk with him about these events, but he was nowhere to be found, and was not available that week for their regular research meeting. When she saw him again, he shrugged off her questions, and suggested they focus more on researching other Irish family connections she might have. He had a huge stack of papers for her, and a list of records for her to check in nearby public offices. She could see it would be enough to keep her busy for weeks.

During the next several weeks, her meetings with Andrew were brief, or they did not occur at all. Sometimes when she showed up, he did not, and he did not let her know when he would not be there. She wondered if he was avoiding her, perhaps feeling embarrassed by revealing his feelings to her. He was much more cordial than he had been in the past, but he continued to keep her at arm's length. Perhaps she should have been more responsive to his statements, but she couldn't be sure of that. Her infatuation with the legendary *McCumhail* grew, although she could not remember any contact with him since the encounter they'd had at the O'hAodha ancestral site.

The next big step in the Irish peace process was the vote to ratify the Peace Agreement. The entire country was abuzz with opinions about whether it would pass. There were discussions in all the stores and all the pubs. The priests called for peace from their pulpits, and the world watched. Colleen wondered how the vote would turn out. An amused smile crossed her face when she remembered one of the conversations she had heard on an outing to the pubs with Maddie. Several men were standing at the bar, and one in particular, was talking about the upcoming vote.

"My Doreen has her mind set on the vote for peace," he was saying. "I don't know what I'm to do."

One of the older widowers fixed a severe gaze on him. "You've a mind of yer own, lad. Vote the way y' want to."

The first man looked a little sheepish. "I think it'll be best if I vote the way she wants. She says if the vote for peace does not pass, it's the last time I'll sleep in her bed."

Colleen's expected that the other men would mock him after this remark, but those she knew to be married only nodded in solemn agreement. She was thoughtful. Was this a unified effort on the part of the women? Could it be that there was a modern-day Lysistrada taking place right here in Ballysheen? With a smile, she turned to Kieran, who was sitting beside her. Her initial glance revealed that he had heard the conversation, too, and he was annoyed by it. When he realized she was looking at him, his expression changed to a neutral one.

"It looked like you didn't agree with him," she said.

"Married men can be so weak sometimes," he said. "Peace isn't going to do anything for us."

"Kieran! I'm surprised to hear you say that!"

He shook his head. "I don't want to talk about it," he said. "Let's talk about something else. Political talk makes for poor conversation."

His tone brought Andrew's warning about him back to her, and she decided that there might be a hot temper lurking under the usually sociable demeanor Kieran ordinarily displayed. After a little more conversation, she excused herself and walked back to Maddie's house.

A few days later, she watched Maddie go off to the polls, and wished her well. After the older woman returned, she and Colleen sat up most of the night, unable to sleep for the anxiety about the outcome of the election.

When morning came, Colleen could not sit still. She threw on her jacket and rushed down to the store to await the morning papers. When they arrived, the deliveryman burst into the store, shouting, "It passed! It passed!" He tossed a paper to Colleen, who placed her money on the counter and opened the paper eagerly. A brilliant smile spread across her face. It had passed. And an interesting fact down in the front-page story caught her eye.

The margin of difference in the vote appeared to have been made up by the women of Ireland. It would not have passed if the women had not voted for peace. Deep inside her, a note of joy sounded and vibrated in her heart. She did not know why that piece of information should mean so much to her, but she found that this was the result she had been expecting. She grinned, wondering how many of the married men had voted in favor of the peace agreement, gathered up the paper, and dashed to Maddie's house with the news. There were others in the store, and she did not notice the dark angry eyes of one who watched her go.

Once in the door of the older woman's house, Colleen caught her hands and danced her around in a circle. She was euphoric. Maddie laughed merrily, and said, "You're not surprised, are ya', darlin'? You shouldn't be."

Something in her tone caught Colleen up short. "What do you mean, Maddie? We stayed up all night waiting because we weren't sure how this would turn out."

Maddie smiled mysteriously. "T'was the women who wanted the peace more than anythin'. You and I both know that. So t'was the women who made it happen."

Something hovered in Colleen's memories, just outside her reach, and Maddie's statement struck a chord. The two of them had not had much conversation about the women of Ireland and the peace process, but it all was so familiar. A small shiver ran up her spine. What was beyond her recall? Why did she feel so connected to these events? If only she could talk with *McCumhail.* But was he even real? She often wondered if she had conjured him up in her imagination.

The night after the news about the election results had spread through the town, she went outside and sat on the steps in front of Maddie's house. People were out in the streets, visiting and laughing, celebrating the result. Even here in the north, this was obviously a turn of events that had been fervently hoped for. She felt satisfied, for the people who lived here, and for the people who lived all over the country. In her American-bred optimism, she believed the election settled it, and that peace would continue, as the cease-fire had. But others did not see it that way, and events were about to make this very clear.

Continuing to sit on the steps long after the people had all gone into their homes, she noted that the sky was hazy overhead. Despite that, she wanted to continue breathing the cool fresh air of the evening. Her pleasure in the outcome of the day was too big to take inside.

Luminescent eyes watched her without her being aware of it, but when the village had quieted, a silhouette disengaged from the other shadows of the night, and moved next to her. Even in the darkness, she knew who it was.

"McCumhail!" She exhaled the name joyfully. "I had begun to wonder if you actually existed!"

"Oh, I'm real, lass," he said, his voice evoking a multitude of emotions. "I couldn't go through *this* without sharin' a part of it with you."

One of his fingers traced the line of her jaw. She shuddered, feeling heat rise in her deepest recesses. He caught his breath, too. How could this man touch her heart in places no one else had ever reached? Her longing to see his face was overwhelming.

"When will you ever let me see you?" she asked.

"You have seen me," he declared.

"Only in the darkness," she responded in frustration. "I want to see you in the light."

"That can't be." The statement was absolute. "It is too dangerous. It is not safe for me to be here with you now. Many things are afoot this night among those who would destroy the peace."

Curious now, Colleen asked, "What do you mean? Doesn't the election settle it all?"

His touch on her face was charged, electrified. "Would that it did, m' love. But it will only make my adversaries more determined. If any of them knew about you, the danger would be upon us both."

Colleen suddenly understood. "Was that who those men were in the woods...the ones you stopped the first time we met?"

"They were."

"But you were aware of them in plenty of time to stop them," she was desperate in her effort to reassure herself.

"They'll see that as an isolated incident. I'm only a single being, and while I have a gift of awareness and strength, I cannot be in all places."

He focused on her with all his intensity. "If anythin' were to happen to you, t'would be the end of me."

Abruptly, his attention shifted. He raised his head as if listening to something in the distance. "It begins!" he hissed, bounding cat-like to his feet, and disappearing into the darkness.

Colleen groaned, feeling like he had been physically ripped from her. She knew his departure meant *McCumhail* was on his way to prevent what violence he could, but she ached with wanting him to stay. Focused on her own pain, she was unaware of a second pair of feral eyes, watching her from the gloom. Drawing a ragged breath, she rose from her place on the steps and entered the cottage. What she did not see was the obscure, lurking figure in the shadowy darkness of the shrubbery by the house. It stayed in place a moment or two more, then crept off into the night.

CHAPTER 21

▼

In the coming days, more news came about the peace process, and its violent opposition. Most Irish people, north and south, continued to hope for real peace. The women were a powerful force, standing for peace at work, in the markets, and in their homes. And many of the men who loved those women and children stood with them.

But some continued to resist in the most brutal ways. For every such event, Colleen heard tales of those instances of violence that had been stopped cold by the mysterious *McCumhail.*

Although he had made her understand that his role was elsewhere, she still longed to see *McCumhail,* or at least wished for some communication with him. Sometimes this line of thought surprised her. This was an inscrutable being, and the ardor she felt toward him was irrational. How could he create so many emotions inside her?

"What's wrong with me?" she wondered. "I've only talked with him on a few occasions, and that's no reason for the desire that wells up in me at the very mention of his name. At this point, I wouldn't be sure he is not a figment of my imagination, except that I hear others tell tales of his exploits."

Perhaps the romance rested in the concept of some sort of superhero, and Irish, at that. It was like a fairytale, and he was an imagined Prince Charming. "I don't even know him," she thought. "If I really knew him, I might not even like him. It's just the mystery and the excitement of it all."

The family history research continued for her, and time passed quickly. While she learned nothing more about these ancestors, more came to light about the status of the country at the time of their departure. Tales of famine conditions and the sheer desperation of the general population at the time drowned her in despair on some days, and buoyed her with inspiration on others. Reading about the hundreds of thousands who starved during the potato blight broke her heart, and stories of those who made it out to opportunities offered by other nations filled her with pride and awe at their courage. Father Callan was stalwart, continuing to provide her with help, delighted to have the diversion from his duties. There was no doubt that he liked this woman. It warmed his heart that she had come from so far away to pour over his church's ancient records. They grew a warm friendship as she grew to love this little man more and more each time she worked with him. In addition to academic help, the feeling that he cared about her as a person became very important. Colleen regarded him as family, in much the same way as Maddie.

July 12, 1998

Then came the first news of an act so dreadful and shocking that it sickened most who heard about it. Three young brothers had been killed in a loyalist gasoline bomb attack in Ballymoney, County Antrim. The boys' mother was Catholic and her live-in boyfriend was Protestant. The horror was so great that people hearing of it could only hope that it would be the last such event. A great public outcry arose against such bloodshed, and the general population was more determined to see the process through to a peaceful result.

The night she and Maddie heard the news, Colleen watched miserably through her own tears as the older woman put her head down on the kitchen table and sobbed inconsolably. Maddie's cries were those of a wounded creature, and they went on endlessly. It was so unfair, Maddie told her. These wee innocents dead, because of some need for posturing on the part of adults who should be better than that.

At last, she lifted her head from the table and looked at Colleen through a sea of tears. "Ah, lass," she moaned. "It is so like when I lost me daughter. That, too, should never have happened. She did nothing to deserve bein' shot."

Colleen stood from her chair and came around the table. Gently putting her arms around the older woman, she comforted her as well as she could. Then she walked with her, almost carrying her, to her bedroom. Maddie collapsed on her bed, continuing to sob. "Leave me alone, now, darlin'," she whimpered. "I'll just cry m'self to sleep."

It hurt to see this sweet woman so wretched, and Colleen knew sleep was the last thing she was ready for. Pacing about the cottage for a while, she finally stepped out into the night air. Taking her usual seat on the steps, she stared at the sky through her tears, and asked the universe a million questions about where the fairness was in all this.

Suddenly, he was there. *McCumhail* stood over her in the dark and placed a hand on her head. Stroking her hair, he murmured to her. "I know, I know," he said "My heart is broken, too. I couldn't get to all of them in time." His voice caught, and she knew he was crying.

"You can't be everywhere," she comforted him.

"I know," he replied. "That's the worst of it. Despite what they say of me, I am only human. Because of this, I must see you one more time, and then no more."

"What do you mean?" Colleen was alarmed. She suddenly could not imagine her world without his touch.

"I must see you at Lughnasadh," he said. "It is a fire ceremony, and you must be there."

"I've heard of Lughnasadh," she mused. Why should such a ceremony have such a strong appeal to her? "Why do you say I must be there??"

"You'll know when the time comes. Prepare for it as you would for the most important revelation in your life. This is why you have come to Eireann."

A chill racked her body. Would this event finally reveal her purpose in being here? How did it connect with *McCumhail*?

As unexpectedly as he had come, he was gone, leaving these questions and many others unanswered. Sighing in frustration, she went back into the house to her room, undressed and slid under the big comforter. But sleep did not come to her that night. As she lay staring at the ceiling, her mind raced back and forth over the words he had said to her in the darkness. If she was preparing for a revelation, what should she do?

Out of the dark recesses of her thoughts, the events leading up to her vision quest came to her with stark clarity. The same should be fitting for Lughnasadh. As dawn arrived, her course was clear. Rising, she showered and dressed, then walked to the kitchen in search of Maddie.

Her host was next to the stove, making a pot of tea. Her appearance looked a little better in the morning light, but her face had aged since the previous night. Through her red-rimmed eyes, she looked at Colleen, and asked her routine morning question.

"What would you be wantin' for breakfast, lass?"

"I won't be eating much for the coming days," Colleen said. Even though it was still 17 days until Lughnasa, she began to mentally fortify herself for the upcoming occasion. She would eat little for the next twelve days, then the last five days would be a total fast, with only water to sustain her. It was a longer fast than she had done for her vision quest, but she knew instinctively that it was to be a much greater event.

She went to the church to talk with Father Callan, and found the little priest gathering some things for what appeared to be a journey. "Father," she said. "Where are you going?"

"Ah, the diocese has called me away," he replied. "They want to talk with some of us in the more rural parishes prior to the 'pagan' holidays like Lughnasadh. Even though the Church has celebrated it as a harvest festival for many years, our rural parishes are viewed with some suspicion, because some of our parishioners hold on to the old beliefs. The diocese wants us to reinforce the Church's teachings, and to work more closely with the people after such festivals. To me, these local celebrations are harmless enough, maybe even necessary, but I must listen to what the leaders have to say, so I'll go. You won't be locked out of me study, though. Andrew has a key, and so does Maddie. Either of them can let you in."

Having had his say, he bade her farewell, shouldered his small bag, and went out the door. Colleen stood for a moment in the soundless sanctuary, and then wandered into the study and opened one of the books she had been working through. The material occupied her for a while, but her attention would not stay focused. When she thought about it carefully, the realization came that every fiber in her being was concentrated on the upcoming fire festival, and she had no idea what to expect. She wished that Andrew were in Ballysheen on this day. He knew so much about these aboriginal Irish events. Even though he did not participate in any of them he could probably explain some of the traditions to her. She looked around Father's study for books on the subject, and did not find anything.

When she realized that she was not concentrating on her work, she leaned back in her chair and stretched. It was nearly evening, and she was amazed that she did not feel hungry. In fact, she felt completely fulfilled and anticipatory. Perhaps Maddie could suggest a source for information on Lughnasadh. She would ask when she got back to the cottage.

The evening was surprisingly warm, and as she walked toward Maddie's, she watched the children playing in the green spaces between houses. Their mothers were probably inside making the evening meal, and some of the men were standing by garden gates, talking and smoking. She was reminded of the little town where she grew up, and she thought about those early days in her life. Even though her own home was on the ranch, she often spent several days in town with childhood friends, and her memories of such peaceful evenings were comforting. She wondered why she had not once felt homesick during this stay in Ireland, and realized that the environment here was so familiar that she always felt at home.

Her thoughts turned to the upcoming Lughnasadh celebration. Why was this an important event? What was it that drew such excitement from the people?

Maddie was waiting for her, teacup on the table, and wonderful aromas coming from the stove.

Once she was seated, she opened the subject.

"Maddie," she said, "Tell me about Lughnasadh. Why is it such an important event?"

The older woman smiled. "Oh, it's a very old celebration, darlin'. We celebrate the harvest, and prepare for the comin' dark months. It's a fire festival."

"So I've been told. What does it involve?"

"You'll learn when I take you there."

The days passed, and finally the first of August arrived. Before leaving the house, Colleen dug into the corner of her suitcase and brought out the medicine bundle. Unrolling the soft deerskin, she examined every object. Gently, she picked up the talisman and turned it over and over, regarding it as it glowed in the palm of her hand. The serpentine twists and turns of the bronze glimmered in the dim light of her room, and she looked at it for a very long time. Then she threaded one of the supple leather strips through it and tied it around her neck. It calmed her inner excitement and made her feel more prepared for whatever might be about to happen. Then she joined the older woman. They stepped onto the path outside the house.

Maddie led Colleen into the woods. After wending their way through the stard of trees, they walked into an opening. Colleen was aware that many people were in the area. They could not be seen clearly, but their presence was palpable, and she could hear the steady rhythm of voices. And there was the music of the trees and wind, as well. Maddie led her to a spot near where the wood was being stacked for the bonfire, and torches here and there lit the area. The mass rose higher and higher as men and boys stacked the logs and branches. Turf was brought, too, and added to the pile. She peered into the darkness, but could not see the faces of those who were building the fire.

A glance at her own body brought the realization and stunned surprise that she was once again attired in the ceremonial garment from Imbolg. How did she change her clothes? She had no memory of doing so, yet here she was. Turning to ask Maddie about this, she found that the older woman had disappeared. In fact, most of the other people faded from view at this point. Then another presence imposed itself upon her consciousness. She could not see him clearly, but her instincts told her...*McCumhail.* Colleen drew in a shaky breath. "Is it really you?" she asked.

Instead of answering, he reached for her hand. The electricity arced between their fingers as they touched, and then shot through their bodies. Colleen's very core was inflamed and ravenous. As she was about to speak, he silenced her by placing his lips on hers. The kiss alone was orgasmic, and signaled that The Joining would be even more intense than it had been the first time.

Now the enormous tower of wood was being ignited by some unseen source. All the torches were extinguished, and only the central pyre was afire. At first the flame was infinitesimal, but it licked at the wood and began to feed. Colleen's soul was filling swiftly with all the sensations besieging her.

The music grew tumultuous and resounding, and began to invade every pore. The infant flame became a fire, then exploded into an inferno. The scent of wood and turf smoke pervaded her senses. The light from the pyre intensified, from glow as pale as that of the moon to a brilliance that impaled the darkness in all corners. It happened suddenly, lighting the grove completely. She came to her senses. If she was ever going to be able to see what *MacCumhail's* face looked like, this was the time. Colleen turned her head quickly. The fire gleamed brighter yet. What she saw defied comprehension for a moment, and then she gasped the name.

"Andrew!"

His hair shone, the brilliance dancing off the silver threads that had become so familiar to her in their research meetings. It really was him. How could she have not seen this? But the two seemed so separate, so different from one another. Could she reconcile this?

As for Andrew, all the shreds of grief for his lost first love, so long a part of him, fell away as his clothing had, and he felt only devotion and yearning for this woman who surrounded him. There was an immense feeling of relief that the deception was over, but it was tempered by fear for what this could mean to the two of them.

He spoke in the cadence of an ancient chant. It was *MacCumhail's* voice, not Andrew's.

"This is the joining of goddess and warrior.
We shall always be one,
Each fighting in our way,
But for one cause...
Peace for Mother Eire."

Finishing, he bent to her and placed his lips on hers in a sensual, deep kiss that touched all her pent up desires.

The memory of Imbolg returned, as did complete recall of her other visions. Now, Colleen knew, they would not slip away from her again. The power of the joining was pervasive. Instinctively, she knew it was happening in hundreds of other locations in Ireland. The seeds for this magic had been preserved in the vast Irish out-migrations throughout history.

Simultaneously, they reached out to one another. Their touch ignited a centuries-old obsession that sealed their fate. *MacCumhaill*/Andrew placed his hands on her body, seemingly touching her in a hundred places at once. Power surged through them, illuminating their minds and their desires with sparks of recognition and fervor.

Again, their clothing drifted away from them, and a tornado of sensations assailed them. Colleen marveled at the knowledge that her embrace enfolded two men in one. *MacCumhaill*/Andrew rejoiced at shedding his pain and loneliness. Both of them were elevated to a level of arousal they had never dreamed possible. The sheltering arboretum of native forest enclosed their passion with cool green drapery, and leaves and mosses spread a soft bed beneath them. The intensity of their joining melded them, body and spirit. *MacCumhail* felt himself surrounded by the hot velvet of her, and Colleen's ecstasy rose level by level until she was sure it would immolate her. Yet there was no stopping. The act of combining their bodies was a force of nature, beyond their control and above the laws of man. The countryside reverberated with the merged cries of their souls while all those gathered for Lughnasa were struck silent with the wonder of it. The act itself was invisible to the other celebrants, save three sets of eyes. Far above their canopied place, in a sacred triangle arrangement, the three magpies kept watch with brilliant black eyes.

"Three for a wedding…"

The night had that odd quality of seeming to go on forever while passing in an instant. When the darkness was about to be invaded by the light of the sun, and the embers of the fire were all that remained, they both knew it was time to go. Neither wanted to separate, even for a short time. Each understood that they were changed forever, and that they were eternally tied together as one.

Finally, Andrew released her. "Now we must be even more careful. I will not return to Ballysheen. What the enemies of peace have planned is not known, but time grows shorter for them, making them more desperate. I will be needed more often in more places, and it will be best if I do not appear so often in the daylight."

"What will I do without you?" Colleen was devastated.

"Remember this night. It must sustain us both."

With a regretful look, he turned to go.

"Andrew! Wait! You must take this to keep you safe!" Colleen untied the leather strip from around her neck and removed the talisman. In trembling hands, she held it out to him.

Taking it carefully from her hand, he stared at it with reverence.

"I've heard of this all my life, but I never thought it was real. I never believed I'd ever be seeing it. It's the key," he stated. "A part of the Goddess's path to peace. It will always be with me. Nothing will ever take it from me as long as I live. Thank you."

Astonished, Colleen asked, "You know this talisman?"

"I have seen many references to it in my studies. It has three sides, symbolizing the warrior, the goddess, and the woman who creates the perfect triune. No one of these entities is strong enough to make peace happen. The three must be joined and their forces woven together to bring peace home to Mother Eire."

Colleen was dazed by this revelation. "It was in my father's medicine bundle. He must have received it from his mother, and she from her mother. It must have crossed the ocean with Margaret."

"Perhaps. The important thing is that it is home now. Nothing will take it from me, no matter what happens."

"I pray that is so," Colleen mused. "It feels right for you to have it now."

Taking her face in his hands, he kissed her one last time, long and profoundly. She could feel the heat of the metal in the hand that held the amulet against her skin, and when he released her, she could feel the pattern the talisman had traced. They parted and went their separate ways, each taking part of the other with them.

CHAPTER 22

▼

September 1998

It was a small sound, but it threw all Colleen's senses into full alert. Lying dead still, she was silent, with ears tuned and eyes staring into the shadows. When the sound came again, she focused on the direction of its source. It was the sound of someone stealthily turning the knob on her bedroom door, then easing it open. Trying to see who was entering, she stared hard, but to no avail. It was not Maddie; the woman never entered her room. *MacCumhail* would have appeared in perfect silence. Besides, he had told her he would not be coming to her. Her extraordinarily acute hearing detected furtive footfalls creeping toward her.

When the intruder was almost upon her, she tensed, summoning everything she could remember from her self-defense training. The invader clamped a hand over her mouth, and instinct drove her response. She bit down hard. He grunted and recoiled enough for her to twist away and clamber toward the far side of her bed, throwing the blanket back over her attacker. A muttered curse escaped from him as he pawed away the impediment and lunged across the bed at her. She stepped to one side, trying to get to the door, but he caught one of her arms in a vice-tight grip, torturing it into a painful position behind her back. In an effort to throw him off center, she moved toward him instead of pulling away, and kicked savagely with her bare foot. A grunt told her she had hurt him, but it wasn't enough.

"Bitch!" he growled, not letting up on his crushing grip. "I'll be breakin' your arm if you keep this up."

Why did this voice sound so familiar? The threats did not deter her resistance. She brought her knee up hard, aiming for his crotch. The breath whooshed out of him, and he struck a glancing blow on her jaw. A burst of cascading lights danced before her eyes, but she refused to lose consciousness. With all his strength, he swept her against the bookshelf like a sack of grain, and even though one of her hands was still free, she could not find a suitable defensive weapon.

Her thoughts came with intense clarity. "I can't let myself be afraid," she told herself. "*MacCumhail* would sense my fear and come here."

The knowledge that his instinct to intervene would place him in mortal danger chilled her. It was her duty to deal with this threat herself. She could defend herself. Her body had never been stronger or more fit. What was available in the room to bolster her defenses? Her free hand continued to search along the shelf behind her. Then she touched a cold, hard item. It was a stone bookend. Grasping it, she swung it hard in the direction of her tormentor. His evasive dodge destroyed her equilibrium, causing her to lose her grip on the bookend as she lost her footing. It thudded to the floor, carrying her hope with it.

His big rough hand grappled with her free arm and he jerked her toward him. In the dark, the rancid odor of his whiskeyed breath washed over her as she heard his deadly calm voice.

"Ye'd best quit fightin' bitch. I'll be tellin' my partner to finish off the old woman."

Colleen's thoughts recoiled. Did they have Maddie? Was it a bluff? She couldn't chance it. She stopped struggling.

The foul voice of her attacker settled over her. "There's a good lass. Now come along quietly, or I'll be glad to lay me fist along your face again."

In a subdued voice, Colleen asked, "What do you want with me? I'm just a tourist."

Her captor snorted. "No friend of the Night Visitor is a tourist," he said.

Suddenly, she understood completely. This wasn't about her. It was about *McCumhail*.

"What does kidnapping me have to do with...what name did you use...the Night Visitor?"

He jerked her arm hard, and spat at her. "You know who I'm talkin' about. We've seen him with you. He comes to you in the night, too, just like he interferes with us in the night. If he knows we have you, he'll come to us...on our terms."

So that was it. She was to be bait for *McCumhail*. What would bring him to her? How would he even know she was held captive? It would be the threads of her fear that would sound the alarm. She smiled, reasoning. If she could keep from being afraid, he would not be aware of her situation, and he would not come. If he did not come, he would not be in jeopardy.

Allowing herself to be led from the house, she looked around and realized that her captor had entered the house alone, and that Maddie was not in danger. Inwardly she cursed, knowing she would have risked more if she had been sure of this.

Once he had her outside, her oppressor moved swiftly to tie her hands. The wet grass chilled her bare feet, and she gritted her teeth as he wrapped the rope around her wrists, jerking it until her hands felt like they were welded together. His next moves wound a blindfold around her eyes, and jammed a dirty gag into her mouth. Dragging her over the stones of the road, he shoved her roughly into the back seat of some kind of car, and drove off into the night.

Colleen lay still on the floor of the vehicle, trying to marshal her thoughts. Staying calm was the utmost goal. It was logical to believe that these people (or was it just this one person?) would not harm her too much. She was too important to their strategy.

After what seemed a short ride, the car skidded to a crunching stop in a graveled area. The man heaved himself out of the driver's side, came around to her door, and half-dragged, half-carried her from the car. Dumping her onto a surface that seemed to be a floor with musty-smelling old blankets on it, he slammed a door behind them and pulled off her blindfold and gag. There was a single, bare lightbulb in the room, and now his face was visible. It was scarred, several days' growth of beard shadowed it, and a mean light shone in his eyes. He leered at her.

"It's here you are, and here you'll stay until he comes for you," he sneered.

"No one will come for me," she replied. "Everyone I know is used to me wandering off for several days, sometimes weeks, at a time. So this is a worthless move on your part."

"We'll see about that," her tormentor laughed nastily. "He rescued you from us once, and he'll come again."

There was no question about it. This was one of the men who had attacked her car on her way to Ballysheen. No wonder the voice sounded so familiar.

"Where's your friend?" she asked.

"He's busy. I knew I wouldn't need him this time."

The man reached into his pocket and pulled out a pint of cheap whiskey. He took a long pull and swaggered from the room, slamming the door as he exited. Colleen's heart sank when she heard the sound of a key turning in the lock of the battered, filthy door. With him out of the room, she looked around. The room was dingy, dirty, and windowless. She suspected that it must be the back room of some kind of storage place, rather than a room in a house. How far had they come from Ballysheen? Or were they still in the little town? The ride had not been far, but it had been far enough to be away from the village. It appeared this room had been used for hiding purposes, or perhaps to hold another prisoner at another time. The blankets were strewn about the floor, and there was a bucket in the corner that reeked of unspeakable things.

Her arms were screaming from the agony of being bound behind her back. She shifted her mind to another plane in order to sidetrack the discomfort. Not knowing what *McCumhail* could sense, she didn't want her pain to sound the same alarm that her fear might have.

Her mind rolled back to the fire festival. All the sensations from that ceremony cascaded over her, and put her at peace with her body. The memory of the pleasure and the power of their joining transported her to a level beyond her immediate pain.

There was no way of knowing how much time had passed. The light bulb remained on, and since there were no windows in the room, she could only occupy her thoughts with images that kept her from worrying, acknowledging her pain, or being afraid. In her younger days, there had been occasion to learn a little about yoga and meditation. Now her memory reached back for these techniques. She hummed quietly to herself, and sat very still on the filthy blankets. Sleep eventually began to descend upon her, and that concerned her even more. Letting a little of the discomfort keep sleep at bay, she concentrated on the details of the room.

Sleep was not an acceptable escape. It would place her mind into a state that she could not control. What would her subconscious do then? If asleep, would her mind seek *McCumhail's* on another plane and bring him to her? It was a risk she could not afford to take. Allowing her consciousness to roam back to the Indian lands of her youth, she permitted her spirit to experience all the feelings of that place. Thoughts about her parents, the ranch, her Indian friends, and, of course, the magpies, paraded through her soul. The sweeping prairies imposed their images. Spring's greenery and wildflowers blazed in her recall, replete with cactus blossoms, shooting stars and bluebells. The call of the hawks overhead echoed in her ears. Peaceful days with her childhood friends glided through her. It had all been so long ago. Would she ever see those places again? Would she ever see her brother and sister again? How much time could go by before someone realized that she was missing?

No. She had to turn her mind from such thoughts. Any worries, pain, fear could trigger his awareness.

The door slammed open, and her captor stood before her again. He leered at her with an ugly, low chuckle. Then he thrust a greasy paper bag toward her, disregarding the fact that her hands were bound.

"Here's your food," he laughed derisively. "and y'd do well to be eatin' it. We're goin' to be here a while, you and me, so y' might as well accept it."

Colleen marveled at how calm she felt, despite his implied threat. Even if he moved to do her harm, or worse, if he molested her in any way, she knew she would be able to accept it. Such serenity would be the only way to protect *McCumhail.* Her mind swirled with possibilities. Intense concentration might help her find a way to escape. Just letting her mind begin to work on possible solutions made her feel better. It appeared that there was only a single captor. Surely there must be a way to get past this one man.

He dragged his flask out of his pocket and took another long pull from it, wiping his mouth with a crusty sleeve. Then he peered at her with red-rimmed eyes and ran his tongue over his lips. She felt like a lamb under the shrewd eye of a coyote.

"Y' know, lass," he hissed, "we could be havin' ourselves some fun while we wait."

Humoring him seemed to be the current method for survival. "What kind of fun do you have in mind?" Her voice was level and non-threatening.

"Don't pretend to be so innocent with me," he sneered. "I know what ye've been doin' with the Night Visitor. Y' could give me a little of the same."

"First of all, I really don't know who you mean when you say the Night Visitor," Colleen replied, "and second, I haven't been doing anything with anyone. I travel alone, work alone and sleep alone."

"No woman who looks like you does any of those alone," he laughed, a low creepy chuckle coming from deep down in his chest. "And if y' do, then y' need a man to show you what yer missin."

Colleen didn't like the direction this conversation was taking, and she didn't like the fact the man was drinking so much. It made his behavior hard to predict. She could hope that he would drink enough to cloud his reflexes, but experience told her a man this size could take in a sizable portion of liquor before losing control. At this point, it appeared he had drunk just enough to make him mean, but not enough to make him careless.

Suddenly, the man cocked his head. Colleen thought she heard the sound of a car arriving outside this building.

"I'll be back to ye later," he spat the words along with a stream of saliva onto the floor. Turning on his heel, he moved quickly out the door of this room, and closed it solidly behind him. The key turned in the lock.

Colleen got herself painfully to her feet and edged toward the door. Putting her ear to it, she listened intently. There were voices on the other side. The man who had brought her here was talking with another man, and she could make out snatches of their conversation.

"Has he come yet?" the new voice asked. She recognized it as her other would-be kidnapper from her journey to Ballysheen.

"He has not," replied her tormentor. "I wish he would, though. The woman's trouble. I don't like taking an American."

"Ye said he'd be comin' if we had her."

"He will."

"When? It must happen soon. He must know by now."

"Give it more time, lad. Here, have a drink."

The talking ceased, and she could only assume they were both drinking. The silence continued for a time, then the conversation resumed.

"Everything else is ready," the voice of the new arrival said. "The peace mongers are goin' to know their cause is without hope when we are done."

"Did ye get the bomb ready?"

"Aye. And it's a big one, too."

"It has to be. It's the only way to make 'em understand."

Colleen felt a cold shiver run down her spine. These men were not just petty thieves or kidnappers. They were terrorists who intended to do major damage somewhere, without regard for human life. She felt sure they would not be like the traditional lads who called in warnings before setting off a blast. These men intended to kill with their bomb.

She continued to listen.

"We've already set the place, the other lads and I. It's a big enough market and the middle of the day will make the explosion effective."

Now Colleen was afraid. She had not been frightened for herself, and it had been her belief that she would be able to survive this episode on her own. But these men were more evil than she had imagined, and they were apparently only part of something bigger. Despite all effort at control, her fear grew and flung itself onto the winds. It seeped under the door of her imprisonment, flowed across the floor of the room where her captors sat drinking, and escaped into the dawning day.

Once free, this emotion took to the air, soared through the trees,rushing on its way. It sought its recipient and found him in the forests where he lived.

McCumhail paused in his tracks. The woods around him suddenly became still and silent. The birds ceased their singing, the wind stopped blowing, the calm was like that before a storm. He sniffed the air, every sense alive.

Something was terribly wrong. Alarm filled his heart. It was Colleen! She was in danger, she was some distance away from where he was, and she was afraid. He could not guess the source of her peril, but only knew that he had to be where she was. He was consumed by the same sense of dread he had felt in Derry when his first love had been killed. This would be his chance to be there on time. He eased into a graceful, swift and silent run, like that of a wild animal. His movements were so akin to nature that the ordinary person would not detect them. He did not pause to consider the possibility that he could be moving toward a trap. He only knew that this woman, the other half of him, needed his help.

It was early in the day, giving him the freedom to seek concealment in the shadows of the less-traveled roads and tracks. On he sped, and as he went, the sense of her grew stronger. All his instincts tuned to her essence, and honed in on her location. His feet found a little-used road in the countryside, although his sharp sight noted that two vehicles had passed over it in recent hours. The grasses that had found a foothold here were crushed and broken, the dew knocked from them in the passage of tires.

The road itself looked like a farm-track, and that turned out to be what it was. It wound between heavy growth of gorse and bramble on each side, and eventually emerged near some farm buildings. One of the structures was an ancient stone house, its corrugated metal roof rusted and bent, weathered doors long since stripped of their paint, and whitewash completely gone. Two older model cars sat in front of it. One was only a little better than the other, but both showed signs of neglect and abuse. The better car was the newer of the two, and although nearly every panel had a dent or a nick, it was in perfect condition compared to the mud-laden, corroded wreckage that composed the second. He recognized the worst one. It was the one he had seen in the woods the night he had rescued Colleen from the highwaymen who stopped her on the way to Ballysheen. He slowed his pace, considering the best strategy for extracting her from this situation.

Walking silently on fox feet, he circled around toward the back of the building like a wolf on the prowl. The far side of the house had a lean-to stone building, attached to the main structure. That addition seemed to emit the strongest signals of Colleen's presence, but it was windowless, doorless, and without any access he could see. Then he looked up at the metal roof. It was old, rotting, and appeared to be poorly attached. He moved up the stone wall effortlessly, and reached up to test the metal. It was as loose as it looked. Lifting up a corner of it, he peered down into the room. Colleen was huddled against the wall, eyes closed, humming to herself. If she didn't hear him, maybe her tormentors wouldn't either.

He pried the roofing up a bit more, and dropped without a sound into the room. She sensed his presence, and opened her eyes. When her vision revealed that it was him, her eyes filled with tears. Her worst fears and fondest hopes were fulfilled at the sight of him. But her desperate wish was not to place him in danger, and now here he was, in virtually the same situation as she was in.

Swiftly he removed her bonds. She flung her aching arms around him, and he held her trembling body for a moment. Gathering herself and taking strength from him, she regained control. When she stepped back, he could see that her resolve was back. Stepping away, he took the light bulb from its socket, plunging the room into total darkness.

Colleen placed herself by the door. Without exchanging words, she knew what she should do. Putting her mouth close to the edge of it, she called out.

"Please let me out. I'll do whatever you want."

Snide laughter came from both men in the next room. "Maybe both of us'll want it," slurred one of the voices, heavy with liquor and bullish gloating.

"I can handle both of you," Colleen baited them.

"Let's just find out about that!"

The key turned in the lock, and the door swing open. The two thugs were looking into the blackness of the room. Why was it dark? How could this woman extinguish the light with her hands tied? Drunk and stupid, they both charged into the tiny cell, only to hear the door slam behind them.

McCumhail hit the biggest one first, then grabbed him by his ragged sweater and slammed him into the wall. When the smaller of the two attempted to come to the aid of his partner, Colleen swing the detestable sewage bucket at the level of his head. Her aim, guided by the sound of his gasping rage, was dead-on. The bucket connected with his skull and brought unconsciousness only a flash before the contents of the bucket poured out and coated the man with a despicable layer. *McCumhail* was a dervish, raining blows upon the lurching leader of the pair in payment for all the pent-up hurt and sorrow he had carried since Derry. The huge man crumpled to his knees, then to the floor, but *McCumhail* did not stop striking him. Colleen jerked open the door to the outer room, and in the light that flooded in, she saw that such blows were no longer necessary. A gasp escaped her when she recognized the second of the two men. Kieran! No wonder he had been so curious about her. The thought that she had allowed him to be so close sickened her.

"Stop!" she pleaded. "Oh God, please stop. Don't become like them!"

He did not seem to hear her, and kept pounding the big man.

She drew a deep breath. "Andrew!" she cried.

The effect of that one word was electric.

McCumhail reacted as if someone had poured ice-cold water on him. He stood, the fury flowing out of him, to be replaced by the relief that he had found her safe, and that she had stopped him before he killed the man.

When she spoke again, her voice was urgent. "I am so sorry you came here."

Puzzled, he turned to her with an inquiring look.

"They used me to throw you off something far worse," she spoke quickly. "They are part of a group that plans a bombing somewhere. I heard them talking about it."

"Did they say where?" *McCumhail's* face was fearful.

"No. They did mention that it was a big market day, and that there would be many people in that place!"

His eyes bored into hers. "I think I know where. I can get there. Take one of these cars and get yourself back as far as you can toward Ballysheen, then drop it off. Go to Maddie's. I'll come to you there."

He kissed her, then turned her away from him.

"Andrew, please let me come with you," she begged.

"No." His voice behind her was gentle, but unyielding. "If I am to win, I have to go alone. Please go back." He gave her a small push.

She turned, only to find him gone. A cold foreboding settled over her. Going over to the cars, she lifted the hood of the older one, and jerked loose one of the sparkplug wires. She threw it as far as she could, then went to the newer car. Dangling from the ignition, the keys waited for her. She got in, started the engine and drove back down the track to the main road. Trying to keep her mind from imagining what could happen to McCumhail, she drove until signposts gave her directions and mileage to Ballysheen. She had been right. The distance she had been transported had not been far.

CHAPTER 23

▼

Colleen barely had time to catch her breath when the news came. It traveled through the village like smoke on the wind. Colleen could feel her skin prickle with it before Maddie flung the door open and stumbled in, blinded by the tears that streamed down her usually cheerful face.

"Maddie! What's wrong?"

"It's terrible, so terrible," the older woman whispered between shuddering gasps. "The peace is over. They've bombed Omagh!"

Colleen's heart froze. She was suddenly cold to her core. No words would come from her throat. Maddie looked helplessly at her stricken face, then fled from her, unable to contain her own emotions.

At that, Colleen came to life. She raced to her room, scrabbled for her car keys and leaped out the door to get to her car. The door latch caused her to fumble for a moment, then she jerked it open, threw herself into the driver's seat and shot down the steep mountain road out of the village.

The trip to Omagh seemed to take an eternity, but it never occurred to her that she should not be going there. This must have been where *MacCumhail* had sped off to. Was it because of her that he had not been able to prevent such a disaster? Was this what he had meant about not letting terrorists know about his personal life? She had never felt so desperate.

When Omagh's edge appeared, she could see that smoke and dust was still rising from one part of the town. People were milling around, emergency crews were digging through the rubble. Instead of a state of panic, the scene was haunting. Women and men alike were standing in shock, some crying, some staring blankly. There was a haze of dust in the air, and rubble was scattered chaotically everywhere. Colleen abandoned her car at the edge of the town and made her way to the scene on foot. She wandered along, stunned, unnoticed by anyone. Everyone else was as fixated on the tragic scene as she was. Some of the injured had already been transported, others were being helped, but the unforgettable thing was the sight of the still bodies lying where they had fallen, some large, some small, some covered by clothing, some by blankets the emergency workers had brought along, some not covered at all.

She approached what must have been ground zero of the blast. There was a profusion of blood stains and fragments of glass and brick and concrete. Suddenly, her eyes were drawn to something metallic glittering in the rubble and grit at her feet. All the light went out of her life when she recognized it.

Bending down, she picked it up. In her trembling hand, almost burning her skin, was the talisman. In her ears, she could still hear *MacCumhail's* voice, telling her that he would never let it leave his possession. She looked around frantically. Was his body here? Was he just injured? But all that seemed to be here was the twisted wreckage that the heart of such a blast exhibits. Anyone standing here would have been vaporized. Her legs ceased to hold her. She crumpled where she stood. One of the paramedics came to her side where she sat on the ground.

"Are y' all right, miss?"

Realizing he thought she was one of the injured, she managed to nod.

"I'm all right. Please go help those who need you!"

Regaining her feet, she stumbled back in the direction of the car. As she shuffled along, denial kicked in and she began to bargain with the facts. *MacCumhail's* instincts were too good. Nothing could have happened to him. She would just wait to hear from him. But she could not shake the fact that she now had no sense of him, no awareness of his life force.

Her only course of action was to go to see Anna and Brendan. Their calm would help reassure her. The drive was slowed by the traffic that was shuttling back and forth to Omagh, but she needed the time to calm herself, anyway. She was hardly aware of the countryside as it flowed past her windows. When she entered Bureen, it seemed abandoned. No one was on the street, and the pub had no cars in front of it. She tried the door, but it was locked. There was no sign of occupancy.

Where were they? In frustration, she slapped the door with the flat of her hand and searched the street again for signs of activity. The town looked back at her silently with blank windows.

The cottage!

As if they had a will of their own, her feet raced up the path into the forest. The track seemed to resist, roots tripping her, stones impeding her progress. A misstep in her headlong charge staggered her, making her choose her steps more carefully. At last, she flung herself into the small clearing in front of the cottage.

The door was open.

Colleen approached, hope rising in her heart. Was he here?

But entering the cottage dashed all such dreams. Anna and Brendan were sitting silently on the spare wood chairs. Both had desperate faces turned toward the door at the sound of her arrival, and at the sight of her, Anna began to keen.

The sound of it broke Colleen's heart. It told her more than any words might have. She threw herself into the arms of the older woman, tearing sobs shredding her soul. After they wept like this for what seemed an eternity, she sat at the feet of these two older people who had loved Andrew/*MacCumhail* for his entire life. All three were silent. Finally Colleen spoke.

"Is everything lost?"

Anna's abject gaze regarded her. She slowly shook her head.

"No, child. The people have had a taste of what peace can be. They will never be content to do without it again. The people will continue to demand it. But for us, we are in dispair. Andrew was the light of our lives, our dream for the future. To lose him this way…" her voice trailed off.

Colleen was devastated. She felt compelled to ask the next question. Fearing the answer, she whispered, "Was he lost because of me?" The idea that she had been friendly with one of his enemies haunted her and ate at her soul.

Brendan shook his head slowly. "His enemies would have kept on until they found him," he sighed. "They only used you to lure him into their trap."

He paused, looking at her stricken face. "You made him happy," he assured her. "It was the first time we ever saw him happy."

Colleen stayed with them until nightfall while they grieved together. She cried until she felt there could never be another tear. The essence of her life was taken from her, leaving her hollow. Finally, she rose from her place at their feet. Hugging each of them in turn, she took her leave. The walk down the pathway had an air of finality for her. She knew what she had to do.

Her return to Ballysheen gave her time to try to sort her jumbled thoughts. All reason for her to remain in Ireland was gone. There was no vision for her here in the future. There was no question in her mind that she had to leave.

Parking in front of Maddie's house, she entered. There was no sign of Maddie, and Colleen was relieved. Facing her older friend would have been too painful. Maddie did not know that Andrew and *McCumhail* were one and the same, and she did not suspect that this could be the man who tried to save her daughter on Bloody Sunday.

Why bring such pain to someone who had been so kind to her? Sinking into the parlor chair, Colleen let her mind sift through the events of the day.

The hours crawled by, but at last the day dawned. The gray wetness of it smothered her and permitted her thoughts to descend into the horror of what Andrew's last moments must have been like. She remembered reading news accounts about the people who were vaporized in the force of explosions like this one. She hoped he had felt nothing, and refused to think he might have been aware of physical pain. Had he realized that he had not been able to avert this tragedy? Did he regret knowing her at that moment, since that association had prevented him from getting to Omagh in time?

There was one more thing she knew she had to do for Andrew. As the light grew stronger, she dragged herself from the chair, pulled on her rain jacket, and stepped out the door. The sodden walk through the rain was mechanical, dulling her awareness of what might have been going on around her. She moved deliberately toward the ancestral grounds of the O'hAodha, the wet grass soaking her boots and the legs of her trousers. Her feet carried her by memory, and she climbed the track with no missteps. At the foot of the ravine, she stared hard into the stream, hoping for a glimpse of the salmon to give her hope, but the bleak light revealed nothing. The water was opaque and the dripping trees and rocks wept their own tears on her uncovered head. The saturated countryside reflected her wretched state.

Shoulders drooping, she plodded on up the path. When she reached the ancient tomb, she stood for a long time just looking at it. Memories of the past months churned turbulently in her head until the empty void within her soul was filled again with tears. Those tears overflowed and spilled down her cheeks for what felt like an eternity. The weeping was for the loss of the hope and joy she had felt with Andrew. She shed tears for the fire he had stirred in her psyche and in her body. Finally, from the depths of her ruined spirit, the age-old *caoin*, the mourning cry, clawed up her throat and out into the thick, wet air. It seemed to go on forever, ripping her larynx and tearing the atmosphere. Then she was silent and devoid of coherent thought.

Fumbling in her pocket, Colleen's fingers wrapped around the battered and burned talisman. The explosion had blackened some of the metal, and dulled the rest. It was cold in her grasp, the heat gone out of it. She fingered it, turning it over and over again in her hands, soot staining her fingers. A precious thing, the memory of what it looked like was carved into her mind. There was no need to have it in her physical possession. At last, with a deep, shuddering sigh, she placed it in the shelter of the portal tomb, and covered it with a large flat stone. It was a fitting tribute to a hero and to her lover. Her father would have wanted it left in this place. Then she stood up, squared her shoulders and turned resolutely to make her way back.

The rain cooled her sorrowful face, and strengthened her resolve. It was time to leave Ireland now. There was no further purpose to her visit here. But in her heart, she still had questions.

Had she been merely part of a pattern in the cycle to set the women on the path to influencing peace? Had her presence been even a small element of the cycle that had held the peace on this island in ancient times?

"The women of Ireland know what is needed," she thought. "They don't need me now, and maybe they really never needed me at all."

Now she heard her father's voice in her ear. "You were important in the cycle, my daughter. Through you, and others like you, those who had to leave Ireland over the centuries were represented. You have made a mark."

As she left the forest, she stopped suddenly. Perched high and regal on the branch of a leafless tree was a single magpie. Just one, alone, and looking at her intensely.

"*One for sorrow…*" she thought, and walked back down to the village, accompanied by the drizzle.

CHAPTER 24

▼

Mechanically, Colleen boarded the plane for the afternoon Aer Lingus flight to Chicago. The past few hours of packing, driving, and ticketing were a blur in her mind. It was amazing that she had arrived safely, since she had wept for the entire drive. The day was dreary and gray, darkly shrouded in mist and rain, visible from the windows of the waiting area. A number of other travelers had looked at her curiously as she sat pale and red-eyed, passing the time until the flight was called. Now she dropped heavily into her seat, relieved to find that the plane was not full, and the place next to her was not occupied. The last thing she wanted was to share the next eight hours with a total stranger sitting shoulder to shoulder with her.

Having now ceased activity, she could no longer avoid contemplating some of her emotions.

"So this is what a broken heart feels like. What a simple phrase to sum up the disintegration of all hope."

A search of her inner feelings found no remaining spark left from the flames that had burned so hot and bright just a few days ago. For all practical purposes, her spirit was devoid of life. Only her ability to weep was alive and well. The flight attendants had looked at her with professional sympathy as she had entered the plane. There had been no way to turn her face away from them. Now that she was seated, one of the uniformed young women paused next to her.

"Is there anything I can do for you?"

A miserable shake of her head, and tears welled up again.

"Will y' be all right?"

"Yes," she replied in a small, nearly inaudible voice, knowing she would never be all right again. "I just need to be alone."

The attendant nodded and stepped away.

Time seemed suspended for the duration of the flight. The people around her, the plane itself, all appeared to have no color. Her vision of everything was in only black, white and shades of gray. The focus was dull around the edges and nothing had any meaning for her. How different from the vibrant trip that brought her to Ireland.

Closing her eyes did not improve things either. It only brought the colors back in horrible clarity. All memory focused on the hideous hues of Omagh. These were clear and vivid and too ghastly to bear. The sight of the shredded buildings in the market, the shades of the victims clothing, but most of all the raw scarlet of blood everywhere. And some of the blood was Andrew's—*MacCumhail's*. This knowledge made the flashbacks unbearable. Would there ever be respite from that remembered atrocity? Would a time ever come when these gruesome images would leave her? This must be how it feels to be haunted, she thought. You live in fear that the ghosts will confront you at any turn with no warning.

At last the plane touched down in Chicago. Luggage claim went flawlessly and she passed through customs without a hitch. After that flurry of activity, she found herself standing aimlessly in the terminal transportation access. Where should she go? She had not thought beyond the point of getting back to American soil. Her apartment was still occupied by the young manager who had been housesitting for her. No one was expecting her back for another month, so she wondered if she should stay here. The realization came to her that she had come this far with no real plan, except to escape her own nightmare.

Pushing her luggage cart ahead of her, she abruptly took the elevator to the shuttle train and boarded it to the domestic airline terminal. Debarking from the train, she scanned the monitors until her eyes came to rest on the flights headed west. A couple more connections and she could be back in Montana. Suddenly, it was the only avenue that made sense to her. After securing a ticket for the next morning's flight, she stored her bags in a locker and called Kathleen.

Her sister answered the telephone before Colleen heard a ring on the line.

"Colleen?" came Kathleen's concerned voice. "Something is terribly wrong, isn't it? I haven't slept for the past week, and I've just had a feeling that something had happened to you. Are you all right?" Kathleen's intuition about her sister was working overtime again.

Weariness dragged at Colleen's voice as she gave an abbreviated reply.

"Physically, I'm fine."

Those few words told Kathleen all she needed to know.

"Where are you?"

"Chicago."

"Well, come home."

"I'm on my way." Colleen sighed, then continued. "I've bought tickets to Billings, and I'll be on tomorrow morning's flight."

"I'll meet your plane," Kathleen assured her. A pause, then she asked, "Should I tell Sean and Mom, or do you need some time?"

"Give me a few days…and, Kathleen?"

"Yes?"

"Thanks. I'm glad you understand."

Kathleen felt physically ill when the conversation ended. She had never heard so much pain in anyone's voice. To hear it in her sister was crushing. Despite the fact that she had no detail, she placed the telephone in its cradle and allowed her own tears of empathy to flow. Things must be terrible for Colleen to call her like this. Her sister was strong enough that she seldom leaned on anyone for any kind of help.

Colleen took a taxi to a nearby bargain motel to wait out the night in privacy. No aspects of jet lag were affecting her. With this much pain, the exhaustion was different, more total, and without hope of recovery. She was afraid to sleep, terrified of what she might dream. The cable television in her room provided a means to occupy her time, although she found it impossible to concentrate on any single program. Sightlessly, staring at the screen as the channels flickered by in response to her restless surfing with the remote, the wait began.

At last the first hint of light came. The mechanized wake-up call shrilled the bell of her room's telephone, finding her already dressed and ready to go. When the shuttle delivered her to the airport, she reclaimed her luggage, then rechecked it through to Billings.

Her flights went smoothly and she arrived in Billings on time. Her sunglasses served a dual purpose, concealing her empty red-rimmed eyes, and giving her a chance to arrive in the baggage area unrecognized by any acquaintances who might be in the terminal.

Kathleen waited there. Colleen's overriding gut response to her sister's presence was massive relief. Kathleen had always been her safe harbor, and never more than today. No words were exchanged between the two women, and they didn't hug each other as they usually did upon greeting. Both of them focused upon retrieving the bags and making their escape from the airport. Once in the parked car, Colleen sank into the passenger seat and leaned her head back, eyes closed. Kathleen turned to her.

"Do you want to go to my house, or somewhere else?"

There was a long moment of silence, then Colleen took off her sunglasses and looked into her sister's eyes. "I'd like to go to your house first, and then how about letting me use one of your cars for a few days? And do you still have my camping gear stowed in your garage? I think I need to go to Yellowstone."

Kathleen examined her younger sibling's face carefully. What she saw alarmed her. Fine lines etched her drawn white face, and the luster was gone from her skin and hair. But it was those eyes that really frightened her. They were empty, the spirit that had always shone from them gone completely.

A gasp escaped Kathleen's lips before she could stop it.

"Are you sure? Should you go alone?"

In the back of her mind lurked the fear that Colleen might be careless, or do herself some harm. This would have been completely out of the question for her indomitable sister in the past. But this empty woman who had returned from her odyssey was a stranger. Her demeanor was vacant, sad and lost. In the depths of her troubled eyes, there was bewilderment, unfathomable sorrow, and total hopelessness. Kathleen had never seen anything like it.

After a long pause, Colleen replied. "Yellowstone is my only refuge. I've never needed to go there as much as I do now."

"Of course you can use one of the cars. Keep it as long as you need to."

Exiting the parking lot, Kathleen finished her thought as she drove them toward the house. "Just promise me you'll call me once in a while, so I'll know you're okay. I hated all the long silences while you were in Ireland."

Colleen gazed at her apologetically. "God, I'm sorry, Kathleen. I really meant to call more often. Time just seemed to slip away from me and the time zone differences really threw me off, too. It was thoughtless for me not to be in contact." Tears stood in her eyes.

Now it was Kathleen's turn to be conciliatory. "Do you want to talk about what has happened to you? I've never seen you like this."

"No."

Colleen's response left no room for discussion, but the tone let Kathleen know this closure was not meant to exclude her. It was obvious that Colleen could not verbalize what had wounded her so deeply.

Kathleen nodded with understanding and contented herself with the knowledge that her sister had returned physically safe.

"I'll run interference with Mom and Sean for you," she advised her. "Since they don't know you are even back in the U.S., I'll just let them continue to think you are still in Ireland. I'll let you decide how and when you tell them you are back."

Gratitude spread across Colleen's face. "If they ask, just tell them I'm okay. I did call Mom a couple of weeks ago, so she won't find this too strange." A long breath shuddered her body. "I just don't have the strength to talk to anyone right now."

With a sinking heart, Kathleen acknowledged this statement with a solemn nod. The sisters needed no more words. The air between them was heavy with melancholy. The secret would be kept, and Kathleen's husband would be part of the secrecy plot. He never questioned the eerie bond between the women, and willingly encouraged it. A good man with a great heart, he empathized with Kathleen in all things. Colleen had always envied and admired their relationship.

Colleen gently refused her sister's offer of dinner and wearily went to bed for the first time in days. Perhaps she could sleep now, in the shelter and protection of her sibling's home. She was dead tired. The past three days and the time since Andrew's death had stretched her thin. "Can you get too tired to sleep?" she wondered.

However, once in the darkness and safety of her sister's basement guest room, sleep was a mercy that covered her like a blanket. Total and dreamless, it claimed her completely and she was lost to the world for the next ten hours.

When she woke, she was disoriented. The room was dark and cool, and she wasn't sure where she was. For a moment or two, she had the happy illusion of believing she was in her room at Maddie's and that none of the events of the last two weeks had happened. It must have all been a bad dream...no, a nightmare. But reality slammed into her immediately, and she was bereft. More tears. Would they never cease? Finally she composed herself, rose and dressed. When she came upstairs, Kathleen was waiting for her with a cup of tea and an anxious look.

Clutching the mug in one hand, Colleen smiled wanly and wandered out of the kitchen to the garage. She crawled up the ladder that gave her access to the rafters where her backpack, sleeping bag and other camping gear were stored. Dragging it down after her, she placed it in the trunk of the car she was borrowing, and shut the lid decisively. Then she sat down with her sister and drank her tea in near silence.

The trip south was almost mindless as she passed through the little mountain ski town of Red Lodge. The only thing she noted as she gazed across the open fields of Rock Creek's winding course was that she did not see a single magpie.

They must have deserted her, too. For a time, her emotions were held at bay, but tears streamed down her face as her climb out of Red Lodge began. The magnificent Beartooth Highway, which had inspired so many pages of effusive prose from writers like Charles Kuralt and John Steinbeck did nothing to lift her crushed spirit. On more than one occasion in the past, she had declared to all within hearing that, if the day ever came that she did not find joy in the spectacle of this mountain pass, her friends and family would know she was dead.

"I am dead," she mused. "There's nothing left for me when even this does not cheer me."

The winding road led her up and up until the raw barren rocks with their first coat of snow greeted her at the summit. A few errant flakes swirled in her path as her descent to the Yellowstone plateau began. Colleen cried until no more tears remained. How could she have such a capacity for weeping? Traveling steadily through Silvergate and Cooke City, her route brought her to the gate of Yellowstone. The ranger looked at her pass, noted that it was still valid, and waved her through.

Lamar Valley sprawled before her, its vista showing the wear and tear of another tourist season gone. Driving slowly, she allowed her eyes to search the terrain that surrounded her. What had she come to look for? What did she hope to find? Comfort was surely out of her reach. Nothing could fill this void in her soul.

Suddenly, her gaze came to rest upon a majestic mountain and she remembered that it had been her father's favorite. He had pointed it out on every trip to the park.

"Look," Magpie," he would say. "That's Druid Peak. I've never found anyone who knows why it was named that, but it sure has enough mystery to have earned the name. It's the most special mountain in the Park."

"Why, Dad?"

"Its secrecy and aloofness, I suppose, and the feeling I have that high up on its slopes somewhere lie the answers to the questions we all want to ask."

"Have you ever climbed it?" The child was curious now.

"Only once. I came here with Black Bird when we were very young," he had replied, eyes distant as he remembered. "We trekked in for a couple of days until we came to a ridge at the base of a rock outcropping. The strangest thing was that the wildlife—the deer and bears—didn't seem to see or hear or smell us.

"When we came there, there were old Indian items placed around the rocks. I was curious, and I asked about it. Black Bird said it was a place he came to look for signs. I thought he meant the petroglyphs, but he went up to the rock and placed his hand into one of the crevices. When he brought it back out, he held something tight in his fist, and I asked him what it was. He said it was something that would guide him, but that it was for him alone. I did not see it, and never found out what it was. He seemed satisfied, though."

Colleen longed to hear her father's voice as she had in the past. What would he tell her to do now? Or was that story his way of telling her long ago, so that she would know now, when things seemed most bleak? But Mike's voice seemed to have left her. Would there be answers for her on Druid Peak? There was one way to find out. Make the journey to the ridge her father had described. But there was not a standard trail head and hiking was discouraged in the area.

For a moment, she wondered about going to obtain a backcountry permit. Ordinarily, she was respectful of the rules and regulations of the park, and followed procedures to the letter. Then something entirely unexpected, something she believed she would never see again caught her attention. It was a single magpie, soaring to and fro between her and the base of Druid Peak. Its black and white plumage beckoned her like a flag, it looped its flight path toward her, then toward the mountain in endless figure eight patterns.

Suddenly, she felt removed beyond the laws of man. Pulling the gear out of the parked car, she put things in an orderly pile. The stack included her backpack, sleeping bag, and compass. After a long look at the mountain before her, her hike began. The magpie (*One for sorrow?*) was no longer in her sight. There were no trail designations, and this was not a recommended hiking area. Walking purposefully, she searched her recall for what had been published about Druid Peak in recent years. Information about all aspects of Yellowstone was continually available on the Internet. The main interest in this mountain since the reintroduction of wolves had been a mysterious pack whose territory included this magnificent mountain. Would she see them on this trip?

Bears did not worry her. Mike had always taught her to be cautious, and to make sure she did nothing to aggravate them. It was her way to pass through the wilderness and leave no sign that she had been there. Many times Mike and she had moved so silently upwind of the animals that they passed bears, deer, elk and mountain lion without alerting them. Such silent movement could be attributed to the tribal brothers who had taught them. If her path crossed that of the Druid Peak wolf pack, they would avoid her, and with such skills, they might not even be aware of her.

The terrain began to climb steeply. The time spent at Ireland's sea level had robbed her of some high altitude stamina, but she measured her energies carefully and ascended at a manageable rate. Each footfall helped her focus upon the destination, and enabled her to set aside some of her grief momentarily. Periodically, a pause to look around gave time to keep her bearings and check her compass.

Since there was no designated track in this portion of the Park, she knew it was up to her to orient as she went along. On the surface, she was convinced that she no longer cared about her safety and well being, but a survival instinct buried deep within still forced her to do the right things. She had packed dried food and water, but she felt little hunger, and was willing to fast as she made this journey.

At one point, the wry thought crossed her mind that she didn't really know what she was looking for. Did she think there would be some guru at the top of Druid Peak to tell her what to do with the rest of her life? Was she here to end her grief and the now-empty misery of her existence? Or was there some need to test herself and see if she was really still alive? It was a mystery. All she knew was that she had to keep moving.

When darkness caught up with her on the trail, she was only partway up the lower slope of the mountain. Noticing that she had arrived at a grove of large spruce and fir that had apparently escaped the fires of '88, she made herself a place under the biggest one. There was good protection where its branches swept the ground and sheltered her from the night air. She rolled out her sleeping bag, hung her pack high in a tree some distance away to avoid tempting any wildlife that might like the smell of what little food she carried.

The physical activity of her day gave her the avenue to slip into a deep, dreamless sleep, and the darkness of her evergreen alcove hid the sight of the full moon coming over the ridge. The sounds of the night were a comfort from her distant past, and the mountain wind whispered secrets between the trees that did not penetrate her sleeping ears.

The sun filtered through the dew-strewn trees and called her back to the world when morning came. She sat up, stretched her muscles, finding to her surprise that there was no soreness from her first day's trek. It began to dawn upon her with the light that she was now absolutely alone. She had broken all the rules of the Park and most of the rules of hiking and camping safety. No one knew where she was, and she was in a non-hiking area. The car was parked near the Pebble Creek trailhead, so if she did not come back, searchers would look for her in the wrong part of the wilderness. A small wave of regret washed over her as she thought about Kathleen and how her sister would worry about her. But her path was set, and it had to be followed now. There was an urgency to this mission that she could not explain.

These thoughts took just a few seconds, and once they were complete, the sorrow of her loss slammed into her with all the force of a locomotive. Tears filled her eyes again, and she cried in desolation for what seemed an eternity. She had never felt so lost or alone. There was no comfort even in her beloved Yellowstone. Finally, empty and spent, she rose to her feet and listlessly rolled her sleeping bag into a tight bundle to attach to her pack. This done, she sipped a little water, shouldered her load, and began to pick her way up the mountain again.

The trip seemed uneventful until she entered a broad meadow where several cow elk grazed under the watchful eye of a magnificent bull. She was in the open area before she actually noticed them, and she scolded herself for being so careless in her approach. They did not seem to see her. All her experience in the mountains and hills of her childhood made her recognize this as odd behavior from these sensitive animals. Perhaps she was upwind from them. She whistled a long, low note. The elk ignored her. She took out her compass and set it flat on a rock. Shock ran through her when she realized that the needle was lazily revolving around and around, not stopping to point in any direction whatsoever.

Taking several steps toward the elk, she was amazed to see that they still did not seem aware of her. Was this part of the phenomenon her father had spoken of in his story about his trek up Druid Peak?

Moving on up the slope, another aspect of her travel caused her to marvel at what was happening. There was plenty of deadfall in the way, but whenever she thought she was at an impasse, a way would open before her. And each turn seemed to lead her in the direction she intuitively wanted to go. All her steps led upward, and there was no feeling of indecision when she came to forks in the route. On she climbed.

The middle of the day found her pausing next to a small brook that meandered down the mountainside, tumbling over rocks and bumping against tree roots. Sipping some water from her pack, she surveyed the terrain. A sleek, fluid form caught her eye just upstream from where she stood. It was a splendid gray wolf. Its green eyes looked directly into hers for a protracted moment, then it lowered its head, raised it again, and ran up the stream. After it had loped a few dozen feet, the wolf paused, turned to gaze back at her, then moved away again. Colleen stood stock still for a moment, then followed the feral creature's route upslope.

The wildlife trail followed the stream for a way, then turned along a jagged jumble of rocks on a talus slope. The going here was rough, but not impossible, and she had seen hundreds of paths like this one in her life. Her sturdy hiking boots kept her feet under her, and she moved with the grace bestowed by years outdoors. The compass she had been scrutinizing so diligently was now in her pocket. Directions were chosen purely by instinct, and she stopped thinking about precautions. If anyone had ever told her that she would someday be so careless in the wilderness she would not have believed them.

It was completely out of character, and deep in her heart she knew it. It just didn't matter. The only thing that did matter was the direction the wolf was traveling. Something told her that she had to follow.

Clouds were beginning to gather overhead. Colleen did not worry about them, since her pack contained a slicker and other waterproof gear. At least she had followed her custom of thorough planning prior to this trip. It would enable her to concentrate on the route, instead of worrying about the effects of the weather. Progress up the mountain was mindless, and with no thoughts entertained as she followed the wolf.

Suddenly, the intriguing animal vanished, leaving no tracks or other trace. It appeared to have merged with the air of the forest, abandoning her to her own devices. And now it began to rain.

Rain in the Rockies is not always what you might expect. There are times when it falls gently on the trees and mountain flowers, but this was not that kind of rain. The skies simply ripped open and dumped a cloudburst of daunting proportions on Druid Peak and the surrounding area. Colleen found a niche in the rock face she had been hiking along and squeezed against the rough surface of the granite. It deflected the worst of the downpour, but did not preclude her getting wet. This rain had the power of the huge cumulus clouds overhead, and the woman caught in it was of little consequence to the storm. Waiting as patiently as she could, water streaming from her hair and down her face, tears joined the rain. The jacket was some protection, but not enough. For a moment, she felt victimized and a little angry, then sadness took over again. It was as if even her constant ability to find comfort in Yellowstone had left her. The day was dismal, she was alone, and perhaps even lost, and now the rain was adding to her misery. Allowing a moment of self-pity, the dark emotional state arose to claim its hold.

As suddenly as it had come, the storm stopped. But the clouds continued to obscure the sunlight. The trees dripped their excess water onto the forest floor as she hefted her pack and began to hike again. The birds and animals who had taken shelter from the cloudburst began to emerge from their hiding places, taking up their lives as if nothing had happened. Envy filled Colleen's heart, as she wished it could be that easy for her to put aside the tumult that had filled her life.

The wet earth gave off a fresh smell, touched by the hint of pine, fir and spruce. A breeze cooled the air and made walking easier. As the trail led around a turn, the sun broke out in those rays that look like stairways to someplace beyond clouds, and illuminated portions of the countryside. From here, the trail began a sharp ascent to a ridge that terminated in a rocky ledge high above the floor of a deep ravine. Breathing hard, Colleen plodded up the steepness and finally scrambled over loose rock and bits of wood to reach the barren perch.

The view was awe-inspiring. A panorama swept her gaze nearly full circle, until she saw something out of the corner of her eye. Just above her, reachable only by precarious footholds in the rock was another ledge. In the past, Colleen would never have considered attempting to reach it. But today, something was pulling at her, and her instincts for self-preservation seemed disconnected.

Stripping off her pack and her jacket, she sucked in her breath. Bending down, she rubbed sand and dirt into her hands to augment her grip, and dug her fingers into a crack in the unforgiving rock. There was no looking down and no looking back.

Crawling up the wall of stone, inch by painful inch, she finally reached the ledge. She pulled herself onto it, and lay panting, partly from fear and partly from relief at having reached this point. Her eyes were squeezed shut as she tried to prepare herself for the sheer drop that plunged down and away from the ledge.

What had possessed her to do this? Finally, there was no choice. Opening her eyes, she peered about, first making sure she had a level place for herself, then taking in her surroundings. Not wanting to look down, she cast her eyes up to the cliffs that stood tall above her. Impossibly high up on the walls were petroglyphs, rock art left by ancient native peoples. They were indiscernible, and still vivid, with their spiral swirls and interlinking serpentine lines. Now she scrutinized the ledge. It was bigger and wider than she had imagined, and she realized that she could move about on it without absolute terror.

In front of her, the landscape revealed a stone cairn, standing at the precipice. In the warmth of the sun, waves of heat rising from it, caused it to appear to shimmer with some kind of internal energy. Indians who used them to mark their travels, or to denote religious and holy ground often left such cairns in the past. Her father had shown her dozens of them in the Big Horn and Pryor Mountains.

As she contemplated it, the hair stood up on the back of her neck and along her arms. The single magpie reappeared, glided down from its spirals in the air, and settled upon the cairn.

(*One for sorrow...*)

Grief stabbed at her heart again. She had not needed the climb to this place to be aware of her pain. But as she watched, something strange happened (or was she hallucinating in her mourning?). The single magpie was joined by a second, drifting down from the heavens in slow motion, a black and white piece of expectation and hope…

(*Two for mirth*…the old chant said).

Getting to her feet, she walked toward the magpies and the stack of stones. Sure enough, there were various bundles deposited there, feathers and rawhide, beads and twisted cloths, and a number of egg-shaped stones laid out in a pattern around the base.

All the rocks that comprised the monument were of the native mountain granite, except for one. It was green, and appeared to be some form of quartz, with a glassy surface. When Colleen put her hand on it, she discovered it was loose. It moved, then fell from its place. Where it had been, there was a gap in the cairn, a hole through which a small niche could be seen.

Colleen stepped back. A ray of sun fell on her and the ledge, and the glitter of metal reflected the light. Without thinking, she reached into the space where the green stone had been. Her hand felt something metallic. It was warm, and somehow familiar. Taking hold of it, she withdrew it from the recess, and then she opened her hand.

What lay within her grasp spoke volumes. It told of the winds and mists of Mother Eire, of the peace process that would continue on until serenity came to that green land again, and of the women who would continue to provide the perpetual force for harmony. It radiated a potent energy that contradicted its most recent, lifeless state. But most of all, it validated Andrew, and the power of love and peace that could not be extinguished.

There in her palm, still blackened and scratched by Omagh's blast, was the talisman.

978-0-595-34933-3
0-595-34933-1

CPSIA information can be obtained at www.ICGtesting.com
Printed in the USA
LVOW08s0043030315

428918LV00001B/4/P